TRAUMA LAND

ALSO BY JOSH SILVER

HappyHead
Dead Happy

TRAUMA LAND

JOSH SILVER

ROCK THE BOAT

This book contains material that some readers may find distressing, including discussions of anxiety, mental illness, medical procedures, knife violence, homophobia, bullying, kidnapping, torture, self-harm, cannibalism and pet death.

A Rock the Boat Book

First published in the United Kingdom, the Republic of Ireland and Australia by Rock the Boat, an imprint of Oneworld Publications Ltd, 2025

Copyright © Josh Silver, 2025
Cover art © Oneworld Art Department
Cover image © Shutterstock

The moral right of Josh Silver to be identified as the Author of this work has been asserted by him in accordance with the Copyright, Designs and Patents Act 1988

All rights reserved
Copyright under Berne Convention
A CIP record for this title is available from the British Library

ISBN 978-0-86154-928-3
eISBN 978-0-86154-929-0

Printed and bound in Great Britain by Clays Ltd, Elcograf S.p.A.

Quotation from *On the Road* by Jack Kerouac. Copyright © 1955, 1957 Jack Kerouac / Copyright renewed © 1983, Stella Kerouac / Copyright renewed © 1985, Stella Kerouac and Jan Kerouac, used by permission of The Wylie Agency (UK) Limited.

Quotation from *Literary Outlaw: The Life and Times of William S. Burroughs* by Ted Morgan. Copyright © 1988, used by permission of W.W. Norton & Company, Inc.

This book is a work of fiction. Names, characters, businesses, organisations, places and events are either the product of the author's imagination or are used fictitiously. Any resemblance to actual persons, living or dead, events or locales is entirely coincidental. Certain long-standing institutions, agencies and public offices are mentioned, but the characters involved are wholly fictitious.

No part of this publication may be reproduced, stored in a retrieval system, or transmitted, in any form or by any means, electronic, mechanical, photocopying, recording or otherwise, without the prior permission of the publishers.

The authorised representative in the EEA is eucomply OÜ,
Pärnu mnt 139b–14, 11317 Tallinn, Estonia
(email: hello@eucompliancepartner.com / phone: +33757690241)

Oneworld Publications Ltd
10 Bloomsbury Street, London WC1B 3SR, England

Stay up to date with the latest books, special offers, and exclusive content from Rock the Boat with our newsletter

Sign up on our website
rocktheboatbooks.com

Dedicated to anyone who is not afraid of this world.
I hope this does something to change that.

1

MY OVERWHELMING EMPTINESS

'Could you repeat that please, Elias? I'm not sure I heard you correctly.'

She heard me correctly. 'I said, I think I'm a psychopath.' I make the final word louder just so she's perfectly clear.

'OK, Elias. That's an interesting choice of words.' Melinda stares at me over the bridge of her glasses. 'Why would you think that?'

'I overheard someone at work say I look like the kind of person that would shoot up a school.' Her face doesn't move. She's good at this. Very professional. 'It got me thinking. What if I actually am that kind of person?'

I don't want to scare her. I like my therapist. I do. But she asked for the truth and I made a promise I'd give it to her.

'So, you think you're a psychopath because someone else said so?' She raises her eyebrows like I'm being childish. She always does that when she thinks I'm being ... well, childish.

'Yes. Exactly.'

It's OK, by the way. We understand one another. I hate her and she hates me, but we love each other really.

'But you have empathy and compassion.'

If I do, I'm currently on the last dregs of it stuck here on this blue swivel chair. 'Sociopath, then. Isn't that the difference? The empathy part?'

'I'm pretty sure you're neither.'

That's promising. My therapist is *pretty* sure I'm neither a psychopath nor a sociopath. No one really knows the difference between a psychopath and a sociopath. Well, I do, but that's because I google these things. Anyway, I digress.

'You don't look convinced, Elias.'

'The guy at work seemed pretty convinced.'

She frowns her thinking frown. 'Is he the one who pushed your head in the toilet while you were cleaning it?'

'No. Different one.' Different one, Melinda. Stay sharp.

'OK, let's see. If you're worried –' I'm not worried – 'let's go through the psychopath checklist.' Oh, fun. 'Do you pretend to feel emotions?'

'No. I just don't have them.'

She raises her eyebrows again. 'Elias.'

'Yes, Melinda.'

'You do have them.'

Never. 'Sporadically.'

'I think you're referring to the overwhelming emptiness we've been working through.'

I didn't name it that, by the way. She did and now it's stuck. Me and my Overwhelming Emptiness meet with her every Thursday at 7 p.m. for fifty minutes, annoy the living shit out of her, then leave. 'Maybe.'

'We've spoken about this.' Melinda is right. We have spoken about this. We've spent forty-three hours speaking about it, to be precise. Every week for ten whole months.

But the Overwhelming Emptiness has gone nowhere and all I've managed to gain is a more profound knowledge of its existence. 'You are making progress. And it's completely normal for you to feel this way after what happened to you.'

'If you say so.'

'Are you cold and ruthless?'

Hmm. Is feeling *nothing* cold? I'll go with yes. I know that ruthless is going to happen at some point soon, too. You'll see.

'I live at home with my mum and dad. I love cats.' I'm a cat person. Don't fuck with cats. 'That doesn't really scream *I'm gonna slit your throat*, does it?'

'No.'

'Could all be a guise though, Melinda.'

'I highly doubt it. And not all psychopaths slit people's throats.'

'That's true.' Told you she was good.

'Are you intent on becoming successful at the expense of others?'

'I work in a café, cleaning the bogs because I failed all three of my A levels.' I put my thumb up. 'So, a firm no to that one.'

OK, fine. I passed one of them. But it was art, which isn't a *proper subject*.

'Next question, Elias. Are you dishonest?' I mean… 'I'll answer that. You're not. You are very honest. Bravely so.' I like that she thinks that. 'Do you try and copy emotions? Imitate them?'

'I…'

That's a weird one. Because since it happened – the reason I'm here – I can't remember how to feel emotions. Instinctively, anyway. I try to summon them, I do. I worry the summoning part is the psychopathic part. Well, no, I don't *worry* because I can't. But I think about it often. Ponder, if you will. *Muse on it*. Sorry. Rambling. Shh, brain.

I should really tell her all this. That would be the honest thing to do. 'No, I don't.'

'And you're not outwardly charming.'

'Wow. OK.'

'You're *genuinely* charming.'

She then looks sad, like she really cares about me. I hate it when she does that. 'So no, Elias, you're not a psychopath or a sociopath.'

'I dream about murdering people.'

She pauses. 'Elias.'

'What?'

'I can't tell if you're joking again.'

Again? Oh, she thinks I was *joking* about the psychopath thing. It's probably better that way.

I am joking now, though. I just want to shit her up a bit. Shake up the session in the closing minutes. I can see by the clock on the wall there are only five minutes left, but the last five are always the worst so I'm hoping she'll just end it. Not all of time and humanity, just the session. (Although that would be interesting.) You get what I mean.

'We've spoken a lot about your dreams.'

Damn it. 'We have.'

'And there's no murder in them.'

'No. I was making a bad joke.'

'Right. Good one.' She puts *her* thumb up this time. 'OK, so can we be serious now?' Melinda closes her notebook, clicks her pen and places it neatly into the pocket of her blazer.

Oh, she's ready. She's ready to get serious.

'Potentially.'

'There's six minutes left.' Five. *Five* left. 'And I want to know how your symptoms have been this week.'

I exhale. 'It's been getting better. The nightmares aren't as bad. The pain is less frequent. The headaches aren't making me feel as sick as they used to. I've woken up feeling more positive and I'm screaming less.' I hope that didn't sound too robotic.

'The screaming at night, you mean?'

Yes, Melinda. 'Less dreaming, less screaming.'

'Well, that's great. Really great, Elias. And the emptiness?'

'It's less.'

'Great. Good. And what about the feeling you've described as *missing something*. You've often spoken about it as a sort of inexplicable *longing*?'

'Yeah.' That's the worst one. 'It's getting better now.'

'It will go fully with time.'

I nod to make her think I believe her.

'And your memory? Is it becoming clearer? Solidifying?'

I blink. 'Yes.'

'That's wonderful. Remember, everyone is safe and everyone is well.'

'They are.'

'Are you keeping up with your therapy exercises?'

'I am. They're helping.'

She wrinkles her nose like she's very pleased and very proud. 'Good. How's Lucas?'

My older brother. Home from uni for the Christmas break. 'He's good. Going to hang out with him tonight.'

'To tell him how awful this has been?'

'You read my mind.'

'God, I would hate to do that.' She grins. 'Right, well. See you tomorrow, Elias.' I scrunch up my face. *Tomorrow?* 'It's going to be a year since the date of the Incident.'

The Incident. She loves referring to it as that. Wait, *what*?

'Yeah. I know.' But I didn't know. I'd actually forgotten. Or blocked it out, probably.

'Good. So, as I told you, it's a group session.' Oh, holy hell. 'With Mum and Dad.'

It makes me feel weird when she calls them that, like they're her mum and dad too. 'Can you call them something else?'

'Right. Sorry. With Mr and Mrs Pew.'

'OK, but no. That's too formal. Like we're going to have a business lunch about my trauma.'

She doesn't smile this time. Probably because she knows that's exactly what we're going to be doing. 'I'll just call them—'

'My parents. Yep. My parents will be there. Got it.'

'It's a home visit. So, if you'll remind them, I'll be at your house at ten a.m.?'

'Does it have to be?'

'At ten?'

'A home visit.' I glance at the clock. We're now running over.

'They're taking the time off work and I know how busy they are.'

'But I just feel like… I dunno. I can't imagine you stood in my kitchen in your own clothes and stuff, talking to my mother about *The Great British Bake Off*—'

'I always wear my own clothes, Elias.'

'You'll suddenly become normal and not the powerful mythic being that you are.'

'I think there's a compliment in there somewhere.' She smiles. I'm good at making her do that. 'It'll be really useful. A pivotal moment in your recovery. We'll show them the progress you've made.'

Not sure. Not sure, Melinda. 'Cannot wait.'

'I'll drop you a text first thing, so you don't forget.'

Yeah. My therapist texts me. She's new wave and edgy like that. She's *available to me at any point, night or day, while retaining appropriate boundaries.* And my parents pay shitloads of money for her. I wish I could say that I haven't had to call her in the middle of the night. But I have. Many times.

I stand. 'See ya, shrink.' And then I leave.

So, another healthy, well-adjusted session with my therapist complete. Time to go home, sit through my family dinner, then escape to my room and rewatch *The Exorcist*. I've seen it over one hundred and forty times. That's one hundred and forty times in the past ten months. This is one of the many things I'll never tell Melinda. But it does help. I'll explain later.

Before that, there's something I must do. And Melinda *definitely* can't know about this. Because I'm going to do something ruthless. Something morally and ethically wrong. Something *bad*.

2

GHOST VAMPIRE

I stand at the bus stop by Melinda's office building, looking at the digital screen inside the shelter. I have six minutes until the 134 to Muswell Hill arrives and takes me back to my house, my parents, my brother and our typically formal family dinner, which I cannot be late for. I can't have them worrying about me. Not any more.

This means I only have six minutes to commit my ruthless act.

I'm going to rob someone.

I'm going to rob them, using force if necessary. Take something of value that they desperately need and will struggle without – they have to struggle, that's vital. Its loss must result in pain and misery – also vital. And I do not have good intentions.

Yes, people can steal and have good intentions. Robin Hood, Aladdin (the Disney version – God, I really fancied him when I was younger). Alas, tonight I will not be joining them in their honourable thieving ways. Tonight I must inflict suffering. (I did fancy Disney Robin Hood too, come to think of it. But that was a cartoon fox so probably best not unpack that now. I'll save it for Melinda. She'll *love* it.)

Just to be clear, this isn't some mindless game. I do *have* intentions – they're just not good ones. I intend to sit and observe my victim from a few seats back on the bus as they realise what's happened and quietly watch their distress unfold.

The screen is saying five minutes now. I scan my eyes over the people congregating at the bus stop, looking for a potential target. I do know this is not a decent or acceptable thing to do. But that's the whole point. Before everything last year, this would not be happening. None of this would.

This isn't just senseless cruelty. It's a little side project, if you will, to go along with all the therapy. It has a purpose. More of a purpose than the sessions with Melinda, but I won't tell her that. She thinks she's doing great and I'd like to keep it that way because I've been lying to her. I'm not as recovered as she thinks I am. I really hate that word, *recovered*.

Anyway, I've decided I'll steal a phone.

I'd initially thought a wallet, because driver's licence, bank cards, cash – all things a person needs. But a phone has everyone's everything on it. And, most importantly, their means to call for help. A phone will do more damage. Yes. This is the level of suffering I must aim for.

I appreciate this might all sound a little … overly thought out. A little … (I'm cautious to use the word because it's a bit serial killer-y, but hey) premeditated. Well, that's because it is.

A few people catch my eye. A few potential targets. I try not to stare at them as I've been told I can appear creepy.

I dyed my hair bright pink last week in an attempt to subdue the creepiness after what that guy at work said, but it only made things worse. Mum had a meltdown and told me I couldn't leave the house until I sorted it out, so I took a pair of scissors to it. Now it's all different lengths and the dye has left drip marks down my forehead that I can't get off. It has a red glow like blood and I must admit I do look a bit mental.

Four minutes now.

I see an old lady with an umbrella. She blinks into the rain and I think: *maybe*. She'll be scared and stranded without her phone. This is the hallmark of a good target. I have found Option One.

I then see a mother with a toddler on her hip, pulling at her hair. She'd also make a good target because, well, the child. Option Two.

I see two boys – all gelled hair and Adidas tracksuits – probably about fourteen. They're sitting on the plastic bench inside the shelter, laughing at something on one of their phones. Hmm. Perhaps. I squint through the pane of glass behind them to see they're watching a TikTok of a man's face being slapped repeatedly by a piece of fried chicken. My forehead accidentally touches the glass, making a soft thud directly behind their heads. Oops.

They both turn. Their laughter stops. They stand.

'What the hell?' one of them says. For a moment he doesn't know what to do so he just spits on the floor. I think it's his way of telling me without using words that although he's just hitting puberty, he's absolutely terrifying. He's even sporting a little fluffy tash on his top lip, bless him.

'A mistake,' I mutter.

'I bet you were,' says the other. It's actually quite a good comeback for someone who hasn't fully grown into his arms yet.

His mate doesn't get the joke but laughs anyway. 'You gay or summat?'

I am, but it's strange for him to have got that from just my head at a bus stop. He smacks his hand on the glass right in front of my face. It doesn't scare me. Damn it.

'What you staring at? You wanna be slapped like that, do you? You like that shit?'

I decide not to answer. I just continue to stare through the glass.

'Hellooo?' The long-armed one waves at me like I'm stupid. 'You dumb? Or just some kind of ghost vampire?'

Ghost vampire? Um. Yes, please. I smile in a way I think a ghost vampire would.

'Freak,' the tashed one says, putting up his middle finger.

I sigh, clouding up the glass. Nope. Stealing their phone would not elicit the response I need because they are, clearly, two little pricks. This means they cannot be an option. Taking their phone would probably do the world a favour. The more vulnerable the better.

I glance at the screen. Three minutes now. Time is ticking.

I perch on the bin and watch the little old lady trying to read the digital board. Maybe Option One is the best option. It often is.

'Three minutes,' I say.

She turns. 'Sorry?'

'It's coming in three minutes. The 134.'

'Does that one go to Archway?'

'It does.'

'Oh, good. Thank you.'

Her eyes hover over my forehead. She frowns. 'What's wrong with your head, young man?'

Now there's a question. 'It's nothing.' I smile. 'Hair dye.'

'No, the … thing.' She points to my temple, tracing a little line through the air with her finger. Oh, she means the scar.

'I was bitten by a shark.' The scar looks worse than it is because the pink dye has seeped into it, so she might believe me.

'In the h-h-head?' the old lady stammers.

'Right in the head.'

She pulls a face at me like *how awful*. She then quickly turns to face the road and stands resolutely, holding her umbrella like a weapon. She should probably use it. Not to hit me with – it's pissing it down and she's getting wet. I kick the bin with my heel.

Two minutes. Not long now. I look for other options.

I see a man in an expensive coat and shiny, pointed shoes. He'll probably have a replacement phone and definitely has the resources to get another quickly. Losing it will mean nothing to him. I watch a man in gym gear shovel a sandwich into his mouth as if it'll disintegrate in the rain if he doesn't finish it in three seconds flat. I can see his muscles through his tight fluorescent T-shirt. No, I can't die tonight.

There's only really Option One: nice old lady, and Option Two: mum with child.

And then I see her.

A girl. Probably my age, a little older at a push, leaning back against the wall next to the entrance of Burger King.

She's wearing a pair of purple wireless earbuds and is nodding along to her music with her eyes closed.

I think she's probably an art student. She looks cool in an effortless way – fishnet tights, oversized checked shirt and Docs – like she has a bit of an edge to her but doesn't really care much about the world outside her own head. (I could like this girl if I didn't have such bad intentions.) I clock her purple phone case sticking out of the pocket of her denim jacket.

Hello, my target.

OK, that sounded a bit Gollum-like. I'm not going to eat her, don't worry.

I look back at the screen. One minute. The time is upon us.

I keep my eyes down on the wet pavement as I hop off the bin and move towards the wall until I'm a metre or so away from her. I lean back and put my foot up against it so my leg is angled. Casual.

I glance at her. I like her thick eyeliner. And I've just bought a pair of Docs that are very similar to hers. We really could have been friends. Shame.

Her eyes are still closed.

I edge along the wall. Other people are gathering now, appearing from nowhere like they have inbuilt bus-tracking systems. A small crowd forms around us. Useful.

I look down the road. The 134, a red double-decker, is moving towards us.

A car drives past and splashes everyone. The noise of Gym Guy shouting *you bastard* makes my target look up. She removes her earbuds and puts them in her pocket with her phone.

As the 134 pulls up, she takes a step forwards and I follow. People push into us, squeezing together.

I move my hand. Put my fingers around the phone. Steady now. Gently.

She turns her head to the bus.

Do it. *Take it.*

And then it's out. It's free. As I slip it into the pocket of my jeans, I realise I'm holding my breath. I feel something. Adrenaline, maybe. A strange buzzing somewhere. A *thrill*.

Earbuds now? Fuck it, why not? They looked expensive.

I wait for the right moment. Until the crowd begins to push again. I then slide my hand back into her pocket. Just as my fingertips brush against the earbuds, the man behind shoves into me, slamming me right into the girl's back.

She turns. Looks directly at me, our faces inches apart.

Not good. My hand is still in her pocket. Casual. *Casual.*

'Hi,' I say.

She frowns. She looks angry. Does she know? Shit.

The man pushes again, pinning us together.

The girl turns her head to him. 'Leave off!'

'It's not my bloody fault,' the man growls. 'Moody cow.'

OK. Now. I clench my hand and pull. One swift movement.

'Prick,' the girl mutters, shaking her head.

I keep my fist balled up, the earbuds inside it. OK, that was risky. *Risky, risky, risky.*

I feel a tingling in my skin. A buzzing in my head. A rush.

'What a tosser,' I say.

The corners of her mouth turn up. I made her smile. I made the girl I just robbed smile.

Don't get cocky now.

The queue in front of us is filing into the bus. We're still pressed together, just behind the old lady who's shuffling towards the doors. Suddenly my victim steps forwards and takes her by the arm. The lady looks startled at first until she realises she's being helped on to the bus by a smiling young woman. I step back, ready to lose myself in the crowd. Nearly there.

But then the girl turns and looks directly at me. 'Could you help us?'

'Um...' Do it. Pretend to be nice. 'Sure.'

I step towards them, smiling like a good Samaritan might, and take the old lady's other arm. As I do, she glances up at me. She looks scared. 'You're the young man who got bitten by a shark.'

The girl narrows her eyes.

'That's me,' I say, still smiling. I glance at my victim and pull a face. *This woman might be a bit off her trolley, the little love.*

The girl smiles again. Wow. I'm so good at this.

When we reach the driver's window, the old lady begins to root through her purse, struggling to find her pass. She drops it.

I instinctively reach down to pick it up, opening my hand as I do.

Oh, shit. Rookie mistake. The purple earbuds fall out and clatter across the floor.

I freeze. Not good, not good, not good.

'Hold on...'

I gaze up at my victim. She's staring at the earbuds, momentarily confused. She then pats her pocket where her phone was. She looks at me and her mouth drops open.

OK. Time to bail. Bye.

I turn and hurl myself at the queue of people still waiting to board the bus.

'Stop him!' the girl screams.

I shove myself into the throng of bodies, colliding with a sea of limbs, bags and umbrellas. As I force my way through the gaps, I can still hear the girl shouting.

A man grabs my arm, gripping my sleeve tight. Shit, shit, shitting shit.

I yank myself free, pushing forwards, dodging more hands, more limbs. Move, move, move.

I see a space in front of me and stumble towards it. Then I run. I run like I've never run before.

I can hear something behind me. Feet pounding right at my heels. Someone, the girl, screaming for me to stop. I glance over my shoulder and she's right there.

Shit, bollocks, shit. I take a sudden left turn, down a side alley.

I twist through the backstreets, chest heaving, ears ringing, rain ripping into my eyes, the pavement blurring. I run until everything turns into an endless grey streak. Until my body hurts. Until I find myself halfway down a narrow passageway between two buildings.

I glance up and down it. Have I lost her?

I duck into a doorway surrounded by bins. Silence. Apart from the rain.

I take the girl's phone out of my pocket. The case is covered with stickers, all overlapping. As I turn it around in my hands, I notice they're trembling. Time to deduce an outcome.

I focus on what I have done. On my ruthless act. And I wait.

But nothing comes.

More. *I need more.*

I close my eyes and picture the girl. I see her crying, asking for help, desperate to get home because ... her mother is sick. Yes. Her mother is dying. That's good. And ... she's poor. Desperate. Working every day to pay her phone bill. Her dying mother bought her this phone. Brilliant.

Nope. Still nothing.

Come on.

I click the side button and the phone lights up. The song she was listening to is now paused.

NISHA'S PLAYLIST

Nisha. That's a nice name.

DREAM 1 (before the wind blows it all away) [Pt.1]
MAX RICHTER

Never heard of it. But actually, this might help. Yes. Good. *Ambience.*

I tap the screen and music starts to play. Soft and gentle. A piano. Not what I expected. I thought something angsty, but this is all rousing and stirring.

I hold the phone close to my chest and feel the vibrations of the music against my jumper. I let it move into my body. Let the music surround me.

Come on. Please, please, please.

I close my eyes again. I can feel my heart thrumming in my blood. And then, something happens. A memory flashes in front of me.

I'm in the garden back in our old cottage in Lewes, before we moved to London last year. Before everything happened. It's night-time. Music is playing from inside the house, *this* music. Dad is with me on the lawn. Mum too, standing under the patio security light. Dad looks angry. And I can hear Mum crying, sobbing…

That's … new. And not at all what I was after.

I still feel nothing. Empty. Numb.

My premeditated act has failed. I have failed.

As I stand in a doorway in a dark alley surrounded by bins with a phone that's not mine, I must deduce this:

I am totally and utterly broken.

3
DING-DONG

I close the front door behind me, shutting out the night. I can hear Classic FM playing from the kitchen. Smell the familiar, lingering floral scent.

'Eli? Is that you?' Mum's voice from the dining room. 'Hi, darling!'

I push the stolen phone down into my jeans pocket, my own phone in the other.

'Got sidetracked helping an old lady get on the bus,' I call back. 'Sorry I'm late!'

'It's fine. Your brother's still in the shower. Dinner's nearly ready!'

'Great!'

I kick off my shoes and check my reflection in the mirror above the side table where a vase of lilies sits. There are always lilies here – Mum's obsessed with them. I sweep my damp fringe out of my eyes and do my ghost-vampire smile. It looks good, *really* good. With the hair dye, it's very Jokeresque. I exhale, then pad across the checked hallway tiles into the dining room.

And there they are. Mum and Dad, Mr and Mrs Pew,

sitting at the dining table – candles lit, four sets of expensive cutlery perfectly laid, napkins neatly folded.

Time to pull out my A game. They must not suspect. Confuse and discombobulate to distract. 'Greetings, sexy earthlings. It is I, your sweet son, descended from a foreign world.'

'Half right,' Dad says, not looking up from the *Telegraph*. 'Me, sexy? Yes. But you, sweet? Not sure.' He smiles.

He's joking, see. Actually, he doesn't think he's sexy but *does* think I'm sweet, which is exactly what I need him to think.

Mum pretends not to have heard. 'How was it?' she says, standing. Her white blouse is all chic and elegant and her eternally blonde hair is in a neat ponytail, as always. Her appearance hasn't changed in my entire seventeen years.

I feel the phone start to vibrate in my pocket. Nisha's phone. *Shit*. I should've turned it off.

'It was good, thanks!' I smile. A warm one.

'I'm so pleased, Eli.' As her arms wrap around me, I smell the faint tang of dusty books and altruism. Mum's a lawyer. A crown prosecutor, to be precise. *Precise* is actually a good word for her. Immaculate. Delicate, but not frail. 'Gosh, you're soaked through.'

'Just a bit damp. How was your day, Mum?'

'Busy. But good.' She kisses my forehead, right where the scar is. She's stopped mentioning it now, to my immense relief. 'I'm going to fetch the food. You hungry?'

'Starving.'

She heads into the hallway and I hear her shout up the stairs. 'Lucas! Dinner! Your brother's back!'

'We were getting a little worried,' Dad says. He doesn't sound it though, and only half looks up from his newspaper. He's wearing his jumper-shirt combo that he thinks makes him look professional but relatable. 'I was about to call the chief of police.'

'Ha!' I say.

He's very clever, my dad. Very perceptive, so I need to play this well. And he probably could call the chief of police because he works for the government. He's a Member of Parliament. The MP for Lewes, to be exact. The town I grew up in – the town we lived in until the Incident.

Dad used to have a job in Big Tech, but the company he worked for loved him so much that they persuaded him to join this new political party they were helping fund. ADVANCE BRITAIN: *a radical party to elicit real change, harnessing and embracing technology as the way forwards.*

Their slogan is burned into my memory from all the campaigning Dad did five years ago. I don't think he actually thought they'd win the election. No one did. But, as Dad so often puts it, people had become desperate. His party offered something new and the nation got on board. Sounds crazy, but it isn't really. It hasn't changed anything for me. Just that my dad is famous now. He signs autographs sometimes – says he hates it, but I know that's a lie.

So, yes. My parents are both honourable, respected members of the community. Which is why this house is so massive. And also why they cannot know about my side project. They wouldn't understand.

I feel the phone start to buzz again. Damn it. *Stop.* I should probably turn it off, but don't want to draw attention to it.

'How's the world doing?' I say, pointing at the newspaper. To distract. Deflect.

'Typically barbaric,' he sighs. He folds it, takes off his glasses and rubs his eyes. He always looks so tired, my dad.

'Why so serious?' I say, like the Joker does. But I don't do the voice.

'Oh, just another day dealing with terrible people doing terrible things.'

'Oh no. The worst type of people.'

'There are more of them than you'd think, Eli.'

'I can imagine.' He starts pouring wine, but not for himself. He doesn't drink or smoke any more – again, very wholesome. 'Maybe don't read the paper then. Out of sight, out of mind.'

'If only that were true.'

He's right. If only that were true of *this stolen phone*.

Dad frowns. 'Is that your phone? Aren't you going to answer it?'

I suddenly feel two arms envelop me from behind, picking me up so my feet leave the floor.

'Hey, Little Broski.'

Saved by my brother. Dad goes back to pouring. *Thank God*.

Lucas smells like a meadow. A masculine meadow. He drops me back down and rubs my head with his knuckle.

'Hey, Luc,' I say, keeping things casual.

'How was the shrink?'

'Good. My head has been perfectly shrunk.'

He grins. 'Brilliant. You're soaking.' He's wearing the same shirt he's been wearing every day since he got back from

Cambridge. Yes: he goes to Cambridge University. Yes: he's very clever. Yes: just like my parents. He's also very nice. He is Perfect Son Material. We are not short of high achievers in this family, except for the black sheep: me.

It didn't used to be that way. There was once so much promise. Then my head was smashed open.

Nisha's phone buzzes in my pocket again.

I quickly sit back down. 'What are we having?'

'Lamb,' Dad says.

Mum brings in the dishes from the kitchen, piled with steaming food. As she sets them down, Lucas sits opposite me and sips his wine in a way that is different to how he did before university. He does it all ... academically.

'How's work going, Eli?' he says in his now even posher voice.

'It's good, yeah.' I see Dad smile. I haven't told them I'm on my last warning at the café. It's not my fault the customers are so messy. The Muswell Hill mums like to bring their children in to cause what I call food tornadoes. It's my job to clean that shit up.

God, this phone.

'No more annoying customers then?'

'I'm learning to deal with them.'

I try to smile as I've been told to. *Be nice. A smile goes a long way, Elias.*

The manager recently had a sit-down chat with me about all the ways I could appear jollier. Laughing is good, she said. So I did. I laughed. I laughed a lot when a customer asked me for a puppucino for her dog because I thought it was genuinely funny. I didn't realise she was not joking.

I got my first warning for that because the customer was very offended.

'You're doing great, Eli.'

'Why, thank you.'

The second warning was for hiding in the walk-in fridge because the dick chef, Dan, kept flicking hot butter at me every time I went into the kitchen. When he found out I was hiding in there, he locked me in. I tried to break the door open, but just broke the lock instead. When the manager finally opened it, she found me drinking a carton of the extra special posh milk with a chef's apron wrapped round my head for warmth, which apparently was really not OK.

'When's your next shift?'

'Saturday.'

It's not. The manager asked me to take Saturday off to reflect on why I think it's OK to drink things that aren't mine. But my family don't need to know that.

I should have thrown this phone in a bush. Please shut up.

I do actually like my job, though. The cleaning bit at least. I find it focuses my brain. To my family, it's *just a stop gap*. A way for me to *regather* myself, after everything. But it's good for now. I have a bit of money in my bank – currently eighty-three whole pounds – and my parents don't make me pay rent because they're nice like that.

'So, tomorrow you're all clear for the group session?' Mum says.

'Yep! Can't wait for that little gem.'

She looks at me warmly. 'I didn't think you'd remember.'

'How could I forget?' Because I have forgotten lots of things.

The buzzes on my upper thigh increase in frequency, like someone's texting the phone at high speed. I feel for it with my fingers and slip it out while my brother talks about how good it's been for me – all the therapy.

I make *uh-huh* noises to show him I'm listening and steal glances at the screen. Messages flash up one after the other. All from the same person.

Boss: I know you stole this phone

Boss: Who are you?

Boss: Fucker

Boss: I'm gonna find you

Wait, is this her? Or is this her boss? Or is *she* Boss? Or someone just called Boss.

Who calls themselves Boss?

'What other shifts are you working this weekend?' Dad says.

'Uh-huh'

'Elias?'

Oh, bollocks. I look up to see him eyeing me as he cuts the lamb. 'Just Saturday.'

'I was thinking…' He glances at Mum as she dishes out green things. I know what's about to happen because he used his soft voice, which means he is about to bring up the Future. 'I wondered if you'd thought any more about going back to resit your exams? Maybe we could discuss it this weekend? No pressure, of course.'

'Let's get tomorrow out of the way first, Gordon,' Mum says with a hint of a warning as she dishes out potatoes covered in herby bits.

'Of course,' Dad replies and I see him go a little red.

I glance back down.

Boss: Ever heard of GPS tracking? Cos that's about to fuck you mate

Oh, God. Not good at all. I am the world's worst thief. How could I not premeditate GPS tracking?

'I have been thinking about it, actually,' I say.

'Oh?' Mum says.

'I want to do criminology.' I appreciate that might seem a little ironic right now, but it's the truth.

'Oh, Eli. That's *wonderful*.' Mum's eyes widen with glee. 'You'd be *so* good at that.'

Boss: I'm gonna find you

'Someone's popular,' Lucas says, seeing me glancing at the phone. *Shit*. 'Made some new friends?' I look up at him and smile coyly like *maybe I have*. He raises his eyebrows in that way he does when he's being encouraging. 'Or is it a boyfriend you haven't told us about?'

The room goes silent. Except for the buzzing.

I notice the hopeful look between Mum and Dad. They want me to find someone lovely. They do. Because I've never had a boyfriend and they think it'll be *really good for me to find someone nice*.

I push the phone back down into my pocket. *Out of sight, out of mind.*

It'll be fine.

People called Boss definitely lie. Just like people called Elias. E-lie-as.

'Sadly not, Lucas.'

I feel the optimism in the room dissipate.

'That's a shame,' Dad says.

'Steve and Paula's son, Peter—' Mum begins.

My brother snorts and grins at me over his wine glass.

'What?' Mum says, glaring at him. 'Peter's nice.'

Peter is nice. Peter lives a few doors down with his parents. He just got a place at UCL to study Social Change or something wonderfully altruistic like that. He's objectively very handsome and wears expensive clothes that don't look expensive, like Prince William. Anyway, Peter asked me on a date. Problem was, he went about it the right way. The polite way. He asked via his mum and dad, which went via my mum and dad. The invitation to go to dinner (at his parents' house, may I add – *why, God, why?*) arrived via the lips of my very own father.

Which all just felt a little … formal. And Steve and Paula are obsessed with my dad because he's famous and they want a famous friend so I actually think they have ulterior motives.

'I just want to be on my own for a bit,' I say.

'You sound like a forty-year-old divorcee,' Mum says, laughing gently. 'Not a handsome young man in the prime of his life.'

'Uh-huh.'

'He's so sweet, Eli. And he's handsome too.'

I slip the phone out again to see if Boss has gone away.

Boss: I know where you live, little bitch

'Fine,' I say to stop Mum talking. 'Maybe.'

Mum's eyebrows raise and her forehead crinkles. 'Brilliant! I'll let them know.'

I feel a sudden flash of blankness, a sharp shooting pain in my head that makes me wince.

'You OK, son?' Dad asks.

'Yeah, all good,' I say, but I can feel my cheek twitching. 'Just one of the –' I point to my head – 'things.' They know what I mean and smile sympathetically. 'How's Ingrid, Lucas?' I ask, to change the subject.

His girlfriend. I call her Intense Ingrid. Because she's really intense.

'She's good, thanks.'

'How's her PhD in Machine-Intelligence-thingy-thingy?'

'Good,' he says, chewing on a potato.

Boss: you're dead

'Does she still think the world's about to end?'

'Yup,' he says.

Mum frowns. Dad blinks.

The doorbell goes.

Oh. Oh, shit.

Mum looks at her watch. 'Who could that be?'

Surely not… Boss is a liar. He has to be. *He's called Boss, for fuck's sake.*

Boss: ding-dong

The doorbell goes again. 'I'll get it,' Lucas says.
'No!' I jump to my feet, scraping my chair. 'Let me.'
'Elias?' Dad says. 'It's probably just Steve or Paula.'
Lucas raises his eyebrows at me playfully.
I feel the smallest twinge of panic. Yes. *Yes!* Oh, sweet panic, I've missed you.
Wait. This could be a problem. A really big problem. 'Um…'
But Lucas is already in the hallway, making his way to the front door.
Maybe Intense Ingrid is right. Maybe the world is about to end.

4

FEEL ALIVE

'There's a girl here.' Lucas stares at the three of us from the hallway. 'Says her phone is somewhere in this house? Used a tracking app or something.'

Dad frowns. Mum's face pinches. I feel their confused gazes turn on me.

'That's brilliant!' I say, standing so quickly that I bang the table with my knee. I take the phone out of my pocket and hold it up – purple case, stickers and all. Hiding it in plain sight is the only way. 'I found this at the bus stop. She dropped it in the queue. I wondered how I'd get it back to her!'

I see frowns. Frowns all around. I look at my brother, scoping for any sign of what she might have told him. 'Is it a girl about my age?'

'Yeah.'

'Denim jacket? Doc Martins?'

'Yup.'

'Great! I thought it might be her. Thank God she has GPS tracking.'

Lucas shrugs. 'She seems nice.'

'Is she out there now?'

'Yeah.'

There's an awkward silence. I really don't want to meet her again. Or Boss. I definitely don't want to meet Boss.

'Why didn't you leave it with the driver?' Dad says. I can see the cogs of suspicion start to turn in his brain.

'Driver was a mean, angry man,' I say. 'I didn't trust him.'

'Right,' he says.

'I'll sort it,' I say calmly. 'One sec—'

'Eli, don't you think—' Before Mum can finish her sentence, I'm in the hall, heading towards the half-open door. I open it fully, but the porch is empty.

Strange. I don't like games. Games I can't win.

I step outside, pulling the door shut behind me. 'Hello?'

I edge down the steps and along the tiled pathway between Mum's rhododendron bushes. When I get to the gate, I stop and look around.

No one. That's—

'Well, you're a slippery little fucker, aren't you?'

Oh. Not happy then.

In this moment I feel nothing but apathy. I really should be concerned, or at least surprised. But I'm not. *Damn it.*

I turn to the shadows behind me, back to the rhododendron bushes. 'I have one question,' her voice says shakily. I hear her sniff. 'Why did you take it?'

She appears out of the darkness and when she enters the light, it's like I'm seeing someone else. She's smaller than I remember, softer. A little *delicate* looking.

Hang on. Is she... Yes, she is. She appears to be *crying*. Well, that's... Not what I expected.

And... Nope. I don't feel sorry for her. Not in the slightest.

She wipes her nose on the back of her sleeve. 'You're clearly rich enough. So, why did you take it?'

'Um... Are you OK?' I murmur. To ... distract. Although I do sort of want to know the answer.

'What the hell do you care?' she says, a stringy bit of snot clinging to her upper lip. Her face looks puffy like she's been crying for a while. Strands of dark curly hair stick to her cheeks. She steps towards me.

'Um... One second. Is your name Boss? Because I swear—'

She raises her eyebrows. '*What?*'

'I just...' I glance back towards the road.

'Answer my question.' She steps forwards again, until she's right in front of me. I glance at the front door. '*Why did you take it?*'

She pulls her hand from her pocket and points something towards me.

Something sharp flashes in her hand. A blade. A little penknife.

I should be shitting myself right now. But I'm not.

And damn it. *Not here.* This could all end very badly.

I put my hands up and step backwards away from her because that's what a scared person would do.

'*All right, all right.*' I keep my voice to a whisper, trying to lead her away from the front door. But she's not moving and she's starting to look fierce again, like the girl who chased me from the bus. And now there's nowhere to run except *at* her. But no, because *the knife*. It's probably best to be honest and hope that's enough to make her leave.

'Um. I...' I'm usually good at this. Why can't I think? 'It was just a ... little project.'

She pulls a face. 'A little *project*?'

'Yeah. I was just trying to ... um ... feel ... something.'

She clenches her empty fist and before I can duck, she smacks me with it right on the side of the head. Wow, that hurt. 'Feel *that*?'

'Yep.' I clutch my cheek. Jesus wept, she's strong. 'Definitely did.'

'Piece of shit,' she says, grabbing her phone from my hand. 'What kind of excuse is that?'

'It's not. I –' ow, my teeth – 'I was trying to feel guilt.'

'To feel *guilt*?'

'Yes. Yep. Correct.'

'Oh, well, that's *normal*.' Her voice echoes down the street. She needs to be quiet. This could *really* mess things up for me... 'And did you?'

'Um... No.'

She shakes her head. 'What is *wrong* with you?'

'That's a good question.' And probably one not best suited to right outside my front door.

'Yeah, it is.'

'Could you just... I dunno – maybe try and keep it down a bit?'

'Keep it *down*? Are you for real?'

'Yeah, just...' Be polite. 'Please. Just ... please.' I check the front door again.

'But you haven't answered me. *Why did you rob me?*'

Because I wanted to feel something. How is she not getting this? 'Look it's... I pictured your mum dying and everything.'

Her face suddenly drops. She goes still. '*What?*' she spits. 'How did you know that?'

No. Don't tell me. Is she joking?

Oh, God. She's crying again. What does that feel like?

'Listen. I'm so sorry. I didn't realise—'

She turns to the house, then back to me, eyes burning. 'Who the hell *are* you?'

'I'm not anyone. I didn't know about your mum. I swear. It was just made up. Which is weird because… Anyway, doesn't matter. I was trying to think of something sad that had happened to you, so I'd feel worse.'

Her mouth hangs open. She looks disturbed, offended and totally baffled all at once. And I can't blame her. 'That's deeply psychotic. Are you aware of that?'

'Yeah. I can see that now.'

'You can see that *now*?' She snorts.

'You have your phone back. I always wanted to get it back to you.'

She starts inspecting it. 'Have you done anything to it?'

'No. Look, if we're going to keep talking – which, you know, is cool – could we possibly do this down the road a bit?'

'No.'

'OK, fine.' I watch her scroll through the screen, muttering about doing something terrible to me if I've so much as opened it. As she removes the purple case, studying it like she's trying to find out if I've infected it with a lethal dose of Batshit Crazy, I scan the stickers littering the back. A slice of watermelon. A smiley face. A glittery star.

One catches my eye – a cartoon rabbit. But not a nice cartoon. It's intense, angry. It's just the head, with big over-ear headphones and black eyes staring right at me, into my soul. Underneath it are the words FEEL ALIVE.

'What's your problem?' Oh, she's looking at me again. 'Why are you staring?'

'I'm not. I just...'

She reattaches the phone case, closes the blade back into the handle of the penknife so it clicks, then pushes past me and steps on to the pavement. I expect her to turn and go, but she doesn't.

Please, just go. It's been lovely, but it really is about time.

'That shark that bit you.' She points to my scar. 'Should've taken your head off.'

'Well, that's mean.' Also, please whisper like me.

'Are you serious? You just *robbed* me.'

'Shh!'

'What? Mummy and Daddy can't know the truth?'

'Exactly.' Damn it. I meant to just think that.

She shakes her head again. 'You really don't give a shit, do you?'

'No.' I do believe honesty is important.

'Right. I see.' Something flickers in her eyes. Anger. I recognise it. Galvanising. Propulsive. God, I miss it. 'I think they should know the truth about their darling son.' She pushes past me, heading back up the pathway towards the front door. 'That he's a complete loony.'

'Wait!' I hiss. I grab her arm and she spins round, eyes blazing. 'Don't. Please.' She laughs like I'm pathetic. 'You can't.'

She folds her arms. 'Oh, yeah? Why?'

'Because, because...' Oh. *Yes.* 'You just pulled a knife on me. I'll call the police.'

She stiffens. 'Self-defence,' she says, but she actually looks a bit scared. She glowers at me. 'How old are you?'

'Twenty.'

She seems unconvinced. I sigh and sweep my fringe out of my eyes.

'What's that?' she says as the sleeve of my top rides up. She's pointing at the stick and poke tattoo on the inside of my wrist.

'It's…' This isn't the time, Nisha. 'It's a bird.'

Her face screws up. 'A bird?'

All right, no need to take that tone. I'm aware it doesn't look much like one.

Suddenly, a click from the door.

'Everything OK out here?' Dad calls from the top of the steps.

I smile. 'All good!' I look at Nisha. *Police*, I mouth.

She frowns, purses her lips, then waves. 'Hi!' She's very over the top, but it's better than nothing. 'Your son has been so *kind*,' she says. 'You must be so *proud*.'

Her voice echoes down the street. But I'm OK with people hearing that bit.

Dad nods. 'We are.'

'Won't be a minute, Dad.'

'Don't be long, Eli. You need an early night before therapy tomorrow.'

Why would he—

He closes the door.

I turn to her and smile. 'Right, so, glad we cleared this mess up. It was nice to meet you and I'm really genuinely sorry about your mum. Let's just call it even and leave it at that, yes? You can go now.'

But I can see she's thinking. 'Wait.' She points to the door. 'Is that the man from the telly?'

'Um…'

'He works for the government, right?'

Bollocks. 'Um…'

She tilts her head. 'Interesting.'

Deflect. 'Where do you live?' I say.

'Are you stupid? You really think I'm going to tell you where I live?'

Be nice. 'I could give you a lift home. Or my dad can, if you're scared of me or whatever.'

'My boss is here.' She points down the road to where I see two parking lights on a banged-up Nissan Micra.

Ohhh. 'Is that Boss?'

'Huh?'

'Boss. Is that his name?'

'Boss is my boss.'

'Oh, right.' At least I now know his parents were kind enough not to christen him Boss. I'll sleep better knowing that. Although I don't really sleep. *Anyway.* 'He seemed quite angry. I'd appreciate you telling Boss not to hunt me down.'

'He's not called *Boss.*'

'Right.'

'He's called Paul.'

Oh, I prefer Boss. Although I'm not sure how much damage a Paul could do. 'OK. Got you.'

'Paul wants to fuck you up.'

Change topic. 'I like your music,' I say.

'Huh?'

'I liked the music. Max Richter. I liked it a lot.'

She looks at me like I'm an entirely new species.

'I actually prefer no vocals. Just sounds. Do you know Brian Eno?' I ask as she begins to walk out of the gate. 'You'd like him.' I realise that's a wild stab in the dark (pun intended), but I think she might. '*Music for Airports*. It's the best album.'

She doesn't reply, which I guess is reasonable. She heads towards the Nissan Micra and climbs inside. I edge back into the darkness of the rhododendron bushes as it drives slowly away, past the house. I catch a glimpse of Paul at the wheel. He looks like a science teacher, like all Pauls do. So that's good.

I head back into the house. When I get inside, Dad is waiting by the lilies.

'Everything OK, Eli?'

Make yourself look surprised. Happy. Anything.

I pull a face. 'Yeah! Great.' I put my thumb up. 'She called me a saint.'

'That's good, son. Quite an eventful time at the bus stop,' he says. 'Lots of good deeds you've done today.'

'I'm a doer of good deeds.'

'You are.' He looks at me for a little too long. 'Like I said, I'm proud of you. Your dinner is getting cold.'

He goes up the stairs. When he reaches the top and disappears round the corner, I turn back to the mirror and go to pull my ghost vampire face again. But as I do, I nearly jump. *Nearly*.

Because as I see my reflection, for a split second, I think it's someone else entirely.

5

THUNDERCLAP

I want you to understand something about the premeditated acts. I do them because I want to know if I can be like I was before.

Since the Incident, I've been numb. Empty. Cold. I need to feel something again to know that I still can. To know that the things I'm missing still exist somewhere in my brain and maybe I can jump-start them back into existence. All of them. Remorse. Guilt. Pain. Fear. And the other ones. The good ones. I want those back too.

Sometimes – very rarely – I have this dream. In the dream, I'm with someone – a shadow. We're lying together on a pebble beach and I feel warm inside like a soft wave of heat is rippling through me. I stand and begin to walk to the edge of the water, the figure right behind me. We enter the waves together and plunge beneath the surface. But when we come up for air, I see its face. It's a bloody, mangled mess. It opens its mouth and gurgles as it tries to speak. Then I wake.

I haven't cried in a year. And bad things have happened that should really have made me cry. Sometimes I'll sit on the bathroom floor and try to squeeze out tears, digging my nails into my temples and pulling at my hair. But it doesn't work.

They say it's the trauma. *The trauma, the trauma, the trauma.* All I know is that it churned me up and spat me out, leaving me a withered mess.

I believe that somewhere in the emptiness there's still a great amount of fear. I hope there is. I really do. Because being numb to fear is not nice. I promise you.

I want to be scared again. I need to be. If I'm not, the thing I should be most scared of is myself.

～

I wake not screaming. I've learned not to make a noise now when the storm of agony takes hold. A stark white bolt of electricity shattering my senses as the pain takes over.

I can feel it in my nails, in every hair on my body. I clutch at my neck, gasping for breath, my fingers searching for something wrapped around it. But it's all inside me. It has a weight to it. Pulling me down into the mattress to take me to some unknowable depths.

This one is a bad one. The pain won't go. It has a name: *thunderclap*. A headache that turns my brain into mush.

I could text Melinda, but I can hardly see. It's late. Or early. And I don't want her to think I'm struggling. *Everyone is fine. Everyone is safe.* I turn to my bedside table and fumble for the foil packet of painkillers.

I place a pill on my tongue and slowly stand. My bedroom tilts as I stagger towards the window – a small rectangle at the top of the wall. My parents call my room *the snug*, but there's nothing snug about it. When we moved from Lewes, they said I should sleep down here in the cellar because it would be easier to access the bathroom if I needed it in the night. But I know it was so they wouldn't be disturbed by the noise.

At first, it didn't work. I was too loud. They'd come down every time and hold my hand while I screamed. I don't want that any more. I push the side of my fist into my mouth, muting the cry that's about to escape me.

When the pain affords me a moment of relief, I lift my hand, click the latch on the window and push so it opens out to the flower bed beside the porch. I draw in gulps of air.

I stand like this for I don't know how long. I crane my neck and count the street lamps to try to regulate. I can't see stars here. I could back in the old house in the countryside where the air was clear. They were so bright. But here the sky is an endless blue ink. And it smells different. Back there it was sharp. Fresh. It opened my brain like I was jumping into freezing water with each inhalation.

I miss that house. I miss before.

Slowly, I start to gather myself. I shuffle back to my bed and plug in the sleep lamp Melinda gave me. The orange stone gives off a soft glow. Crystal salt. Himalayan. Peaceful.

My floor is covered in clothes. Random things I've bought from charity shops for dressing up. I know that sounds childish, but I enjoy becoming someone else. My desk is covered in paints, pastels and half-finished sketches of deconstructed brains.

I stare at the wall opposite my bed. Pictures of me growing up are pinned with tacks as a reminder of who I am. Or was.

Then I do what I always do and reach under my bed to pull out my laptop. But I stop when I see the familiar wooden box next to it, with its handwritten label.

GUILT BOX

No one knows about it. No one can.

I slide open the lid to reveal the various mobile phones and wallets, along with a few bank notes, that I've taken as part of my side project. There's a little slip of paper inside, with the heading:

TALLY OF HOW MANY TIMES I HAVE FELT GUILT/FEAR/SHAME

The rest of the page is blank. Not once have I felt anything. Not once.

I'm going to have to go bigger. Be more ... creative.

I put the lid back on and shove the box so it slides out of sight. I then take my laptop and wrap my quilt around my shoulders. I open it up to reveal a paused screen and press play.

As I watch what I objectively know is gruesome and terrifying, I remind myself that there was a time when *The Exorcist* made me hide behind the sofa. Sometimes I get the odd glimmer of the fear I felt before. It starts with that buzz I found today at the bus stop. That rush when the doorbell went. But it never leads to more.

Tonight, all I feel is indifference.

I press pause just as Regan is levitating off the bed.

The silence of night simmers around me. Then an image comes into my brain. A rabbit.

A cartoon rabbit, staring and intense.

I open the internet browser. Hover my fingers over the keys. And then I type: *feel alive.*

I'm met with endless search results: adverts for multivitamins and supplements, a YouTube video of a song by someone called KAMRAD, a blog post called *how base jumping saved my life*. I begin to click through further browsing suggestions. *What makes a person feel alive? Does music make you feel alive? How can I feel alive again?* I read advice on Reddit encouraging me to find something I'm passionate about, something that gives me a *thrill*.

There are so many answers and no rabbits.

I go back to the home screen and I type: *feel alive rabbit*.

Reams of veterinary advice, interspersed with children's songs about bunnies.

I go back. I type again: *feel alive intense rabbit headphones*.

Something about Gordon Ramsay grilling roadkill. A post called *this is disgusting: be warned*, showing pictures of malnourished rabbits in tiny hutches. Headphones for children with bunnies all over them.

I type once more: *I want to feel alive. I am numb. Rabbit hole.*

I click on images. There aren't many of them. Maybe fifteen on the whole of the internet. *Alice in Wonderland.* Johnny Depp in a red hat. A poster for a Nicole Kidman film…

And then I see it. The rabbit from Nisha's phone case. The exact one. I feel a tiny vibration inside me. I move the cursor, hovering it over the picture.

A web page pops up: a black page with an even larger picture of the rabbit. Close up, I can see its whiskers, the mouth seemingly smiling – but in a strange and sinister way – and its piercing eyes never leaving me. Beneath it, there's white writing.

TRAUMALAND

FEEL ALIVE

I click the words. Nothing happens.

I scroll back up to the rabbit's face and click again. This time, the screen changes. Another black page with more white words.

DARE TO COME DOWN THE RABBIT HOLE?

Fridays/Saturdays | 9 p.m. onwards
Feral St, London SE1
Beneath the railway bridge | White door
Dress appropriately
18+, ID required
Payment by bank card only

TraumaLand. I stare at the word, repeating it over and over in my mind. Friday and Saturday… Interesting. Because tomorrow is Friday.

I shut the laptop, lie back and watch the ceiling swim in the glow of the lamp. As I do, I can't stop thinking about Nisha's face. Distraught.

And all I can think is, I want that.

6 (66)

There's this bit in *The Exorcist* where the mum is fighting with the doctors, the psychiatrists, about what's happening to her daughter Regan. They tell her Regan has had a complete personality change because of a rare lesion on her brain.

But Regan's mum is convinced it's nothing to do with that because her daughter has got a green face and is acting all possessed and stuff. There's this great moment where Ellen Burstyn, who plays the mum, looks like she's about to go full-on nuts because she suddenly understands that no one really has a clue. That moment makes me realise that so much of the brain is unknown. Often people are just grasping for answers when it comes to the brain. Guessing about this thing that is so important and complex, delicate and extraordinary. People just ... make shit up.

That scene is probably my favourite bit in the whole film. Well, that or the bit where Regan scuttles backwards down the stairs on all fours then vomits blood everywhere while upside down.

I like that bit too.

It's three minutes to eight, which means Melinda is due to arrive in approximately two hours. I still have absolutely no idea how I'm going to get through it.

Eli's Trauma Processing Day.

Melinda coined that term. She likes doing that – naming things. I'd think it was quite a cool name for a day if I wasn't so directly involved. Anyway, it seems to have caught on because Mum wrote it in big fat marker pen on the Lake District calendar pinned to the fridge.

ELI'S TRAUMA PROCESSING DAY!
10 a.m.

At 10 a.m. the Incident will be recounted and processed just in time for lunch. Trauma then a tuna baguette.

Mum put a bright orange Post-it on the calendar, just in case we missed it, with the words all family members must attend underlined twice.

First I need to remember what it feels like to be completely and utterly terrified. I need to experience a potent injection of fear in order to convincingly re-enact my trauma in front of my whole family. Because if I'm unable to convince the attendees of today's festivities that I understand what happened to me – that I can *move through it step by step, experiencing the feelings in real time, then leave them behind with love and kindness* – then I'm screwed. More therapy, more family meetings, more concern, more lying.

And I don't want that any more.

So, I've concocted a plan. I'd thought about smashing my face into the wall a few times, or stepping into moving traffic (not fatally, just enough to know how bad it could be) in order to evoke the Terror. But sadly they'd notice the bruises and blood, and I can't have that. They need to think I'm not being sneaky when it comes to my trauma-processing journey. That I'm the opposite of sneaky: open, honest and willing.

I've spent the night hyper-fixating. Everything is a bit fuzzy at the edges and I have a strange, sleepless metallic taste in my mouth. But the hyper-fixation has served me well and now I know exactly what to do. I'd be excited, if I could be.

Maybe I am excited because my fingers are tingling. But that might be from where I've been twisting a rubber band around them for the past ten minutes while waiting for Mum and Dad to leave the house for their morning run (which they do every day, together, *willingly*). They turned purple. My fingers, not my parents. I was interested to see if they would burst. They didn't.

Something keeps pulling my thoughts back to the image of that hell bunny on the website. *TraumaLand*. Why is it so appealing? So *seductive*? Is it the mystery? Is it the rabbit?

I think it's the rabbit.

I hear the front door slam and look at the digits on my phone.

08:00

Like clockwork.

I peer up through my grid window to see my parents' running shoes trotting down the path, completely in sync.

They turn left out of the gate, their matching fluorescent hi-vis running jackets flashing as they speed off.

They'll be half an hour exactly. They're very exact about these things.

It's *go* time.

I creep up the little flight of steps and unbolt the door. As I creep out on to the ground floor (I don't know why I'm creeping, but I like it), I glance back down the steps into my bedroom. My Dark Underground Abode. I've painted a raven on the stone floor so that it's the first thing you see when you look down. Edgar Allen Poe would be proud.

I make a point of showing it to Mum's friends when I give them the grand tour. Of my cell. Not the rest of the house. The rest of the house looks like something from an interior design magazine.

Oh, I forgot to say. I'm dressed as the Joker.

I found an old waistcoat, made a tie out of paper and stuck it on to a paisley shirt. I then coloured my hair green with a marker pen (took ages) and used some old face paints to make the smile. I'm the Joaquin Phoenix version. It was a toss-up between his and Heath Ledger's, but I don't own a purple coat. The costume isn't an intrinsic part of the plan. I just thought it would be fun – and appropriate. What with me being like him now. You know, a psychopath.

I'm also carrying two wire clothes hangers. These are relevant to the plan. You'll see.

I go up the stairs to the first-floor landing where the walls change colour from beige to light green (smoke-sage, apparently). I can hear Lucas in his bedroom talking on FaceTime to Intense Ingrid, which is useful. They like to talk intensely for a very long time so he'll be tied up. Not literally. Although Ingrid is a little dark-sided so maybe she's corrupted him.

I creep along the hallway (still creeping, still fun), past Dad's study and Mum's 'closet' where she keeps about six hundred versions of the same outfit – the silk shirt and trouser set she loves – towards the next flight of stairs. The house is three-storeys tall. Four, if you count the attic. Five, if you count my cellar.

As I make my way up the second flight of stairs, I'm suddenly hit, mid-ascent, by the smell of what can only be described as My Parents. It's not gross – it's just *them*. Their clothes. Their auras. It should make me feel *at home* and *safe*, but all I get is lavender hand soap and hard work, which is just a bit… Actually, yeah. Gross.

I tiptoe along the landing towards their bedroom, the colour of the walls changing to a chalky pink – calming, apparently. I don't often come up here. The last time was maybe half a year ago, in the dead of night. I was screaming in agony and could hardly breathe, so Mum made a bed up in the hallway so she could keep an eye on me. She said the calming pink might help. Sweet of her, but also wrong.

I look up at the ceiling – at the hatch to the attic. Mum's study. I know how to open it because I stared at it the whole time I was up here screaming, but it's going to take a little skill, which is why I'm carrying the hangers.

I don't know where Mum and Dad keep the long pole thing to open it. I assume their bedroom, but no way am I going in there. They seem to spend a little while in the bedroom after their joint run (no, please, just no) and Mum is a complete order freak, so she'd know if it had been so much as breathed on.

Hence the hangers. Sneaky. Shh.

I start untwisting them, which is actually really hard as I don't want them to snap. I then twist them round each other to make a long, thin wire with a hook at the end. I'm quite proud of myself. I lift it up and manage to hook the end on to the latch.

I pull, but the latch doesn't budge. I can feel myself sweating. In part because of the too-tight trousers I'm wearing for my Joker costume, but also because the clock on the wall says ten past, which means my parents will be back in twenty minutes.

When I pull again, the wires nearly come apart under the strain, but then I hear a click as the hatch opens. A wooden ladder drops down to the floor with a thud, about an inch from my face, nearly taking my head off.

I don't even flinch. Just feel a waft of air move my fringe.

I drop my trusty attic-opener, then climb up the ladder until my head surfaces into darkness. I clamber through the square gap and feel a cord dangling into my face. As I pull it, a soft light flickers from the ceiling.

I've been up here before, when we'd just moved in, but I forgot how bougie it is. All fluffy beige carpet, freshly painted walls, dark woodwork and soft furnishings. Then I see something. Something that wasn't here the last time.

There are stacks of cardboard storages boxes lined up in the eaves, perfectly ordered and neat, just like Mum. I notice an armchair tucked into the corner – expensive looking, dark wood, with brass plating and beige linen cushions – a reading lamp behind it, donning a blue flower-patterned shade. Very Virginia Woolf, but the comfortable version.

What's in the boxes, though?

No time. Need to move. Stick to The Plan.

I look up and see what I need. The window in the slanted ceiling. Bingo. My passage to the roof.

I take off my shoes, pull the chair beneath the window and stand on it. The chair creaks a little like the wood is splitting. *Oops.* I reach up, push my thumb on to the metal button on the handle at the bottom of the frame and twist it open.

Easy. So easy. When I push the glass, the window tilts up into the grey sky and tiny raindrops tickle my face.

I hoist myself up through the gap and out on to the tiles. I nearly lose my handmade paper tie in the process, but just about manage to keep it in place. I slowly stand and balance on the tiles, trying not to slip. The roof is wet and more slanted than I'd expected.

I am exactly where I need to be.

I look out across the sky and see the surrounding rooftops pointing up into the perpetual grey. But I feel no fear, just an appreciation of the view. London looks great from up here.

Damn it. OK. Terror reminder.

Now, look down.

I turn my gaze to the front garden and the road below, but the world just looks smaller. Not scarier.

Nothing. *Nothing.*

I conjure up an image – my mangled, twisted body on the grass, shattered bones and brain matter splatted all over it.

And… Is that…? Is that panic I sense within?

I think… I think it *is*.

More. *More.*

I picture an ambulance turning up, paramedics, chest compressions as I splutter blood.

Mum crying.

Dad crying.

Yes. *Yes.* This is it! I feel bad. I feel bad!

Oh my God, this is amazing. I knew this would—

'*Elias?*' Oh, bollocks. 'What on *earth* are you doing?'

7

BIRD IN FLIGHT

Two people step into view, staring up at me.

'What are you doing up there?' the woman calls, panicked. 'Are you crying?' I wish. 'Do you need help?'

It's Steve and Paula. The neighbours with the son that fancies me. Oh joy. And … yep. There he is, joining them.

All three of them gawp up at me. OK. This could be an issue.

'Hi!' I wave.

They look tiny. Like terrified finger puppets. I, in contrast, am not even remotely scared. *I was so close—*

'Why are you dressed like that?' Paula shouts. She turns and I see her lips move as she mouths something to her husband. I don't catch all of the words, but two of them definitely read as *potentially psychotic*. She turns back to me. 'Is your mum in, Elias?'

'No – she's out running with Dad. It's all fine. Honestly!' I wave again. *Just wave.*

They don't look convinced. Paula is whispering to Steve, while rooting through her handbag. She takes out her phone. I can't quite bring myself to look at Peter, but I know he isn't taking his annoyingly kind eyes off me.

Wait. Paula's calling my mum. *She's such a snitch.*

'Stop!' I cry. My feet slip a little on the tiles. 'You don't need to—'

'I think it's best your parents know, Elias. They might be worried.'

'There's nothing to worry about!'

'Oh, yes, I know!' She smiles patronisingly. 'But let's just make sure.'

'But—'

'I love your little costume!' She cuts me off. 'You look very sweet.' Pipe down, Paula. I never liked you.

I smile back, mirroring her condescension. 'It's not sweet, Paula. I'm a mentally ill clown who's lost touch with reality and has the simple mission of wreaking anarchy and chaos.' Oops. Couldn't help it. They all look petrified. 'The character – the Joker. Not me.' Well, maybe a little bit. 'I just like dressing up.'

I sound like a three-year-old.

'OK, Elias!' Steve puts his hand up like it might stop me from hurtling to the ground. 'You look very cool!' He assumes his wife's patronising tone. Not you too, Steve. I believed you were different. 'We're just going to call your mum. Just want to make sure everything is A-OK!' He makes an OK sign with his fingers.

God, can these people back off and let me feel the fear of a ten-metre drop alone? *I was so close.*

'Honestly, it's all fine! Don't be concerned! I'm in the middle of something and can't be disturbed. Neither should you be.' I nod encouragingly. 'Please, on with your day, good people.'

Paula stares. Steve stares. Peter stares, but in a gentle way. Why are they not moving? *Quick*, think of something. 'This is part of an art project!'

'*Art* project?' Paula sounds confused.

I must un-confuse her. 'Yes!'

'Oh? And what project is that?'

'It's called ... Mangled Perspectives.' Just keep lying. Good things happen to those who lie. 'I want to document how different the world is from up here.' More. They need more. 'I'm going to apply to art college with it. Goldsmiths.'

'*Goldsmiths?* Elias! That's wonderful news!'

'I know! It's a great day for everyone!' I lower my voice and pull a concerned face. 'But my parents can't know…'

Paula raises her eyebrows. 'Why not?'

I pause. 'Because, Paula… I don't…' I shake my head sadly. 'I don't want to disappoint them if I don't get in. I'm still quite…' I make the next word sound like it's very painful to say, '*vulnerable*.'

Paula's face softens. She lowers her phone. 'Oh, Elias…'

Oh, Paula. So fickle.

'I know,' I say. 'I hate disappointing them.' I wipe my dry eyes.

Paula looks like she might cry herself. 'Your mum told me how good at art you were. That's so lovely. She'll be so pleased.'

Peter's eyes are lingering. Kind. So kind. Please stop.

'Well, let's see. I hope I can live up to her expectations.'

'OK, Elias,' Paula says, then winks. I watch the phone go back into her bag. 'I think what you're doing is very brave.'

Brave. Yes. Yes, I am, Paula. I always liked you. 'Will you get down safely? And we won't say a word.'

'But of course.'

She nods. They're all nodding. Please leave now.

Steve looks at me cautiously. 'So, you're going to climb down the drainpipe, Mr Poppins?'

Shut up, Steve. 'No, I came up through the—' Hang on. They can't know I've been in the attic. They might tell Mum. 'Yes. *Exactly*, Steve. Chim chim cher-oo.'

'We'll leave you to it,' Paula says, taking Steve's arm.

'Have a wonderful day!' I shout.

'Do you fancy hanging out at some point?' Peter suddenly says.

Paula's face looks like it might melt with the reality of what this would mean. The course of her future altering as she understands she could potentially invite this unstable man-child into her family.

'No need to rush anything, Pete,' she says quietly. I watch her take his sleeve and together they begin to head off up the street.

When they've gone, I take a small step back to resume my trauma-experiencing position and find myself dropping backwards, falling down through the open skylight. My back cracks on the wooden frame of the chair.

It takes me a second as I lie sprawled across the carpet. A second to feel the pain. And fuck my life does it hurt. That's more like it. The chair didn't break. My back might have.

Once I've stretched it out, checking all bones are still working correctly, which they annoyingly seem to be – a broken back might have made me feel scared – I stand.

Nothing. What a kick in the teeth. Actually, a kick in the teeth might have been better.

As I regain my focus, I scan my eyes over the storage boxes, each neatly labelled: MISCELLANEOUS, BOOKS, KITCHENWARE, ADVANCE BRITAIN. My gaze fixes on to one in particular.

MEDICAL DOCUMENTATION
E.G.P.

Elias Gollum Pew.
OK, fine. My middle name is Gordon, but I've submitted an application to the Deed Poll office to change it to Gollum. It has a better ring to it.

A whole box of my very own medical documentation. I hadn't realised there was so much of it. I know I was in the hospital for a while, recovering. But still.

Before I can stop myself, I'm hobbling across the carpet towards it, ignoring the shooting pain in my back. The box is open. A cut line runs though the Sellotape that joins the two cardboard flaps, revealing a small gap through which I can see a heap of papers. A Stanley knife lies on the carpet beside it.

My first thought is: there seem to be an increasing number of knives in my life lately. My second thought is: I know Mum said she wants to try to support me as best she can, but do my medical records really need to be her night-time reading? Can't she just enjoy something a little more commercial like Jane Austen or Sally Rooney?

Something behind the box catches my eye, where the slanted roof meets the carpet. Another box. It's tattier than the rest and there are drawings all over it. Vampires, gargoyles and other gruesome winged things.

I kneel down to get a better look. There's a label stuck on its side, but this one is handwritten.

The handwriting is my own.

MY STUFF – DON'T TOUCH

Huh? My body involuntarily shudders. A real shudder.

OK. That's ... new. Or old. Depending on how you look at it.

I pick up the Stanley knife. And then I'm crawling (creep crawling) until I'm right in front of the box. I click the knife so the blade shoots out of its safety and press the tip into the Sellotape. It makes a small, satisfying puncture sound: a slow pop. I move it along the tape until the cardboard flaps open. When they do, I'm hit with something. A smell.

I smell paint.

My stomach clenches. All my old paints. So many tubes of them.

I sift through them. Half used. Endless leaking colours, lids missing, paint now dried. There's something at the bottom of the box.

A sketchbook.

I turn in the direction of the hatch. No sound of my parents as yet, but I don't have long. For some reason, this strange feeling in my stomach pulls at me. A dull ache that feels... Well, it *feels*.

I take out the sketchbook, brushing off flecks of dried paint, and open it.

Pages have been torn out. I flick through the back ones. Blank, mostly. Then I stop as I see a sketch, done in charcoal. It's only half of one. Torn like someone has pulled at it in a hurry, leaving the remaining paper crumpled and smudged.

Half a picture.

Half a body. A chest. A torso. Naked.

No face.

The remaining hand is turned upwards. On the inside of the wrist is a tattoo – a silhouette of an m-shaped bird in flight. I look down at the tattoo on my own wrist. A self-portrait. Interesting. I never liked drawing myself that I can remember.

It seems like I've been very generous with the muscle definition.

I lift it up so I can see it in the half-light beneath the eaves. As I do, the smell of the paper, the feel of its texture on my fingertips, does something to my brain. Suddenly, a flash of memory. Me. Drawing. In a room I don't know. And someone is there. Someone I can't quite—

A shadow. A familiar shadow.

My breath catches and then I sense it. A faint pulse. Deep and tender, dangerous and sharp, right in the centre of me.

I know this feeling.

The pulse grows into a terrible throb and I'm overwhelmed by the pressure – its veracity making me dizzy, its familiarity knocking me sick.

This is fear. *This is terror.*

I know it so well. It's unmistakable.

Yes. *Yes.*

But why now?

Something falls from behind the torn page on to the carpet in front of me, twisting as it descends like a helicopter seed.

A photograph.

Tatty and worn, with creases through it like it's been folded and unfolded many times.

I lean down, squinting.

It's my family. Mum, Dad and Lucas, beaming into the camera. A long time ago, back in Lewes.

They're standing on the gravel drive of our cottage, in front of Dad's green Cadillac with the yellow stripe. He looks so proud – arms folded, shirtsleeves rolled up. Mum is smiling, actually smiling. Not the hard smile she uses for other people, but the soft one she reserves only for us – her family. Lucas has his head back, mouth open, eyes tightly shut, mid laugh.

They look so happy.

I don't feel anything. I know I should be filled up by its warmth, but nothing comes.

I think I must have taken it. I have a vague recollection of the day Dad got the car. I must have been about twelve.

I pick it up and turn it over. There's something on the back.

Handwriting. My own again, but shaky and scrawled like I was rushing when I wrote it.

Don't forget. Never. <u>Never forget.</u>
You can't – please – remember him.
Shave your head.

The air catches in my throat, a sudden heat drying it out.

I don't ... remember writing this. It's intense. And unsettling.

Remember *him*? Shave your head?

Suddenly, a bang from somewhere downstairs. The front door. Shit. My perfectly exact and in-sync parents are back.

Always keep your eye on the time.

I'm about to put the photograph back when I pause. I fold it and slide it into my pocket. Quickly – *carefully* – I slip the sketchbook into the box and push the lid shut. It won't stick, but that's fine – it'll have to be.

And then I'm moving the chair back into place and hurriedly climbing, creeping, back down the ladder. When I'm at the bottom I give it a shove to make it fold in on itself and disappear up into the ceiling. I close the hatch with my attic-opener then turn to the window. I throw the coat hangers out of it, down into the back garden, then descend the stairs.

Shit. I forgot to close the skylight.

My parents stand in the hallway, by the lilies, their matching fluorescent hi-vis jackets flashing at me. Sweaty, energised, ready for the day.

They mumble to each other about an important meeting Dad has later. Something to do with public-private partnerships. They then look at me and stop.

'Have you been upstairs?' Dad frowns slightly as he wipes his dripping forehead. 'Elias?'

'Yeah, sorry,' I say. 'I wanted to feel calm before the session with Melinda.' My voice sounds odd. Far away. 'The hallway by your room. The colour of the walls.'

'Oh, sweetie,' Mum says softly, walking towards me.

As she places her hand on my shoulder, I ball my fists and shove them in my pockets. She tells me that I'm going to do brilliantly. That she thinks what I'm wearing is possibly a little inappropriate, but that if it makes me feel comfortable, I should keep it on. I nod and smile. Because that is what we do in this family. All the while, I feel the photograph against my fingers, sending a tingling up my arm and into the back of my neck.

As Mum tells me she's going to set up the living room and put some croissants in the oven to warm them up, I feel that flicker of fear lingering deep inside. But I still have no idea why a flimsy piece of paper, rather than a ten-metre drop to the ground, was the thing that ignited it.

8

THE INCIDENT

I relate to Regan MacNeil, our possessed protagonist from *The Exorcist*. In fact, I'd go so far as to say that I have a connection with her. Here's why.

In the book version – which, yes, I have read – the doctors give Regan a prescription of Ritalin as they think she might have some form of ADHD that's causing her bizarre behaviour. Now, I don't believe possession is anything like ADHD, but part of me thinks it would be fun if they were linked in some way. Because, now brace yourself.

I have ADHD.

Tell me something I don't know, I hear you say.

Well, it was news to me.

I used to hate it – that diagnosis – *really* hate it. I was ashamed, embarrassed, back in the days when I could feel those things. But then I realised something. Those four letters could actually help me. Help me get away with stuff. With murder. Not *literal* murder – although, maybe. I understood that the symptoms could be incredibly useful. I found I could use them when people felt my behaviour was questionable. I'm not talking about *constant fidgeting* or *an inability to sit still*. I'm talking about the good ones. *Speaks without thinking. Lack of behavioural self-control. High impulsivity.*

Then something happened.

Three months before the Incident, I was put on medication to treat the ADHD because my behaviour was becoming noticeable and *problematic*. The meds helped, I suppose, at first. Calmed me. But after a couple of weeks, as the dose increased, something shifted. They sort of did the opposite of what they were supposed to do. They exacerbated the symptoms. I started to feel a bit buzzy.

Apparently, when combined with my anti-depressant, I had way too much serotonin suddenly pumping through my brain, which was fun for me – just not for everyone else. I've since been told that I was experiencing something called a *hypomanic episode*. I remember it very clearly. In fact, it's the last thing I remember before my memory suddenly stops. Before the blankness. The Gap.

The Gap of two months.

Two whole months. Gone.

But the hypomanic episode remains, clear as day. It went a bit like this.

It was January 8th. We were still living at the old house. It was cold, crisp, the days still short. My thoughts began to move very, very quickly – more so than usual – and I didn't want to sleep. Sleep was the last thing on my mind because I suddenly had so much to *do*. I'd been awake for five whole days. I was energised. Motivated. Alive. I thought I was invincible. Completely and utterly indestructible.

And it felt amazing.

During those five days I did many things. I did thirty-two trips to the local Tesco, on foot. It was a mile away so it was a good opportunity to get my steps in. I borrowed cash from Mum's purse (I'm supposed to use the word *stole*, but I didn't see it like that) to get chocolate and sweets to share with my family because I felt such an overpowering sense of love for them and I wanted to show it. And I bought some cushions and throws that I thought Mum would like. She didn't.

I also bought lots of hair dye. I dyed my hair six times, six different colours, which made my forehead blister from all the bleaching. I bought bulbs and planted them in the garden. Many, many bulbs. I felt an incredible creative surge too. I bought paint and paper and felt-tip pens from the kids' craft section and drew eighty-five pictures of distorted and dying bats.

I then decided it'd be fun and really helpful to continuously clean the whole house from top to bottom. I jet-washed the patio at 2 a.m. along with some of the neighbours' driveways, even though I didn't really know them, because I had a sudden, overwhelming desire to give back to the community.

But then Mum and Dad got annoyed – or scared, I suppose – because I went into their bedroom while they were sleeping. I woke them up when tiptoeing around the bed holding a spade (from late-night bulb planting) wearing only an apron over my underpants with fluorescent blue hair. I then asked them to come and see my good work. That made them worry. They got worried I was going to do something stupid and dangerous.

I guess they were right.

The last thing I remember is getting them to follow me into the garden at 10:30 at night.

I remember nothing else until I walked through the front door of the new London house, two months later.

January 8th until March 8th.

Exactly two months. *Exactly*. Nothing.

Which is a bit strange, don't you think?

Apparently, the Incident was so brutal that my brain decided to erase not only the night it happened, but the whole two months after it. I've been told. The erasure was because of the biological damage caused to my brain. Also, it was a form of self-protection. My mind wanted to protect me from the pain of it all. The guilt. The regret. *Post-traumatic dissociative amnesia*, Melinda calls it. I think it's kind of amazing that your brain will do that for you.

But now I want it all back. Those memories are mine and I'd like to have them again.

My parents have given me so much. Patience. Generosity. The hospital fees. The therapy fees. Melinda. They moved to London. For me. *A fresh start for Eli*. I need them to think I'm fine now.

I don't feel guilty, but I know I should. I don't feel anything.

I did back then. Everything. I felt everything. So much, all at once. It could be really painful at times. And you might think that's worse, but I don't.

⁓

Melinda sits in the armchair directly in front of me in our living room, framed by the heavy curtains hanging on either side of the bay windows.

It's here. It's happening. Therapy D-Day is upon us. It's Trauma Time.

'How's your morning been so far, Elias? Nice and relaxed?'

Melinda is wearing her posh blazer today and her hair has an extra static frizz from where she's overused the straighteners. Both these things mean that she is in the mood for serious business.

This is all we have worked for. Together.

I'm sitting on one of two dining chairs that have been placed side by side in the middle of the room on top of the rug where the coffee table usually is. Melinda smiles at me, her professional smile. I find it hard to reciprocate because I'm holding myself completely still. So still I'm hardly breathing or blinking. My family are huddled in a row on the sofa to my left, staring at me, all sad and earnest, hands in their laps, heads slightly bowed, like they're in a cold and uncomfortable church. The Pews, on their pew, expecting a miracle.

Or an exorcism. An exorcism of my pain.

'It's been pretty normal,' I say.

Melinda looks to the sofa for confirmation of my claim. Lucas looks at Mum. Mum looks at Dad. Dad looks at my paper tie and face paint. 'Yes, normal for Eli.'

Melinda's eyes scan me up and down. 'So, the Arthur Fleck outfit is for—'

'Fun.'

Melinda nods. 'Of course.'

It doesn't surprise me that she knows the real name of the Joaquin Phoenix Joker, the person I've come to my own exorcism dressed as. Unlike Meddling Paula and Vanilla Steve, Melinda is actually quite perceptive and, dare I say it, cool. I have a hunch she was a bit of a wild one in her day. Sometimes I can see a hint of chaos flickering within her. She's drawn to it, I can tell. It's why she likes me.

'I think there should be an element of fun to this, don't you?' I say hopefully.

She tilts her head sympathetically. 'I just want you to be comfortable, Elias. We all do. Today is about being comfortable, which, in turn, will allow the uncomfortable to be exposed.'

Therapy talk, how I despise you. 'Well, that does sound like fun.'

She doesn't react. She seems different in front of my family. More poised. 'Are you comfortable, Elias?'

No one is, Melinda. We are en route to my fabricated hell. 'Yes.'

'Then you are dressed appropriately.'

Dress appropriately. TraumaLand.

'We're all here for you.' Melinda's voice is soft and kind, but it makes me want to scream, *I'm going to fail, Melinda. Do my family really have to be here to see it happen?* 'Your family are here to support you as you forge the memories once and for all. After today you will move on from them with a healthy sense of acceptance and separateness. Not to be forgotten, but to be controlled.' Her eyes shine hopefully. 'And remember, there is no blame today.' She leans towards me. I try to lean away from her, but the back of my chair stops me. 'There is no blame from anyone, OK?'

To me that implies there is blame. 'Sure.'

Melinda places her hands on her knees and inhales sharply through her nose. 'OK,' she says. 'It's time to begin.'

I don't dare look at the sofa, but I can feel the anticipation aimed in my direction. I keep my eyes on Melinda and make one last-ditch attempt to make this stop. 'Are we sure this is a good idea? Collectively? Unanimously?'

She nods, but it is loaded. *We've been through this many times. You know what to do.* 'Now, please, close your eyes.'

Right. So. Yep. There is no escape. 'Well then, let the exorcism commence.'

She frowns. 'Excuse me?'

'Nothing.'

I hear anxious shuffling from the Pews' pew, but I yield and shut my eyes before I can see who it's come from.

'I'm now going to ask you some questions, Elias. Keep your answers factual and without any emotion for now.'

For now. 'Right.'

'I want you to think back to the day of the Incident.'

The day of the Incident. Great. 'OK.'

'How old are you?'

Facts. Easy. 'I'm sixteen.'

'Good. What day is it?'

'Sunday.'

'And what time is it?'

'It was … late.'

'Try and stay inside the memory, Elias, if that's OK? Talk about it as if you're there. As if it is now.'

'Oh, right. Sorry. It *is* late.'

'Good. And be more specific. We need specificity.'

I think of the night. The sky. Dark and cold. 'It's ten thirty in the evening.'

'Good. And where are you?'

'At our house in Lewes.'

'Describe it.'

Doable. 'It's at the end of a small country road with only five other houses. It's detached. Aesthetically very pleasing. More of a cottage, really. Ivy covers the outside walls. It's always reminded me of something from *Midsomer Murders*. It's right on the edge of the South Downs, at the top of a typical country hill. The garden is sloped and long, leading down into fields, with a wooded area right at the bottom. It's two storeys tall. There's a garden at the front with a pebble driveway and a garage where Dad keeps his classic car. The green soft-top Cadillac. Anyway. Yes. It's … calm. Sleepy. I really liked it there. Made me feel—'

'No emotions, Elias. Just the facts.'

'Right, sorry. No emotions.' Got that covered, Melinda. Don't you worry.

'What are you wearing?'

'I…'

'Be specific.'

The sofa squeaks nervously. 'I'm stood in the garden, wearing my underpants, one of Mum's aprons and nothing else. Oh, and I'm holding a spade.'

This is the last thing I remember. I only have Melinda's reminders to guide me now. That and her leading questions. *Please keep leading the witness, your honour.*

'But then I go inside and get changed. Sorry, I *change*. I put on some trousers and my shoes. But I remain topless.'

'Why do you do that?'

'Remain topless? I think I was just a little overexcited.'

'No, why do you change?'

Oh. 'Because I want to go out.'

'Yes. Good. You're doing brilliantly.' Oh, wonderful. 'Could you talk me through why you want to go out?'

More noise from the congregation. I try to focus. 'Yeah, sure. So, I've just cleaned the whole house, done a bit of gardening and I wanted – sorry – I *want* to go back to Tesco. It's about a mile down the road and I've previously been walking there because I like the fresh air and I'm feeling very –' *invincible* – 'energetic. It's late and cold now, but I know there's a grout cleaner in the domestic household products section that would work wonders on the grey bits between the bathroom tiles that I can't get out.'

I see the tiles in my mind. Repeating white squares and dirty grout.

That's good. *Good.*

Melinda's voice is steady. Soft. 'You want to clean the grout because you think it'll be a nice thing to do?'

'Yes.'

'OK...' There was more. I can hear it in her voice. We went over this bit a lot.

'But also, I...' What was it? 'I feel like I *need* to.'

'*Yes.*' She sounds pleased. She waits a moment, then, 'Perhaps you've become a little fixated?'

That's a leading question, Melinda. But I'm not complaining. 'Yes. *Fixated.* The grey bits are all I can see now and I want them gone.'

'And so, you decide to drive yourself to Tesco?'

'That's right.'

'Have you passed your driving test?'

I swallow. My Adam's apple suddenly feels huge, like it

might choke me. Power through. 'No. But Dad has insured me on the Volkswagen Golf and we've done a few practice sessions together, so I feel ready. I realise I'll need to use the car if I want to get to Tesco before it closes and it's important that I do.' I hear birds through the glass behind Melinda's head. 'They shut at eleven so I only have half an hour left to get there.'

'Why don't you just ask your dad to drive you?'

Because I'm indestructible. 'I think it's a good idea for me to practise… I tell my dad that.'

'Yes. You do. And where is this conversation taking place?'

'We're in the kitchen now.'

'Brilliant. Really well done. And what happens next?'

'Dad says no.'

'He does. Why is that?'

'Because it's dark. And illegal.'

'And?'

'Because my behaviour is currently a little…' Pathological. No. What's the word we use? 'Erratic.'

'Good. Why?'

'I…'

'Specific.'

'I am experiencing a hypomanic episode.'

'Great. *Very* good.' Not really, Melinda. 'You are unwell.'

I am. She's right about that. 'But I didn't… I don't know that.'

'No one does. Your mum has suspicions.'

Suspicions. 'Yes.'

'Your family are concerned about you.'

'Yes.'

'What else do you say?'

What else? 'I say I'm fine.'

'You do. You become...' She waits for me to finish her sentence.

Leading. *Good*. Shit, what do I become?

Oh, yes. 'I become ... *insistent*.'

'Good, Elias. So, you're in the kitchen with Dad.'

Please don't say it like that. He's not your dad. 'Yes.'

'Mum joins you?'

She's not your mum. *I don't remember*. 'Yes. Dad has put music on to try and calm me down. But I mess with the record player and nearly break it. He tries to stop me, but I'm ... again I'm *insistent*. And then...'

'Then?'

Oh, hell. Here we go. 'There's an argument.'

Melinda pauses. I'm not really sure what is happening outside of my own head, but I have a feeling the congregation is currently making eye contact with my Trauma Exorcist. Shuffling. Lots of shuffling.

Eventually, Melinda speaks again. 'Can you see it, Elias? Are you able to see it playing out in front of you?'

No. I see nothing. 'Yes.'

'You can start to feel the emotions now.'

Damn. 'OK, great.'

'Just take a moment.'

I need to look scared. Ashamed. I put my hands over my face and tilt my head forwards. This is what ashamed looks like, isn't it? More. *Do more*. I make my breath shudder a little.

'It's OK, Elias,' Melinda whispers. *Phew*. But she actually sounds kind of happy. 'What do you say to your parents?'

I don't remember. 'Um...'

'Something about how they make you feel.'

Leading. *Thank you.* 'I say they're suffocating me.' I strain my voice for good measure.

'Yes. You do.' I make what I hope sounds like a regretful gurgle. 'Be gentle, Elias. Stay gentle with yourself. What happens next?'

'There's lots of shouting,' I croak.

'Yes.'

'I become a little...' Make it hard to say. 'Out of control.'

I hear my brother sniff. Is he crying? Jesus, he can't be crying before me. That's just unfair. But it's also good. Good that I'm making him cry.

'What do you do that is out of control?'

Oh, God. This bit. 'Um... At some point during the shouting, I get angry. I suddenly *switch* –' her word, not mine – 'and I pick up a glass.' I push my knuckles into my eyes in an attempt to make them water. 'I turn round and throw it at my mum. It misses her and shatters on the wall behind her head.'

I stop. The room is silent. No one moves or speaks.

I think they're expecting a reaction. *React.*

I feign a sobbing noise and try to make it phlegmy.

'Yes, Elias. Very good. What next?'

I force my knuckles deeper into my eye sockets. 'Mum is really upset. Scared.'

'Can you see it? In your mind's eye?'

'I can.' I can't.

'That's *brilliant.*' Strong choice of word, Melinda. 'Where's Lucas?'

'He's gone back to university early to study. He doesn't know about … any of this.' I hear him sniff again.

'What next?'

What next? Something to do with the shovel… 'I pick up the shovel and start screaming that I feel trapped.'

'Good.'

Good! 'But Dad tells me to put it down. He says we can walk to Tesco in the morning together, that it would be a nice thing to do. But I say no, I don't want that, I need to go now.' Melinda told me to say something else at this point. Oh, *yes*. 'Mum and Dad are now both really worried that I'm going to hurt them.'

'Yes, they are.' Fantastic. I'm on a *roll*. 'Go on.'

'I'm screaming. It's chaotic. Dad manages to get the shovel out of my hand, but I grab the car keys from Mum's handbag and run for the front door. I run to the Golf, which is parked on the driveway. I open it and get into the driver's seat.'

'Can you feel the emotions?'

'Yes,' I lie. I make another small murmur, my face still in my hands.

'Good. Let it out. Let all the emotions out, Elias. And name them.'

Oh, bollocks. 'Anger.' I say quietly.

'Anger, yes. Keep going.'

'Guilt.'

'Yes.'

'Sadness.'

'Yes.'

'Shame.'

'Shame. *Yes, shame.*' All right, Melinda, calm down. 'And then?' Why does she sound so excited?

'As I put the keys in the ignition, Dad is suddenly there, in front of the car, waving his hands at me to stop. He gets into the passenger seat next to me.'

'Gordon,' Melinda says gently. 'If you would now like to join Elias.'

Um, *what*? Objection, your honour. This is… I wasn't told about this bit.

'Of course,' Dad says, his voice full of something that sounds like emotional pain. The smell of lavender and hard work waft over me as he sits on the empty chair beside me, his arm pressing into mine.

I flinch.

'Sorry,' Dad says quietly.

'No, I'm…' I don't finish.

My body is shaking. I guess that's good. That's… That's good. Right?

Wait. Is it my body that's shaking, or his?

'So, Elias,' Melinda says. 'You're now both in the car.' In the car. Yes. *Yes.* 'What does your dad say?'

'He says… He says…' I can hear him breathing right next to me. 'He says *please don't drive, son.*'

'Gordon?' Melinda's voice is extra gentle now. 'Could you please say that to Elias?'

Can we maybe not—

'Please don't drive, son,' Dad says softly, the emotional pain increasing. But I feel nothing. Other than how I want to move off the chair and go far, far away.

'What else does your dad say, Elias?'

'Um. He says…' What was it? 'He says *I think you need some help, son.*'

'Gordon?' Melinda sounds like she might cry now. Can everyone stop crying before I do?

'I think you need some help, son.' Dad's voice shakes. 'Let's go back inside where we can talk this through.' OK. Curveball. Dad's improvising. We're in unchartered territory.

It's all unchartered territory.

'Good, Gordon.' Melinda seems to like it. 'Very good.'

Maybe I should improvise. 'No, Dad. I want to get the grout cleaner and there's nothing you can do to stop me.'

Bit much? This is all a bit much.

Dad goes with it. 'Then I'll drive, son. Why don't you let me?'

Um… Best respond. 'Because I want to drive. It's only a mile.'

'Why won't you let me, son?'

I don't know, Dad! I wish I did. 'Because this is my plan and you treat me like a child.'

'Very good, Elias.' Melinda is pleased again. 'What else does your dad say?'

'I…' God. Do we have to? 'I think that was it.'

'It wasn't, Elias. He tells you something.'

'It's difficult to remember…'

'Gordon, maybe you could remind him?'

'Of course.' I feel Dad's hand on my forearm. He squeezes it.

I flinch again. 'Sorry.'

'We care about you. We love you. Don't do this.' His hand remains around my wrist, his fingers steady.

I make a stifled fake sob into my hands, but I'm worried he won't feel the tears. Because there are none.

'Does that help remind you, Elias?'

No. 'Yes. Thank you, Dad.'

'Keep going,' Melinda whispers.

'I don't listen to him. I'm still not thinking straight. I'm still out of control.'

'Good.'

'I put the key in the ignition and I start to drive.'

'Yes.'

'Dad is telling me to stop.'

'Gordon?'

'Please stop, son. Please just stop.'

'And you reply, Elias?'

'I say no.'

'Say it.'

'No.'

'Louder.'

'What?'

'Say it louder. You were screaming. That's right, isn't it, Gordon?'

'Yes. He was screaming.'

Was I? OK. 'No. No. *No!*' My voice reverberates through the room.

'Good,' Melinda says. 'This is it, Elias. Tell us what happened next.'

Dad's palm is clammy on my skin. I can do this. Just facts. 'I take a left turn out of the driveway and we're on the road. It's dark, no street lamps. I can only see the headlights ahead of us. The road is windy, trees on either side. It's a narrow country lane. I start to press my foot down on the accelerator because I'm scared that Tesco will close and I really want the grout cleaner. Dad is still telling me to stop. To slow down. To put my seat belt on. But I don't listen. My legs are shaking because of the adrenaline. I can't really hear anything. I am in a –' what was the word Melinda used? – *'trance.'* That's it. 'Hyperfixated.' *That's it.* 'I feel no fear. I just want to get there. I think it's the right thing to do. I round a corner, going very quickly. When I see the other headlights coming towards us, I panic.'

I think I recited that perfectly. Near perfectly.

'Describe it.'

'I am.'

'The panic.'

Fuck. 'It … stuns me. Disables me. Everything stops.' More. More. This is it. *Convince them.* 'I feel a heat in my stomach like a claw clenching. It grips me so hard that I freeze. I can't find the brake with my foot. The other car swerves past us, just misses. I then realise we're no longer on the road. We're still travelling very quickly, only now down the bank next to it. The ground is icy and the tyres skid. I see the headlights light up the trees. The wheels hit something and the car flips.' I stop and remove my hands from my face. I look at Dad.

He's crying. Oh, God.

'Yes, it flips,' Melinda says. 'Go on…'

Dad nods at me. 'Go on, son.'

'We tumble down the slope. Over and over. And then I feel the impact. The car stops, but my body doesn't. When I open my eyes, I'm no longer inside it. I'm on the bonnet, on the other side of the windscreen, covered in glass and blood.'

I'm panting. Sweating.

'It's OK, Elias. Picture it. Tell us. *This is it*. Visualise it. Tell us what you see.'

I see nothing. 'I see Dad is still inside the car.'

'And...'

'A low branch from the tree we hit is sticking straight through the windscreen, where the glass was. When I look into the passenger seat, I can see Dad's head is sort of drooped down, lolling forwards, and the branch is sticking straight into his stomach.' I push my knuckles as hard and deep into my eyeballs as I can. 'The branch has...' Melinda said I have to use a specific word. 'The branch has *impaled* him.' I can feel my saliva dribbling over my hands. They're wet, but not with tears. I nearly killed my dad and I can't even cry. 'And then I pass out.'

'Well done, Elias.' Melinda's voice is clear. Assured. 'Let all that pain out. Let it out. Because it's done. You are done.'

I pretend to weep – deep, guttural sobs. Dad keeps his hand on my arm.

Suddenly, an image shudders into my thoughts, clear as day. It elicits a sudden involuntary gasp from my throat.

'Oh, Eli...'

It's my first memory of the aftermath of the crash. Ever. I've had dreams, flashes of the forest, but this is new. It's real. Dad is lying on his back on the ground in the woods. Blood pours out of his stomach and I'm kneeling over him...

'You can stop now, Elias.'

But someone else is here too. A dark shadow next to me.

'Wait,' I croak. 'I think...'

'What is it?' Melinda sounds hesitant.

'I think – there's more. Dad's on the ground. In the forest. And I think someone else…'

I'm met with silence. OK, I've gone massively off-script.

'You're done now,' Melinda says quickly. 'We don't need any more. You can open your eyes.'

'But I think…' We never talked about this.

'Elias, we've finished.'

Another pair of hands, next to me. Bloody.

'But I can see it. I can actually *see*—'

'The paramedics came.' My mum's voice comes from the sofa. Calm. Precise. Gentle. 'There were lots of people. You were in and out of consciousness by that point.'

'Oh.'

I've been told countless times that Mum was with them when they arrived. Apparently, she called the police as soon as we left so it didn't take them long to find us. It would have been fatal, if she hadn't.

Mum saved us.

'Thank you, Heather,' Melinda says softly. 'Time to open your eyes, Elias.'

'But—'

'Now, please.' There's an edge to her voice.

When I do, the room is darker than I remember. Melinda is looking directly at me, tears glistening, her face taut with pain and pride. My own face feels fucked. Hot, puffy and angry. Which is good. Isn't it?

Oh my God, I'm terrible. But I don't feel terrible.

I can't look at Dad. At any of my family. I focus on Melinda's static hair.

'Now, just one more thing to help the memory recall,' Melinda says. 'I'd like you both to do something, if you're willing. I'd like you to reveal your scars.'

Um. No. Please.

I didn't sign up for that. No way…

'Sure,' Dad says quietly. 'Whatever will help Eli.'

I don't think this will.

Melinda nods approvingly. 'It will.'

'I'm not sure that I need…' I start, but I see Dad is already lifting up his top. Before I know it, his pale stomach emerges next to me. It's so bizarre that it doesn't seem real. *None of this seems real.* In the centre of his pale skin a fat red circle of scar tissue protrudes outwards like a bulging blister.

Melinda keeps her eyes on me. 'Make sure you look at it properly, Elias. It's important.'

When I do, I see small red dots surrounding it from where the doctors stitched him back together. There are some burn marks too. I can't remember how he got those. I don't think she said.

'I'm sorry, Dad,' I whisper. 'I'm so sorry. I didn't ever want to hurt you.'

Dad pulls his top back down. 'I know, son.' He turns to me. 'You don't need to blame yourself. I want you to move on from this. I forgive you.'

'Thank you, Dad.'

'Thank you, Gordon,' Melinda says. 'Forgiveness is an important part of the healing process. Now, Elias. Would you show yours?'

'I…'

I look at Lucas, still crying. I look at Mum nodding. Tearful.

It's OK. Nearly there. Nearly there, then no more of this. Just do it.

I point to my head. To the scar on my temple. 'This is from where I went through the windscreen.'

'Yes.'

'And...' I stand, my legs heavy. Leaden.

I quickly lift my top, pulling it all the way up so it's gathered under my chin. I look down at the burn marks across my tummy and chest. Webs of taut, shiny skin. The place where my left nipple once was now a smooth, pale blotch like a piece of wafer-thin ham. 'These are from when I hit the bonnet. I was scalded by the steam and battery acid that were leaking from it. The burns were so bad because I wasn't wearing a top.'

'Or your seat belt,' Melinda says, a little too forcefully.

'Right. Yes.'

'Yes. You and your dad would have died, if the doctors hadn't acted so quickly.'

I turn to Dad. 'Dad, I...' I mumble. 'I'm so sorry.' I don't know what else to say.

'It's OK, son.'

'I... I'm glad you didn't die.'

'Me too.' And then his arms are around me, strong, pulling me into him. And I feel – nothing. 'I love you, son.'

'I love you too.'

Maybe you hate me and I get that. I do.

'Well done, both of you,' Melinda says. 'How are you feeling, Elias?'

Dad releases his grip. I turn to her. 'Um...'

'The memories are all there. You've proved that. And you've processed them.'

'Yeah...'

'And now you can begin to move on from this. The memories exist and the pain is real. But you are capable and strong and you, Elias, are *not* a bad person.'

I do everything I can not to tell her how wrong she is. How deeply mistaken. 'Um... Thank you, Melinda. For everything.'

'You're very welcome. Now –' she turns to the sofa – 'why don't you all join together in the centre of the room?'

Mum and Lucas slowly rise and make their way to the rug. They both look exhausted. Melinda says something else and then I realise I'm standing in a circle with my family, Dad holding my left hand, Mum my right. 'Remember,' Melinda says from somewhere on the periphery, 'pain makes us stronger. You are united as a family. And you will continue to support each other.'

As we stand in our little post-exorcism circle, I catch Lucas's eye. He gives a small wink. I need to make him think I appreciate and understand him, so wink back.

'Shall we hug?' I hear myself say. 'Group hug?' That's what appreciative people do, isn't it? They group-hug.

Everyone is looking at me a bit funny. Have I gone too far?

I do it anyway, pulling them into me.

'I love you all very much and I'm grateful and appreciate you,' I say like a weird machine.

When the group hug is over, I don't know what to do.

I look at Mum. She smiles sadly. Gratefully.

She turns to Melinda. 'Thank you,' she says. 'For all you have done.'

'You're very welcome,' Melinda replies.

'Right,' Mum says. 'Now, who'd like something to eat? Are you a fan of croissants, Melinda?'

Melinda beams. 'Sounds wonderful.'

Wonderful. I watch them all make their way towards the door.

Lucas turns. 'You coming, bro?'

'Yeah, just need a second.'

Once he's gone, I stare at the wall. I'm broken. The crash has broken me. It might as well have killed me.

What am I going to do?

I feel the photograph in my pocket. A pang of heat moves through the fabric, up my leg, into my stomach, where it stops and twists like it's punctured my insides.

Never, never forget. Remember him.

I feel like I might burst into flames. Or tears. Actual tears.

For the first time since the crash, I think I'm about to cry. My whole body aches. Not from physical pain, but from something else, somewhere deep in my gut. For the briefest moment I feel completely in pain, completely in my own body. *Alive.*

'Eli!' Mum's voice from the kitchen. 'Croissants are ready, darling!'

And then, it's gone. The emptiness returns.

But I've tasted it. And now I'm craving it. I want more.

There's only one thing for it.

Feel alive.

TraumaLand.

Tonight.

9

PART OF

Here's something I do remember. It's a nice thing, I promise.

I didn't have loads of friends when we were in Lewes. Still don't. The ones I did have dropped off after the move, but I work better as a lone wolf anyway.

Lewes was a very nice town – near enough to Brighton to be cool, but far enough away to feel safe and rural middle class. When I was twelve, Mum and Dad thought I was lonely because I just sat inside and painted all day. If I wasn't doing that, I was on my bike. I loved my bike. It was yellow. I used to just ride round in circles on the driveway for hours and hours.

I think they grew concerned that I wasn't socialising. So, they said *they* would be my friends and asked me what I'd like to do. I said I wanted to go into the woods and build a tepee. I was half joking to see how they'd react, but they said OK. *That sounds like a nice idea.* And so, we did. We went out into the woods at the back of the house, the three of us, found fallen branches and built.

I loved it. We'd spend days out there, building these tepees right in the middle of the woods. It was nice spending time with Mum and Dad. I remember thinking they were so clever, teaching me how to tie all those knots with the rope, showing me which branch to put where. Dad brought his toolbox out and started to really take it seriously – using his drill, shaving the branches down into points so they would dig into the ground (impale it). He even let me use the nail gun to pin them together at the top, which I thought was so cool.

What I really loved was that they'd let me dress up however I wanted in stuff from my dressing-up box. As elves, gnomes and other friendly woodland creatures. (Yes, I was different back then too.) We tried to get Lucas involved, but he was too busy with his actual friends who were his actual age.

Then something amazing happened. Dad said we could try and make a proper hut.

It took weeks. It had a real roof, an actual floor, a window and four walls, which we painted in colourful patterns. We hung curtains and put a rug down. It even had a proper door with a lock. It was like a miniature house.

Dad helped me paint a whole solar system on the ceiling – each planet a different colour. Not childish, though. Detailed. The moons and rings and craters all there. It looked incredible. It took us about a month to finish it, every night after school. Dad said I could use it as my artist's studio.

I was so happy.

But then Dad was elected as MP for Lewes and we stopped going. He even had a driver. This big bloke with a bald head, who always wore a leather jacket and leather gloves. His name was Karl, which I thought was a funny name, but now I realise that's very judgy. I liked Karl a lot – he was always kind to me. He loved Dad. Said Dad had given him a chance and he'd always be loyal to him. He was a bit like a biker but not (actually ex-military), with a thick, south London accent. Gentle Giant, Dad called him.

There was this one night I was up in my room when I heard Dad rush outside and get his Cadillac out of the garage. He got back really late. When he got in, he was dead tired and a bit *grey*. I asked if he wanted to go with me to the hut the next day to get some fresh air, but he said no, that sadly he didn't have time. He was very busy. His new job as MP for Lewes was very important. I didn't ask him again.

I went back to the hut a few times on my own, but it wasn't as fun. Then I just stopped. I wish I'd gone more. I don't even know if it's still standing. Anyway, I think what I'm trying to say is that my parents have always tried to look out for me.

After the crash, I was in hospital for two months while they monitored my brain and did the skin grafts on my torso. Dad was also in the hospital, but he got out sooner than I did. They said he was lucky. The wound was deep and had caused internal bleeding, but the doctors who operated on him were able to stop it.

Because of his job, things had to be kept quiet. There was no announcement. Nothing in the press. I think people in the government helped. They told the staff that Dad had a hernia operation, which they said would deflect any questions. Dad didn't want me to receive any backlash, he said. He was worried people would get angry with me.

Dad's now the Secretary of State for Health and Social Care, you see. I don't know if I told you that. So, yeah. Important. Lots of people know who he is.

Dad is very liked by the public. He's done lots of good things, for lots of people who need it. I think having a mental son isn't really the image his party want for him, which makes sense. So, they made it all go away. I actually think they're helping to pay for Melinda, but I might be wrong.

So, Dad had his hernia op, then was back to the House of Commons and sat next to all the other important politicians like nothing had happened. Which is just how they wanted it to be. Keep calm and carry on. I *hate* that saying.

When I left the hospital, I came straight to the new house. Mum, Dad and Lucas had already moved in, so I never went back to the cottage in Lewes. I didn't speak for weeks, if you can believe that. I just felt like a zombie. Lobotomised.

Mum and Dad moved us here to help me, to give me a fresh start. They loved the old house. We all did. Things were simple there. Everyone was happy. And it was my fault that it changed.

I don't blame the meds. I don't blame my ADHD. Not for this. This isn't like getting bollocked at school by the head teacher for setting off the fire alarm to escape an exam. This isn't constantly forgetting to do homework. This is different.

I take complete responsibility for the crash. For nearly killing my dad.

I know it's my fault. I'm fully aware. My actions, my choices. I was out of control, but I should have listened to Dad. I should have got out of the car.

And while I don't feel any guilt, I'm sorry. I really, really am.

Shave your head.

I stare at my reflection. My face is sweaty but cold, the face paint claggy on my skin. As I push the uneven strands of my choppy mullet back from my forehead, the white paint smears into it. I hold my hair back and widen my eyes, then blow out my cheeks, making the red Joker smile morph and grow.

I look ill.

To be fair, this bathroom lighting isn't helping. I always look a mess in here. But that might be because I typically am a mess in here. The pain of the thunderclaps has often brought me blindly fumbling up the cellar steps and into the ground-floor bathroom. I've found myself scrambling to get to the sink in time, but falling short and collapsing into a pool of vomit on the marble floor.

I catch the reflection of the wallpaper behind me. Green swirls with gold triangles repeating across it. It's expensive, but thankfully wipeable. I've wiped a lot of my own sick off that wallpaper. The pattern makes my head swim. I involuntarily gag.

I glance down at the floor, by the toilet, where the pile of books sits. Mum's strategically placed a quote book at the top – a Christmas present from Lucas. I've read it over and over while lying on the tiles.

I resume eye contact with myself in the mirror and trace the tip of my forefinger over the bumpy scar on my temple. A raised line, two inches long, clinically straight, just above my eyebrow.

Shave your head. Fine. *Fine.*

I open the cupboard door beneath the sink and root through the spare toilet rolls, the posh hand soap and room spray until I find a small basket at the back. Mum's *for emergencies* box.

I consider this an emergency.

Inside I find Dad's spare beard trimmers. I take them and pull off the length comb so it's just the bare metal blades. The short ones. I click the button and it begins to buzz.

As I push the vibrating blades into my tangled hair, I feel my whole head shake. They nip at my scalp, but I don't stop. I move it slowly backwards over the curve of my head, watching the matted and uneven strands drop limply into the basin in front of me. It's difficult at the back where I can't see what I am doing, but I get the hang of it. I begin to speed up, ignoring the sharp nicks. It takes less time than I thought it would.

When it's all off, I stare at myself. Interesting.

I pull the photograph out of my pocket and place it in the basin on top of my pink-hair pile, face down.

> *Don't forget. Never. <u>Never forget.</u>*
> *You can't – please – remember him.*
> *Shave your head.*

It's very intense. But I guess I am intense. *Remember him.*

If I was referring to the old me, perhaps I thought shaving my head would make me a blank canvas that I could rebuild from. *Remember that sweet, innocent boy and bring him back.*

I stare at my scrawled handwriting. I don't know when I wrote it. It must have been some time after the crash, in the middle of the Gap when I was all a bit hazy. Not hazy. Blank.

Maybe I was referring to Dad. Or Lucas. It would be a shame to forget either of them.

Or maybe I was referring to the paramedic I think I half saw in my memory. Maybe I fancied him. Tried to get his number and failed because I was too busy bleeding out. Maybe this is true. Paramedics are hot.

Shave your head. Why so earnest, Past Eli?

Maybe I just thought I'd suit it. That I urgently needed to remind my future self how good I'd look with a skinhead. Well, Past Eli, you were wrong. I look like a clown who's suffering a long and invasive illness.

I don't know what I was expecting. That's a lie. I was expecting that with each clump of hair that fell from my head a new emotion would come flooding back, one by one, filling me up.

My phone pings in my pocket. Strange. I rarely receive texts these days.

Melinda. Oh. Unexpected.

Hi Eli,
Well done today. You seemed a little flustered at points.

Flustered? I wasn't flustered.

This isn't a bad thing, just something I was aware of. It can be tricky to end therapy and the journey you're now on could potentially feel isolating. I wondered if you'd like to join an online aftercare support group that I run. It starts at 6 – so soon – just for an hour.

There'll be people who are in a similar position to you. Some of them are my patients, others just want to connect as part of a shared experience. I think you'd really benefit. I've cleared it with your parents. We think this might help you move forwards. To see that our sessions have worked. I'd like to see that too. You might find your tribe there. Your people. It's good to feel 'part of'. I've emailed you the Zoom link. Hope to see you at 6.

Melinda

Part of. No, thanks. I compose my response.

I'm good. Don't worry. I feel fine and ready and great. Thanks though. For everything!!!!
You therapy Jedi! I'm cured!

I hover my finger over the send button.

'Eli!' Dad's voice comes from behind the door. 'We're going to eat at six. Melinda has just messaged about the support group – we think that sounds really helpful. What do you think? It might be good for you to meet some people who get what you're going through.'

A shared experience with trauma victims, or a shared experience with my family. Maybe one is the lesser of two evils.

Potentially feel isolating. Like-minded people.

'I think I'll do the support group… But I'm actually feeling –' nothing – 'fine.'

'OK, son. It's really good for you to be getting life back on track, speaking with other people who've struggled too.'

Sounds horrendous. 'Thanks, Dad.'

'Don't worry. There's nothing to worry about now.'

As I hear him head into the kitchen, I delete the message to Melinda, then gather up the hairs from the sink, shove them into the toilet and flush them away.

Back to Operation TraumaLand. Which reminds me, I need to prove that I'm an adult. *ID required.*

I slide my phone into my pocket and creep through the hallway, checking that Lucas is in the kitchen with my parents. I then tiptoe up the stairs into his bedroom and open his bedside table. I half close my eyes in case there's anything I absolutely do not want to see, but it appears to all be fairly innocent: paracetamol, a nasal spray, Vaseline, his mouth guard for teeth grinding and *bingo* – his wallet. I lift it – expertly avoiding the other items like I'm playing a game of Operation – and take out his driver's licence.

Twenty years old. I can pull that off. His blonde curls and wide eyes make his mugshot look angelic, which may be a problem. However, without my hair I can now say I'm going through an identity crisis, which isn't a lie.

I feel something under the tips of my fingers behind it. Along with the driver's licence, I've lifted out a business card of some sort.

TEAR Solutions
Contact us for support
Helping your loved one can be difficult.
We are here to guide you

TEAR? Like *cry*? Or like *rip*?

Neither are filling me with much confidence. Or clarity. Or joy. I flip it over. Nothing. I guess Lucas needs help too. I hadn't really thought of that.

The clock on his bedside table beeps.

18:00

I pocket the driver's licence, slide the business card into the wallet and place it back inside the drawer. I hurriedly creep out of Lucas's bedroom and down the stairs to my cellar, bolting the door shut behind me. I then get my laptop out, open my emails and find Melinda's Zoom link. I hover the cursor over it.

Your tribe. Your people.

'Fine,' I say out loud. '*Fine.*'

I plug in my headphones and click the link.

10

GUESS WHO?

Twenty-five faces stare back at me from the screen, each one in its own little square. It's like a real-life game of Guess Who? – the Trauma Edition.

I flick them down in my brain as we wait.

Do they have brown eyes?
Are they wearing a hat?
Do they have a big nose?
Hmm...

I'm not doing very well. The faces are too small to determine eye colour, there are lots of people wearing a hat (mildly interesting), and we don't nose shame in today's society so this is not a useful line of questioning. I need to be more specific.

Do they look like they've had a near-fatal blow to the skull?
Better...
Flick. Flick. Flick. Flick.
Do they look like they were dropped on their head as a small child?
Definitely some.
Flick. Flick. Flick.

Do they look like they're dead behind the eyes?
Flick. Flick.
Oh my God, Melinda was right. My people. My tribe.
Do they look like they're confused and uncomfortable?
Flick. Flick.

'Welcome.' The speaker is a softly spoken and serious man whose display name reads Dr Konstantinos Athanasiou. He's conventionally handsome with a tan and a rugged beard with a bit of grey in it. Probably about fifty.

Melinda isn't running the session, but I can see her in her own little square in the bottom corner of my screen. She has her glasses on and a more casual top than the one she was wearing at my exorcism – a knit pullover with a turtleneck. When she sees me, she smiles and opens her eyes in a way that says *I'm a little surprised, but glad you came*. At least I think it's aimed at me. Her display name reads just Melinda. Too cool for a surname. Like Socrates. Or Jesus. Or Madonna.

'You can call me Dr A,' Dr Konstantinos Athanasiou says. A few of the faces relax. Clearly they were afraid that attempting to say his name would elicit another Major Traumatic Experience. 'Thank you for joining us. I'm here with Melinda.' Melinda waves from her square. A few people sheepishly wave back.

'Some of you may know me and some of you may know Melinda from therapy. For those of you I've not met before, I'm a psychologist and have worked extensively with victims – or survivors – of trauma for over twenty-five years, particularly those who struggle with memory loss around the incidents that have caused them pain. For those of you who don't know Melinda, she is a widely celebrated psychotherapist who also specialises in trauma. We've created this group to give you teenagers an open and relaxed space to connect and share your truth.' I try my best not to pull a face at this.

'Some of you may know each other from previous support groups, but many of you haven't met before. Please try not to be nervous – you're all in the same boat.' He smiles gently at us. 'A few rules of the group to begin. Everything you hear here should be kept anonymous, for the safety of each person. Please do not cross-share, which means mentioning any other participant, offering them advice or referencing them in any way when you speak. This is not a space for debate, but for support. Listening is our way of doing that here.'

As Dr A continues, I can see Melinda staring at me. I mean, she could be staring at anyone. But it's definitely me. 'If you'd like to share, use the raise hand function you can find at the bottom of your screen and we'll call on you when it's your turn. If you're not sharing, please be respectful and keep your microphone muted.'

I look at my own square. I've put a hoodie on, so Melinda won't see I've shaved my head. She might be alarmed by that. Or not. She might not care, but I don't want her texting my parents about it. I've wiped off most of the face paint, but it's still a bit smeared around the edges. My skin actually looks grey, the light above my bed highlighting the bags under my eyes.

Dr A lays out more sharing rules, about staying empathetic to ourselves, not going into too much detail about the trauma in case we trigger one another, keeping things broad and not discussing where we live or mentioning surnames. My chat box blinks at me.

Melinda (host):
Hi Eli. I'm so glad you came. Did you tell your parents?

I lock eyes with her and she gives a discreet smile. I type back.

Elias Gollum:
No. You were right.
I want them to know I'm fine now. Because I am fine now.

I smile broadly and watch her frown in her square.

Melinda (host):
Let me know if you need me during this. Or if anything makes you feel uncomfortable. Or wobbly. Anything at all.

Wobbly. I don't get wobbly.

Elias Gollum:
Will do. But I am cured now ☺

Melinda sits back. I don't see her typing to anyone else, which makes me feel a little bit special and a little of a charity case all at once.

A few yellow hands appear next to people's faces.

'Annabel, you were first,' Dr A says. 'Would you like to share?'

I search for Annabel and find her at the top of my screen, fiddling with her keypad probably trying to find the unmute button. She's around my age, with dark curly hair and a very nice set of straight white teeth.

'Hi, yes. Thanks, Dr A. My name is Annabel and I'm a trauma survivor.' Everyone waves silently back at Annabel. 'Thanks, everyone. It's really good to be here. So, I just want to say thank you to Melinda for guiding me through this past year.' Melinda smiles. 'Like we've been instructed, I won't get into the gory details of the incident, but a year ago I was involved in an accident. I fell from a roof, three storeys tall, at a party.'

I squint at Annabel. I think I can see a small scar on her forehead. *Your tribe. Your people.*

'I have since experienced post traumatic dissociative amnesia.' That's different to mine. That means Annabel can't remember the period of time before, not after, her incident. 'I've been able to piece together the memories with Melinda and I'm moving forwards. The most important thing I've learned during this journey is that the feelings and emotions that have at times felt muted are gradually coming back. I feel like I'm now living in the real world again. It took a little time, it is ongoing, but acceptance is the most important thing. And I'm learning to trust again. I suffered this freak accident and I'm angry that it happened, but I'm still here.'

I can see her eyes glistening. She seems to be feeling something, which is good to see. I mean, I don't want her to be sad, of course I don't. 'I'm alive. And I'm so grateful for that. Keep going, guys. Life is for living. We must remember that.' Her voice cracks slightly as she finishes. She puts her thumb up to the screen and is met with twenty-four thumbs up reciprocating, including mine.

Well done, Annabel.

Next, a boy named Max shares. 'Hi, I'm Max and I'm a trauma survivor.' Max looks about sixteen and fell off the roof of his school. He suffered such bad injuries to his head and his retrograde amnesia was so extensive that he's been piecing together the past two years of his life. *Two years*. He says there were certain friends he couldn't remember, but his family have been supporting him through it. At least he can feel things now. He often feels lonely, like no one quite understands, but he's now feeling much better than he did.

Dr A is helping him see the beauty in life again. He's able to see things like the colour of the grass or the sky, or smell things like strong coffee and appreciate them. They now make him feel good. He knows this might sound silly or simple, but he says it's important. When he does, I realise my life has been in greyscale since I got back from the hospital. I like Max. He seems a little confused, but his passion for getting better makes me know that he will.

I think I have it too. That passion. That desire.

The shares go on and I study the faces in their tiny squares, all listening intently and nodding supportively. A patchwork quilt of ages, genders, ethnicities, hairstyles, facial structures and postures. Some lean on both hands, some just one, others sit upright like they're in class. But all have exactly the same expression. It's hard to name. A blend of empathy, pride and thinly veiled confusion. Some people still look a little blank.

I check my own face in my square. A little blank too. But my brow is furrowed. A big crease has appeared between my eyebrows, which happens when I'm interested. When I'm listening.

Next, it's a girl and a woman's turn. Willow and Sandra. Two faces side by side in their square. The girl, Willow, looks about fourteen and the woman appears to be her mother. Willow had a trampolining accident and has been struggling with anterograde amnesia – forgetting the period of time after the event, like me.

Her mum holds her hand throughout her share, in which she talks about being reintegrated to school and socialising with friends again. She smiles and laughs as she talks, saying that Melinda has helped her move forwards and find a new path outside of trampolining. She was good enough to be picked for the Olympic squad, Sandra tells us, and people start to clap silently. But this makes Willow uncomfortable. 'I'm moving past it now,' she tells us and the silent clapping stops.

As the shares continue, I learn that most people here have hit their head. Been in a fall, a horrific accident – a few motor collisions, someone got struck in the face with a brick during an unprovoked attack by a drunk. One girl shows her scars, but Dr A steps in to gently remind her to keep her share broad and unspecific.

Some don't want to discuss their incidents at all, but focus purely on the recovery. They talk about the positives and the *solution*: how much their memory recall and emotional processing has helped. Many mention the trauma-processing event (or, as we call it, the pain exorcism) as a turning point in their journey. This makes me feel broken again, but I also want what they have. I'm jealous without feeling it.

Dr A and Melinda nod empathetically, always listening, always watching as the sharers tell their truth.

'Hi, I'm Jack and I'm a trauma survivor.' I look at Jack. A boy with a beanie about my age. I'm not here to virtually flirt – that would be inappropriate – but I find myself shuffling to find a better position beneath the light so I look less like a devil. Typically, I wouldn't mind that, but Jack is cool and handsome, albeit not in a conventional way. Which, you know, is cool. His face is slender and he has sunken eyes, but also a softness to his features. It's a little like he's been hollowed out, like the previous version of him was fuller in some way. But his shoulders are broad. He was one of the people I kept up in my game of Guess Who? – the Trauma Edition as appearing dead behind the eyes.

'So...' he says quietly. 'I think honesty is important. And while I'm so pleased for you all – really, I am – for getting to a place where you can move forwards, the truth for me is different. I still don't remember anything.'

This makes me sit up. I lean forwards towards the screen. I watch as others sit forwards too. Melinda's eyes are flicking over her screen like she's joining dots between the onlookers.

'And it's pissing me off,' Jack goes on.

Out of the corner of my eye I see someone named Toby waving his hand. The little red microphone with the cross through it disappears as he unmutes himself. 'Hi, Jack. Let's remember to keep it positive! Dr A and Melinda want us to focus on—'

Jack pulls his beanie forwards slightly. He doesn't look embarrassed. He looks a bit – nothing. 'Right, yeah. Thanks, Toby. I just wanted to share my truth and all.'

Toby looks very pleased with himself. 'Well, I don't think people want to—'

'I want to hear it,' I say out loud.

I freeze. Oh, thank God. I'm still on mute.

'Let him speak,' Dr A puts in. 'Go on, Jack.'

Toby nods apologetically.

'I dunno. I just… I'm here for the truth.' Jack fiddles with his fingers. 'That's what I want. And I'd be lying if I said I'd moved on in any way because I don't know what I'm moving on *from*. Not really. I've been told, but I have absolutely no reference point. Just other people's words.' He pauses. 'I don't want sympathy. Or empathy. Whatever those things even are. But I feel isolated. Melinda keeps telling me that's normal but…' He's one of Melinda's patients too. 'But I don't have a… I don't…' He scratches his cheek.

'Look, I don't have lots of other people to help me remember, so I'm doing it on my own and it's not easy.' I see nodding heads pulling sympathetic faces, some narrowing their eyes compassionately like they're transmitting their deepest condolences through the screen. I catch Toby put his thumb up and mouth *you got this, mate* like the patronising twat he is. It makes me bristle. He should hang out with Paula and Steve.

'I sometimes see flashes,' Jack continues. 'I won't go into the *gory details*, but there aren't many ways to say it. I was found by someone on the bank of a river, beneath a bridge. Apparently, I'd tried to end my own life.' The squares all go immediately still. Mouths hang half open. 'But I can't remember any of it. I don't really feel like I belong here. Or anywhere right now. It's no way to live – in a vacuum. I'm trying to appreciate the smaller things, but I'm numb. Blank and numb. The past is a mush. Completely hazy. And I feel like if I don't figure this out soon I...' He stops again. This time I wonder if his connection is broken because he goes very silent and still, his face like a vacant doll. But then he slowly shakes his head. 'I just want to get to the bottom of this. The only thing I really feel is that something is missing. A sort of longing.'

Wait. I said that. *I said that.*

'Thank you, Jack,' Dr A says gently. 'You may feel alone, but we're here for you. All of us. That's why we have created this group. So, you can understand that you're *not* alone.'

Jack smiles emptily at the screen. 'Thanks. Yeah.'

'Olivia, it's your turn...'

I can't stop looking at Jack as he lowers his head. I watch his hand take hold of something dangling round his neck in front of his hoodie. It catches the light as he begins to turn it between his fingers. I lean towards the screen. Hanging from a silver chain is a wooden pendant. A rose. It looks a little odd, misshapen, perhaps home-made, but also kind of beautiful in a twisted way.

I glance at the room behind him. It looks big. I can see a bunk bed and a poster on the wall with the words TURNING TIDES TOGETHER beneath an image of a wave. I hover the cursor over his face, clicking, trying to find a way to message him. I open the chat box, but the direct messaging function has been disabled and I can only message the hosts. I tap his face with my finger as if it might make him look up, but he doesn't.

I unmute myself.

'Jack,' I say, cutting off Olivia. Oops. This is bad. But also he looks up, so good.

He sits up straight, his eyes searching for the square my voice has come from. When he finds it he squints at me, unsure. Most people are doing the same. I try not to look at Melinda's expression.

'Elias,' Dr A's voice says. 'It's Olivia's turn. You can use the raise hand function at the bottom of the—'

'Yeah, I know. Love the raised hand function. Love democracy. But I just wanted to say...' *What did I want to say?* 'Jack. Um. Thanks. And keep going.' He looks at me blankly. I smile, doing my best to look ... nice. He nods, mouths *thanks*, then drops his head back down.

Olivia shoots me a look so severe it's like she's trying to cause me another head injury. 'Sorry, Olivia...' I say, then quickly mute myself again. I don't have to look directly at Toby's twat-head to know he's performatively shaking it with disapproval.

'As I was saying, I'm really grateful...' Olivia begins again. I chew my lip. Oops. Oh well. I liked what he said, and I think—

The bottom of my screen blinks.

Melinda (host):
Are you OK, Eli?

I find her face in the tapestry. Frowning, concerned.

Elias Gollum:
Yes, great. I feel really settled and great and excited to move on to the next chapter.
Felt worried for Jack there!

More frowning. She doesn't believe me.

Melinda (host):
You seem a little unsettled.

Elias Gollum:
I'm not. I wasn't.

Melinda (host):
Did something Jack say upset you?

Elias Gollum:
No. Not at all.

Melinda squints at me.

Elias Gollum:
It's sad what happened to him. He seems nice.

Her face is closer to her screen now.

Melinda (host):
He'll get there. Like you are.

Elias Gollum:
Good luck to him.

I watch her nod, then smile.

Melinda (host):
I'm glad you came. It's been really useful.

Elias Gollum:
Yes, Melinda. In realising how fucked I truly am.

I'm joking. I don't type that. But I want to.

I see Melinda's attention has shifted away from me, back into the virtual room. She's now nodding along as Olivia shares her truth about being kicked in the face by a horse.

I glance around the screen, searching for Jack. I go through each square, one by one, but after a few minutes of checking and re-checking, I realise he's gone.

There's a knock at my cellar door and Mum's voice comes from behind it. 'There's someone here for you, Eli.'

11

PISTACHIO ICE CREAM

I was wrong.

I said it was more appropriate for me to have dressed as the Joaquin Phoenix version of the Joker rather than the Heath Ledger one, but I'm having second thoughts. You see, I think that Phoenix represents someone who's deeply messed up by his past, while Ledger just commits to a full-out psychopath.

Heath Ledger gives the image of someone who's quite literally missing the capability of being and feeling normally, like he's been broken, a switch flicked within him that cannot be switched back. And I think I need to commit to that, like Heath did. I think that's probably more appropriate.

It's a shame I didn't have a purple coat. But hey.

I slam the laptop shut.

'Who is?' I shout. 'Who's here?'

That twinge of heat, that fleeting thrill, emerges in the pit of my stomach. Could it be Boss? Boss here to fuck me up, like he said?

That could bring terror. That could bring *immediate* terror. Yes. *Yes.*

'It's Peter,' Mum says. Huh? Peter? As in, *Nice-Neighbour Peter*? Peter who wants to take me on a date. The promise of terror is instantly snuffed out, replaced by an impending sense of *this is going to be awkward as hell*. For him. I don't feel awkward. 'Steve and Paula's son, Eli. You know Peter—'

'Yes! Of course I do. Well, how lovely.' Why do I suddenly sound very posh, just like Peter? 'What does he want?'

'He wondered if you'd like to go for a walk…'

'A walk?' A *walk*? What middle-aged tomfoolery is this? 'Oh, right… What, now?'

'Yes, now.'

God. Really? Now? I have to prepare for tonight. 'But it's…' I look up out of my window. 'Dark.'

'He said he wants to take you for an ice cream.'

Ice cream? It's freezing. This guy is very bold. So bold, Peter. 'But it's … cold.'

'Wear a coat, then.' I'm running out of excuses. Think. *Think*. I hear Mum sigh. 'I can tell him no, Eli. He said he just thought you might want to do something together. And it might feel good to be out.'

It might feel good. *Feel good.*

Wait. *Wait*. I've been so obsessed with feeling *bad* that feeling *good* – which I suppose *is* a feeling – hasn't really entered the landscape of my side project. Yet.

I stare at the pictures of myself pinned up on the wall opposite my bed. Me, younger. Me, smiling. Me, *emoting*. Happily.

My brain goes into overdrive.

This could be utilised as an offshoot of my side project. An impromptu opportunity. If I go on this walk with Peter, maybe I'll feel something good. Maybe I'll even fall in love. *Love.* That's an emotion, isn't it? An emotion I've never felt. Perhaps I'm only broken where it comes to emotions I've felt before. Perhaps I can generate a fresh one. Perhaps Peter will save me. Perhaps he'll unlock my potential of being a fully fleshed, empathetic, emotional, normal human.

It's not how I saw this evening going, but it might be time to try something new.

'He's still here, Eli. Should I tell him to leave?'

I'll have to keep it short in order to get ready for TraumaLand, but hopefully it's possible to fall in love in the space of thirty minutes, max. Should be doable. I bet it is. And Peter is handsome. So I've been told, many times, by my mother. 'Um... No.'

'No?'

'No. I'll come up, Mum.'

'Oh! OK. *OK.* Wonderful, darling.' I can hear her trying to stifle her excitement. 'I'll tell him to wait on the porch.'

Shit. I jump up from the bed.

OK. A walk. A walk-*date*. What does one wear on a walk-date? A hat. A nice hat to cover my messy head. Shame it won't keep what's inside it hidden, but one can hope. I swap my hoodie for a big, woollen jumper – no time for a T-shirt – and my jeans. I look at myself in the mirror and point. Hey. Hey, *you.*

OK, no. That's gross.

I bound up the stairs. When I open the door, Mum is still hovering outside.

'Hey,' I say. Oh, OK, Dad is here too. And Lucas, lurking in the dining-room doorway still holding his fork. They're all here. Fun. 'Everyone OK?' Lucas is looking at me funny. 'Why are you looking at me funny, Lucas?'

He shrugs. 'Oh, nothing. Just...' He points his fork at me. 'Little Broski, overcoming his past, moving on with his life. I'm proud of you.'

'Calm down, it's just an ice cream.' There's a long pause as they stare at me, smiles fixed. 'OK! Well, this hallway family meeting has been sufficiently needless.'

'You two seem to have a nice spark,' Mum says, eyes bright. 'You and Peter.'

I'm pretty sure she's never seen us together. 'Um... Yeah. Sure.'

'He's very charming.'

Is he? 'He is.'

They wait for me to say something. 'OK, so I'm going to leave now.'

'Yes! Don't let us keep you,' Mum says.

'Thanks. I hope you all have a wonderful evening and manage to make it back to the dining table before your pudding goes cold.'

'Just have fun, son. Try and enjoy yourself.'

'Will do!'

I step out on to the porch and pull the door shut behind me, closing it firmly on my family.

'Hi, Eli.'

Standing on the tiled path by the rhododendron bushes, hair gelled, smelling of cologne, is Peter. He looks really sweet. If I had a heart, it might break.

'Hi.' Try and sound warm. *Warm is good.* 'You look nice.' OK not like that – that sounds like a creepy Sunday school teacher. 'I like your shirt.'

'Oh, thanks.' He self-consciously pushes his fringe out of his eyes. He's wearing one of those distressed light-brown shirts on top of a large white T-shirt with wide jeans. The whole outfit probably cost more than a car, but looks like he found it in a bin, which I think is the point.

Say something. *Anything.*

'Ice cream,' is all I can think of. I blurt it out loudly. He looks a little startled. He's quite a bit taller than me. Six foot? 'Ice cream tonight?'

'Um… Yeah, there's a new dessert shop opened on the Broadway. You fancy it?' His hair is all swooshy, like an American jock.

'Sure, sounds great.'

He nods. 'Great.'

I don't fancy him. That much I know. I can see he's objectively very handsome, but I don't feel anything. Maybe that will change. He still has half an hour to cure me.

'I have half an hour,' I say, to be clear.

He raises his eyebrows. 'Just a quickie, then.'

I think he's tried to make a joke, so I laugh. 'Ha!' His mouth screws up a bit and his brow furrows. I don't feel uncomfortable because I can't, but he sure as shit looks it. Never mind. 'Let's get to it, then! A lot can be achieved in thirty minutes!'

It's true. It can. I hope. Please cure me, Peter.

We walk down the path, side by side, and out of the gate where Nisha nearly stabbed me. We take a right up the hill, moving in and out of the pools of light from the street lamps. His arm keeps brushing mine. Every time it does, I try and notice any sort of ... tingling – sexual chemistry, emotional connection, love, love, *love* – when our arms meet. But all I feel is the itchiness of my jumper against my skin.

Maybe I should try and hold his hand? That's what people who are in love do, isn't it? Fuck it.

In the name of Love, I brush my fingers against his. This is the kind of thing song lyrics talk about. He quickly pushes his hand into his jacket pocket.

'Sorry,' I say.

He gives an uncomfortable laugh, more a snort. 'It's all right.'

As we near the top of the hill, just before the Broadway, he stops.

'So, where's this dessert place?' I say. Maybe I should feed him some of my ice cream. That's what they do in the films.

'One sec,' he says. I glance back to see he's leaning against a lamppost. He doesn't answer my question, just looks me up and down. Maybe he's about to snog me? People do that under lampposts, don't they? Then fall madly in—

'What was it like?' he says, lowering his voice.

'Huh?'

He makes that snort-laugh again and points to the scar on my forehead. 'The crash.'

'Oh, that.' Is this conversational foreplay? 'Well, it was...' Oh, wait, I have no idea. Maybe a visual representation is better. 'Do you want to see my other scars?'

Maybe they're hot. Maybe Peter is into that.

I see his features contort into a small grimace. 'You're kind of strange, aren't you?'

'Sorry?'

'Just… You're strange. I heard that before you moved here you were different.' He looks all shadowy beneath the yellow light. 'What were you like before the crash?'

'What was I *like*?'

'Yeah. Don't take this the wrong way, you just seem a bit of a robot.' In his defence, I might actually think that's quite cool – being a robot – if I wasn't so desperately in need of feeling more human. 'Have you always been like that?'

'No. I don't think so. Sorry.'

'Sorry? What for?'

Not entirely sure. 'Sorry … that I haven't been a robot from birth.'

He raises his eyebrows. 'That's not what I meant.'

'So, you just—'

'I just wanted to know if this is you, or a product of the crash.'

Jesus, it seems ice-cream dates are really not about the ice cream. 'It's a product of what happened, yeah. But I'm fine. Totally fine. Sorry if I don't seem—'

'Stop apologising.'

'Right – yes. Sorry.'

'Stop,' he says forcefully. That's OK. Perhaps this is all part of the excitement. *Yes*. The heat of the moment giving way to passionate responses. Maybe this is how love begins. Peter, you dark horse. 'Someone told me you killed a cat.'

'Excuse me? I love cats—'

'Dan. The chef you work with. Saw him in the pub the other night. He said you kill animals and stuff.'

'Wait. What?'

'And I dunno… That's a bit weird, Eli. A bit messed up. But you've kind of got that vibe. And the thing is, I can't tell if that's what you want – to appear a certain way for shock value, to appear edgy or cool. Or if you genuinely have no idea how you come across.' He runs his hand through his hair. 'Don't take this the wrong way –' why does he keep saying that? – 'and it wasn't me who said it, it was Dan. But…' He looks up at the night sky.

Is that the end? The end of the conversational foreplay? OK. So… Not sure this date is going *super well*. Not feeling *super sexy*. Yet… There's still time.

'What did Dan say?' My voice is monotone. Just like a robot, damn it.

He doesn't look at me. 'He said it's like you've turned into one of those guys from a Netflix documentary that ends up in prison because body parts are found under his floorboards.'

Oh. 'Well, that's … mean.'

He scuffs his feet. Then, after a long pause. 'Your brother Lucas was there.'

'Huh?'

'At the pub the other night. He got annoyed at Dan.'

'Oh… Right.'

'He was very drunk.'

'Dan was?'

'No, Lucas.'

'Right.' That's not like Lucas.

'And then he started...' Peter trails off. He shifts uncomfortably.

'He started what?'

'He started getting mad, telling Dan to keep his mouth shut.' Thank you, Lucas. 'He was slurring something – blind drunk – I only caught a bit of it.' He narrows his eyes as if trying to remember. 'He said no one knows the truth.' He pauses, thinking for a moment. 'And then I swear I heard him say that not even *you* know the truth. And that you never will.'

'Well... People thought that. But I do know it now.'

'He looked scared, your brother. Upset. And very angry.'

Protective. 'Well, yeah. I was confused about what happened for a while.' Peter doesn't react. 'But I've worked through it with my therapist. And now I know.'

'Well, that's good, Eli.' Is it? Is it good? 'You seem normal.' He raises one eyebrow.

I feel a shift inside my chest, an immediate and desperate *need*. My mouth moves before I can stop it. 'Have you ever been in love, Peter?'

He looks up at me, startled. Like he might lose his balance. 'Huh?'

I step towards him. 'What does love feel like?'

He steps sideways, away from the lamppost, away from me. 'Um... I dunno, Eli. That's very random.'

'Is it?'

'Yeah.'

'Why? We're on a date, aren't we?'

Something appears in his eyes. A flash of terror. And I want it. 'No,' he says quickly. 'This isn't a date, Eli.' He then mumbles under his breath. 'This is *definitely* not a date.'

'So, you're here to gawk at me?'

'Huh?'

'At the robot?'

He swallows, hard. 'What? No—'

'Ice cream is a date. You don't have to be a human to understand that.'

I step towards him again.

He steps back. Runs his hand through his hair again. 'All right, Eli. Look, I'm sorry—'

'Now *you're* apologising. Stop it.'

'I just … don't want to upset you.' His voice is quieter now as I keep stepping forwards and he keeps stepping back, down the slope of the hill. 'So, you've never felt love?'

'What are you talking about? Can you just … back off a little?'

I quicken my pace. He speeds up. 'Just answer me.'

His eyes widen. 'Fine. No. I've not been in love, Eli. I'm seventeen. No one's been in love at seventeen.'

He thinks I'm ridiculous. I can hear it in his voice. Maybe I am.

'Same,' I say. He frowns. 'Same, same. I'm seventeen and I've never been in love either.' I raise my hand and click my fingers. 'Snap.' His body makes a small jolt.

'Jesus,' he whispers. He turns to see how far he has to go until he's back in the safety of his parents' arms.

I don't want to scare him. I don't. But actually, I really, really do. There's something about seeing it on his face, beneath his skin, that's pulling me towards him. I can almost smell his fear and like a vampire – a ghost vampire – I want to suck it all out of him. I want to keep it. To let it live within me. *What's it like?*

'Are you OK? You look scared,' I say.

He keeps his eyes on my face, too afraid to turn his back to me. *That's it.* 'Just… Let's leave it, Eli.'

I quicken my pace, gaining ground. 'Why did you invite me for ice cream?'

'I… I just think you're interesting,' he says, nearly tripping backwards. 'You're hard to make sense of.' I laugh, loudly. Not because it's funny, but because I want to shit him up a bit more. He flinches.

'This is all quite hard to make sense of,' he mumbles.

'This is hard for *you* to make sense of?' I add bite to my words, for effect.

He puts his hand out towards me like a defence barrier. 'I don't know, Eli. Can you… Can you stop moving for a minute?'

'I'm just walking home. Like you. Why are you in such a rush? We didn't get our ice cream.'

'Christ.' Peter is panicking now. *Panic.* 'My parents are worried that I'm even here with you.'

I knew it. I never liked Steve and Paula. 'Maybe they should be.'

'Sorry?'

'Nothing.'

'It was your mum and dad who wanted this to happen.'

'Huh?'

'Yeah. They've been trying to get me to date you for weeks. Your mum even offered me some kind of internship with her work.'

'*What?*'

'Look, Eli. I think you're great. Really great.' Oh, he's grovelling now. Sadly, ghost vampires hate that. It only spurs them on. 'And I don't want you to take this the wrong way…' Here he goes again. 'But I just wanted to see if—'

'See if what?' He goes to reply, but the words get caught in his throat. 'See if what, Peter? If I'm a *psychopath*?'

I suddenly stop and his eyes widen. Then I bark like a dog.

I laugh as his entire body spasms.

'Jesus, Eli. What the hell are you *doing*?'

'Having fun. Dates should be fun.' I mean, I assume. Never been on one.

He's nearly at his front door now. He turns his head to check.

'I don't have floorboards.'

'What?'

'In my bedroom. To hide bodies under. I have concrete. I live in the cellar.' He nods like *yeah, OK, that's fine, forget I even said it…* 'You can come and see, if you like?'

'It's getting late.'

'It's six thirty.'

'Well, yeah. But I'd better get inside… It's been nice, though.'

'It has, hasn't it? So nice.'

He's made it to his garden gate now. I smell his relief.

'OK, Eli. Jesus. Dan was right. You are a freak.' With that, he turns and heads up the pathway towards his house. My chances of feeling love disappear with him into the shadows of the porch.

I hear Peter slam his front door, then I head for home.

Well, I don't know about you, but I think that went rather well for a first date.

'Oh! Hi, darling!' Mum calls as she hears me come in. She sounds a little surprised. 'That was quick!'

'Hi!' I shout, bright and cheery. I kick off my shoes. Casual. *Casual*.

'We're in the living room!'

I can hear my dad's voice too, but I realise it's coming from the TV. I poke my head round the door.

They're all here, sprawled out on the sofa watching the news. Dad is on the screen, speaking to a bunch of people in the House of Commons. He looks very assured. Very passionate. Lucas looks at me and frowns. Dad – my real dad, not the telly dad – turns his tired eyes to me.

'It was just a quickie,' I say, trying the same joke Peter used. It doesn't land, just like Peter's didn't.

'How did it go?' Lucas says.

'Yeah, it was nice. He's nice.'

Mum smiles and stands. 'He is, isn't he?' She joins me in the doorway. 'Did it feel good?' she asks hopefully, studying my face.

Feel good. I have no idea what that means. 'Yes,' I say absently. Like a robot, I suppose. 'It felt good.'

'Did you get ice cream?'

'Pistachio.'

'Cute,' Lucas says.

'I'm proud of you for going.' Mum puts her hand on my shoulder. I can smell lavender, fresh and clean. 'It's lovely to see the Eli we know coming back to us. After everything. Coming back to your old self, aren't you?'

Peter was right. Not about the animal killing – that never happened. Like I said, I'm a cat person. But he was right about one thing: I am strange.

I turn away from my family as they stare after me and head for my cellar to instigate my original plan. Because I don't have any other options now.

No more procrastinating. I must follow the fucked-up bunny.

It's my last chance.

My last hope.

12

NDA

The house is finally quiet.

It's later than I anticipated, but it's given me time to prepare.

Not *prepare*. That sounds like I'm about to make homemade soup.

It's given me time to premeditate. To strategize. To scheme.

Yes, I like scheme. That's the right word for it. For Operation TraumaLand.

I'm pretty certain my family are asleep now. Mum and Dad like to go to bed by ten. Mum read in some self-help book that it makes you more emotionally stable. I would try it, but you can't become emotionally stable without emotions to stabilise. Therefore I am resolved that not sleeping before 2 a.m. is fine for me.

I snuck up to the kitchen half an hour ago to eat the leftover sausages Dad left for me in the oven and all the lights were off. I could hear Lucas in his bedroom on FaceTime to Ingrid and I left a message in the family WhatsApp group saying that if anyone wants me, they should text first because I need a good night's sleep after today. Mum replied with love heart emojis, Dad a thumbs up and Lucas said *sleep well, bro. We love you.*

I waited at the top of the cellar stairs and listened through the door until the muffled sound of footsteps and toilet flushes finally stopped. They won't come down now until morning. My door is bolted shut.

Everything is set and ready.

I close my laptop, the screen still displaying my Google search for TEAR Solutions. I found nothing. Except a website for an American health company that sells medicine to people who have a condition called 'dry eye' because, get this: they lack the ability to produce tears, and the medicine *helps them cry*. Yes, I know what you're about to say. *That would have come in useful for you in your trauma exorcism this morning, wouldn't it?* Well, all I can say is irony can be such a bitch. But it doesn't matter. My family are convinced that I'm fixed. For now.

After my googling, I concluded that TEAR Solutions must provide therapy. Melinda said that Lucas might find all this difficult, but I hadn't realised just how difficult. He's been away at uni so I didn't notice. I feel bad that he's been struggling.

Well, I don't. But you know what I mean.

I take his driver's licence and shove it into my Adidas backpack, along with my phone and bank card and a marker pen for my costume, where I've already strategically – no, *schemingly* (if it's not a word, it should be) – placed them. What did the TraumaLand website say? *Payment by bank card only.* I can only hope eighty-three pounds is enough for whatever's waiting for me there. Fingers crossed, a whole new personality.

One thing's for certain – I'm about to find out.

I catch sight of the photograph of my family I found in the attic, which I've placed on my nightstand. *Never forget*. I take it and shove it down into the side of my sock, then go to the window.

It's just big enough for me to get out of. I've done it before. I unlock the handle.

When I lift the pane of glass, the cold night air makes me shudder. Using my chair to stand on, I shove my backpack through the gap, then stick my head out so my chin presses into the grass. I push myself up, my feeble arms trembling under the strain, until my feet follow and I'm crouching in Mum's newly planted pansies. Trying not to crush them, I lower the grid, wedging it with a rock so it stays slightly open.

When it's secure, I blow a kiss to my cellar. It feels like something I'd do in the film version of my life and a small part of me does wonder if I'll ever see it again. I then sling my backpack over my shoulder.

This is easy. Turns out I'm very good at getting out of windows.

Hugging the rhododendron bushes, I tiptoe down the path, watching the front of the house. Mum and Dad's room is dark behind their William Morris curtains, exactly as it should be. Nothing to worry about.

I head up the hill towards the bus stop, where I wait for the 43.

It's very cold and I'm not wearing much. Why, you ask? Well, tonight I'm dressed as Regan MacNeil.

Dress appropriately.

I found some green contact lenses I was saving for Halloween and drew on thick black eyeliner to make them really pop. I then fashioned a nightgown out of a bed sheet, poured green paint down the front of it (for the sick) and rubbed black charcoal on my teeth from my art set. It tastes bitter as anything but looks absolutely brilliant. Sadly, I didn't have a wig.

Regan's face is ghostly white and she's pretty much hairless, but don't underestimate her.

Tonight, she is ready. Tonight, she is ready to go to a place she knows well.

Hell.

～

I'm freezing my bollocks off. The night bus is like a moving fridge and Regan's gown isn't doing much to protect me from the cold. I could feel something damp on the seat through the thin cotton so now I'm sitting on my bag. I won't question why the seat is damp. Never question that.

'*Alight here for London Bridge.*'

I press the bell, pull my bag over my shoulders and make my way to the doors. As they hiss open, I wave at the driver. He blinks, clearly thinking *yet another freak*. I get out my phone, open Google Maps, then push on down the pavement.

I hug my arms around me, avoiding the prying eyes of strangers. There are loads of nutters in London so I briefly wonder why I'm attracting attention. I guess with the backpack I look a little like a small, skinhead devil child on its way to small, skinhead devil school. (God, I wish that existed.)

TraumaLand is not easy to find. I keep circling back on myself beneath the arches of the bridge as the trains rattle above, Google Maps insistent that I've reached my destination. I pass the same couple for the third time, pressed up into a corner of a wall, seemingly eating each other's faces off.

Time is ticking.

'Hello!' I shout to the Face Eaters. 'Sorry to disturb you.' The male one peels his mouth from the female one. He turns to me, head lolling, eyes glazed, completely ... high? 'Dude...' he says slowly. 'What the hell...?' OK, yep, definitely high.

'Hello, dude.' I don't suit saying that, but want to appear relatable. 'Can you please tell me where Feral Street is? I'm a little lost.'

He squints. 'What the fuck *are* you?'

'I am no one,' I say politely. (Regan says that in the film. Well, the devil does, through her.)

'Whoa...' he mumbles. 'That's so deep. For a second, I thought you were my nan. She looked exactly like you the day she died.'

Aw, I like this guy.

The girl taps him on the shoulder. '*Don't encourage it,*' she whispers. 'It might put a curse on us.'

I wish. 'OK, not to worry!' I say. 'Have a nice evening, Face Eaters.'

The man whispers to the girl. 'Hayley, this thing is so real. In more ways than one.'

She shakes her head. I think she might be less high. Her eyeline drifts to something behind my head. 'You mean there?' she says, pointing.

I turn to see a small archway in the brick wall with a sign above it, barely visible.

FERAL STREET

Yes, I do mean there, Hayley. 'Thank you,' I start to say, but she's back to dining out on High Man's face.

I step towards the archway. Well, hello.

It appears Feral Street isn't actually a street. It is, in fact, a narrow brick passageway with little doors and wall-mounted lamps running down either side. A low fog has gathered in the entrance, which is … eerie as fuck.

I love it.

I keep my eyes on the doors as I move quickly along the cobbles. It's deserted, save a pissed clubber necking a blue WKD. As I pass, he gives me a wide berth, saying, 'Bro, the asylum is that way.'

Big flirt.

I stop as a particular door catches my eye: white and covered in faded graffiti. Block lettering, skulls, tags, colourful swirls, all blending together into one washed-out confusion. On top of the graffiti, painted in neon pink, is something that is very hard to miss.

A rush shudders through my body. A thrill. Adrenaline.

Yes. *Yes.*

A hell rabbit.

The paint drips down to merge with two words, filling me with so much promise.

Feel alive.

I'd like to, door. I really would.

What now? Maybe knock? That seems like the appropriate thing to do.

'Hello.'

I spin round to see a man inches away from me. There's a gaping gash across his face, oozing blood. I reach for my rucksack to get my phone and call an ambulance because he definitely looks like he needs one.

'Let me guess,' he says casually, pointing to my pale face. 'Uncle Fester.'

'Um...' His gash shines in the lamplight. It looks ... syrupy. Oh, I see. *Dress appropriately*. Wow, that's realistic. 'Almost. I'm Skinhead Regan.'

'Oh, niche.' He puts his hands into the pockets of his long, dark trench coat. 'Love it.'

'Thanks. What about you?'

'Roadkill.' He tilts his head and lolls out his tongue. 'Hit by a truck. Didn't make it.' Interesting. A lot of road trauma for one day.

'It looks very real.'

'I do all my own prosthetics,' he says proudly. He seems older than I'd initially thought. Pushing thirty, well spoken, clean-shaven beneath the spatters of blood.

'Nice.' I glance down at my bed sheet. 'Mine was a bit ... rushed.'

He narrows his eyes and steps towards me. 'Have you been here before?'

I can smell the glue holding the gash on to his skin. 'Nope. First time.'

He nods and a spark of something mischievous, almost wicked, appears in his eyes. 'Hmm. Curious.' Is it? 'People get really into it. You'll see.'

Nonchalance is key. 'Yeah? Can't wait.'

'This place isn't easy to find.' I said that. 'But once you do find it, it'll stay with you forever.'

'So,' I say, like this is all completely ordinary. 'What now?'

He pauses. His eyebrows are thick with blood. 'What do your instincts tell you?'

They tell me to *go to any lengths to feel again*. But I won't say that.

'Would you go to any lengths to feel again?'

I shrug like I hadn't considered it. 'Yeah, sure. I mean, why not?'

He smiles. 'Then let's go inside.'

Yes, I agree, Roadkill Man. But how?

He stares at me like I know what to do. 'I don't know—'

'What do your instincts tell you?' he repeats.

I won't say that my instincts told me to just knock on the door because I have a feeling that's not the correct answer and I'm going to look stupid if I say it. Maybe I should say something mysterious and intriguing like *my instincts told me to say TraumaLand three times, spin round, draw blood with a knife and smear it all over—*

Oh, OK, so he's knocking on the door. 'Pretty simple,' he says as he raps three times.

'That's what my instincts told me,' I say quietly.

'Follow them,' he whispers, his eyes fixed on the bunny. 'Like the rabbit.' A smile creeps across his face. 'Trust your gut. Down the hole we go.'

I hear the noise of a key in a lock, then the door begins to creak open. A woman peers through the gap.

'Yes?' she says flatly.

'We want to go down the rabbit hole,' the man says.

The woman looks us both up and down. 'Are you together?'

'No,' he says quickly.

The woman glances down the alleyway. She must be about fifty. Hair pulled back in a neat bun, stern features. 'Right, you first.' She points to Roadkill Man, then widens the gap.

'See you down there, I hope,' he says as he disappears.

The woman looks at me. 'Wait here.' She closes the door.

I dig my toes into the cobbles to try and keep myself warm. I'm not freaked out, by the way. I have no fear. But logically I feel – well, not feel – I am becoming increasingly aware that something might be a bit off here.

'Skinhead Regan?' The woman's head reappears.

It startles me. Slightly. 'Me?'

'You see any other Skinhead Regans out here?'

Good point. I step through the gap into near blackness. It smells like mildew and I hear the low thrum of a noise, a beat, below my feet.

A torch clicks on. The woman is now standing in front of a wooden lectern with a slanted top covered in sheets of paper. She opens what appears to be a ledger, licks her finger and turns the page. 'ID,' she says.

I pull my backpack off and root around until I find the small, shiny driver's licence.

She takes it from my hand and studies it, squinting into the torchlight. 'Name?'

'Lucas Arthur Pew.'

'How old are you, Lucas?'

'Twenty.'

She glances up at me. 'You look different.'

She knows. I need to say something charming. Something witty. 'That was before I lost my mind.'

The woman pauses. Then the corners of her lips turn up into a tiny smile. She hands the driver's licence back. 'You're funny.' She looks back down at the lectern and begins to scribble with a pen. 'Come here,' she says sharply, the smile gone. 'You need to sign this.'

'What is it?'

'An NDA.'

'A what?'

'A non-disclosure agreement.'

Oh, I've heard of those. They're what important people make less important people sign so they can't tell anyone things. Things they've done to them – typically something horrendous. Stops them telling the truth, basically.

'Sure,' I say.

She keeps the torch pointed at the lectern so I can read the words.

NON-DISCLOSURE AGREEMENT
TRAUMALAND

I, The Receiving Party, named LUCAS ARTHUR PEW, hereby agree not to disclose anything witnessed or experienced in TRAUMALAND. This refers to any and all third parties, including via the use of social media, talking to the press, people in the public eye, or any medical professionals. I understand that breach of this contract will result in appropriate action taken by TRAUMALAND LTD, which they will determine as they see fit: action may include banning, lawsuits, or financial reparations. At TRAUMALAND, secrecy is key to safety.

All responsibility for any physical, emotional, or psychological damage occurred shall remain entirely mine.

I have full capacity to make the decision to enter. My state of mind is not impaired by the influence of drugs or alcohol, nor do I have any mental health illness (to my knowledge) that may compromise my judgement. I have not been forced, nor am I experiencing any blackmail or external control. The choice is made by me and me alone. I enter TRAUMALAND out of my own free will and desire.

Signed:

I look up at her. 'Is this legally binding?'

Her voice is quiet, but each word she utters is crystal clear. 'You don't want to mess with these people. Believe me, Lucas.'

My instincts are a little conflicted, I must admit. But, hey. *Feel alive.*

I press the pen into the paper and sign Lucas's name.

'OK,' the lady says. 'Phone.' She holds out her hand.

'Sure.' I hate my phone anyway. I reach into my bag and take it out, along with my bankcard. 'Is there an entry fee?'

'No,' she replies. She opens a drawer in the lectern. I glance down to see it's filled with phones. She puts mine inside, on top of the others. Just before she closes it, I see one I recognise. Purple. Stickers all over.

Nisha's. *Nisha is here.*

'I need to search you. Backpack, please.' I hand her my bag and she roots through it, the torch between her teeth. She then drops it on to a pile of other bags. 'You can pick it up when you leave. Arms up,' she says, her words muffled by the torch.

She proceeds to pat me down through my makeshift nightgown. My thoughts begin to speed up, jumping from one to the other: Nisha, Lucas, TEAR Solutions, the photograph – still in my sock. I start to feel dizzy as the blood churns in my brain. I can hear it slushing between my ears. I'm about to ask if I can sit down when—

'All done.'

She missed the photograph.

She takes the torch from her mouth and points it into the darkness behind me. At the end of the tiny, brick-walled room is an alcove. 'In there.'

Right. *Right.* I begin to follow the shaft of light, trying not to sway as I do.

'Oh, and Lucas?'

I turn, squinting into the torchlight. 'Yeah?'

'I hope you find what you're looking for here.'

I hope so too or I don't know what I'm going to do to continue on in this world feels a bit much. So I just say, 'Thank you.'

'Follow the staircase down to the bottom. Be careful not to trip. You'll reach a door. Everything will make sense when you go through it.'

I nod. 'Great.'

I do exactly as she says. As I begin to step slowly down the twisting stairwell, her words echo in my mind. *Everything will make sense.*

Nothing makes sense.

Through the door is a small room with a bar at one end. A three-headed woman sits at the counter. Next to her is Snow White, drinking a Martini, having vomited blood all down the front of her dress. Beside Snow White is Pennywise, the murderous clown from *IT*, eating a bag of salted peanuts. In the centre of the room are twelve circular tables. Freddie Krueger sits at one of them, doing a crossword. Ghostface from *Scream* is here. And the Babadook. Alex DeLarge from *A Clockwork Orange*, drinking a glass of milk.

There are evil dolls too – JIGSAW, Chucky and Annabel – all sitting silently together, while M3GAN dances around them to the slow, jazzy elevator music that's playing from invisible speakers.

Oh my God. Is that ... Jason? *Jason Voorhees is here.* I'm in the same room as Jason Voorhees, who's doing a sudoku in the corner, smiling to himself behind his mask.

Well, holy shit. Melinda was wrong. *This* is my tribe. *These* are my people.

I look for Roadkill Man and find him sitting with the girl from *The Ring*. She keeps having to part her long black hair to take sips of her cocktail through a straw. I put my hand up to him. *Hi.* He sees me and reciprocates. *You made it.*

The room is lit with candles: on the tables, on antique-glass wall mounts and chandeliers. The wall to the right of the bar is covered in a deep red curtain.

I don't see Nisha.

Behind the bar is a small man in his late twenties, wearing wire-rimmed glasses. He is very slight, his baggy white T-shirt tucked into a little waiter's apron. He looks up at me, smiles and beckons me over.

'What you having, pal?' I notice a slight accent. Northern. Scouse.

'Sorry?'

'What would you like to drink?'

Well, this could be fun. 'Um… Triple vodka coke, please.'

He raises his eyebrows. 'We don't serve alcohol. There are plenty of other places you can get that.'

'Oh, right.' I glance at Snow White's Martini.

'Mocktail,' he says. 'We get our kicks differently here.'

I look at the name badge pinned to his apron. CASIMIR. Something about him is familiar. I swear I've seen him before. Maybe he's an actor and this is his part-time job to pay the bills. They do that, don't they, actors? Come to think of it, he does look like the kind of guy that'd die first in a horror movie. 'Do you do cranberry juice?'

Casimir smiles. 'Now you're talking my language.'

As he busies himself putting ice in a glass, I scan my eyes around the room. It all feels slightly … not what I expected. Everyone looks – well, *bored*.

'Here you are.' Casimir hands me the drink.

'Thanks. How much?'

'This one's on me, pal.'

'You sure?'

He nods. 'Save your money for the good stuff.' He then picks up a dishcloth and goes back to work.

I lean forwards slightly over the bar. 'Casimir?'

'Yeah,' he says, head down.

I lower my voice to a whisper. 'Is this it, then?'

He looks up. 'What do you mean, pal?'

'You know…' I try to sound nonchalant. 'So, this is… This is *TraumaLand*?'

'*This?*' He smiles. 'No, my friend. This is the holding area.' His eyes move to the clock on the wall. 'Three minutes, then you're in.'

Holding area. *Interesting.* 'Oh! Right. Yes, of course. I forgot.'

He folds his arms, not buying it. 'First time?'

'Um… Yeah.'

He winks. 'Hold on to your bollocks.'

'Will do!' I plaster on a big fat smile.

He stares at me for what feels like far, far too long. 'Yeah,' he says quietly. 'You're in the right place.'

I sip my cranberry juice, counting to sixty three times. When I'm done, nothing happens. I must have been off, damn it. But then I hear the tinkling of a bell. I turn to see the red curtain open.

Behind it is another door. But this one is iron. Bolted shut.

People begin to stand, remaining completely silent. A queue forms and I join it, right behind Nurse Ratched and Harley Quinn. Casimir steps out from behind the bar.

'It's time to feel.' He pulls the bolt and the door opens. 'Welcome to your worst nightmare. Welcome to TraumaLand.'

13

TO FEEL IS TO LIVE

It comes at me in flashing snapshots.

Strobe lights, blazing through the darkness. The rapid thump of trance music – a furious and incessant heartbeat – shakes the room.

No. Not a room. An underground vault.

Perfectly circular, the depth of a tennis court. Pulsating with energy, dangerous and volatile. Fluorescent lights hang suspended from horizontal steel beams that run overhead, floating in the dark, spelling words that take my breath away. CHOOSE TO FEEL EVERYTHING – FREEDOM IS HERE – TO FEEL IS TO LIVE. And the rabbit, multiple rabbits, in neon pink, blue and yellow.

The vault is teeming with people. Characters I know, some I don't. A heaving mass of bloody, distorted faces, painted and prosthetic, bruised and bandaged. All appear half dead in the blinking light. But these people are not dead.

They are well and truly alive. And they're dancing.

Jumping, moving together as one, completely synchronised with the heavy bass – the relentless heartbeat of this underground world. Up and down, arms thrown into the air, a melee of twisted, turning shadows. The vibrations of the music move up through the floor and into my body. *Dmm. Dmm. Dmm. Dmm. Dmm.* With it, that rush, that thrill enters me, filling my every fibre, possessing me. I can hardly breathe. I feel… I *feel*…

Alive.

A hand touches my shoulder. Roadkill Man's face flickers through the strobes. *Good luck*, he mouths. He points to the circular brick wall surrounding the vault, then pushes into the crowd until he disappears.

I see what he was pointing at.

Doors.

So many of them. Arched like entrances to small cells, repeating the entire way around the vault. Above each door, a single glowing word. They're seemingly random, but something about each word makes my skin bristle awake.

GUN. GRIEF. FOREST. FIGHT. FIRE. AXE. GRAVEYARD. BUCKET.

More. On and on.

CLIFF. BOX. CHEAT. BULLY. KNIFE. HELICOPTER. BRIDGE.

There must be at least thirty of them.

Directly opposite, a projection of a large digital clock shines on the wall, ticking backwards.

03:59… 03:58… 03:57…

A countdown. *What is this place?*

In the centre, people are congregating around another bar. Small and circular, a glowing neon island in the sea of chaos. I step into the throng of sweaty bodies, dodging thrashing and flailing limbs as I make my way towards it. Everything *feels* fast but *looks* slow. Like time has been altered and is stalling, juddering in unison with the throbbing beat. Half of reality in light, half in darkness, alternating so quickly that I no longer know which is real. The darkness, or the light.

Then I see her. *Nisha*. Behind the bar. Handing out drinks to the gathering swarm.

I push forwards, watching her as she works: wiping her forehead, cleaning spills, putting ice in plastic cups, taking payment with a card machine. She moves efficiently and automatically like she's in a trance, always keeping her eyes on the ticking digits on the wall.

'Nisha!' I shout, but she doesn't reply.

Part of me wonders if this is a good idea, if any of this is a good idea, but the doubt is drummed out of my head by the pounding beat. I'm drawn to her like a moth to a fluorescent flame, her image offering refuge among the mayhem – *she threatened to stab you* – a familiar anchor – *she knows where you live* – something I recognise, however vaguely, within the unknowable. '*Nisha!*'

She turns to me. Panic flashes across her face. 'How do you know my—?'

'It's me!' I shout, but she doesn't recognise me as Skinhead Regan. I lean forwards over the bar. 'It's Eli. From the bus stop!' Again, nothing. 'I stole your—'

Her face changes. Now she remembers. She glances over her shoulder at the short man with a purple mohawk behind her, who's busy serving a woman with tyre tracks across her wedding dress. She then looks back and taps her name badge warningly. It reads VIOLET.

She leans towards me, shouting into my ear over the noise. 'What the hell are you doing here?'

'Same as everyone else.'

'Did you follow me?'

'What? No.'

'Then how did you—?'

'I saw the sticker on your phone case. The rabbit.'

She glances back at her colleague again, then reaches down into a fridge beneath the bar. She brings out a Red Bull and begins to pour it into a plastic cup in front of me. 'You shouldn't be here,' she says, not looking up.

'I want to apologise. Properly.' Her eyes remain focused on the drink. 'And I wanted to know what this place is. Where am I, Nisha?' She shoots me a threatening look, then taps her name badge again. Violet. 'Where am I, *Violet*?' I repeat.

She doesn't answer. Her eyes move back to the digital clock ticking down on the wall.

00:22… 00:21… 00:20…

'Listen!' I shout, trying to keep her attention. 'I really am sorry. I stole your phone because I wanted to feel guilt. I'm sorry you were the victim of that. But you need to understand. I want to feel again. And for some reason your phone – or the universe – brought me here.'

Suddenly she turns, slamming her hand down on top of mine. 'Stop.' She leans her face right into mine and puts her mouth right next to my ear. 'I don't want to hear your little sob story, OK? I'm not interested. If you insist on being here, you have to promise me – don't tell anyone what happened. No one can know it was you who took my phone. OK?'

'OK, but—' She pushes her weight down on to my hand. 'Ow. Jesus. OK. I promise.'

'You don't know me. We've never met.'

Fine. 'Fine by me.'

She lets go of my hand and holds up the plastic cup. 'That'll be five pounds.'

I don't take it. 'What happens in those rooms, Violet?'

Before she can answer, the music suddenly stops. With it, the bodies around me do the same and a deathly stillness falls. The strobe lighting ceases, leaving only the fluorescent glow of the rabbits above.

I turn to the clock. Everyone does.

00:00

A voice booms out from a speaker in the ceiling. It's deep and crackling and sounds like it's been distorted by a computer.

'The world is dying. It is removing our ability to know what it is to be human. You have each arrived at this place for your own reasons. Some of you are tired. Others detached. Desensitised. Bored. Empty. Numb. Whatever it may be, all of you know there is something missing. But here, you can choose to live. To feel again. To experience life in all its fullness – every part of it. And so, welcome to TraumaLand. It is time for you to choose your story.'

There's a sudden pushing around me. People begin to split off, darting in all directions, colliding with each other as they rush through the half-light. They stop only when they arrive at one of the doors.

I turn to Nisha. 'Go on,' she says.

I trace my eyes over the doors, each word bright through the darkness, queues of people forming outside them.

GUN is the most popular. Followed by AXE. And then BRIDGE.

I glimpse a door that no one is waiting beside. HAMMER.

I give Nisha one last glance – her arms folded, frowning at me – then make my way towards it.

I stop and stare at it for a moment. Dark wood, black bolts, arched at the top. On the wall alongside the door is a card machine with a small plaque beneath that reads:

£10 PER MINUTE.
MAX FIVE MINUTES.
USE THE KEYPAD TO CHOOSE HOW LONG
YOU WOULD LIKE YOUR STORY TO BE.
THEN TAP YOUR CARD.

£10 pounds per minute? No shit Casimir gave me the cranberry juice for free. I deserved the whole carton.

I turn to see the person to my right, outside the door labelled FIRE, eagerly pressing the up button on the keypad. *Two minutes, three minutes, four minutes, five.*

Fifty quid for a full story?

The voice booms out again, echoing across the vault. '*Your selection will be locked in ten seconds.*'

Fuck. The screen is set to one minute. I quickly press the up button until I reach three and tap my card. It beeps affirmatively.

Payment approved.

The door swings open and I step inside another brick room. This one is tiny. No bigger than the fridge the chef locked me in at work. It's actually more a cell, which is right up my street, but something feels a little... I don't know. *Disconcerting. Unsettled. Odd.* A single light bulb hangs from the roof.

The room is empty, save for something on the floor. A pair of goggles.

They're like the ones I used to wear to swimming lessons, only the strap is thicker and the Perspex lenses are completely black. Connected to the rubber strap are two wires, each with a white pad at the end, the size of those cotton things Mum uses to remove her make up.

They have words written on them.

One says: ATTACH TO FOREHEAD.

The other says: ATTACH TO BASE OF SKULL.

On the sides of the rubber strap are two earbuds.

I stare at the device for a moment. It looks like something from a sci-fi film, but not. It looks almost home-made.

The vault behind me goes quiet and I look back to see the door is closing. As it shuts completely, I hear the clunk of bolts slotting into place. I'm locked in.

Only three minutes. How could anything possibly change in three minutes?

I position myself dead centre, right in the middle of the room where the goggles were, and – *please God let this work* – pull them over my head and stick the pads into place. It takes me a moment to figure out how to get the earbuds in. When I do, the silence is so deafening, I forget to breathe.

Just as I inhale, bright white words flash in front of me through the darkness.

> YOU HAVE CHOSEN HAMMER.
> YOU ARE NOW AMY.
> HELLO, AMY.
> YOUR STORY WILL START IN
> 3... 2... 1...

The world shifts in front of my eyes. I'm no longer in my own body. My own reality. I am a voyeur inside someone else's.

The story begins.

14

NO AIR

– AMY –

I open my eyes, but it's pitch-black.

I see nothing. Hear nothing. There's no light. No noise. Other than my heartbeat thrumming against my ribcage.

'Hello?'

I'm lying down. On my back. There's no breeze. No air.

My head pulses with a cocktail of adrenaline and fatigue. I want to sleep. Have I been asleep?

I'm thirsty. So thirsty. I move my tongue against my lips to wet them.

There's something covering my face – a coarse material, some sort of bag. I can feel it against my ears, the top of my head, bunched up around my shoulders.

Panic floods into my every pore. Where am I?

I turn my head slightly and feel something hard behind it. I try to lift my foot, but it's stuck.

There's something around my ankles.

I try to raise my arms, but they remain fixed by my side. As I twist my wrists, I feel leather against my skin.

Straps. I'm strapped down.

'Hello?' *I try again. My voice sounds hoarse and thin, muffled by the bag.*

No response. Nothing. My body is shuddering. It's so cold.

I can smell something strange. Copper. Or iron. Or … blood. Panic lurches in my chest.

Move, Amy. You need to go. Now.

I fight against the straps around my wrists and ankles, tears and dribble now covering my cheeks and chin. But it's no use.

I hear a noise. A door latch.

My stomach drops. My body goes rigid.

The door creaks, slowly opening.

I feel the presence of someone. I want to scream, but my voice is stolen from me. Who are you? What is this? *I want to say, but the words won't come. Fear has me in a chokehold.*

Heavy footsteps move towards me.

Please don't hurt me. *Say it, Amy. Scream it.*

I can't.

Another noise. The strike of a match. I strain against the straps again as the sting of sulphur hits the back of my throat.

More footsteps. Careful and precise, circling me. They're close now. Too close. Right here.

'Please…' *I manage. My voice trembles.* 'Just let me go… I'll do anything if you just let me go.' *No reply.* 'Please…'

I can hear their breath.

And… Then…

Fingers on the material, pulling the bag off my head.

The first thing I see are the hooks hanging from the dark beams above me. And then the tools. A hand saw. A cleaver knife. A hammer.

'Hello, Amy.'

A man stands over me. Tiny, shining black eyes like beetles, staring. A beard. A checked shirt. A dirty face.

He's smiling.

'What is this?' I breathe.

'I'm here to help you.' He turns away.

I look down the length of my body to see I'm not on the floor. I'm on a table. A wooden table.

Oh my God.

'Please! Please... Tell me what—'

'Try not to struggle.' His voice is calm. Steady. It makes me feel sick.

I watch as he reaches his hand up and takes hold of the hammer.

Move, Amy.

I turn my head to see my hand is strapped down by a belt.

I wriggle it, twisting until I can feel a slight movement. A gap. My hand slips down, looser now.

He turns back. I go still.

'What do you want?' I say. Calm, like him.

'Like I said,' he whispers. 'I am here to help. You shouldn't be jogging in the woods alone, Amy. Has no one ever told you there are bad people out there?' There's something in his eyes. Compassion. But it's not real. He's enjoying this. 'You need to learn.'

I look at my feet, bound tight. 'What are you going to do to me?'

He steps towards the table, the hammer in his hand. 'I just want to teach you about bad people, Amy.'

He pauses, looking at me with his beetle eyes.

Then, suddenly—

Smash. *He slams the hammer down on the table next to my head.*

'*Stop!*' *I yell.*

Smash.

Again, he smashes it down.

Smash. Smash.

He moves around me, slamming it into the wood. Over and over. The vibrations shuddering up through my body.

Smash. Smash. Smash. *Closer and closer.*

'*Stop! Please don't hurt me.*'

He stops and looks up at the ceiling. '*Time for something else, don't you think?*'

I pull my hand and it slips free from the belt. The table creaks.

As he looks back down, I throw my fist at him with all my might. It lands squarely in the side of his neck.

He chokes. Splutters. Stumbles backwards.

I pull at the buckle binding my other hand, freeing it. I sit up, blood surging to my head, threatening to make me pass out.

I grab for the belt around my legs, fumbling with the buckle. It's tight. Too tight.

Come on. Come on.

I tug at it, digging in with my fingernails until they feel like they might break off.

Come on. Please.

And then, his voice. Right next to me once more.

'*Bad decision, Amy. Very bad.*'

Before I can scream, the hammer smashes into my shin.

TIME ENDED

I yank the headset off. What the—?

I'm on the floor – *sprawled on the floor* – my chest heaving, my body alive with adrenaline. A pressure pounds against my temple, blood drumming at the veins in my neck. Ow, my nails. My fingernails. As I raise them to my eyes, I see they're cracked and bloody.

I look down. There are scratch marks on the concrete floor.

Did I do that?

Amy... What happened to her? What happened to Amy? It was like I could hear her thoughts.

'Is she OK?' I hear myself rasp, not entirely sure who I'm asking. My voice bounces off the brick. There's no reply.

I stand and regain my bearings. The single light bulb. The door, still shut. The vault outside. I feel as if I've been a million miles away. Three minutes. *That was only three minutes.* But I felt so different, so far removed from this. From myself. I was in her thoughts, her feelings, her entire life.

I could hear her thoughts. Actually hear them. Not a commentary – more subconscious. It was like I *was* her.

And I do ... feel. Something inside me is fluttering. It hurts – not a physical pain, but something else. I'm *worried*. About Amy.

Yes. *Yes. Worry.* I remember it. Like I'm balancing on a cliff edge and could fall at any second.

Who was that man?

'Hello?' I shout. No answer.

I pace around the room, back and forth, back and forth, trying to order my racing thoughts. The remnants of Amy's panic, her terror, fuelling them. What happens now? Who was she? What happened to her leg? What is this place?

Slow down.

'Let me out!' I yell.

Again, nothing. I'm still locked in.

I begin banging on the door, her story looping in my mind, over and over.

There's a loud clunk. I flinch. The hammer.

But it's not the hammer.

The door swings open and I stagger out of the cell to see the others piling back into the vault. Some are crying. Some are retching. Others are crawling on their hands and knees, trying to catch their breath.

The strobe lights blaze – *dark light, dark light* – as bright as the glare from a machine gun. The trance music thuds into us like bullets.

The digits on the wall suddenly light up. They begin to tick backwards again.

04:00… 03:59… 03:58…

Oh my God.

'Bloody hell,' wheezes a girl as she stumbles out of a room called FIRE. She's weeping. *Weeping.* She turns to me, eyes puffy and red. 'Oh, fucking hell,' she whispers through shallow sobs. 'That one is *crazy*. You need to try it.'

My brain is buzzing. I feel…

It's awful to admit it, but I definitely feel… Awake. *Alive.*

I look for Nisha. Not at the bar. Where are you?

I scan my eyes around the vault, searching, then see her between the doors CHEAT and BULLY. She's holding something in her hands. A mop and bucket. She locks eyes with me, tilting her head. *Get what you wanted?* I start walking towards her, to tell her *yes, yes I did*, but also *what the—?*

She begins to move away and I pick up my pace, legs trembling as I push through the crowd. When I reach her, I take her arm. 'Nisha. What the hell is this place?'

She spins round. 'Don't ask me about the stories. I don't know anything about them. Even if I did, I wouldn't be allowed to tell you how they end. So don't—'

'Just ... tell me. Who are those people?' I say. 'Who are the people *in* the stories?'

She tries to pull away, but I don't let go. 'I'm not allowed to discuss them.'

'Nisha, please. I just want to know she's OK.'

She sighs, then lowers her voice. 'Listen, I'm not meant to ... *break the illusion*, but I really need you to let go of me.' She pauses. 'They're actors.'

'Holy shit.' I almost laugh. 'But it was so *real*.'

She raises her eyebrows. 'That's the whole point.'

'I could hear her thoughts. It was like I was thinking them...'

'That's the sensory pads. I hear it's amazing.'

'It's mental. It's completely...' What I want to say is that it's completely genius and incredible – like a found-footage horror film mixed with a trauma-porn slasher. Only it's better, because you're actually living it through their eyes. The camerawork is unbelievable and the actors are phenomenal – even the slight distortion in the voices makes it feel more intense. I could understand Amy's fear like she was whispering it into my brain.

Instead, I say, 'Very cool.' I can feel myself smiling. 'How many do we get to watch?'

She gives a shrug. 'As many as you want. Until your money runs out.' Her eyes move to the digits.

01:45… 01:44… 01:43…

'Now I need to—'

'Wait!' I keep hold of her arm. 'Have you…?'

She sighs. 'Have I *what*?'

'Have you watched them?'

'Why would I watch them?'

'I dunno. To experience it?'

'No. I've not. Now—'

'You don't know what happened to the girl in HAMMER Amy?'

'I don't know what happens in any of them. You can go back and find out. Now let me do my job.'

'You should—'

Before I can finish, her mohawked colleague from the bar appears. 'Everything OK?' he says, eyeing me cautiously. I notice he's holding a first-aid kit. His name badge reads AJAX.

I drop Nisha's arm. 'Sorry. Yeah, I just—'

'It's fine.' She cuts me off. 'Same as always. Wants to know the end of the story.'

He looks me up and down. 'You have to pay for that. If you go back to the same door, you'll have to watch from the beginning. Understand?' I nod. OK, boss. Actually, where is Boss? Ajax turns to Nisha. Or Violet. Whatever her name is. 'Vomiter in CRASH, fainter in AXE.' She nods and then they disappear in opposite directions.

I turn back into the room. The air is thick with adrenaline, charged, volatile and sharp. There's a shriek and I see a topless man howling up at the ceiling like a wolf, beating his chest with his fists. Next to him, two girls grip each other's hands, spinning in circles – laughing or crying, I'm not sure – like children in a playground.

00:37... 00:36... 00:35...

I nearly laugh. But not because this is funny. It isn't. What it is, is *insane*. This place is completely insane.

And it seems to be ... working. I need more. *I need more of it.*

I look back at my door, HAMMER. A man is loitering outside, waiting for the countdown to finish. Damn it.

But also, I want... Look, don't hate me. *I want to try a different one.*

00:14... 00:13... 00:12...

'Did you get a good one?' Roadkill Man suddenly appears next to me, eyes wide like he's high. High on pain. On trauma.

'Um... Yeah, yeah I did...'

He puts his hand on my arm. 'You feel it?'

I'm about to ask *feel what?* But I know what he means. *Feel what they felt.*

'I did.'

'Feels *good*, right?'

Maybe we should define *good*. But for me, in my current situation... 'Yeah. It really does.'

The music stops. The lights cut out. The voice bellows from the ceiling. '*It is time to choose your next story.*'

Another story.

I can't help but feel ... *excitement. I'm excited.*

Whoa. I'd forgotten it. What a thing to forget. I feel utterly invigorated. I feel life happening inside me for the first time since the crash. *Life.*

Tears sting my eyes.

The crowd disperses, people fighting to get to the doors. I scan the room and find the door the weeping girl stumbled out of. *That one is crazy. You need to try it.*

FIRE.

There's no one in front of it. My feet carry me there. I press the button like I'm on autopilot.

Three minutes again. Just another taster. That's all. That's all I need.

Then the door opens and I'm inside.

It's exactly the same as the last room. I pull on the headset. Take a deep breath. Here we go.

YOU HAVE CHOSEN FIRE.
YOU ARE NOW BELLA.
HELLO, BELLA.
YOUR STORY WILL START IN
3… 2… 1…

And, just like before, in an instant, reality is no longer mine.

15

THE SOLAR SYSTEM

– BELLA –

I bang the door with my fist so hard that the skin on my knuckles splits. 'Sam? Sam!'

I try the door handle, but it doesn't turn. It's locked.

'Sam!' I yell again, but the smoke catches in my throat, making me splutter. I fumble in my pockets for the key card.

It's not there. Oh, shit.

I hear footsteps and turn to see a man sprinting towards me down the corridor.

'Stop!' I shout. 'Please! Help me!'

He runs straight past me. 'You need to get out of here!' he shouts over his shoulder. 'Now!'

'But my brother—'

'It's coming from the lift shaft!' I watch him disappear round the corner, in the direction of the staircase. I hear the crackle of flames from where he came.

'Sam!'

No answer. Shit.

I take out my phone, hands trembling. Dial 997. Fuck. No.

999. I hold it to my ear. It rings once, then clicks.

'*Emergency. Which service do you require?*'

'*All of them! I need all of them—*'

'*Slow down, miss.*'

'*I need help! I'm on the fifth floor of the Jasmine Hotel. Room 512—*'

'*Destination?*'

'*I just said—*'

'*Which city are you nearest to, miss?*'

'*Birmingham! I'm in Birmingham!*' *I bang the door again.* '*Sam! Please, Sam!*'

'*Miss, you need to calm down. Is someone in danger?*'

'*My brother. He's locked inside the hotel room. There's a fire—*'

'*Do you have keys?*'

'*You think I'd be stood out here if I had keys?*' *I don't recognise my own voice. The smoke is getting hotter. Heavier.* '*Sam!*'

My fist feels like pulp. Tears cool on my cheeks.

'*How old is he?*'

'*He's twelve. He's fucking twelve!*' *Oh my God, oh my God.* '*Sam!*'

'*Calm down, miss.*'

'*Don't tell me to calm down! He's going to die if I don't open this fucking door!*'

'*I can see that the fire brigade, ambulance and police have already been dispatched to your location. Now listen to me carefully. You need to ensure your own safety.*'

'*No, I need someone to help me get him out!*'

'*You need to leave immediately.*'

'*No!*'

'Now, miss—'

I drop the phone. It hits the floor, still connected. 'Sam, I'm coming in.'

How? How?

I take a few steps back, until I'm against the corridor wall. I hear the growing roar of flames to my left.

I lurch forwards and throw myself at the door. Again and again and again. Over and over and over.

Screaming his name. 'Sam! Sam! Sam!'

The smoke chokes me. It's hard to breathe now.

I keep going until I hear a splitting sound as the wood begins to crack around the lock.

I pummel my whole weight into it. 'Argh! Fucking – open!'

Suddenly, I'm inside.

I can hardly breathe. 'Sam! Where are you?' I run into the bedroom – empty. Check under the bed. Not here.

'Sam!'

In the wardrobe.

No.

'Where are you, Sam?'

I bolt to the bathroom. Open the door.

There he is. Flat on his back in the bath with his fingers in his ears.

'Sam!' His eyes are black with terror. 'We need to go! Now!'

He's frozen in shock.

I grab his arms and pull, but he's a dead weight. I sob into his hair.

'Please, Sam. Let's move. We can go together.'

TIME ENDED

I pull the headset off, gasping for air. My throat sears with pain. The bulb above me flickers, making the room quiver around me.

I struggle to catch my breath. I feel sick. *I'm going to be sick.*

Sam. *Sam.* He looked so scared.

Is he OK? Is he going to be OK? *And Bella.*

My shoulder. I pull the collar of my nightgown down. Red marks. Fresh bruises. Everywhere.

I've been throwing myself against the wall.

Wow, OK. That was *insane*. And ... *amazing*.

I try to sit, to lie down, but every position hurts. My whole body feels beaten. Two minutes till I get out. I lower myself down with my back against the wall and wait. I think about Bella and Sam, and that idiot who ran for the stairs. I close my eyes, trying to go back, back inside her head.

How did they film it? I could taste the smoke.

At last the door clunks open.

As the music and lights start up again, I wait outside for the countdown to finish.

01:12... 01:11... 01:10...

I feel a tap on my arm. It's the girl from before. 'I need to watch it again,' she says.

'I was going to go back—'

'Please.' Her bottom lip trembles, her eyes filling with tears. 'Please, I just... I need to go back. I need to—'

'What happens to Sam?' I say.

'I can't...' She shakes her head. 'I won't spoil it for you. Can't you just watch another one?' I look at the clock.

00:22... 00:21... 00:20...

'But—'

'I feel very connected to Bella.'

Well, so do I. *So do I.* 'I feel the same.'

Her face suddenly flashes with anger. 'Tough shit, this one's mine.' She steps in front of me, putting her hand on the door. 'You'll need to find another.'

00:00

The lights stop. The music stops. The distorted voice booms. *'It's time to choose your story.'*

She won't budge.

I turn and find the closest door with no one outside it. I look up.

BUCKET.

Bucket doesn't sound as good. It doesn't sound as good at all.

Fine. I press the up button on the keypad, two minutes – that's all I can afford, damn it – and tap my card.

Same as the other rooms. Same goggles.

But as I put them on, something feels different. The excitement, the thrill, is replaced with what I can only describe as some sort of dread. It's as if a shadow has entered with me.

My stomach tightens as I pull the headset on.

> YOU HAVE CHOSEN BUCKET.
> YOU ARE NOW JACK.
> HELLO, JACK.
> YOUR STORY WILL START IN
> 3... 2... 1...

– JACK –

My head is underwater.

I'm going to die. I'm going to—

A hand grabs the back of my neck and yanks me up. I splutter, dragging the cold air into my lungs. They rage in agony.

A man speaks from behind me. 'Are you ready to agree?'

'No way,' I say. It hurts. I try to move my hands to push him away, but they're tied behind my back.

I look down. There's a bucket on the floor in front of me. Ice cubes floating on its surface. I feel the cold on my chest. Inside it too.

I squint into the room, but it's too dark to see.

'Well, we'll be here until you do,' he says in a thick south-London accent. 'We have all the time in the world.'

His fingers tighten around my hair and he pushes down again – hard – submerging my head back into the icy water. I want to twist my body, but he's too strong.

I try to keep my mind blank. Not to panic.

The pressure in my chest makes me push back against him. He shoves me further down into the water.

I'm going to die. I'm going to die…

Finally he pulls me up and drops me to the floor. I turn on my side, spewing up water, my eyes streaming.

I watch his feet – black military boots, the bottom of his trousers now flecked in mud – slowly step around my head. Then he stops. His face leans into mine.

I see the collar of his leather jacket. His bald head. Stubble. Dark eyes.

'Leave me alone,' I splutter. I try to scream, but I can't. 'Help me!'

He makes a small laugh. 'No one can hear you, mate.'

'You're evil.'

He crouches down next to me. 'You're going to be a real problem for us, aren't you?'

'Let me out of here.'

He shrugs. 'I don't take my orders from you.' I try to move away from him, across the wooden floor, but his gloved hand pushes the side of my head down with a thud. He holds it there. 'What's this?' he says, lifting the pendant that I wear round my neck. I watch him studying it in his fingers.

'Don't you—'

'A rose.' He begins to laugh. 'Sweet. Fitting, I suppose. Did you make it?'

I turn my head and focus on the ceiling. There's a solar system painted across it. Each planet a different colour. It's faded, bits of moss growing through the cracks in the wood, but I can see it was once so detailed, so beautiful.

I have no idea where I am.

'You like that?' the man says. 'This hut was built years ago. He painted it.' He smirks.

'Fuck you.'

His foot slams into my stomach. 'Manners, Jack.'

But then, there's a noise. From outside. In the woods.

A voice I know.

'Jack!' It's him. He's come. 'Jack!'

'I'm in here!' I scream.

The bald man snaps his head to the door as it smashes open. I see him framed in the doorway, with his fluorescent-blue hair. He runs towards me and drops to his knees. 'Jack. What've they done to you?' He looks up at the bald man. 'What have you done?'

He grabs me, pulling me into his chest.

He's here. He's here. I see the bird tattoo on his wrist. The one I did for him.

'Please—' I start to say, but before I can finish, he pushes the man with the bald head. They struggle together in a blur – fists flying, legs kicking, yelling, scrapping. Then a loud thud.

The boy drops to the ground next to me, groaning in agony. Blood dribbles from a straight line, clinically straight, across his forehead.

I look up to see the bald man holding a piece of wood in his hand.

'You sick bastard,' I scream. 'You can't do this.'

I see a shadow behind him, lurking in the doorway. A man. Shirt tucked into smart trousers. Shiny shoes.

I know who he is, but I can't see his face. There's a balaclava pulled over it.

'Good God,' he mutters as he steps into the room. 'Thank you, Karl,' he says. His voice is clipped. Posh. 'I'll take it from here.'

His eyes land on the floor – on the boy with the fluorescent-blue hair, now seeped with blood.

'Eli?' I nudge his side with my arm. There's blood everywhere. 'Eli?'

TIME ENDED

I can't move. I'm paralysed.

Tears are pouring down my face. I'm sobbing. Deep, guttural sobs.

How? *How?*

Jack. *Jack*. The pendant. The wooden rose. Jack from Melinda's support group. The boy who remembered nothing. Like me.

The solar system. The hut. The hut I built with my parents.

And then me.

I saw myself, clear as day. Enter the room and kneel down next to Jack. In our hut in the woods behind the old house.

I have no memory of it. None. My mind is reeling. She said they were actors.

Jack. I knew … *something* when I saw him. But it was so faint, so distant.

Matching tattoos. The drawing in the attic.

But what makes me retch, makes my head spin out, is the man in the balaclava. I know that voice. I know that voice so well.

Because it was my dad.

16

WONKY

Hands take hold of my wrists and pull me along the concrete. 'You can't be in here any longer.'

I lift my head and peel open my eyes. Ajax, Mohawk Man. He lets me go, then pushes open the door. 'Vomiter in BUCKET!' he shouts.

I can feel my sick, a layer of it seeping into the bed sheet, between my fingers, my teeth. Wet and lumpy. When I see the strobes through the doorway, they stab into my retinas, making the nausea swell.

Ajax turns back and the door swings shut, bringing with it darkness and quiet. He begins to pull at my arms again to lift me, but I'm a dead weight.

The story. Jack's story.

I'm in his story.

I know him. I know him from before.

I retch.

'Get up,' Ajax says. 'You can't do that in here. You can sort yourself out in the bathroom.'

'Wait,' I manage. 'Please. Just…' My dad. What was my dad doing there? 'Wait.'

Ajax sighs, looking at his watch under the low light of the bulb above his head. 'The countdown is almost over. We need to clean up your mess before the stories go again.'

Go again. I need to see what happened.

'I'm staying here. I need to watch this story again. *I need to watch more.*' Dribble runs down my chin.

'You have to pay if you want to watch more,' Ajax says as he struggles with my arms, trying to lift me. 'You can't just lie here.'

'I...' I don't have any more money. 'No. *No.* I'm not leaving.'

'You have to *pay*.'

'*I have to stay here!*' My voice is so shrill that I hardly recognise it, but it makes Ajax stop. He lets go of my arms and takes a step back.

'*For fuck's sake,*' he hisses. I hear the click of static as he steps into the corner and speaks into something in his hand. '*Hi, Cas. Ajax here. Can you send security down to BUCKET. We've got a wonky one...*' A walkie-talkie. '*He's fine – just the usual. Doesn't want to leave.*' A voice mumbles back to him. '*No, he only did two minutes... I know... Yeah... He's harmless, just needs a breather. Right... Yes, boss.*'

Cas. Boss. Casimir is Boss.

I knew I recognised him. He's the man who was driving the Nissan Micra, who came to my house with Nisha.

Nisha. Where is she? Where the fuck is she? I push myself up on to my knees. 'Where is she? *Where's Nisha?*'

Ajax clicks the walkie-talkie and the static stops. He turns to me, scowling. 'Where's *who*?'

'*Nisha.*'

'Who the hell is Nisha?'

My brain. It hurts. *It hurts.*

'The bartender. Your colleague.' Her name badge. What did it say? '*Violet*.' That's it. 'Where's Violet?'

He clips the walkie-talkie back on to his belt. 'Listen, you have one minute to get out of here, or you'll have to be taken by force.'

'I'm not leaving until you tell me what this place is. *You have to tell me!*' I'm yelling again. '*I won't leave.*'

'Jesus, these people,' he says under his breath. 'Security are coming and you will be removed.'

'No.' I crawl away from him, towards the back wall. 'You can't. I'm in this story. *I am in this story!*' I slam my finger into the floor like it'll make him understand. 'How did this happen? Why am I in it?'

He watches, staring blankly like he's seen it all before. 'OK, mate. You need some fresh air.'

What's wrong with him?

The headset. Where's the headset?

I scan the room and see it on the floor in the pool of light beneath the hanging bulb. I scramble forwards, grab it, fumble with the strap, desperately trying to pull it back over my head. But Ajax's hand is on it too, trying to wrestle it from my grip.

We pull the headset back and forth, slipping on my sick. '*Lunatic*,' he mumbles. 'Where do these people come from? I can't be arsed with this.'

Then someone steps into the room. Nisha. Clutching her mop.

'What's going on?' she shouts over the music.

'Close the door,' Ajax says, letting go so I fall backwards with a thud. 'We've got a wonky one.'

'Stop calling me *wonky*.'

He wipes his forehead and turns to her. 'Security are coming. This one has completely lost it.'

I pull myself up, using the wall to support me, the headset still in my hand. I point it at her, my hand shaking. 'Nisha. Tell me what the hell is going on here. *Tell me right now!*'

She looks back at me, completely impassive. 'Who's Nisha?'

My head. *My head.* '*Violet!*' I shout. 'Whatever your name is *I don't care*. Just please, *please*... If this is some game, or some joke, I need to know. I need...' But I can't finish. I'm sobbing again, buckling forwards on to my knees. I heave.

'See?' I hear Ajax say, almost bored. 'Lost it.'

'Why am I in it?' I cry. 'Who's Jack?'

'Who *is* Jack?' Nisha asks Ajax.

'I guess the character in the story,' Ajax replies. 'He thinks it's real.'

I push myself up. '*It was real – I was in it!*' I'm smashing my finger into my chest. 'Me!' What don't they understand? 'You said they were actors, but I know these people. I am one of these people.'

Nisha takes a small step back, frowning, and I wonder if she might take pity on me. But she folds her arms. 'You just need some fresh air,' she says. 'You've gone too deep. That happens, OK? You'll be fine.'

'I don't need *fresh air*—'

The door opens again and I'm hit by the electrical storm of strobes and trance music. The pressure shifts behind my eyes. A stark white pain flickers. I feel weak and brittle like I'm adrift, a dead leaf in the wind about to crumple into nothing.

More people enter. Two heavyset men in white T-shirts and black trousers grab my arms. '*No! No – you don't understand—*' Somehow the headset is no longer in my hand. I try to squirm free, but the two men are strong – much stronger than Ajax, and bigger.

'Come on, mate,' one of them says. 'Let's get you out of here. You're just a little confused.'

'I'm not confused!' I shout. But they aren't listening. Together they lift me, a hand under each armpit, until my feet are no longer touching the floor.

I find myself moving out of the room, back into the vault, past the twisting melee of dancing bodies. The words above the doors flash past me: CRASH, AXE, KNIFE. We stop outside one.

SMOKERS.

Nisha opens it.

As we move through the doorway I see there isn't a room on the other side, but a corridor, then a staircase with lots of steps – '*Get off me! Get off me!*' – a fire-escape door at the top. '*Let —*'

Nisha bangs it open and the cold air smashes into my body, stealing my words.

Another alleyway. We must be at the back of the building now. The bouncers dump me down on to the cobbled ground, but I hardly feel it. I'm crying. I can't stop. 'Let me back in! I need to watch more!'

One of them turns to Nisha. 'He can't come back in. Not tonight. I'll tell Cas it's under control.' He goes back through the fire-escape door. The other folds his arms and waits beside it.

Nisha stays in the open doorway.

'Please, Nisha. You have to hear what I'm saying. *I was in that story.*'

'Just stop!' she snaps. As she steps towards me, her eyes scan the alley. I see small groups of people around me, some smoking, some crying, some crouched, retching, while others rub their backs.

'Nisha, please—'

She leans down and grabs my arm. 'Stop using my name,' she hisses.

'But—'

She shakes her head. 'You're bad news. I want nothing to do with you.' I hear someone vomit behind me. 'Listen. This is going to be quick. You're keeping me from my work.' She glances back at the bouncer, who is now in conversation with a zombie Mary Poppins. 'You should never have come here and you must never come back. The experience can be very real for some people, especially if they're vulnerable. It's not for the faint-hearted. People watch the stories and can sometimes think it's them. They typically just need a breather and then they're fine. That's what's happened to you.'

'No, it's not.'

'Yes, it is.'

'You're lying.'

'I'm not lying.'

'I was in the story.'

'That's impossible.'

'I know.' We stare at each other for a moment. 'Have you watched it, Nisha?'

'No.'

I grab her hand. Her eyes widen a fraction. 'Watch it, Nisha. Just watch it. The first two minutes is all you need—'

She tries to pull away, but I don't let her.

'Are you on drugs?'

'No. Why haven't you watched it?'

'*Because*...' She looks a little frightened now. Frightened of me. 'I'm not allowed.'

'Why not?'

'I don't need to explain.'

I squeeze her hand. 'Yes, you do. You do need to explain.'

She turns back to the bouncer, but he's still speaking with Zombie Mary Poppins. 'I need you to leave.'

'Answer my question first.'

She leans down so she's crouched right in front of me. 'Fine. If that's what it takes. Because of the NDA.' She keeps her voice low. 'To keep it a surprise for the guests. To keep it special. Now will you go?'

Our faces are inches apart. 'Special?'

'You know what I mean.'

'Not really.'

She sighs. 'It's an immersive experience for thrill-seekers. We don't want the thrill to be ruined.'

'The *thrill*?'

'Yes. You found it thrilling, didn't you? From what I saw, you were loving it.'

'That was before I found out they were not *actors*.'

She shakes her head. 'No.'

'No? You can't just say no. Do you think I'm mental?'

'You're not exactly the definition of sanity.'

Fine. That's a fair point. 'I know what I saw.'

She scrunches her face and I watch her studying mine for a moment. 'How old even are you?'

'That's not important.' I pause. I need to know more. 'Where do they get the stories from?'

'It's actors.'

'Stop. Stop *lying*.' Why does everyone keep lying to me?

'I'm not.'

'I don't believe you.'

'You don't seem to believe *anything*.'

'How can I? Who is Jack?'

'I said I don't *know*.' She yanks her hand from my grip and moves back towards the door. 'Don't let him back in,' she shouts to the bouncer. He nods as she passes him. 'I need to deal with his mess.'

She disappears, the door slamming shut behind her.

I stare at it for a moment.

It's a blur. Everything is. Like I'm swimming underwater.

The graffiti on the door slowly comes into focus. But there's no rabbit on this one. Just a star. A butterfly. An alien with a speech bubble that reads *the truth is out there*.

I lift myself up from the ground and make my way towards the bouncer. 'Please—'

He holds up his hand. *No.*

'Skinhead Regan!' a voice calls from behind me. I turn. 'Whoa, what happened?' Roadkill Man, holding a can of Red Bull in one hand.

Maybe he can help. 'I just… I need to get back inside.'

'Whoa, fella.' He takes a step back, scrunching his nose. 'Wow.' He wafts the air with his hand. 'You don't smell great, bro.' He looks at me and smiles sympathetically. 'Oh, shit,' he says softly. 'Skinhead Regan went in too deep. Got a case of the wonks.'

'Why do people keep saying that?'

'You'll feel better in a minute.' He keeps his distance. 'Sit down, fella. Take some deep breaths.' I feel my body sink back down into the ground. 'That's it.' I cross my legs, pulling my arms around my chest. 'I'll give you a minute.' And then he's gone.

As I sit on the cobbles, I stare at the back of the door. The star, the butterfly, the alien. *The truth is out there.*

The truth. I need it. I need it now. How do I get back in?

I try to think but my brain feels like it's unravelling. Like it's a piece of string and someone is pulling at one end. I fight desperately to gather it up, to bring it back in to me. But the more I do, the faster it moves, hurtling out of my grasp.

Wait. My hair was blue in Jack's story.

My hair was only blue around the time of the crash. I dyed it three days before it happened. It wasn't blue when I remember arriving at the new house in London from the hospital.

So, what happened in the hut must have happened around the time of the crash. *Did it happen?*

I put my head in my hands and look down at the ground. The noise of people talking around me mixes with the sound of retching. I can see my body is trembling, but I don't feel cold.

I sit and wait. I wait for it to make sense, but it doesn't.

Suddenly there's a bang. I look up to see the door being smashed open. Nisha steps out, heading straight towards me.

I bolt upright, swaying from the rush of blood to my head. 'Nisha—'

Her face is different. It's so harsh – so intent – that it stops me dead. She grabs my arm. 'Listen to me,' she says quietly. 'Go to Polly's Diner in Soho. They know me there. Go straight there, right now. It's open till three. I finish in an hour. I'll meet you there.'

'Did you watch it?'

She doesn't answer. Instead, she throws something at me – a balled-up hoodie and a tatty pair of joggers. 'Put these on.' Then she turns and disappears back into TraumaLand.

Did she watch it?

Fuck. My head.

I try to lodge what she's said into my unravelling brain. Polly's Diner. Soho. Now.

'I like your tattoo.' I turn to see Roadkill Man standing behind me again, a cigarette hanging between his lips, the prosthetics coming loose from his sweaty face.

'Sorry, what?'

'I said I like your tattoo.'

'What tattoo?'

He points to my head. 'The one on the back of your head. Behind your ear?'

'Wait, *what*?'

'Did you stick and poke it?'

'What are you—?'

'It's hard to do words.'

Oh my God. *Shave your head.*

I step towards him. He steps back.

'What does it say?' I can hear the panic in my voice.

He laughs like I'm completely mental. 'You really need to chill – and have a wash, fella. Splash some water on yourself. You're talking crazy. You don't even remember what your own tattoo says?'

'Tell me! *What does it say?*' I scream. Everyone's looking at me, even the ones mid-vomit. I grab the collar of his trench coat. 'If you don't tell me now, I swear to God—'

'OK. OK.' He backs away from me, hands in the air like I'm about to hit him. 'It says *remember Jack.*'

17
POLLY'S

The truth.

It's a funny thing. Or not, I suppose. Depending.

People's relationships with it can definitely be funny, though. And by funny, I mean deceitful. Now isn't that a mind fuck? A deceitful relationship with the truth.

I admit I've been deceitful. With my parents. With Lucas. With Melinda. But not with the truth.

I hope you can see that. All my plans, my side project, are geared towards it. That is the ultimate goal. The plan is to find the truth. It ends there – this journey. I hope it does. Because it's really the only thing that I want.

Hindsight is also a funny thing. Depending. Because now I know about the lies – the lies that are not mine – I can see them very clearly.

I can feel them. Sense them. Hanging in the air in my house, in the boxes in the attic, in the perpetual scent of lilies that fills the hallway. It exists in the space between myself and my family. In their tiny exchanges of looks, their careful pauses before replies.

I thought it was me. I thought it was all me.

Their lies are not little like mine. I know it.

Mum and Dad used to tell those – little ones – and it always made me uncomfortable. There was a time when I fell while playing with Lucas on the driveway. I must have been six. He was teasing me, like he always did, and then he kicked the back of my foot. I landed face down on the gravel and my tooth went through my lip. Mum made me promise to tell people I'd tripped. And so, I did.

Then when Dad would come in from his meetings. His important meetings in the city. Sometimes I'd sit at the top of the stairs and hear him talking to Mum late at night about how everyone lies in politics and how it's important to be seen a certain way.

And his drinking. He lied a lot about that. I could smell something strong on him after work. Sometimes before work. Dad said it was his cologne, but I knew he was lying.

There is something else. Something that has become clear to me now. That night I mentioned – the night Dad left in his Cadillac and came back tired and upset and didn't want to go to the hut with me the next day. Well, that's not the truth. Not really. I omitted things. I lied by omission. I must've blocked them out or chosen to forget.

That night, after he left, I heard Mum on the phone to him. Yelling. Telling him to come home immediately. When he returned, he was drunk, which wasn't unusual back then. I heard him and Mum having a fight. A big one. I could hear them trying to keep their voices down, but Mum was fuming. There was lots of shouting and tears, which was unusual. Even Lucas went down and got involved. At one point I heard him crying too, which was *very* unusual.

I just put my headphones on and kept painting.

In the morning when I asked them about it, they said they were watching a romantic thriller on the TV. But they all looked a bit grey like they hadn't slept a wink. Then I noticed my yellow bike that I liked to circle around the driveway for hours was missing. I was absolutely gutted. Mum said Dad broke it, which was weird, but I didn't question it. And it was never spoken of again.

I can feel fear now. It's so potent. So wretched and painful and very, very confusing.

I asked for it. I pursued it. I desired it.

I'd forgotten what feelings do to you. I can't help but wonder if it was better before, when I was numb. But it is true. It's the truth. Finally, things are real. Only, it's not what I thought it would be.

Welcome to your worst nightmare.

It's not my handwriting. The tattoo. A blotchy, hastily done stick and poke, just like Roadkill Man said.

It's hard to tell from this angle in the bathroom of Polly's Diner, but I know I can't have done it. The two words are located along the skin above the protruding bone at the base of my skull behind my ear. It would've been near impossible for me to do it.

Which means someone else must have done it, which also seems impossible. But then, most of the past few hours seem impossible.

My vision goes hazy as I stare at the two words in the circular make-up mirror I'm holding up in front of my face, reflecting them from the mirror above the sink behind me. I asked one of the waitresses for it – said I needed to find an ingrown hair. This request definitely grossed her out. This was exactly what I wanted because she handed it over without asking questions.

I can see two words now. A reflection of a reflection of a memory I don't have.

REMEMBER JACK

I'd take a picture of it, but I don't have my phone. Or my bag. They're both still with the stern woman back at the club.

Not having my phone made finding Polly's Diner difficult. Due to my brain being mangled like a piece of mashed-up Blu-Tack, I didn't make much sense when I asked people for directions. They either ignored me or moved away, thinking I was blind drunk. One woman actually asked if I was homeless and needed support with drug addiction. She said she could call social services, or my parents, if I wanted. I just cried. It felt so strange, because this is what I'd wanted, but it was awful.

No, don't call my parents, I told her. I said I was twenty-one and I was fine. She just shrugged and said something like *people are so lost these days*.

I was lost, but not in the way she meant. Although, maybe. I cried because everything hurt. It still does. I've been struggling to align my thoughts, to make them make sense. I need to remember every detail of the story. Jack in the hut, my dad saying *I'll take it from here*. The matching tattoos. But the pain is so new, or so old, that I'm struggling to make sense of it.

When eventually I found the diner, down one of those side streets off Old Compton, the waitress at the counter said I couldn't sit inside because I smelled funny. But then she saw I was crying and rolled her eyes and said *come on in. Just don't be a nuisance. I can't deal with more chaos tonight.*

And I thought *you have no idea.*

Polly's Diner isn't the classiest of establishments, all squeaky floors, strip lights and the strong, persistent smell of bleach. The other people all look like I do – pale and sick – which is useful because I can blend in. Late-night pissheads munching on their end-of-night scran. Exhausted taxi drivers. A table rammed with a group of women desperate to keep the last dregs of a hen-do going in a mess of pink wigs and glitter.

But it's quiet in here. In the bathroom.

REMEMBER JACK

Jack.

I didn't remember him in the meeting on Zoom, but I was drawn to him. There was something about him I liked. His energy, maybe. His sadness. I felt like I recognised it. But not his story. That I didn't recognise. He said he'd tried to end his life by jumping off a bridge. He said that was what he'd been told, but he had no memory of it.

He was honest. That's what I liked. I liked his honesty.

He said nothing made sense. He said that's just the truth. Blank and numb. I remember how he said *the only thing I really feel is that something is missing. A sort of longing.* That's how I've felt – or not felt, *sensed* – for so long. That sort of longing.

I don't know if I liked him because he was saying the exact same things I was thinking, or if there was something more beneath it all. No, *no*, that's ridiculous. This whole thing is insane. Nisha will give me some rational explanation.

As I stare at those two blurry words, I keep thinking of a quote from Mum's book in the downstairs loo. The one I read over and over as I tried to calm the residue of the thunderclap headaches. I can't remember all of it, or who wrote this specific one, but for some reason the quote is churning round in my brain.

There are no coincidences and there are no accidents—

The bathroom door smashes open, startling me. I clip the mirror shut as a man in a white vest and denim shorts stumbles past me. 'Don't let me stop you putting on your lippy, hun. You're in Soho, be free,' he slurs, then sways towards the urinal.

Be free.

I turn to the tap and scrub my hands and face with soap, then take a proper look at the hoodie Nisha gave me. It has NIRVANA on it in yellow letters and a faded picture of a woman with wings. It's warm and there's the faint smell of something sweet and clean. The joggers are pink and tatty where the elastic is, or was. They keep falling down around my hips.

Who is this girl?

I push the swing door and step back into the diner. I'm met with the screech of laughter from the hen-do table as one of them attempts to balance a burger patty on her forehead. I make my way towards the frazzled waitress at the counter.

'Here.' I hold out the mirror she lent me.

'That's OK, sweetheart. You keep that,' she says, while crossing something out on her notepad. 'I have a spare.'

'Right,' I say. 'Thanks.'

'Did you get it out?'

'Get what out?'

'The ingrown—' She stops, looks back down. '*Damn it.*' She shouts through the kitchen hatch behind her. 'Ben, it's four waffles, not three! Sorry!' She begins to type something into the touchscreen on the counter.

She looks up and notices I'm still standing there. 'You OK? You seem a bit confused.'

I'm more than a bit confused. 'I'm just … waiting for someone. She said you know her? She comes in after work.' The waitress frowns. I want to say Nisha's name, but I don't know if it's the right one. 'Twenty-ish. Arty type. A bit emo—'

'Nisha?'

'Yeah. That's it.'

'Ah, we love Nisha.' I assume when she says we, she's including me. 'She usually comes in to do her studying after work.'

'Studying? In here?'

'Are you…?' She stops and frowns.

'Am I what?'

'You know…' No, I don't know. 'Never mind.' She observes my puffy eyes, clearly assuming that I'm some forlorn ex-boyfriend here to beg for Nisha's love. 'Well, she takes that table round the corner where it's quieter. It's free. We keep it for her.'

'Um… Yeah, sure.' She looks at me funny. 'Oh, shall I go now?'

She scrunches her eyes, slots her pencil into the rubber band holding her messy ponytail and smiles kindly. 'You're not OK, are you, sweets?' I don't answer. 'Well, whatever it is that's happened, it'll all work out.' She thinks I'm broken-hearted. That Nisha broke my heart. 'What do you want? Coffee?'

'Vodka.'

The smile leaves her face. 'Sorry, it's after hours. And don't you think you've had enough tonight?'

'I haven't had a…' Being drunk is a better explanation than *I was in a locked room and saw a story about me that took place from inside someone else's head*. 'Coffee is good.'

'I'll bring it over.'

As I head in the direction she pointed, past the kitchen and the smell of sizzling fatty food, I try to make myself as invisible as possible. I don't want to talk to anyone.

Except Nisha. I need to talk to Nisha.

She'd better come.

The table is half hidden behind a dying potted palm. It's quieter here and the lighting is less harsh. My brain likes it.

The photograph.

I push my way past the brown leaves and sit, lean down to my sock and take it out. I place it on the table, flatten out the creases. I feel tears welling in my eyes as I stare at it. At some point the waitress places the coffee in front of me. I say thank you, but I don't look up.

Don't forget. Never. <u>Never forget</u>.
You can't – please – remember him.
Shave your head.

The more I stare, the more my brain begins to unravel again. I try to shut it off by studying my hands. My cracked and bloody nails. The bird tattoo on my wrist. Stick and poke, like the tattoo on the back of my head. I think of my drawing. The drawing of myself, but different, more muscular, well built. It wasn't me. The drawing wasn't of me. He said it in the story. Jack said it. *Matching tattoos*. The drawing was of *him*.

'Hi.'

I look up. It's Nisha. Hair tied back, coat wrapped around her, eyes glaring. For a moment we stare at each other. Me with my hands face down on the table, her chewing the inside of her lip.

'You can't scream at me like you did back there. If you scream like that again, I'll leave. And if you follow me, I'll call the police.' Her voice is firm.

'I'm not going to scream.'

She nods, then pulls out the chair opposite so it grinds against the lino floor. She clears her throat. 'So, what is it that you want?'

'What is it that *I* want?'

'Yes.'

'You asked me to come here.'

'Because you were causing a scene and I needed you out of there.'

'But...' I consider the myriad questions I have for her, deciding to lead with the most urgent one. 'What the hell is happening?' I can hear my voice shake. She doesn't answer me, just studies my face. Fine. I'll try a different question. More specific. 'Why were you at the bus stop that night? Were you following me?'

'What? No. I knew nothing about you until you robbed me and began to make my life hell.'

'I've made *your* life hell? I've just *been* to hell, Nisha, and that's because I followed *you*.'

She recoils. 'You *followed* me?'

'No. Yes. Does it matter?'

'Um… If I'm getting stalked then yes, it matters.'

'I followed the rabbit. The sticker on your phone.'

She frowns. 'Coincidences—'

I cut her off. 'Don't say that. There are no coincidences and there are no accidents.'

'What?'

'Nothing.' Ask something else. 'Where does TraumaLand get those stories from? I need you tell me, *now*.'

'Keep your voice down,' she hisses. She glances through the leaves towards the other diners chatting loudly at their tables, all mashed off their heads.

'They can't hear us,' I say. 'Look at me. Please, *look at me*.' She flinches and I see it – a flash of fear – then she turns her head.

My mouth opens and begins to spill words. 'I need you to help me, Nisha. I assume that's your real name, but at this point I don't give a shit. I need you – whoever you are – to help me, OK? Good. I'm Elias. I'm seventeen years old and I used my brother's ID to get into TraumaLand because I wanted to feel alive. That's what it promised and that's what I wanted.

'Last year I was in a car crash and I have no memory of it. I have no memory of two months of my life and my brain has stopped working properly ever since. I've felt numb, blank, *nothing* – until today. Until I entered that room called BUCKET. I ended up there because of *you*. On Thursday night I was waiting at the bus stop and I took your phone – granted, not brilliant, but I have apologised. Somehow, out of *all* the people at the bus stop I could have chosen to rob, I chose *you*.'

I lift the photograph off the table and hold it up to her, my hand shaking. 'Look at this. This is my family.' I turn it over so the writing on the back is facing her. 'And this is a note to me, from me, that I have no memory of writing.' I watch her eyes scan the words, then turn my head and point behind my ear. '*Shave your head*. I did that and this was on my head. See?' Her eyes remain fixed on me, unwavering. '*Never forget Jack*. I was in *his* story, doing things I have no memory of. And I don't remember him.'

'Elias—'

'I met him earlier today, in a group support session for victims of head trauma. I thought it was the first time I'd ever laid eyes on him. But it wasn't. That story suggests, *proves*, that I have seen him –' *felt for him* – 'before today. And you're going to tell me how the hell—'

'*Elias—*'

'Let me speak. I need to speak.' She narrows her eyes. 'And not only that, my *own dad* was in that story. He was doing something terrible – or about to – and I have no idea why. And now I don't know what's real and what's not, and I'm scared. I know that the people in that story aren't actors. And unless I've had a complete psychotic breakdown, which at this point I'm sure some people wouldn't put past me…'

She keeps staring at me, unblinking. 'I need to see more of the story. I need to go back to TraumaLand. I'm aware I probably look mental to you right now, but you have to understand that I'm very, very certain. I'm certain that I can't trust anyone. I'm certain that I'm actually not crazy. Whatever happened last year changed me. It made me this way.' I point at her, my finger trembling. 'And I'm certain that *you* know more. You have to tell me what you know. Whatever's happening, it's not right. It's bad. Really bad. Fucked up is an understatement. But you know that, don't you?'

Her eyes flicker, but she holds my gaze. There's something she's keeping back. *What isn't she telling me?*

'Pancakes?'

I turn to see the frazzled waitress. Nisha keeps her eyes on me. 'Nice to see you, Nisha, love,' the waitress continues. 'You look knackered. Here's your coffee.' She places a steaming mug down on the table.

'Cheers,' Nisha says. 'That's great, Polly.'

'Kitchen's closing soon. You want your usual?'

'Not eating tonight, thanks.'

Polly looks at me. 'What about you? Hungry? Pancakes?'

'No, thanks.'

'OK. Well, it seems like you two are having a bit of a *moment*, so I'll leave you to it.'

'We aren't going to be here for long,' Nisha says. 'Are we, Elias?'

'Hopefully not,' I say.

Polly glances at Nisha in a way that says, *you want me to get rid of him?*

Nisha shakes her head. 'It's fine, Polly.'

'You know where I am if you need me.' She turns on her heel, clearly confused. We sit in silence until she's disappeared round the corner.

Nisha, what do you know? I hold her gaze as she lifts up the mug of coffee and takes a gulp. Her hands are shaking too. The coffee spills on her, but she doesn't react.

Something burns in my stomach, a need to persist. 'Why did you ask me to meet you, Nisha? You must know something or you wouldn't be here. You clearly hate me, so why did you tell me to come?'

'*OK*,' Nisha snaps, looking straight at me. 'OK.' She exhales slowly. 'OK.'

'You're going to need to say more than that.'

She leans back. 'I watched it.'

'What?'

'I watched Jack's story.'

'You watched it?'

'Yes.'

'How much?'

'Two minutes. Like you said. It's all I could manage without getting caught.'

That's enough – *two minutes is enough*. 'And?'

'And I believe you.'

I slump back down into my chair. 'Why didn't you lead with that, you absolute nutter?'

'Elias, you haven't given me a second to speak.'

'That's not...' OK, maybe it is true. Move on. *She believes me*. 'So, you went back in and watched it?'

'You seemed very upset and *convinced*. I've never seen anyone react like that before. And I just wanted to see if—'

'See if I wasn't completely batshit?'

She nods. 'Yeah.'

'So, you saw me in the story? You saw that it's not actors?'

She glances over at the other tables. 'Yeah, I saw,' she whispers. 'It was you.'

'And you always thought it was actors?'

'Yes,' she says quietly. 'But clearly...' A look of concern crosses her features. 'Clearly it's not.'

'Oh my God,' I say, putting my head in my hands. '*Oh, thank fuck.*' I feel like I might float away or evaporate entirely. As the tension disintegrates from my muscles, I'm aware that what I'm feeling is *relief*. Relief, for the first time in so long. I'd forgotten how light, how incredibly *light*, how warm, how *bright* it is. This is the first proof I've had that I'm not actually losing my mind. That I'm not completely off my rocker – well, maybe slightly – and it's so *freeing*.

'I know Jack,' Nisha then says.

It takes me a moment to compute her words. 'Sorry? What did you just say?'

She leans forwards across the table, her voice barely a whisper. 'I said, I know Jack.' Her eyes are darker. 'I recognised him. I know him, Elias.'

'Hold on. *What?* You *know* Jack?'

'Yes.'

'But...' My brain stalls. *How? How?* 'How?'

'We were...' She shakes her head. 'Years ago, Jack and I were in foster care together.'

'You *what*?'

'You heard me.'

'You were in *foster care* together?'

She frowns. 'Do you have a problem with that?'

'What? No, I'm not saying...' I don't know what I'm saying. It came out all wrong. '*When?*'

'When we were about fourteen. Well, I was. He was a little younger than me.'

Oh, my brain. My mangled brain.

'OK... But...' I feel a tightening in my stomach, my chest, like I might cry again. It's so raw, so intense, that it makes me feel – *feel* – that I am *here*. I am here and this is real. 'Where?'

'In Brighton.'

'Brighton?'

'Yes. We were both in foster care in Brighton.'

'I lived in Lewes.'

'Not far.'

'Not far at all... This is insane.'

'Yeah, it is.'

'So, we actually agree on something.'

'Seems that way.' A smile flickers on her face.

Hold on. 'Does this mean we've met before? Me and you?'

'No. I have no memory of you.'

I don't know if that really means anything. 'Is this all linked? Me, you, Jack... *How?*'

Nisha shakes her head. 'I don't know.'

'Are you being honest?'

'Yes, Elias.'

'I need to trust you.'

'That's your choice.'

We sit in silence for a moment and I watch her bite her lip as she thinks. I can see that she's also—

Scared. Confused. Lost.

In pain, somewhere beneath it all. But honest.

I exhale, my breath quivering. 'Can you help me?' I stammer. '*Will* you help me… To understand…'

'I…' She pauses. 'We need to be careful.'

'Why? What's there to be careful about? We should go to the police.'

'No.' I see fear – more than fear, terror. 'No, we can't.'

'Why not?'

She lowers her voice again and practically mouths the word, 'Casimir.'

'Casimir. The man from the holding bay at TraumaLand.'

She nods.

'Paul.'

'Well, yes, but you shouldn't know that.' Fear, again.

'Paul is also Boss, right? The man in the car. He's your boss.'

'Yes.'

'He was the one who texted your phone after I stole it? Telling me he'd kill me?'

She chews her lip. 'Yes.'

'But he seemed so nice in person. Friendly.' She raises her eyebrows a fraction, in a way that says *no*. No, he is not. 'Can we talk to him? Tell him? Figure out what the hell is—'

'No.'

'Why not? Stop being so—'

'So what?'

'Obstructive to the plan.'

'The plan?' Her eyes widen. 'Elias—'

I hate that. 'It's Eli.'

'Eli, listen to me. Casimir is a very…' Her eyes dart around like she's searching for the right word. 'He's a very *particular* man.'

'What kind of particular? *Dangerous* particular?'

'Maybe.'

'That's encouraging. Who is he?'

'He just owns the place.'

'Well, he's clearly off his nut and dark as hell, owning a place like that.'

'It's very popular.' She leans back in her chair, folding her arms. 'You're not the only person who's ever felt numb, you know.'

'But this is different.'

'Why?'

'Because I was *in one of the stories*!' I slam my hand on the table. Anger. Yep. That's definitely anger. She frowns, *keep your voice down*. 'Something happened to me. It was against my will and everyone is lying to me.'

'I'm not lying to you.'

'Has he known who I was all along? He acted like he didn't recognise me at the bar.'

'You look different to how you did in the story.' Her eyes take in my shaved head, my pale make-up. As she picks up her teaspoon and starts to fiddle with it, I notice the chapped skin around her nails – from the cleaning, the bleach, all the vomit she's scrubbed off the floor. 'They vet the names on the door and your ID said your brother's name. He won't have been looking out for it.'

'You're scared of him.'

'I don't want to get on the wrong side of him and neither do you.' Her eyes move to the scar on my temple. 'Is that from the crash?'

'Apparently.'

'It's right where the man hit you in Jack's story.' She bites her lip. 'Who was he?'

'A man named Karl.' Karl. Karl who I knew as a child, with his military boots and moustache and thick south-London accent. *Gentle Giant*. 'My dad's driver for years.'

'And your dad was the man who came in after? With the balaclava?'

I feel a jolt as I remember. 'Yes.'

She picks up the photograph and turns it over. 'Your dad's a famous politician.'

'I'm aware…'

'Very famous. People love him.' She seems annoyed at this.

'Also aware…'

'Well, some do.' Nisha leans back in her chair again. 'When did you say the crash was?'

'A year ago.'

'And you have absolutely no memory of it?'

'Some flashes – small things – but mostly only what I've been told happened.' I lift up my top, showing the burns on my stomach. 'And these.'

Her eyes hover over my scars. 'I see,' she says quietly. 'I'm sorry.' For a brief moment something crosses her face. Pity, or some kind of understanding.

'I don't have a nipple either.' I go to lift up my top. 'Wanna see?'

'I'm good, thanks.'

'So, you're going to help me?'

She bites her nail. 'You are the strangest person I've ever met.' It's so matter-of-fact, so candid, that for a moment I really like her. 'My life has become very fucking strange since I met you.'

'I could say the same for you. Although mine was already all over the place.'

'Yeah,' she says. 'Mine too.' She then looks like she wants to take the words back.

I lean forwards. 'Have you ever needed something so desperately that you'd do anything to get it?' She doesn't reply, but there's something in the way she shifts in her chair that makes me think she has. 'In response to your first question, *what do I want?* the answer is this. I want the truth. Are you in the business of finding it? Because if you are, I need you to tell me what you know.'

And then I say something my dad once told me. 'We are only as sick as our secrets. We should be free of them.' I feel strange using his language now, but it's true. She hesitates, conflicted. 'I know you're a good person, Nisha. I know you are. Please. *Please* help me.' *Come on.*

I suddenly realise something. It sends a shock through my body, raising the hairs on my arms. 'Nisha, if my story is real, doesn't that mean all the others are too?' She looks up at me, her eyes wide. I think of Amy with her mangled leg, Bella in the hotel, her brother Sam, hiding in the bath. 'They're awful, Nisha. Horrific.'

She takes a sip of her coffee, her gaze fixed on me. Then I see something change inside her like a switch has been flicked. She picks her bag from the floor, unzips it on the table and takes out a screwed-up backpack – mine. She hands it to me, then stands. 'Your phone's inside.' She turns and walks past the dead palm tree. 'Follow me,' she says, without looking back.

I take my phone and pull my bag over my shoulder.

I have to run to keep up because she's fast, which I already knew. I soon realise we're not going back to TraumaLand. We're going somewhere else. We wind through the streets, dodging people stumbling out of bars and clubs, food delivery drivers on bikes, until she stops.

I feel an overwhelming sense of dread when I look up at the building in front of us.

We're on Tottenham Court Road, right outside Melinda's office, right by the bus stop where I first saw her.

'Why are we here?' I glance up at the fourth floor and find the room where I meet her every Thursday. Melinda.

Nisha looks up and down the street, checking we haven't been followed. She breathes out shakily.

'I need to show you something.' She turns and begins to walk down the little street round the side of the building.

Why *here*?

Wait. William S. Burroughs. That's who wrote the quote. *There are no coincidences and there are no accidents.* And I can remember the end of it now. *Nothing happens unless someone wills it to happen.*

'Eli, come on.'

I follow Nisha into the shadows.

18

LIKE CRY, OR LIKE RIP

Nisha steps along the passageway directly behind Melinda's office block, dodging discarded McDonald's wrappers and Starbucks cups. As I follow, I glance back up at the floor where I have my therapy every Thursday. I've never seen it from this angle, having only ever entered through the revolving doors at the front where it's all modern and smart. From here, it looks the complete opposite: grey and oppressive. It's dark in this alley. I can only just make out Nisha stopping halfway down it, in front of a door.

I hesitate. Fucking doors. I'm really beginning to hate them.

'Hurry up,' she hisses.

I weave my way through the litter, trying to look through the unlit windows on the bottom floor next to me, but all I can see is my reflection in the black glass. Tear marks streak through the face paint on my cheeks and one of my contacts has fallen out. One eye is green, the other back to my normal brown.

I really do look a mess.

'Why are we here?' I say as I join her. 'I don't understand—'

'You asked me what I was doing that night.' She cuts me off. 'And I'm going to show you.' She pulls her bag from her back and begins to unzip it.

'It's weird that we're here,' I whisper.

'Why?'

'Because I have therapy in this building.'

She stops and looks up. 'What?'

'I have therapy in this building. Up on the fourth floor.' I point to the windows above us.

'In *this* building?'

'Yeah. That's why I was at the bus stop. I was in a therapy session before I robbed you.'

She frowns. 'I was in this building before you robbed me too.'

'What?'

She suddenly looks scared again. 'Yeah. I come here every Thursday.'

'To this building?'

'Yes.'

'For therapy?'

'No.'

'But…' My body is tingling, firing with adrenaline. 'Nisha, why were you here?'

'Just wait.' She reaches into her bag and pulls something out. A vape. The passageway is illuminated in a glowing red as she takes in a long drag of air. She exhales shakily. 'I'm going to tell you everything I know.'

'OK,' I say. 'Good.'

'But that's it, OK? I can only tell you what I know. That's where this ends.'

'Yeah, that's all I need.'

'You can do what you want with the information, but you have to promise not to drag me into any more of this. Not to follow me. To leave me alone, OK? And you have to promise not to repeat this to anyone.' She steps towards me, holding my gaze. *'Promise me.'*

A heat lingers in the pit of my stomach – apprehension, maybe? Concern? 'I promise. I won't tell anyone.'

She takes another drag. When she speaks again, the vapour leaves her lips in thin wisps, weaving their way around us. I can smell it. Cherry. 'Casimir works in this building as a cleaner during the week. I come here every Thursday, before the weekend begins, and he gives me something. I then take it to TraumaLand. I'm here for no longer than ten minutes.'

'Hold on. Casimir works as a cleaner?'

'Yeah.'

'Casimir, your boss?'

'Yes.'

'Casimir who owns TraumaLand is a cleaner in *this* building?'

'You seem confused.'

'Well, yes, Nisha.'

'Can cleaners not own businesses too?' she says, like I'm being a judgy little posh boy again.

'That's not what's confusing,' I say. Although there was a lot of money flying around TraumaLand so I don't quite follow why he'd need another job. Why would he be a cleaner too? 'What's confusing is that it's the same building where I get my therapy.'

'It's probably a—'

'Don't say it. Coincidences aren't real.' She glowers, then takes another drag on her vape. 'What do you pick up?'

'A file.'

'Like a ring binder?'

'No. A digital file. I've not brought you back to the early noughties.'

Funny. 'What, a chip?'

'Yes.'

'From here?'

'Yes. From Casimir.'

'From Casimir the cleaner?'

'Jesus, Eli. Do you have—?'

'ADHD? Yes.'

'OK, that makes sense.'

'Nothing makes sense.' I realise we're very close together now. 'What's on the digital file?'

'The stories.' Oh my God. The stories. From TraumaLand. 'I think this is where the stories are made.'

'*In here?*' Melinda works on the fourth floor. 'Where does Casimir work?'

'On the first floor.'

I turn to the door. There's a combination lock and a metal panel attached to the wall next to it inscribed with the words: HARPER HOUSE: DELIVERIES. There's also an intercom with a list of business names behind plastic covers, each with a buzzer beside it.

Floor 6: JPR Recruitment Co.
Floor 5: QuickTaxi Call Service Centre
Floor 4: Melinda Parry Therapy

I've never clocked that's her second name before. Parry. Seems so … posh.

Nisha points to it. 'Is that your therapist?'

'Yeah.' I continue to scan down the list.

Floor 3: Canary Marketing LTD
Floor 2: Harlow and Gross Solicitors

As I reach the bottom, I point. Her eyes follow the line of my finger.

Floor 1: _____

It's blank.

'Why's it blank?' I whisper.

'I don't know…'

I blink. 'What's the name of the company he works for?'

'He didn't say. Just that it's some digital analysis thing.'

'Didn't you ask him?'

'I don't ask questions, Eli.'

'Why not?'

'Because…' She pauses.

'Because he's a very particular man.' I frown as I study the door. 'Do you know the lock combination?'

She shakes her head.

'Can you text him? Ask him for it?'

'No way,' she says sharply. 'What don't you understand? I just do what Casimir tells me to, OK?'

'Why?'

Her eyes look momentarily blank. Void of anything. She exhales sharply. 'Look, it's just a job. I've never been beyond this point. He hands me the files here, then goes back inside.' She points up to a circular camera over the door.

'Shit.'

'Don't worry, he disabled it.'

'Right,' I say. 'The cleaner who disables cameras.' She gives me that look again, like I'm being judgemental. 'And before you say it, no, I don't assume that cleaners can't disable cameras. But it's odd that he did, don't you think? Since he also, you know, owns a live experience trauma-porn club.' *Wait*. 'Was the chip in your phone when I robbed you?'

She cocks her head like I've caught her out. 'There was one tucked behind the case.'

'So, that's why you pulled a knife out?'

'I was defending myself.'

I step towards her. 'Do you still have it? The chip?'

She puts her hand out. 'Wow, calm down...'

'Why doesn't Casimir just take them there himself? Why do you do it?'

'I don't *know*, Eli. Jesus. Stop asking me questions.' She slings her bag over her shoulder like she's about to leave.

'*Wait*.' I put my hand on her arm. She flinches and I remove it. 'Sorry – I didn't mean to... Please, just wait a moment.' Her body goes still. 'Don't you want to know what this place is?'

'I don't know,' she says quietly. That blankness suddenly returns. 'I think I need to go now.'

Fine. 'Fine. Bye, Violet. I'm going in.'

She frowns. 'Eli...'

But I'm already concocting a plan. I look back down the alleyway at the windows. I'm good at opening windows. Adrenaline fires in my stomach.

'Don't you think they're alarmed?' Nisha says.

I have no idea. All I know is that smashing one probably isn't a good idea. I stare at the deliveries panel. Interesting.

'Look, I'm going to leave.' No you're not. 'This is really stup—' As I press the buzzer, the noise cuts her off. 'What are you doing?'

I press it again. Come on.

The intercom clicks. *'Hello, QuickTaxi.'*

'Hi,' I say. 'I have a food delivery. Nom Nom's burgers?'

'I don't think we ordered any,' the voice on the intercom says back. *'Hold on, I'll just ask.'*

'I'm in a rush, mate. Can you just open the door and I'll leave it inside? I've got a load more to get through and it's fuckin' freezing.'

I hear muffled noises as he puts his finger over the mouthpiece. I strain forwards, my ear pressed against the speaker.

'Hey, boys, this delivery man thinks we ordered food.'
'What is it?'
'Burgers.'
'I'll have a burger.'
'Me too.'

More sounds. Then the voice, louder again. *'Hey, mate. Don't you need a code from us or whatever?'*

I pause. 'Nah.'

I can feel Nisha's glare as I assume a cockney accent. To be honest, I think it's good. Convincing.

'OK. Cheers, mate.' A pause. 'Just leave it there. We … er… We paid on the phone.'

'Yeah, that's fine.'

The door clunks and swings open an inch.

I look at Nisha. Her face says *you're batshit*.

But brilliant mine says back.

'You coming?'

I step inside and she follows me, into the bottom of a concrete stairwell lit by stark strip lights. I begin to bound up them, two at a time, turning where it bends round, on up another flight of stairs. There I find a door.

It has a small gold plaque nailed into it. My chest feels as if it might rupture. Not fear this time. Panic. Cold, brutal panic.

On the gold plaque there are four words.

Floor One
TEAR Solutions

TEAR. Like *cry*, or like *rip*? The card from Lucas's wallet.

'TEAR Solutions?' Nisha says. The buzzing in my brain is at such a high frequency I can't formulate a reply. All I know is I'm glad she's here.

'Eli? What is it?'

'I've seen that name before.'

'What does it mean?'

I think, Nisha, we are about to find out.

I feel a burning heat in my stomach, my chest, my gut.

The door is slightly ajar.

I push and it opens.

19

USABLE

The corridor ahead is long and dark.

I look down to see a carpet beneath my feet, fluffy and beige. It smells like fresh linen and new paint. It feels so clean in here. Too clean. And *wealthy*.

Nisha joins me, swinging the door shut behind her.

'Don't close it,' I hiss. 'Leave it as it was.'

She uses her arm to stop it from slamming. 'You sure about this?' she whispers.

I can hear a low, mechanical hum – air conditioning or electrics – in the walls. But there's something else too. I can sense it. Something dark and unsettling, almost *powerful*, lurking within the concrete, hidden behind the layers of fresh paint. 'Let's go.'

'Eli, maybe we should go back…'

We can't. Not now.

I begin to head down the length of the corridor, Nisha trailing behind me, glancing at the rows of doors on either side as I pass. More gold plaques, each with the same lettering:

Data Collection Room 1

Data Collection Room 2
Data Analysis, Data Sorting
Clinic Room 1
Clinic Room 2

The further we get, the darker it becomes. A heaviness descends and a pressure seems to build. The walls feel denser, like they're penning us in. The air is thicker too. I can hear every movement, every rustle of clothes, every breath.

'Eli…' Nisha says from behind me. '*Stop.*'

But I can't. I see other smaller corridors leading off from this one. This place is so *big*. Like the floor above with Melinda's office.

Melinda. How much does she know? Can I trust her? Should I ever have trusted her? Does she know about Dad? She knows Jack. He was in her therapy group. Why hasn't she told me I knew him?

Then my brain empties as one particular plaque catches my eye.

Cleaner's Room.

Casimir.

'Eli.' Nisha's voice comes from directly behind me. '*Look.*' A sharpness in her tone makes me glance up. She's pointing down the corridor, her face fixed in an expression of something I recognise. Panic. Light spills out of a frosted-glass window in a door up ahead of us, illuminating a plaque beneath it that reads *Security Office*.

Behind the glass is a shadow, pacing back and forth. There's someone here.

'Eli—'

I take Nisha's arm and pull her towards the cleaner's room. I grab the handle, pushing it down until it clicks.

Loudly. Too loudly. *Fuck*.

I snap my head up to see the shadow behind the glass stop moving.

'*What was that?*' A voice, low and muffled. A man's. '*You hear that?*'

My body tingles with fear. Actual fear.

And then another voice, somewhere out of view. '*Probably just the ventilation.*'

The outline of the man leans towards the glass, peering into the darkness. '*I think I heard a door open.*'

Nisha gasps. 'Eli, we need to—'

Without giving her time to finish, I bundle her into the cleaner's room. I close the door behind us – gently, *gently*, holding my breath – until it shuts and we're plunged into complete darkness. We press our backs up against the door.

'Eli—'

I squeeze Nisha's hand. *Shh*.

'*Hello?*' The man's voice, nearer now. '*Who's there?*' I hear the heavy tread of his footsteps until they come to a stop directly outside.

I keep my hand on Nisha's. She's trembling, her breath rattling with each intake.

'*Is there a night cleaner tonight?*' the voice shouts back down the corridor.

Nisha flinches.

'*Sometimes they no-show on weekends.*' The other voice, further away. '*Check the data rooms. As long as they're secure, we're fine. Probably just the pipes.*'

The man sighs, then mumbles to himself. '*Why can't this place just have cameras?*'

He has a point. Why doesn't this place have cameras? What's it hiding?

Nisha and I wait for what seems like an eternity as the footsteps move off. Only when I'm sure he's gone do I allow myself to move, my jaw aching from where I've been clenching it. I scan my eyes around the room but can only make out the small green dot of a smoke alarm on the ceiling. I smell something sharp that tickles the back of my throat, like bleach.

This room makes me feel … something. I *feel* something. Uneasy. Very, very uneasy.

'What do we do?' Nisha murmurs, her voice coarse with the residue of panic.

I feel it too. Fear. I swallow it down. 'Find what we need.'

'And what do we need?'

'Answers.'

I run my hand across the wall next to the door, searching for the light switch. *Fuck's sake, where are you?* I hear Nisha unzip her bag, fumbling inside. A light appears – the torch on her phone. She scans it over the wall.

'Got you.' I see the light switch and click it on. A strip light flickers above us, stark white.

I blink a few times, shielding my eyes with my hand as I adjust to its severity.

The room comes into focus. I don't know what I expected, but this cleaner's room looks just like … a cleaner's room.

Long and narrow, with shelves on either side, holding reams of different products in uniform rows: bleaches, anti-bacterial surface sprays, disinfectants, air fresheners, Dettol wipes, toilet cleaner. It smells sharp. Clinical. Beneath the shelves are a washing machine and a tumble dryer. Mops and buckets and brooms neatly lined up, alongside a grey plastic trolley with rubber gloves and dust cloths folded on the top.

When I was hypomanic, I would've *loved* this. This would've been my idea of heaven. I wonder if they have grout cleaner.

'I don't know about this, Eli,' Nisha says. She's standing by a little desk at the bottom end of the room. There's an empty Tupperware container and some cans of drink on top of it, their straws still poking out of them. Casimir *is* particular. A cleaner who likes Dr Pepper by day and runs a club appealing to the needs of trauma addicts at night. Who is he?

I begin to search through the sprays, trying not to move them too far from their very particular positions, looking for something, *anything...*

I stop in front of the washing machine. The door is slightly ajar. I kneel down and peer inside.

That's strange. A long, thin white box, about the same size and shape as the container Dad keeps his poker chips in.

'Nisha,' I say. 'Look at this.' I lift it out of the drum and hold it up.

'Eli...' she says hesitantly. 'Maybe we shouldn't touch anything.' She looks tiny again, hunched over, shoulders up. I place it down on the desk next to the empty cans.

On the lid a white sticker, with one word:

USABLE

I pause, feeling my body tingling with anticipation. It seems to be making up for lost time, every fibre fizzing with the unknown.

Do it. Open it.

I lift my hand.

'Eli, wait.'

Ignoring her, I flick the clip latches. I lift the lid to reveal a series of compartments in a grid formation, separated by thin plastic dividers. Inside each one are what look like SIM cards. Two, three at the most.

The fizzing swells. 'Is this them?' I say, my voice shaking. 'The digital chips?'

'Eli—'

I lean forwards to look closer. On the inner side of each compartment, scrawled on the plastic, is a name.

TOBY
BEA
ALEXANDRA
JEREMY
MAX
SHILO
KEIRAN
BELLA
SCARLETT
WILLOW

'What the hell?' Nisha says.

Willow. A name I've heard before. Recently.

I know who that is. The girl from group therapy, who was with her mother.

Toby. *Twat-Head Toby*.

These people were in the group therapy session. *I know these people.*

FRANK
JEREMY
TAMIA
JAI
KEIRAN

Then I see two names in the bottom right-hand corner and something sears into me. Heat. Pressure. Like a needle into the side of my brain, pumping something both euphoric and dreadful into its folds.

JACK
ELIAS

Nisha makes a small gasp.

'What is this place, Nisha?' My voice sounds far away. Outside of myself.

'I think he's stealing them. The chips. He's stealing them from Tear Solutions.'

I look back at the box. Some of the compartments are empty. Tamia's. Keiran's.

And Jack's. Jack's compartment is empty.

Usable. What does usable mean?

I look at the chips beneath my name. Two of them.

I lift one out and hold it close to my face. A date is scrawled on it.

JAN 8TH

I'm shaking so much I nearly drop it. 'This was the day of the crash.'

'What?'

'This –' I turn to her, holding it up – 'is the day the crash happened.'

Nisha glances back at the door to check no one's coming. I know I'm speaking loudly, but I don't care. I take out the other chip.

JAN 16TH

I don't remember that day. I study the chip for any more writing. 'What are these?' I turn to Nisha, who is now standing beside the tumble dryer. 'How do I watch them?'

She has a strange expression on her face and I see she's holding something in her hand. A pair of black goggles with wires and pads just like the ones in TraumaLand. A headset.

'Where did you get that?'

She points to the drum of the dryer, sheets now spilling out of it. 'In there.'

A bang from the corridor. A door. Nisha flinches.

'How do we get the chip in?' I say, urgency fuelling me.

'Eli—'

'Quickly, Nisha!' I hiss, holding out my hand. 'Pass it to me.'

'Fine, fine. I'll show you.' She lifts the headset in her shaking hands and presses something on the side of the rubber rim of the left goggle. A tray shoots out, like the kind you'd put a SIM card into on a phone.

'OK,' I say. 'Great. I'm watching it.'

'Eli. I don't know if this is a good—'

Before she can stop me, I snatch the headset and place the chip marked Jan 8th inside the slot. I attach the pads to my forehead, to the base of my skull, and pull the goggles down. Then the world goes black as I enter another reality.

One I do not know.

My own.

20

SYCAMORE

ELIAS
JAN 8TH
TIME: 22:30
LOCATION: LEWES
USABLE

I'm dancing.

In the garden, my bare feet in the mud. It's been hardened by the cold, which has made it difficult to dig and plant the bulbs that lie scattered on the ground. There's music playing in the kitchen. Soft and gentle.

I turn. Spinning. Laughing.

It's beautiful. A piano.

I hold the shovel like it's my dance partner. Dip it low in my arms. 'Dance with me!'

'Eli, please stop.' I turn to see Dad standing beside me in his dressing gown. 'You're going to wake up the neighbours. Come inside.'

'I don't have time.'

'It might help you calm—'

'*I don't want to calm down!*' *I shout. It's true. I don't. Not now. I have lots to do and so little time.* 'Tesco closes at eleven, so I need to get there quick. I've had a google and no other shops are open within a twelve-mile radius unless it's a garage, but they won't sell what I want.' *I can hear myself talking rapidly, but I need him to understand.*

Dad looks at the woman standing under the security light of the patio at the back of the cottage, her blonde hair in a tight ponytail. I can see she's crying.

Mum.

She never cries. She raises her eyebrows at Dad in a way that says no way. Not now.

He turns back to me. 'We can walk to Tesco in the morning, Eli. It'll be a nice thing to do together.'

'No, I need to go as soon as I've finished planting these.' *My brain is buzzing, alive, firing on all cylinders. Everything – every colour and shape and sound – is clear and bright and fills me with life.*

I am alive.

I am indestructible.

'Please put the shovel down,' *Mum says quietly, but her voice is strong. Precise.*

'No, Mum,' *I say firmly.* 'I'm just trying to be helpful. The bathroom needs cleaning and I need a specific product. It's very important that it's the right one. You'll see what I mean when it's done. I know you'll love it.'

'You've dug up half the garden, Eli, and it's ten thirty at night. This has been going on for days.' *She pauses. Then quieter,* 'You need to see a doctor. A psychiatrist.'

I drop the shovel so it falls with a thud in the dirt. 'No. No psychiatrists, Mum.'

'*Eli—*'

'*I'm fine, I promise. In fact, I'm the best I've ever been.*' There's a tremor somewhere inside me, vibrating, desperate to find its way out. '*I feel amazing.*' I start to laugh. Because this is so clear to me now. Everything is so clear.

'Look at yourself, Eli,' Dad says calmly. I glance down at my body. Shirtless. No shoes. Mud between my toes. Only wearing an apron and my underpants. 'Your hair is blue.'

'I like it,' I say.

'Let's go inside and talk,' Mum says. 'It's freezing.'

'Can I go to Tesco?'

'If you calm down, come inside, maybe your father will take you.' She glances at him. He nods.

That's good. Great! 'OK,' I say. 'We'll need to take the car.'

'That's fine,' Dad says.

I follow them through the patio doors and into the kitchen where the music is louder. I stand next to the kitchen island. Dad shuts the patio door behind us and locks it. Mum stands back, arms folded, against the wall.

'Well done, Eli,' Dad says. 'Now let's try and have a rational conversation.'

'That's all I want,' I say. 'I'm here for exactly that.'

He pauses, then says, 'We're going to call a crisis team to come and assess you.'

I slam my fist on the countertop. 'No.'

'We think your new medication has caused this. It's necessary.'

'No, Dad. What's necessary is … is…' I've forgotten. This music is driving me insane. The relentless plonk of the piano. I *go to the record player on the side table in the corner and look down at the spinning record.* 'Who put this shit on?'

'You did, Eli.'

I pull the arm so the needle scratches across the vinyl. All I want is for the noise to stop.

'You'll break it.' *Dad steps towards me.* 'Just leave it, Eli!' *But the needle keeps scratching.*

'I want something more lively. This is sucking the life out of me.'

He's right in front of me now, grabbing my arm.

'Gordon!' *I hear Mum shout, her voice shrill and panicked. She never shouts. She is never shrill or panicked. But Dad keeps trying to pull me away from the record player.*

I turn. 'Get off me!' *My thoughts are like beetles, scurrying over details, moving relentlessly, but I don't mind. They make me faster, which is important.*

I punch him right in the face. Oops.

'Eli!' *Mum screams.* 'Stop it!' *I see her reaching for her handbag on the kitchen island, but before she can, I grab it.*

'No, Mum!' *I shout. Things are juddery, the room is convulsing around me, as I tip out the contents of her bag on to the floor. Keys, keys, come on, keys…*

There. I snatch them, just before Mum's hand can take them. She grabs her phone and scrambles to turn it on, stepping away from me.

'Yes?' *she says into it.* 'I need an ambulance. As soon as you can. My son is having a manic episode and I think he's going to do something dangerous.' *She looks at Dad, who's on the ground with his face in his hands. I think I broke his glasses.*

'No, Mum!' I scream. I realise I'm next to the sink and I have a glass in my hand.

Do it, something tells me. She doesn't understand.

'...he's been acting manic for the past few days and is now seriously out of—'

Do it. Now.

I throw the glass.

It hits the wall a few centimetres above Mum's head. I watch the glass shatter over her like rain.

She screams, dropping the phone. She never screams. Never.

'Wait,' *I say.* 'I didn't mean—'

I can see Dad standing. He's staring at me with so much anger, so much loathing. Before I know what's happening, he launches himself at me. I dodge him and run for the kitchen door, skidding on the shattered glass.

I still have the car keys in my hand. Yes.

I run through the hall and pull open the front door. Outside on the driveway, I see the blue Golf.

I'd rather take Dad's green Cadillac – to ride in style – but that's in the garage, locked away. My old bike would have been perfect, but that's gone.

This'll do, something says to me.

A voice. From within me, but also not. Somewhere next to me. Above me. Behind me. One I do not know. An actual voice.

This is good. It's time to go. Leave these people that do not understand you.

I fumble with the keys in the lock. Come on.

The door opens and I get into the driver's seat. I push the keys into the ignition, hands shaking. The headlights flick on.

'Eli, please!'

Dad is suddenly here – how did he get here? – standing in their glow, waving his hands at me, blood on his upper lip. He looks panicked. Afraid. He moves to the side of the car. As I try to push the lock down – 'No, Dad' – he opens the door. Then his hands are on me, pulling me, dragging me out of the car and on to the driveway.

I jump up, scrambling out of his grip. I climb on to the bonnet. Then up, on to the car roof.

'Get down, Elias!' His voice is strong. Angry.

'No, Dad.'

He grabs my foot and pulls. I tumble off it, landing on top of him. As we wrestle on the ground, I can feel that I'm crying. He puts his whole weight on top of me.

'You're suffocating me!'

His foot is in my back, his hand is on the side of my head. He pushes it into the ground and my mouth fills with gravel. I can't move. 'You need some help, son. You need some help,' he keeps repeating. The keys are no longer in my hand. I look up and see Mum on the phone, in front of our house, our beautiful country cottage in leafy Lewes, her hand over her mouth.

Everything judders.

I hear the sound of sirens, the sounds of tyres grinding to a halt on the gravel. The driveway becomes doused in a blur of red and blue. There are people in a green uniform – are they paramedics? – lifting me into the back of the ambulance.

'You're safe, Elias. We're taking you somewhere you will be safe,' the paramedic says.

And then I'm moving.

I'm screaming and yelling, strapped down. 'I'm sorry, I'm sorry, I'm sorry. Please, where are you taking me?'

SESSION ENDED
USABLE FOR ELIAS'S STORY
HOSPITAL

I'm in the cleaner's room, lying on my front. The stark white of the tiles shatters into view. I bolt up, panting, tears wet on my face. My ribs. They ache.

My head. I can't think straight.

A hand touches my arm. I jump.

Nisha stands over me, panic in her eyes. Confusion. Terror. '*Shh.*'

'Nisha, I...' I start to say, but the words get caught in my throat. This is...

This is bad. This is very, very...

'What was it?' she whispers. 'What happened?'

'I... I...'

'You were writhing around on the floor.'

'Nothing they said is true.'

She kneels down next to me, places her hand on my shoulder. 'What do you mean?'

'There was no car crash,' I say, my throat thick with phlegm. 'It never happened.' I drag myself up, my arms struggling to hold me.

'Stay quiet—'

'I was taken away in an ambulance before I drove the car. I never drove it. I tried to, but my dad pulled me out before I could.'

I can see her biting her lip, thinking.

'They lied.'

They lied. Why?

Nisha frowns, studying my head. 'But if there was no crash, how did you get the scars?'

My scars. My chest. My stomach. My nipple.

The hole in Dad's stomach. From the branch.

But there was no branch. There was no fucking branch. How did he get it?

'Eli—'

I crawl away from her towards the desk, the headset still in my hand. I fumble through the white container until I find the other chip in my compartment.

JAN 16TH

'Eli, wait. They keep walking past.'

But she can't stop me. Nothing can. I'm already pushing it into the headset.

'You don't need to be here,' I say. 'If you don't want…' My voice falters, emotion gripping me – so deep and painful I can't quantify it. I catch something in her expression, something I've not seen or felt for a long time.

Empathy. Real empathy. Warm against the stark whiteness of everything else.

'I'm not against you,' she says quietly and I know she means it.

'OK,' I say. 'Thank you, Nisha.'

'Just… I need you to stay quiet. Sit under the desk,' she says. 'You nearly threw yourself into the shelves.'

I point at a pillowcase on the floor that she pulled out of the dryer. 'Pass me that.'

She does and I begin to twist it.

'I'll stay by the door,' she says. 'If I hear anything, I'll pull the headset off.'

'OK.' I crawl beneath the desk. 'If I scream and it comes out, shove it back in.' I take the pillowcase and push it into my mouth, tying it behind my head. Just before I pull the headset back on, I look at Nisha and for the briefest of moments I feel a sense of calm wash over me.

I think what I feel is *comforted*.

Then I pull down the goggles once more and she is gone.

⌒

ELIAS
DATE: JAN 10TH
TIME: 10:06
LOCATION: SYCAMORE WARD
USABLE

'Do you know where you are, Elias?'

The man standing in front of me is wearing a crisp white shirt, no tie, top button undone. Behind him are four large men in light-blue polo shirts with the letters 'NHS' embroidered where the pocket should be. The walls are a soft cream colour. The room is empty, except for these people. These people I do not know.

'I'll take your silence as a no,' the man in the white shirt says. 'You are currently in a seclusion room at Sycamore Adolescent Psychiatric Unit in Brighton, about ten miles from your family home. My name is Dr Dexter and I will be your responsible

clinician. You are currently unsafe. You are a risk to yourself and to others, so you need some help.'

I'm crouched on the floor, wearing clothes that are not my own.

A gown. A hospital gown, tied around my waist. I can see the top of my thigh through the slit. My blue boxer shorts.

'Let me out of here,' I say.

I watch the four men bristle.

'I just want to speak with you,' the doctor says calmly. 'We're going to take your vitals, then bring you some food and some medication. I need you to stay at the back of the room while we do that, OK? To keep everyone safe.'

'No.'

'Elias, you are not very well. You have been sectioned here and you are very confused, so we will have to—'

'I'm not confused. I need to get to Tesco.'

One of the men behind the doctor stifles a laugh.

The doctor doesn't take his eyes off me. 'Are you still hearing voices?' he says. 'Are they telling you to do things?'

I don't answer.

He sighs, looks at his watch, then turns to one of the men. 'Blood pressure, please.'

The man who laughed steps towards me, holding something in his hand. A grey box with a rubber wire coming out of it.

'This is a blood pressure—'

'No!' I yell. 'Don't come near me!' I'm standing now, my body screaming in pain, my head thick with racing thoughts. 'Just let me go!'

'Elias, we can't look after you if you resist. Work with us,' the doctor says, stepping backwards behind the men. 'We are helping you.'

The man with the grey box is strapping something attached to it by a grey tube around my arm.

'Please—'

And then I see the door on the opposite side of the room, with a small, square window in it. It begins to open. A lady steps into the room carrying a tray.

'Who are you?' I yell.

No one answers.

On top of the tray is a plate of food and, next to it, a needle.

'No!'

I grab the rubber tube attached to the grey box, pulling it from the laughing man's hand.

'Oi!'

I swing it, feeling its weight, as I back away from him into the corner.

'Restrain him!' the doctor shouts. 'He has a weapon!'

I wrap the rubber tube around my hand, the grey box hanging from it like a mace. I look at the four men. 'Don't you touch me or—'

Suddenly, it feels as if a brick wall has pounded into my body. I fly backwards, landing on the floor with a crack.

The four men are on top of me, grabbing for my limbs.

I twist my body, sliding along the floor, dodging hands, between their feet. Then I'm up, running, past the man in the shirt and the lady with the tray and through the open door, out into a corridor.

I run, run, run, slamming into walls, turning corners, past other people in hospital clothes staring at me blankly. A ward. I'm in a ward. Rooms with people's names on them – KELLY'S ROOM, MOHAMMAD'S ROOM, ELISHA'S ROOM – fly past. I can hear the four men behind me, feet slapping on the lino floor.

My body crashes into someone.

'Sorry, sorry, sorry.' A girl with a bloody mark on her forehead. 'Can you tell me which way is the—'

'Move, Rosie!' I hear. She steps aside just as a body slams into mine from behind. I fly forwards.

All I see is the ceiling. And hands. Hands on me, gripping hard like they're trying to snap me in half. I feel each finger as they dig into the muscles in my arms, my legs, as I'm picked up and dragged back through the corridor. I scream and thrash, the skin on my knees burning as they skid across the lino.

Then I'm back inside the cream room. I'm dropped down on to the cold, hard floor.

My head bounces off it and I smell the sharp tang of metal.

I try to stand.

White dots swarm as two of the men appear on either side of me. They pull me down with them until they're lying straight on either side of me, pushing into me with their bodies.

'No! No – no!' I feel a crushing weight across the back of my legs. 'Get off me!'

'OK, Elias,' a voice says. A female voice. 'It's OK.'

I'm able to turn my head just enough to see her standing over me – the lady in the blue nurse's uniform who was holding the tray.

'Help me, please!' I see the needle in her hand. 'No!'

'Work with us, Elia—'

'Don't!' I scream. 'Don't you touch me!'

The white spots begin to merge. I can no longer see her face. Just a white blotch.

And then I feel my gown being pulled down, below my back. I try to kick and kick, but I can't move. There's something heavy on my back. A knee. My chest hurts. I can't breathe. I can't...

My lungs feel like they'll explode.

I can see the man on my left is smiling. Smiling like this is funny.

I gasp for air. 'Help me—'

A sharp pain radiates into my upper thigh.

'Stop...' My voice is small. The white is closing in on me.

The man laughs again.

'Just one more...' the nurse says brightly.

Another sharp pain. The other thigh.

The two men stay lying on either side of me, until I hear the door open.

The weight on my legs lifts. The man on my left lets go.

The man on my right stays, holding my arm, now crouching next to me.

'That fucking hurt,' I say.

He smiles. 'Don't fight next time. It'll be easier.'

And then he is gone.

The lights flick out. I hear the door slam.

I turn to it. The small, square window is the only thing I can see.

I drag myself up off the floor and stagger towards it. 'Help me,' I say, leaning my forehead against the glass. 'Please, help me.'

No one.

Wait. Yes. There is. A little down the corridor with his back to the wall.

A boy. My age. It startles me slightly when his eyes meet mine. I look at him – tall with broad shoulders, his face slender with sunken eyes, yet soft somehow. He's wearing a beanie and a hospital gown like mine. 'Help me,' I say. 'Please.'

He frowns, opens his mouth as if to speak – and then I see a hand on his arm. Someone pulls at him. The nurse who stabbed me with the needle. 'Come on, Mr Quinn.' She pulls at his arm again. 'Jack, this way, please.'

And he's led away. Out of sight.

I feel sluggish. Exhausted.

As my body pulls me down on to the floor, I see something slide underneath the door.

I hear the nurse's voice. 'Your parents wanted you to have this.'

A photograph.

One I took. Dad, Mum and Lucas in the sun outside our house, in front of Dad's green Cadillac with the yellow stripe down the bonnet. They all look so happy.

I pick it up and turn it over, wondering if they've left me a note on the back. Some kind words. An apology.

But it's blank.

I fold it and hold it pressed into my palm as I stare at the walls.

Cream. All around.

And endless silence.

TIME ENDED
STORY NAME: HOSPITAL

21

CLASSIFIED

I open my eyes. Rip off the headset.

I'm panting, gasping for air, the pillowcase still in my mouth.

I spit it out, saliva dribbling down my chin as I inhale. My head rages, full to bursting, brimming over with thoughts and questions that spin and spiral away from me. What the hell was that?

'Eli?' Nisha kneels in front of me.

I'm still under the desk. 'Was I loud?'

She shakes her head. 'You were thrashing around, but the pillowcase stifled your screams.'

'OK,' I say, relieved. *Relief*. She watches me as I catch my breath, her face riddled with concern. 'I'm OK.' I am. 'It's OK.'

She crawls underneath the table and sits next to me, crossing her legs. 'What was it?' she says. 'What did you see?'

'I was in a hospital. But not Royal Sussex County Hospital, like they said. There was no amnesia. No head injury.' I pause. 'I was in a psychiatric unit.'

'A *psychiatric unit*?'

'If this is true, I...' My head. It hurts. So much. 'Jack was there too.'

She tilts her head. 'Jack was in the hospital with you?'

'Yes.' I watch her eyes studying mine. 'He was a patient.' Beanie, broad shoulders, his eyes meeting mine through the small, square window. 'He was there.' My chest constricts. 'When was the last time you saw him?'

'Years ago,' Nisha says. 'Maybe three or four years...'

'What the hell is happening?' I hold up the headset and see it trembling between my fingers. 'What are these stories? *Is it real?*' My voice cracks. 'I was in a room, locked in a fucking room. They were using my name, so it was me – *it was definitely me*. They injected me. Said I was hearing voices. That I was unsafe to others and to myself.' Dribble and snot begin to drip down my face again. I wipe it with the back of the sleeve of her hoodie, covering it in a slimy film. 'Sorry,' I say. 'Argh...'

I try to pull the hoodie off because I'm hot. *It's so hot.* But it gets stuck on my head, digging into my neck, strangling me.

'Hey, Eli – *Eli*. Just slow down...' I feel Nisha's hands on mine, stopping me, then gently lifting it over my head.

'I can't... I don't... I'm sorry...'

'It's OK. It's just a hoodie. Breathe, OK?' I inhale through my nose heavily.

She picks the hoodie up from the floor and begins to wipe my face with it. 'You can keep it,' she says quietly. My head lolls forwards and I feel it meet her shoulder. I leave it there for a moment, continuing to inhale through my nose. Her hand presses firmly, securely, into the back of my head, holding it steady. 'Jesus, Eli,' she whispers.

My brain feels like it's malfunctioning. 'Is it a lie?' I say into her shoulder. 'Is it a deepfake? Some computer-generated – I don't know – *game*?' She leaves her hand where it is. It feels nice. I hate that word, but it's true. 'What is Casimir, Nisha? Because he clearly isn't a cleaner.'

'Yeah,' she whispers. 'You were definitely right about that.'

I lift my head. 'Promise me you're telling me everything you know.' I can hear the desperation in my voice.

'I am. Of course I am,' she says and I can hear the certainty in hers. 'It used to be someone else who picked up the files. He worked behind the bar too. But one day he just wasn't there any more. Casimir said he was "removed" from his role because he couldn't be trusted. Then he asked me to start doing the pick-up. Said he could trust me to keep my mouth shut. And he knows…' She shakes her head, dropping her eyes. 'Look, I've not had the most perfect life. I've done some stuff. Bad stuff. I've done bad things and… Well, he knows about it. He said if I break his trust, he will make my life hell.'

'So, he's blackmailing you?' She stares at her legs, crossed beneath her. Begins to pick at her DM boots. I notice they have holes in the bottom. I can see her socks through them. Purple. 'And the reason he was so mad that I had your phone was because he wanted his file. He didn't actually give a crap about you.'

'Maybe,' she mumbles.

'He doesn't seem to give a crap about many people.'

'I don't want you to think I'm a bad person. If you ever find out… If he ever—'

'I don't care what you've done, Nisha.' I don't. 'We need to find out what Casimir's doing and stop it.'

She nods. 'I found something else. While you were watching it.' She crawls out from under the table and I hear her lift something off the top of the desk. When she kneels back down, she has something in her hand. She places it on the floor between us.

Another box. Slightly smaller than the other one. It's black with a sticker of a bunny on it just like the one on the back of her phone.

'Where did you find it?'

'It was hidden,' she says, pointing. 'In that bucket. Covered by an old mop.'

I take it from her and look down at the words written in marker pen in Casimir's handwriting.

NEW PROJECT – classified

'Have you opened it?'

'No,' she whispers. 'I was waiting for you.'

I undo the clips, lift the lid and look down to see more compartments. But this time each one has a pair of names on the plastic.

JONNY AND EMILY
TERRY AND JOAN
SIERRA AND JASPER
ELIAS AND JACK

Elias and Jack. A single chip inside our compartment.

'Nisha…'

Suddenly the door clicks. I whip my head round to see the handle moving.

Nisha is up, already flicking the light off. As we're plunged into darkness, adrenaline sears into me. I push myself back against the wall beneath the desk, still clutching the headset and the box.

A crack of light spills through the partly open door and a man's head emerges. Nisha grabs the handle from the inside, stopping it from opening any further.

'*Jesus*,' the man says, startled.

'Hi,' Nisha says, suddenly warm. Friendly. 'Security?'

'Yes.' The wrinkles in his forehead deepen. 'Who let you in here?' He's sceptical. Very.

'I'm covering the weekend shift,' Nisha says casually.

He nods, still frowning. 'I've not seen you before. Paul didn't mention you.' He's still uncertain. 'We vet all our staff. What's your name?'

I see the muscles in Nisha's neck flicker. *Shit*.

'Oh, d'you know what,' she says, her voice remaining casual. 'I'm an idiot. I must be on the wrong floor. Is this QuickTaxi?'

'You need the fifth for that…' He pauses. 'How did you get in?'

'The door was ajar.'

His eyes flash into the room. 'Are you with someone?'

I hold my breath.

'No, just me.' Nisha remains where she is, blocking the man from entering. 'Oh my God, would you look at me, stumbling into your lovely offices. I'm so sorry. I get confused with all these floors.'

His eyes move to her face. 'Don't worry.'

'So, floor five?' she says, smiling.

'Floor five.'

'Oh, brilliant. Thanks.' She laughs, a little gormlessly. He steps back, about to turn away.

'Wait,' Nisha says, opening the door a fraction. 'What is this place? Looks posh.' She laughs again like she's stupid. Like she's too stupid to worry about.

But this girl is not stupid. Quite the opposite.

I hold myself completely still in the pause that follows, waiting for his answer.

'Data collection,' he says. 'Nothing interesting.' Then, 'I'll see you out. I'll just get the keys.'

'Sure!' she says brightly. As his footsteps fade away, she turns to me. 'Quick. Put everything back. Casimir can't know we've been here. *Now, Eli.*' She turns back to the corridor, loitering in the half-open door.

I pull myself out from beneath the desk, placing the black box and headset on top of it, next to the box marked USABLE. I quickly make sure all the chips are in their correct places and shove it back into the washing machine. I then pick up my bag.

'Hurry up, Eli.'

When I return to the desk, I glance down at the second box. NEW PROJECT – CLASSIFIED. I stare at the compartment labelled ELIAS AND JACK. The single chip inside it.

I have an idea. One Nisha won't like.

I check to see that she's still looking through the gap in the door. And I take my opportunity.

I grab the chip between my fingers, stuff it inside my bag along with the headset, then zip it shut. I turn to the tumble dryer, shove the pillowcase back inside and put the black box in the bucket beneath the mop.

Nisha glances back. 'Everything where it should be?'

I nod. 'Yep.'

I sling my bag over my back and join her in the doorway. She peers out once more. 'OK. He's in the office. Let's go.'

I feel her hand take mine and then she's pulling me out the door and back down the corridor, in the direction we came. I glance over my shoulder to see the security guard put his head round the office door. 'Wait! Who's that with you? Stop!'

We hurtle past the golden plaques, one after the other. As we run, as the man shouts after us, my blood feels electric. Something chemical courses through it – terrible and charged and fantastic all at once.

We dart out the front door and back down the concrete steps, smashing the delivery door open. As we're met with the bite of the early-morning air, my skin prickles awake.

'*Keep going!*' Nisha screams up ahead and I follow, charging through the McDonald's wrappers and Starbucks cups, rounding the corner and sprinting down the street. Tears streak down my cheeks. I don't know if it's the cold, or something else – it doesn't matter because I'm momentarily weightless.

Nisha stops in front of me, doubling forwards, catching her breath, and I have to stop myself from flying over her. I suddenly laugh, an explosion of relief forcing its way out of me. I'm fizzing with life. I can hear it in my ears. Taste it on my tongue. Exhilaration and terror, confusion and hurt and…

'What's so funny?' she says.

I don't know.

None of this is funny. It's fucking awful.

But I can't help it. I laugh and laugh. She stares at me like I'm a complete and utter nutcase.

But I'm not. What I am is this: I am living. I feel alive. I guess TraumaLand achieved something.

'What now, Eli?' she says and my laughter subsides.

That's a good question. I inhale the cold, sharp air and with it comes the reality of the night ahead.

'I have an idea,' I say. 'But I could do with a hand.' And the company. I like her company, but I won't tell her that. There's something about her, her separateness from everything I've known – or know – that makes me feel safe. Because I now see that it's the people I'm closest to that I should be most afraid of. 'You want to come with me or not?'

22

A BRIGHT FUTURE

We're standing on the roof of my house.

I can see the city lights in the distance, stretching out for miles. This city is so big. This world so enormous. All those people, so many of them, living their lives. People I will never know.

'Eli,' Nisha whispers. 'What the hell are you doing? Stargazing?' She has her arms outstretched as she balances on the tiles, the wind threatening to topple her. 'What now?'

'In there,' I say, pointing to the skylight in the slanted roof, still slightly open where I forgot to close it earlier. 'But land quietly. My parents' room is directly beneath it.'

'Are you kidding me?'

I shrug. There is no other way in. I ran through all the options on the night bus on our way here. We stashed our bags in in the rhododendron bushes, then scaled the drainpipe. Nisha wasn't too happy about that bit of the plan (the drainpipe), but she was very good at it. Better than me. I lack upper-body strength. She clearly does not.

I didn't tell her about the fact the attic is above my parents' room. Thought I'd save that bit till now. I check the time on my phone. 05:38. Christ. They'll actually be up quite soon.

'Eli.'

'Sorry.'

I crouch down and open the glass panel until the gap is wide enough to fit through.

Nisha gives me a look. *Who first?*

I nod. *You.*

She rolls her eyes, but I know part of her is enjoying this, the excitement, the danger. So am I. The consequences could be bad – disastrous, in fact – but I can feel the thrill burning in the pit of my stomach.

I watch as she perches on the edge of the skylight, dangling her legs into it. She then lowers herself into the darkness beneath, her movements confident and exact. I hold my breath, waiting to hear the thud as she lands, but there's nothing. *Good, that's good.* I have the impression that she's done this kind of thing before. By that, I mean accessed a locked house that is not her own.

I've done bad things.

'Eli, I'm in.'

I follow her, lowering my body and feeling with my feet until they meet the soft carpet. The glow of the inky-blue sky above makes a perfect square on the floor. I reach for my phone and turn on the torch to find Nisha.

I nod. *OK?*

She nods. *OK.*

I tiptoe towards the lamp and click it on. The attic is exactly as I left it.

Nisha widens her eyes, taking it in. Who has an attic like this? *Rich people*, her face says. *That's who.*

I point to the boxes tucked in the eaves. *In there.*

She frowns.

But quiet.

Together we creep towards them, painstakingly slowly, one foot in front of the other across the thick carpet.

'That one,' I whisper.

MEDICAL DOCUMENTATION
E.G.P.

Nisha stares at the box for a moment. I can feel questions lingering in the air, heavy and important. From this moment, things could be very, very bad. Is it better not to know? Should we just go back? Leave this attic – this night – in the past? Pretend it never happened?

If we look inside, what will change? But I already know the answer: everything.

The past changes everything.

I feel Nisha's hand on my arm. *Come on.*

I lift the box and place it at our feet. We kneel in front of it carefully. I open the cardboard flaps and look down.

Loose pages, hundreds of them, covered in typed words in the same font. All laid out in neat boxes with dates, the blue NHS logo in the top-right corner, next to two words: SYCAMORE WARD.

I remember the doctor with the crisp white shirt.

Do you know where you are? You are currently in a seclusion room at Sycamore Adolescent Psychiatric Unit.

We begin to lift them, one by one. As we do, I realise that they're printouts of nursing notes. *My* nursing notes.

'So, it did happen...' Nisha says quietly.

It's here. Proof. It was real.

My throat constricts as I run my eyes over the words. There are so many pages, each covered in examinations and opinions of me. My *Mental State*, my *Engagement with Others*, my *Food and Fluid Intake*, my *Compliance with Medication*.

Jan 8th – EP admitted on Section 2 due to manic episode induced by ADHD medication...

Jan 10th – EP still exhibits signs of elation...

Jan 11th – EP's behaviour remains challenging...

Jan 13th – EP lacks insight into why he needs to be at Sycamore...

Jan 14th – Pressured speech, excessive talking, thought disordered...

Thought disordered. That sounds about right.

I root through the box, down to the bottom, pulling out more.

Feb 13th – EP gaining insight...

Feb 18th – EP becoming far more settled on the ward...

Feb 20th – New medication having good effect on Eli...

Feb 27th – EP needs a few more weeks to improve...

All the way down to the last one.

March 4th

And then, no more. March 4th. Exactly four days before my memory returned.

'The dates are pretty much the exact dates I can't remember,' I murmur. 'Nearly the whole gap of two months, I was here. In this hospital.'

Except those four days.

I look at the single note on the page headed March 4th.

EP was taken out of our care by his parents and handed over to a private provider.

'Look at this,' I say, my voice barely a whisper. Nisha leans over my shoulder.

'You were taken out of the hospital and placed somewhere new?' she says, matching my volume. She takes it out of my hand, squinting at it. 'And you have no memory of that place either?'

'No.'

'What did your parents tell you?'

My parents. I look over at the hatch and listen for a moment. Nothing. Both of them fast asleep, directly beneath us.

'They said the crash caused *post traumatic amnesia* and that I was in Royal Sussex County Hospital recovering for two months, unconscious for most of it, in a coma.'

'But … why lie?' She pauses. 'Are they ashamed that you were there?' I don't know. A shiver runs down my spine. 'Is there any mention of Jack?'

Jack. I scan over the papers, looking in the boxes titled *Engagement with Others.*

– *EP can be abrasive*

– EP can be very talkative and persistent

– EP is kind when you get to know him but struggles with boundaries

– Not many of the patients warm to EP, which he has a hard time with, as he can come across as overbearing

And then I see something.

Two letters – JQ – dotted throughout the pages.

I remember what the nurse said to the boy, outside the seclusion room. *Come with me, Mr Quinn.*

JQ. Jack Quinn.

– EP has become close to patient JQ

– EP and JQ remain friendly, boundaries healthy, seem to be encouraging one another. Staff to continue to monitor. Nil concerns currently.

– EP's demeanour is calm and relaxed around JQ in particular, often smiling and in general good spirits when together

– EP and JQ went on escorted leave together today to the local supermarket accompanied by staff, both in bright spirits, engaging well

– EP and JQ spend most evenings together playing card games in the de-escalation room

– Nursing team suspect EP and JQ are developing a relationship that is more than platonic… Monitor.

'What does it say?'

'Hmm?' I move the page to the back so she can't see. 'Yeah, he's in here.'

'And?'

'I'm not sure yet...' I say. 'It doesn't make much sense.'

'Is *JQ* him?'

'Yeah... I think so. Jack Quinn.'

'Look.'

– Since the escorted leave to the beach, EP and JQ to be kept separate at EP parents' request. To be monitored at all times, boundaries asserted and no contact between the two.

– Parents are worried about JQ's influence on EP.

Escorted leave to the beach? What beach?

'So, you and Jack were in this hospital in Brighton together the whole time,' Nisha says.

'Apparently.'

'Why were your parents trying to keep you apart?' She looks at me, eyes wide. 'Just before you were moved out of the hospital?'

I really don't know. 'What was he like, Nisha?' I say. 'When you knew him?'

'He...' She chews her lip. 'He was ... quiet. Lots of stuff had happened to him. His parents gave up on him and his little sister when he was young. His sister died. I remember him being really cut up about it.'

'And you don't know anything about him now? Where he is?'

'No. I haven't heard about him since I moved on a few years ago.'

Something slips from the pages in my hand. A piece of card just like the one Lucas had in his wallet.

My heart jumps. A ringing sounds in my ears.
'Shit, Nisha. Look at this.'

TEAR Solutions
Private Healthcare
Scan QR Code

Keep hidden from patient

She reaches into her pocket for her phone. 'Well, I guess we're about to find out what TEAR stands for.' She opens the camera and goes to scan the QR code.

'Wait,' I say. Wait for what?

'It's OK,' Nisha whispers. *Is it? Is it really?* I'm trembling. *Stop it.* 'Eli, it's OK. I'm going to help you,' she says gently. 'Whatever this is … I want to help you.'

And I believe her. My eyes are stinging. 'Thank you,' I say.

She scans the code and a webpage appears with a single white box, a triangle in the middle of it.

TEAR Solutions
Press to play.

I can't feel my hands. I'm overwhelmed. *Filled with complete and utter dread.*

That's the correct phrase. My insides are trembling now. All of me is.

'Turn the volume down,' I whisper shakily. 'They might hear us.'

Nisha reaches into her pocket and takes out her purple earbuds, handing me one of them. She then places her phone on the carpet, screen up.

We lean over it on our knees. She hovers her finger over the triangle. 'Ready?'

I glance back at the hatch. Still shut. Of course it's still shut.

I have the sudden urge to go down the steps. To knock on my parents' door. To ask them what the hell is going on and then to be given a rational explanation.

To be given clarity. To be given a hug.

To be told something awful must be going on, but they can help me. That's what I want. But now I know that's not what would happen.

'Eli...' Nisha takes my hand in hers.

Then she presses the triangle with her finger and the video begins to play.

23

MARKED *ANONYMOUS*

Two adults sit at a dining table across from a teenager. The teenager is crying. Calming music plays, some kind of mellow flute. A well-spoken male voice begins to talk over it.

'You are watching this because you are worried about your child.'

The parents lean across the table to take the teenager's hand, but she moves back in her chair. She looks out of the window, a single tear falling down her cheek.

'Your child has been through an unimaginable trauma and it seems to you that they will never pass through the pain of it.'

The mother gets up and walks around the table, but the teenager stands too, backing away from her. She storms out of the room, slamming the door in her mother's face. The mother turns, her face taught with worry.

'You are desperate to help them.'

The father has his head in his hands and is rubbing his eyes.

'Here at TEAR Solutions, we have the answer.'

The parents look up as a woman enters the room from out of shot. Pinned to her knitted cardigan is a badge that says

TEAR Solutions. She's smiling. The parents smile back at her, relief flooding into their eyes.

'TEAR Solutions offer a fast, effective and painless way of removing life-altering trauma.'

The woman sits down at the table opposite them, where the teenager was. The mother hands her a cup of coffee and she sips it gratefully. The woman then opens her bag and takes out a brochure, placing it on top of the table. The front cover shows lots of smiling teenagers.

'Healthcare is rapidly changing. TEAR Solutions are at the forefront of that change. We have developed and harnessed the use of something called optogenetics.'

The camera zooms onto a page in the brochure. The voiceover continues as it scans over the words.

'By merging genetic engineering with the use of light, we at TEAR SOLUTIONS are able to control the activity of individual neurons using a process called optogenetics. This is achieved by using engineered viruses, which are transferred into a specific part of the brain. Through this, almost every human memory can be read and saved. Or erased. Simply put, we locate your child's specific traumatic memory and remove it. And the whole process is swift and painless.'

The parents frown thoughtfully. The mother then glances sadly at the door her daughter slammed. She looks at her husband and nods. He takes her hand in his.

'Optogenetics is a cutting-edge neuro modulation that has been approved for its first clinical trials. Here at TEAR Solutions, we offer that trial to you.'

The woman in the cardigan hands the parents a pen and a slip of paper.

They sign it, smiling.

'Once the trauma has been removed, then comes the "replacement" period. This is done using therapy, which our skilled psychotherapists, Dr Melinda Parry and Dr Konstantinos Athanasiou...'

Melinda's face appears on the screen. I squeeze Nisha's hand, hard.

Oh my God. Melinda.

'That's my therapist...' I whisper.

'What?'

'That's Melinda, my fucking therapist. From floor four. I told you there are no coincidences.'

She's standing next to Dr A, her arms folded, wearing her expensive-looking blazer, the one she wears when she means business. They're both looking directly to camera: stern, professional, trustworthy.

'...will undertake an intensive form of "replacement therapy" that will lead the patient to believe that something less traumatic – typically a car accident or a blow to the head – is the reason for the memory gap. In order to maintain this new narrative, they will work closely with the family and any others that are aware of the initial trauma to make sure the patient remains ignorant. Discretion is vital. As your child's parent, only you can understand the importance of this.'

The parents look up, nodding like they understand the importance of this.

'Typically, traumatic events happen in very brief moments – sometimes a matter of minutes. Some, sadly, are more ongoing. But here, we can find the specific time periods and remove *them. The prognosis suggests fantastic outcomes for patients. They will move forwards freed from their trauma and into a healthy and happy future in the absence of the memories that are causing deep, emotional pain.'*

The well-spoken man stops speaking.

The teenager reappears on screen, hugging her parents, smiling. Everyone begins to laugh.

The woman in the cardigan is gone like she was never there.

The screen goes white. Words appear.

TEAR SOLUTIONS
Trauma Extraction and Replacement

A quick, effective and innovatory new therapy, set to revolutionise mental healthcare.

No trauma, no pain.
Only a bright future.

Cost of the treatment is dependent upon the length of the trauma and the amount of therapy the patient requires moving forwards.
Terms and conditions apply.

The video ends. I stare at the blank screen. My brain crackles like static.

'Shit,' Nisha whispers. I can't look at her. I can't move. 'Holy shit. You've had your memory *wiped*?'

'I don't…'

'This is so messed up, Eli…'

'I don't understand…'

'And then that woman, Melinda, your *therapist* made you think you were in a car crash? A whole lie to cover for it? How is this *legal*?'

'I don't know...'

She starts to root through the box, but I can't compute what she's doing.

How could my parents do this?

When was BUCKET – Jack's story from TraumaLand? When were we in the hut in the forest behind the house in Lewes? After the psychiatric hospital? In those missing four days?

'Look,' Nisha says, holding something up in front of me.

'What is it?'

'Some kind of invoice, I think...'

I look down at the piece of paper.

MR G. AND MRS H. PEW
INVOICE

Transactions:
PAYMENT 1:
PEW, ELIAS GORDON
Time period of trauma removed: Feb 8th– March 4th:
£26,000
Ongoing trauma replacement with Melinda Parry: £15,000

PAYMENT 2:
JQ – MARKED *ANONYMOUS* ON ALL
DOCUMENTATION
Time period of trauma removed: Feb 8th– March 4th:

£26,000

Plus one historical episode (1 day) a further £10,000

Ongoing trauma replacement with Melinda Parry: £15,000

Special requirements: EP and JQ to have nil contact under any circumstances.
Monitored by Melinda Parry.
Additional £5,000

Total: £92,000

'*Oh my God...*' I breathe. 'They did it to him too. Look.'

'Fuck...' Nisha says in a low voice. 'That's a lot of money.'

Yeah. It is.

'It's the exact same dates for both of us.' I look up at her.

'It's like they've literally had you removed from each other's brains and called it trauma.' I remember what he said had happened to him. That he'd had a blow to the head. That he'd jumped off a bridge. Is that what Melinda's been feeding him? That lie? This is sick. 'But *why*? Why would your parents do this?'

'I have no idea...'

'I don't remember him being like this, but do you think Jack did something to you? That this was their way of protecting you from him?' I remember the way I felt when I was in his story, in Jack's mind, in the hut in the woods. As he cradled my smashed-open head.

'No.' I shake my head firmly. 'It's not that.' It can't be. My eyes return to the invoice. 'They made an extra payment for Jack.'

'Huh?'

'They made an extra payment for him.' I point to it. 'It says *plus one historical episode – one day*. Why?'

Suddenly, a noise from below. My parents. I grab Nisha's arm.

She goes deadly still.

Footsteps, then a door opening. More footsteps along the hallway. The click of the bathroom light.

My chest might spill out of my throat. *Move*, I mouth.

We silently place the papers back in the box, then gently close the lid. We pad across the carpet, holding our breaths, until we're under the window. I can hear whoever it is, Mum or Dad, just a few metres below, running the tap.

I point up.

Nisha nods. She looks petrified. *Go. Now.*

We clamber through the skylight and steady ourselves on the roof. I feel myself sway, the cold air billowing into Nisha's hoodie. Together we begin to edge back down the tiles.

I stop halfway down. 'The skylight. Shit.' I try to pull myself back up again.

'It's fine, Eli. Let's just go.'

'It's not fine. It needs to be shut.'

'You can come back later and shut it.'

'You don't know my parents.'

'Yeah, well, neither do you.'

She's right. I have no idea who they are.

'Eli, we need to get off this roof.'

I follow as she half steps, half skids down the slates until she reaches the gutter. I watch her cling to the drainpipe and clamber down it, fast and agile as a cat.

I slowly turn, copying her. I feel strange. Thin. Barely here. I hardly notice my hands as I descend, my fingers automatically searching for the grooves in the pipe as I scramble down it. All I can think of is Jack—

My dad was there. That night. In the hut. He must've known Karl nearly drowned him.

And Melinda. Melinda knew all along too.

I hear Nisha's feet hit the gravel beneath me, jolting me back into the moment.

I join her, collapsing into a heap on the ground. I pull myself to my feet and look up at my parents' bathroom window. The light is still on behind the blinds. Nisha pulls my arm and we crouch, making our way towards the rhododendron bushes where we stashed our bags. She takes hers and turns towards the path. I stay where I am.

'What are you doing, Eli? Let's *go*.'

'Where?'

'Anywhere but here.'

I want to. I want to run. But…

'No.' I glance back at the bathroom window. I can see steam against the glass, hear the faint grumble of the shower cistern. It must be Dad. Sometimes he showers early when he can't sleep. 'I'm not leaving. They can't know anything's wrong.'

'So, what? You're just going to pretend everything's fine?'

'Yes.' That's exactly what I'm going to do.

'Don't you want to tell…' She trails off.

'Who?'

'I dunno… Maybe someone who will help?'

'You mean the police? And say what?'

'Um … maybe that you got your mind messed with – *against your will*?' She stresses that last bit like I'm not aware. Like I'm unclear what has happened to me.

But I'm not. I'm very clear.

'I was sectioned, Nisha. They're not going to believe a word I say. I wasn't in my right mind. I was unwell. It was treatment.'

She looks back at the house. 'So, what are you going to do?' she whispers. Scared. She's scared of them.

So am I.

'Make a plan.' Because that's what I'm good at. I start to feel oddly calm, because I know what I have to do. 'They think I'm working today. I'll say I'm going in like normal. I'll make them think everything is normal. And then I'll go and find Jack.'

'Eli, are you serious?' She shakes her head.

'Yes.'

'But … what if he chose this? You can't—'

'It doesn't seem like he *chose this*, does it? According to the invoice—'

'OK, well, what if he's turned into a complete nutter? Maybe that's why your parents did this. To keep you safe from him?' She steps towards me, but I've made up my mind. 'When bad things happen to people, it can change them. Maybe it's good you don't remember—'

'What bad things happened to him, Nisha?'

'I don't know. But I remember he was very angry.'

'Angry?'

'Yes.'

I pause. 'How well did you know him? He's had months of his life erased by my parents. I feel responsible for that. Even if he is a *complete nutter*, he deserves to know.'

'Just listen, Eli—'

'*No, Nisha.*' I cut her off, my voice louder than I intended. We wait for a moment, watching the bathroom window. 'I'd think he'd want to know the truth.' I can hear the certainty in my voice. 'Do you have any idea where he lives now?'

She shrugs. 'Haven't a clue.'

'I'll find him.' I will. 'And then I need to go back to TraumaLand. Tonight.' *Tonight*. 'I need to watch the rest of BUCKET to see what my dad was doing. And so does Jack. He needs to see the truth.' My breath mists in front of us. 'I can't trust anyone else.' My parents did this. Melinda helped them. Lucas has their card in his wallet. There is no one else. 'I need *your* help.'

She nods slowly. 'OK.'

'OK?'

'Yeah.'

Good. *Good*. 'Are you working tonight?'

'Yeah.'

'Can you make sure I get back in?'

'The bouncers already think you're mental—'

'Everyone in that place is mental.'

'That's true.' She pauses. 'If I make sure you get in, Casimir can't know anything.' Casimir. I think of the chip and headset in my bag. '*Eli?* Do you hear me? *He can't know*, or we – both of us – are screwed. I told you what happened to the last guy.'

Disappeared. Gone.

'Of course. Will you come with me? To find Jack?'

'I can't...'

'Why not?'

'I live with…'

Hold on. 'You live with Casimir?'

'Not like *that*,' she says, but a darkness descends. 'He's been helping me.'

'Helping you?'

'It's complicated. After the foster placement in Brighton, where I met Jack,' she says, her voice flat. 'I came up to London. I wanted to get out. Fell into some bad habits… I was just trying to get what I needed. Survive, I guess. It was all … chaos. I don't really remember much of it.'

'Drugs?' I need to work on my delivery.

She ignores me. Fair enough.

'But then I met Casimir,' she continues. 'He was friendly. He took pity on me. Said he'd help me. He gave me a job. Had a spare room. Took me in. Said he'd help me get my A levels done, apply to uni. Get back on my feet. In return, I'd work for him at the club. Then eventually he asked me to do the pick-ups, the drops.'

'Keep his secrets.'

She turns to me. 'I swear I didn't know about any of this, Eli.'

'Is he blackmailing you?' Her eyes move to the ground. I place my hand on her sleeve. 'Well, it seems to me you've got it figured out. You're doing good, aren't you? Life is better than it was before?'

'I guess so, yeah.' Her eyes narrow.

She's tough. I can see that. This world has toughened her.

I feel weak, incapable, in comparison. Look, if you find out anything … text me, OK?'

She hesitates, then takes her phone out and unlocks it, hands it to me. I punch in my digits and add my name.

TRAUMA BOY

I hand it back. 'So you don't forget.'

'I don't think I'll be forgetting you any time soon, Eli,' she says. Her eyes land on the bird tattoo on my wrist. 'Did you do that?'

'Yeah. I mean … I think I did.'

She half smiles. 'I like it.'

I can still hear the water of the shower running in the bathroom. 'You want one?' I grab my bag, rooting through it – careful that she doesn't see the headset – until I find my marker pen. The one I used to draw my eyeliner with. 'Lift up your sleeve.'

'Um…'

'Go on. Kindred spirits now.'

She doesn't laugh.

As she slowly rolls up the sleeve of her checked shirt, I see a scar.

'What's that?' I ask before I can stop myself.

'Cigarette burn,' she says. 'From the … before.'

'Before you met Casimir?'

'No. *Before* before.'

Oh, I see. 'I'm sorry.'

'It's OK.'

She exhales. 'Go on, then. Hurry up.' I start to scribble away. 'Jesus, what are you doing? I didn't ask for your whole life story.'

'Well, lucky for you I couldn't give it, even if I wanted to. Done.'

I look at my handiwork.

The truth is out there
And it's not what you think.
Signed,
Elias Pew
Property of TEAR Solutions, Floor 1, Harper House

'Funny.'

'Isn't it?' Then I remember. 'Oh, wait.' I draw the bird, like the one on my wrist, in the exact same place on hers.

She pulls her sleeve back down. 'Will that ever come off?'

'Probably not. We are now bonded for life.'

I hear the low grumble of water pipes suddenly stop. My dad has finished his shower. I look up and see the bathroom light is now off.

'OK, I'm out of here—'

I take her arm. 'Listen, thank you, Nisha. I like you. You're very kind.'

She frowns at me and I think she's about to tell me I'm the weirdest person she's ever met – again. Instead, she says, 'I like you too.'

I suddenly panic. 'I'm gay, by the way.'

She laughs. 'I wasn't going to suggest we start shagging in the bushes.'

'Oh.'

She shrugs. 'And your mind seems elsewhere.'

She gives me a knowing look, then turns and heads down the path and out of sight.

My stomach twinges. *Jack*.

I grab my bag, the headset and chip inside it. Shit. I feel bad now – guilty that I haven't told Nisha. Guilt, *there you are* and you are not fun *at all*.

Then I creep towards my cellar window. I pull it open, duck down, shove my bag through and climb into my bedroom.

The room feels so still.

It's like it's been years since I was last here. My face-paint sponges still sitting on the dressing table. The pile of clothes, the scissors, the paints. All exactly where I left them. Nothing's changed.

Except everything.

I get my washbag and take out a handful of face wipes, then stand in front of the dressing table and stare at myself in the small, oval mirror. I begin to scrub my face, harder and harder, until all the paint, the grime, the eyeliner, every trace of the night, is gone. Erased.

But I can still see the scar on my forehead, clear as day. A shiny streak. A reminder that will never go.

I feel a well open up inside me, and with it, an emotion runs deep into the core of me. I know this one immediately. *Anger*. My hands begin to shake as it seeps into my blood, as it poisons me with its bitterness. I can taste it at the back of my throat.

How could he do this? What is he trying to hide?

I turn to my bed, sit on it and pull out my phone. Three per cent battery. I fumble for the charger, shove it in and open Google.

I think back to the Zoom call. His beanie, his broad shoulders. What did he say? *Think*.

Nothing. Blank.

Wait. Hold on. There was something in his room. Something behind him, on the wall. A poster.

What did it say? There was a symbol of a wave. Something about water…

And then I remember. I type in the words TURNING TIDES TOGETHER. And hit enter.

The top search result shows a link.

COUNCIL SUPPORT – ADOLESCENTS IN NEED

He's definitely an adolescent in need. I click on it.

It takes me to a page with a photograph of a rundown house, with peeling paint and dirty walls, on some kind of back street. There's a broken sign above the door, with the wave painted on it and the words:

TURNING TIDES TOGETHER
SUPPORTED HOUSING
BRIXTON

Supported Housing? Brixton? I've never been to Brixton, south of the river. That I know of.

I scroll down to see a series of pictures. Adolescents eating cereal together in a little kitchen, standing around bunk beds, smiling. *Wait*. Bunk beds. Just like the one behind Jack in his square. And the poster.

It's right there. Pinned to the wall behind the teenagers.

This is where he was…

There's a knock at my door. I spin round.

'Eli?' Dad's voice echoes down the concrete steps. 'Can I have a word?'

24

IN CASE OF EMERGENCY

I pull my cellar door open.

Dad stands outside in his dressing gown and slippers, squinting at me without his glasses.

The anger and fear merge together, bubbling inside me. Confusion too. And pain. *Hide it.*

'Morning, Father of mine,' I say as brightly as I can. But it's not the same. *Don't let him see.* ''Tis early, even for you.'

'I...' His eyes search my face. I try to make it appear relaxed. He frowns. 'Hold on, something's different.' Panic now. *Shit*. 'Eli, did you shave your head?'

Oh... 'Yep.' I smile. Big grin. 'New me, new hair!'

'I see...'

'Since yesterday I am a changed man.'

At least that's true. I am. Just not in the way he thinks.

I can hear my heart in my ears as he looks me up and down, taking me in. I know this look. This look of uncertainty. Of suspicion. 'How are you feeling this morning?' he says.

I suddenly see an image of him wearing the balaclava, standing over Jack in the hut. *What have you done?*

I bite my lip to stop the question spilling out. 'Great,' I say. 'Never better.'

'I thought I heard you knocking about down here.'

'Nope. I was sleeping soundly.' My legs are shaking.

'Good. Well, sorry if I woke you.' His eyes are still clouded with doubt. They lock on to my ear. The left one. The one with the tattoo behind it.

Remember Jack.

He begins to lift his hand.

No. I instinctively grab his wrist.

Oops. Fuck.

He frowns, surprised.

Calm down, Eli. Be cool. Think like a psychopath. I let go.

'Face paint,' he says and laughs.

'Oh!' I blurt out. 'The residue of a remarkable day.'

He reaches into his pocket and takes out a tissue. 'Here.' He rubs my earlobe with it roughly. As he does, I fight against the shiver that runs through my body.

'There we are. Gone.'

'Why, thank you, Father.'

But I can see he knows something is different. That something's wrong. 'Is everything OK, son?'

'Of course.'

'You seem a bit fidgety. More so than usual.' He pauses. 'Since Thursday.'

'Honestly, Dad. Nothing's—'

'Since after that girl came round.'

Shit, *shit*. 'What girl?'

He pushes his hands into his dressing-gown pockets, tilting his head. 'The girl whose phone you found on the bus?'

'Oh, yeah!' I say. '*Her*. I forgot about her.'

'Right,' he says. He's not convinced.

I can no longer convince him.

Convince him. 'I've been too focused on the group therapy.' I lean back against the door. Casual. 'She didn't seem that important.'

He might like that. He does think some people are less important.

'Hmm.' He pauses. 'Don't take this the wrong way, Eli, but something tells me that you're not being honest with me.'

'I am.'

'Have you been having more headaches? More dreams? It's OK – you can tell me.'

'No.'

'Any … flashbacks?'

I pause before answering. There's a slight edge of trepidation in his voice. He's worried – maybe not worried because he seems far too calm – *concerned*. That I might be able to remember. Remember the truth.

'Nope. None.'

'Something's changed.'

Yes. I'm now scared of you. I am terrified of you. I have no idea what you're capable of. 'Well, it must just be because I feel a lot better.'

'So, yesterday, with Melinda, it helped? It … worked?'

'Definitely. I've processed the trauma and I'm now moving on, fully equipped with knowledge of the truth.'

Careful.

He frowns. 'You're not feeling manic again, are you?'

'No, Dad.'

'You'd tell me, wouldn't you? I have a really busy day with work and I don't want to worry.'

'Of course.'

'I do worry about you sometimes.'

'Well, you don't need to. Really. You don't.' My voice is firm. A little too firm.

Dad nods. 'OK, Eli.' He sighs. Rubs his tired eyes. 'Work today. For both of us.'

Deflect. Move it on. 'What's on the agenda in the world of government?' I make myself sound proud.

He laughs modestly, like he always does when someone mentions his work. 'Oh, you know.' No, I don't actually, because I don't know you at all. 'Helping people.'

Something about the way he says it makes my skin prickle. 'Like always.'

'Oh, I don't know. We do the best we can.'

'Of course you do.'

'A lot of people need help, Eli.' He sounds the faintest bit annoyed that he has to do that. Help people. 'That's why people voted for us. And why the party received so much investment. Because we deliver it. Radical change.'

'That's good.' *Don't. Don't say it.* 'I suppose having money helps with clearing stuff up.' *Stop, Eli.*

'Not always.'

'But if you've got it, why not snap your fingers and make the problems go away?'

I'm angry. I'm so angry. It's fuelling me.

'If only it were that simple,' he says.

'If only.'

'How's Karl getting on?' I blurt.

'Karl?' His face doesn't change. His eyes don't so much as flicker.

'I always liked Karl.'

'I don't need a driver any more. The commute to work is much shorter now.'

'How is he?'

'Karl?'

'Yes.'

'I should really text him. See how he's doing.'

'Say hello from me.'

'I will.'

Careful. *Careful*.

We stare at each other for a moment.

'What about you?' he says. 'What time does your shift start?'

'At eight.'

'Well, let's both have a good day today. Try and get everything back to the way it should be.'

'I'd like that,' I say.

'We all would.' He tilts his head sympathetically. 'It's been really hard for you, hasn't it?' He turns into the hallway and is about to go up the stairs when he stops. 'We love you, son. You know that, don't you? We're so proud of the man you're becoming.' He winks. 'Who knows, maybe one day you'll end up like me.'

I swallow hard. 'Yeah. Maybe.'

'Just remember, when it comes down to it, we only get one chance to be who we want and we mustn't let anything get in our way. You're doing great.'

And then he leaves, trudging back up the stairs.

I open my cellar door, wait for a moment, then slam it closed again, loud enough for him to hear. When I hear his bedroom door shut, I exhale. *Holy shit.*

Then, I move. *Quick.* Time is of the essence.

First things first, I have no money. I'll need some to find Jack and then to watch the rest of his story. I tiptoe into the kitchen and start opening the drawers under the kitchen island, searching through them. Nothing.

Wait. *I know.*

I head back into the hallway to the downstairs bathroom. I pull open the door and kneel in front of the cupboard under the sink. Where are you? Then I see it. The little box right at the back *for emergencies*. I pull it out and root through the items.

Bingo. A small leather wallet.

Inside are five bank cards. Little labels on each of them:

IN CASE OF EMERGENCY
IN CASE OF EMERGENCY
IN CASE OF EMERGENCY
IN CASE OF EMERGENCY
IN CASE OF EMERGENCY

Who *labels* bank cards? And who has *five*?

My parents, that's wh—

'You OK, bro?'

I smack my head on the top of the cupboard. Damn it. I turn. 'Jesus, Lucas.'

'What are you doing?' He looks at me, all stuck-up hair and crumpled pyjamas.

'Just… Um… Looking for some soap.'

'Soap? Why?'

'Because I like to be clean, Lucas.'

He pulls a face. *No, you don't.* 'You shaved your head.'

'I did.' I put my head back into the cupboard, quickly clench my hand around one of the cards, grab a bar of soap in the other and stand. I close the cupboard door with my knee and turn to face him. 'Found it.' *Be collected.* I lift up the soap, holding my other hand behind my back.

'Why's everyone awake so early?' he groans.

'Because, Lucas, the Pews are *go-getters*,' I say. I sound a bit like my dad.

Which is… Actually, let's not.

'Right…' he says. 'You're being weird.' He pauses. 'Well, you know. Weird for *you*.'

'Talking of weird,' I say, then lower my voice. 'Can I ask you a question, bro?'

'Of course, Elven One.'

That's his nickname for me, since I used to like elves as a kid. It means he's being nice. 'Right, well, you know Mum and Dad…'

'A little, yeah.'

'Well, this is going to sound strange but…' I pause. This is important. I do need to know.

'What is it?'

I lower my voice. 'You don't think they've ever had a problem with me being gay, do you?'

His eyes widen. 'What?' He laughs like it's a stupid thing for me to say. But is it? 'Bro, what? *No.* Where did *that* come from?'

'I don't know...'

I do know.

He looks at me sympathetically. 'God, Eli. Listen, sure they can be a bit ... *traditional* at times. But no. No *way*. They would *never* have a problem with that.' He puts his hand on my arm. 'You heard them the other night. They can't wait for you to get a boyfriend.' He smiles. 'They want you to find someone who makes you happy. They don't care who it is. You know that's true, right?'

'Yeah. Yeah, I do.'

I do. They can't have done it because of that. What, then? Does Lucas know?

He nudges my arm playfully. 'So, what about Peter?'

'No. Not Peter.'

'Poor Peter.' He smiles sadly.

'He's just so ... nice.'

'He's not weird enough for you.'

'No,' I say. 'I like a bit of ... weird.'

'I know you do, Eli.' Lucas smiles.

'Right, well. Better get ready for work.'

'All right, little brother. Have a good shift today.'

'Thanks.'

I push past him, into the hall, folding my arms so that the bank card remains hidden. I start to walk towards my cellar door, when—

'Eli?'

I turn back. 'Yeah?'

'Who's Jack?'

My body feels like it's alight. My cheeks flush with panic.

Don't show it. Don't show anything.

I cock my head. 'Hmm?'

'Who's Jack?' He stays in the bathroom doorway. 'Behind your ear, bro. It says *Remember Jack*.'

I see a flash of something behind his eyes. Concern. Worry. Fear? Before I can decipher it, he blinks it away.

'Does it?' Think fast.

'Yes, the tattoo.'

'Oh, *that*.' I smile. Big grin. Why didn't I cover it up with face paint, damn it?

'It's...' I clock the pile of books behind him, by the toilet. Mum's quote book. 'The only people for me are the mad ones: the ones who are mad to live, mad to talk, mad to be saved, desirous of everything at the same time, the ones who burn, burn, burn like fabulous yellow Roman candles.'

He stares at me. 'Huh?'

'Jack Kerouac,' I say. 'Founding member of the beat generation, with William S. Burroughs. I love that quote. It's in Mum's book. The one you gave her.' I point to it. 'Read that thing a million times during the madness and I wanted to remember it.' The madness. 'And he was very handsome and cool and *weird*. So, yeah.'

He shakes his head, but then I see he's smiling. 'I guess that makes sense.' Silly old Eli. 'Is it permanent?'

'Umm...'

'Actually, you know what.' He holds his hands up. 'Don't tell me. I know nothing.'

'Yeah, I was gonna say.' I lower my voice to a whisper. 'Probably best not to mention it to them.' I point up to the ceiling. 'Can't be arsed with the aggro, you know what I mean? They think I'm doing really well.'

He narrows his eyes. 'Are you?'

'Yeah. I am.'

'Good. I'm glad. All you need to do now is find yourself a Jack.'

'Huh?'

'Kerouac.'

'Oh, right.' Jesus Christ. 'Yeah. Yes. I do. I need to find myself a Jack.'

Lucas smiles. As he heads to the kitchen, I go into my cellar and bolt the door behind me.

Does he know?

I don't have time to worry. I don't have time because he's right. I need to find Jack.

Brixton. Not far. Just south of the river. An hour on the tube, max.

But before that, I need to know. To know who he is. A threat? A danger, like Nisha suggested? And if so, I need to be prepared.

I take out the headset, along with the single chip from the box marked NEW PROJECT.

ELIAS AND JACK

I flip it over. More of Casimir's handwriting. Tiny, hardly legible.

IN DEVELOPMENT:
JACK AND ELI'S STORY

Fingers trembling, I slot it into the headset, place the pads in position and pull the goggles over my eyes. I then rest my head back on the pillow and am taken away.

As I enter this unknown world of my own past, I weep behind the goggles. My tears flood them.

But I don't stop watching. I can't.

25

A STORY

DATE: JAN 12TH
TIME: 16:00
LOCATION: SYCAMORE WARD

I watch him lean back against the wall, his face in the only patch of sun in the garden. It's not really a garden, even though they call it one. Just a small concrete yard in the centre of the building with a few pot plants and benches, which is shaped like a polo mint. I saw a poster on the wall that said the circle shape of Sycamore Ward symbolises the 'continuity of life'. But really it's shaped like this so none of us can escape. Unless, of course, they climb on to the roof. Someone recently attempted it and failed. Wire mesh was put around the rim to stop it happening again, so now there's no chance.

The person who attempted it was me. That was last week. It's pushed things back a bit in terms of my discharge planning. Oh, well.

'Hi,' I say.

He doesn't reply. Doesn't even open his eyes. He's holding a polystyrene cup of the instant coffee they give us. It tastes a bit like the floor, but I'm getting used to it.

I hardly see him around the ward. He seems to stay in his bedroom most of the time. But I have noticed a few things about him. I've noticed that he comes into the dining room once everyone has eaten to pick up a banana and a packet of crisps. I've noticed that he'll then quietly ask the kitchen staff for two slices of bread, like he's almost embarrassed, before taking everything back into his bedroom.

I've noticed that he only wears one outfit – a baggy grey jumper, a pair of light brown cords and some scuffed New Balance trainers. He always wears his sleeves pulled down over his hands. But sometimes when he reaches for something, like the bananas or the bread, I can see bandages poking out of the bottom of them, wrapped around his forearms near his wrists. Sometimes when the alarm goes off, particularly at night, the nurses rush into his room with various implements that I don't know the name of, but can only guess what they're used for, like the hooked scissors.

I noticed that once, when one of the patients was screaming so much that the nurses piled on her and injected her, he took her a glass of water as she sat huddled in the corner afterwards and spoke to her until she smiled. I've noticed that he rarely smiles himself. In fact, never. He has shoulder-length hair that hangs over his face, mousey brown, hiding his soft features like a form of protection. A shield from the world.

I've also noticed that when he goes into the clinical team room on a Wednesday, which is when we all do – Wednesday is the only part of the week that seems to matter to the staff, Ward Round Day – he doesn't have any friends or family to join him, like the rest of us. He goes in quietly, comes out quietly, then goes straight to his room. He could easily be missed. I think some of the patients haven't even noticed that he's here.

But I've noticed.

There's something about him I can't help but feel drawn to, my eyes constantly looking for him. He's the opposite of me, which I find interesting.

Quiet. Private. Gentle.

'Can I ask you a question?' I say. He doesn't answer, but I decide to ask it anyway. 'Do you make crisp and banana sandwiches?'

He reclines his head slightly so the sun hits his forehead, his eyes still shut. 'Sorry?'

'I just wanted to know if you make banana and crisp sandwiches. I've seen you take the ingredients into your room and I'm intrigued. I can't figure out if it'd be good because of the mix of textures, or if it all just turns into mush in your mouth. I'd imagine the crisps act as a sort of mush barrier, but I guess it depends on which crisp. If you go for Wotsits or Skips, you'd struggle – they'd just disintegrate. But if you go for something more sturdy like a bog-standard Walkers, or even a Pringle, then maybe you're getting somewhere.'

He blinks his eyes open. I half expect him to tell me to back off, that I'm talking too much, like the rest of the patients tell me. But he doesn't. He narrows his eyes in the sun. 'Doritos,' he says. His voice is barely audible. Soft.

I like the word soft. People think it's a bad word, but I don't.

'Yeah. See, I get that,' I say. 'I fully get that. For the necessary crunch.'

'For the necessary crunch,' he repeats. He leans forwards so the backs of his shoulders leave the wall, then takes a small step

to the side, making space next to him in the light. 'You want some sun before it goes?'

'Yeah, go on, then.' I stand next to him and turn so my back is against the brick, just like his. I feel the small rectangle of warmth on my face. It calms me. Makes the buzzing in my brain subside a little. 'It's nice,' I say.

'Uh-huh.'

'Do you like that coffee?'

I see him smile. 'I fucking love coffee,' he says gently.

'That stuff tastes a bit like the floor.'

He smiles again. 'I'll take what I can get.'

Neither of us says anything for a while, leaning back in silence. All I can hear is his breath next to me and the occasional shuffling of the support worker sitting on one of the benches in the shadows. He has someone assigned to him at all times. They call it 'one-to-one support', but it really means they're there to stop him from doing something dangerous. He really doesn't seem to be the dangerous type, but then I don't know him very well.

I look at her, sitting on her phone, not watching him. Most of the support staff help him by sitting on their phones. Sometimes they have their earbuds in and when I walk past I can see they're watching a film, scrolling, even FaceTiming a friend.

I like standing next to him. His energy. It feels... I don't know. Non-intrusive somehow. And in this place, that feels kind.

He seems kind. But maybe not to himself.

I feel the sun going down behind the top of the building and don't want it to.

'So,' he then says in that quiet way, barely moving his lips. 'Since we've got the important question out of the way, can I ask a boring one?'

'Sure.'

'Why are you here?' He says this without hesitation. It surprises me a little. It's an unwritten rule on the ward that you don't ask that question and people spend most of their time trying to figure out why the other patients have been admitted. But I'm more surprised by his bluntness. It makes me feel safe somehow. No pretence. No ulterior motives.

'Oh, I...' How do I do the short version of this? 'I had a bit of a giddy spell.' I heard one of the nurses say this once and I've decided to use it myself because it's simpler. 'I think I've been a bit ... chaotic, or whatever – that's what they keep saying – and just needed some support to get back to myself. I don't think I'll be here long, though. Should be out soon. I hope.'

He nods.

'What about you?'

He exhales slowly. 'I've been in and out of these places for a few years now. Since I was about thirteen.'

Oh. 'I'm sorry.'

'Don't be.' He raises his shoulders in a small shrug. 'It's not your fault, is it?'

I wait for a moment. 'Did something happen?' I say and immediately regret it, but he doesn't seem to mind. He keeps his head back, eyes closed.

'Yeah, it did,' he says. 'They then diagnosed me with PTSD, or something. I dunno, it keeps changing.' I can sense the faintest hint of embarrassment in his voice. He turns to me and opens his eyes. They meet mine, and I suddenly feel like

I want to smile. Not because of what he's saying, but because he seems to want to talk to me. To me, not at me, like I do to everyone. I like that. It's different – it's nice – and makes me want to try it.

'They say I need to want to get better,' he says. 'But that I don't seem to want to.'

I look down at my shoes. 'Do you?'

'Yeah,' he says. 'I do. Of course.'

Good, I nearly say. I probably should, but I don't.

'I'm a bit ... stuck,' he says. 'In one place. This place in my head...' He trails off.

I wonder what to say to this. Whether I should say no, you're not stuck, you'll get out of here in no time. Or don't listen to these people, they don't know what they're doing. This place is bullshit. No one really gives a crap...

Instead I just say, 'I'm Eli.'

'Jack,' he says. 'Nice to meet you.'

He holds out his hand. As I take it in mine, I hear a noise from the shadows.

'No touching,' the support worker shouts, glancing up from her phone.

We let go of each other, but our shoulders remain inches apart, still in the last patch of sun. We wait for her to go back to her phone.

'Apparently someone got pregnant in here once,' Jack whispers.

'No way.'

'She clearly doesn't want that to happen again.'

I laugh. 'Yeah, she's just being good at her job.' I watch her tapping away at her screen.

We stand in the light until it disappears, the cold gradually replacing the pool of warmth as the shadows cover us. The support worker tells us to go inside for our evening meds.

'See you around,' Jack says as he turns to head down the corridor towards his bedroom.

'Yeah,' I say. 'I'd like that.'

He shrugs again. 'Who knows? Maybe I'll come to art class.'

Does he know I'm the only one in that class? 'Yeah,' I say. 'I'd like that.' *Oh, wait. That was a bit…* 'Or, not. I don't care. You should – you know – do what's best for you.' *My ears feel hot.*

He continues back to his room, tugging on the sleeves of his jumper, followed by the sighing support worker.

'Jack,' I shout.

He turns. 'Yeah?'

'Would you ever try it with Monster Munch?'

He pauses and I see him considering this. 'Sounds a bit … chaotic. A lot of chaos for one mouthful.'

'True,' I say. 'But maybe sometimes we need a bit of chaos?' I try. 'Just to keep things … alive?'

His mouth turns up in the smallest of smiles. 'Yeah,' he says. 'Maybe you're right.'

⁓

DATE: FEB 9TH
TIME: 14:03
LOCATION: SYCAMORE WARD

'Eli has been working on some woodwork,' Cameron says, rolling up the sleeves of his checked work shirt. Jack nods, *loitering in the doorway. 'Come in, Jack. It's very chill in here.'*

Cameron loves to say the word chill, but he's right. It is chill in the art room and he's probably the most chill staff member. I like Cameron. He doesn't try and make me say things that I have no intention of saying, which is nice. And the art room is quiet. It's hard to find quiet spots here.

Jack tentatively shuffles into the room and perches on one of the little stools around the worktop.

'The brief is to make something meaningful from your past.' Cameron hands him a brown work apron. 'But you don't have to follow it, Jack, if you don't want to. Eli hasn't.'

'No, I have not,' I say proudly.

'Why?' Jack says, tying a brown work apron around his waist. 'What have you been making?'

'I've carved an elf.' I try to mute my excitement, but it just comes out of me. I stand and lift it off the shelf behind me. When I turn to show him, my cheeks are tense with excitement.

'Whoa,' he says quietly, raising his eyebrows. He has one of them pierced, which I really like. A small hoop. 'That's really good.'

I hold it out to him.

He hesitates. 'Are you sure? I don't want to break it,' he says. 'It looks delicate.'

'Course I'm sure. Take it.'

He opens his hands and I place it in them. He holds it like it's made of glass, turning it in his fingers, running them over the grooves of the wood – the leaf headdress, the cape, the pointed ears.

'I like fantasy,' I say.

'Like Lord of the Rings*?'*

'Sure. Me and my parents made this hut out the back of the house in the woods when I was younger. I used to love going there and pretending I was an elf.'

He smiles at this. 'Well, it's brilliant.'

'Thanks.'

He's quite elf-like, actually.

He passes it back to me. 'Well, that seems meaningful enough.'

'I said that,' Cameron said.

'It's not that important,' I say. 'It just reminds me of...' I look at Cameron and smile. 'Simpler times.'

Cameron winks. 'Ah, simpler times.'

I laugh.

'Can you think of something meaningful, Jack?' Cameron says.

'Um...' A flash of anxiety crosses his features. 'Maybe I'll just watch for this session, if that's OK? Join in next time.'

'Sure,' Cameron says.

'No music today?' I ask Cameron.

'Shall we let Jack choose?'

'Yeah, course.' I place the elf on the table and pick up my carving tool. I then pull out the little box of wood from under the work station that I've saved to make his bow and arrow. As I rummage through it, I hear Jack scrolling through Cameron's Spotify (Cameron is a bit of a maverick – he lets us hold his actual phone and pick actual songs, even ones with swearing in them, God forbid) until classical music starts to play out of his little Bluetooth speaker.

'Good choice.' I look up to see Cameron nodding his head.

I don't know it, but I pretend I do. Slow synths, more like a soundscape. It's almost hypnotic.

I work along to the music as Cameron carries on carving his own bowl that he said he's been working on for months.

'There is something that reminds me of simpler times,' Jack says.

'Oh, yeah?' Cameron remains nonchalant, not looking up. 'Go on.' I know what he's doing when he does this. He's done it with me. He's trying to encourage him to open up.

But Jack doesn't resist like I do. He rolls up his sleeves and I see the bandages around his arms – a few places where small splotches of red have seeped through.

'A rose.'

'A rose?' Cameron says.

'Yeah.'

'Why?'

'It was my sister's name,' Jack says quietly.

Was.

'That's lovely, Jack,' Cameron says.

'Jack and Rose,' I say. 'Like in Titanic.'

Jack smiles. 'Yeah, it was my mum's favourite film.'

Was.

'You have good memories of being with your sister?' Cameron says.

'Some,' he says. I take a small piece of wood and my carving tool and begin to shave around the edges. 'We grew up round here. Not the posh part, though. On one of the estates.' He sounds a bit embarrassed.

'Nothing wrong with that,' Cameron says.

'Before my sister died,' he says slowly, 'I'd take her to the beach sometimes. But I find the sea quite scary. Something about it… I'd never swim in it, no chance. There's something about

how endless it seems that terrifies me.' He pauses. *'So, instead, we used to jump on the train or a bus and go to all these places to get away from the foster placement we were in. We'd hide in the toilet so we didn't have to pay the fare, then just spend the day together, dossing about. Me and Rose. We'd go and stare at all the massive houses in these country villages and pretend they were ours. See all their nice things on their nice lawns. All their cars, swing sets, those huge, outdoor seats with fireplaces. They all had these mad names. Hassocks. Ditchling. Lewes.'*

'I'm from Lewes,' I say, then feel a bit stupid. I go back to focusing on the wood in my hand.

'It's bloody nice round there,' he says. 'There was this one time –' he makes a small laugh, remembering – *'Rose was literally playing on someone's front lawn with their hula hoop. This woman came out and yelled at her. Her kids were all stood in the doorway in their little jumpers, looking like they were watching a crime scene. The mum saw me and said I should be ashamed for letting my sister break the law. Trespassing. She just kept saying the word "trespassing" – and it was making me and Rose laugh. I was about to apologise, but Rose gave her the middle finger and called her a stuck-up cow. Her kids looked like they were gonna shit themselves.'*

Cameron laughs. 'Wow. Ballsy.'

'Yeah.' Jack smiles, his eyes a little glazed. 'I was scared we'd get in trouble with the police, so we got back on the train and laughed the whole way to Brighton, crammed in the toilet. Felt like such rebels.'

'She sounds great,' Cameron says.

'Yeah.' The music keeps playing as Jack speaks and I keep carving, shaving, twisting the wood around in my hands. 'She

was funny. Really naughty, though. Jesus. Got herself in lots of trouble. At the placement. At school too. I'd have to intercept all the letters they'd send. Some of them were hilarious. She'd get called into the head teacher's office for causing trouble, nothing awful, just for being loud and talkative, and she didn't respond well to authority.' I already like the sound of her. I look up at Jack, his eyes glistening. He shakes his head and pulls his beanie down over his forehead, shifting his fringe to cover his eyes. 'Sorry,' he says.

'Don't apologise, Jack,' Cameron says. 'Memories are important. They shape us. Make us who we are. We need them.'

Jack wipes the back of his sleeve on his nose. 'Yeah.' He keeps his head down.

'Here.' I hold out the piece of wood I've been shaving in the palm of my hand.

He moves his eyes down to it. 'No way.' He looks up at me. 'Have you just done that?'

'Yeah,' I say. 'Sorry, it's a bit rushed.'

He takes it in his hands. 'It's perfect,' he says, looking at the little rose I've carved. 'Sort of scrappy, just like her.'

I nod. 'You can keep it. I made it for you. I put your name on it.'

He looks at the four little carved letters.

'Thanks.' He slides it into his pocket. But there's a look in his eyes that's a little unsure, a little sceptical, uncertain. Like there might be some sort of catch. Like he isn't used to being given something without needing to give something in return.

'I don't want anything back,' I say. When I hear it, it sounds a bit strange, but it seems to make him relax.

I can feel Cameron looking at me. 'That's a lovely thing to do, Eli.'

'Yeah,' Jack says. 'Really. Thank you.'

DATE: FEB 22ND
TIME: 22:42
LOCATION: SYCAMORE WARD

'*I like the nights more,*' Jack says. '*It feels more relaxed than the day. Less management around. The staff are nicer.*'

'*I like them too,*' I say.

We're sitting on the blue beanbags in the room where everything is blue and soft because blue is, apparently, the most calming colour.

I look at the sign on the wall.

DE-ESCALATION ROOM

'*I'm glad they let us sit in here now,*' I say. '*It's been fun to de-escalate with you every night for the past two weeks pretending to play cards.*'

He smiles. '*Same to you. And what do you mean, pretend?*' *He puts a seven of hearts down on top of the pile on the floor.* '*Car,*' *he says.*

'*Interesting.*' *I place a queen of spades on top of his seven.* '*Jungle.*'

'*No.*' *He feigns a gasp.* '*Not jungle.*'

'*I'm afraid so,*' I say. '*That means three cards to me.*'

He looks up. 'Three? Why?'

'Um… Lost. You're completely lost.'

He sighs, shaking his head. 'Nice move, Pew.'

'Thanks.'

He hands me three cards, then puts a two of clubs down. 'Uh-oh.'

'What?'

He pulls a face like something disastrous has happened. 'Apocalypse.'

'Shit,' I say. 'Now?'

'Right now,' he says. 'Two of clubs. Means card of death.'

I nod slowly. 'So it does. How many do I need to give you to stay alive?'

'Seven.'

'Seven?' I say. 'That's a bit extreme…'

'Yeah, but…' I watch him trying to think of a reason. 'Because of … all the zombies and stuff.'

'Why do I always forget about the zombies?'

He shakes his head. 'You should never forget about the zombies.'

The door swings open. 'Hey, lads.' It's Fola, one of the night nurses. She smiles kindly at us. 'Just doing checks.'

'No worries,' I say.

She turns to Jack. 'You must be happy to be off one-to-one, Mr Quinn?'

He nods. 'Yeah, I am.'

'You're doing well. Keep it up.'

'Thanks, Fola.'

'So, you're on fifteen-minute intermittent observation now, glad to hear it. All going in the right direction.'

A small smile flickers on his face.

'It's nearly eleven.' Fola ticks off something on her clipboard. 'You know the rules on a week night. You need to get to your rooms.'

'Bit longer?' I ask hopefully.

She sighs, but smiles, pointing her pen at us. 'Ten minutes, but that's it. Jane is working, so best behaviour, please.'

Jane is like an army corporal. She seems to be allergic to teenagers. I have no idea why she works here.

'Thanks, Fola,' Jack says.

She cocks her head. 'It's really nice to see you out of your room more, Jack. And keeping this one –' she points the pen in my direction – 'distracted so he doesn't bother us.' She winks at me. 'Ten minutes. That's it.' Then she leaves.

We sit in silence for a moment. I look at Jack. He has his head down.

'You OK?' I say.

He puts his cards on the floor and starts picking at the grippy bits on the bottom of his blue hospital socks. We all have them. I don't know why they make them grippy – it only helps us run away faster.

'Can I show you something?' he says slowly. 'It might be a bit weird.'

'Yeah. Of course.'

He shuffles his beanbag towards me, then checks behind him, looking for the camera in the corner of the ceiling, shifting his position so he has his back to it.

He slowly lifts his sleeve up. No bandage this time.

Scars. Lots of them. I try not to react, keeping my face still. Some white and shiny – maybe months, years old. Some fresh and pink, but healing.

'No new cuts,' he says quietly.

'How long?' I say.

'Six days.'

I feel a lump rise in my throat. 'Well done, Jack. That's amazing.' I realise that might be why I haven't heard the alarms going off so much at night.

He pulls his sleeve down. 'I really want to get out of here,' he whispers. 'I want to get out of this system. Start my life properly, even if...' He trails off.

I watch him take out the wooden rose I made him from his pocket and turn it between his fingers.

'Jack?'

'Yeah,' he says, a little absently.

'How long ago was it?' I say. 'That she died?'

'Five years.' He looks up at me. 'I know it seems a long time – everyone keeps telling me that. But I can't help but still feel...'

'What?' I say.

'Guilt.' He leans his head forwards and exhales slowly. 'I was there when it happened.'

He's never told me what happened. 'You aren't to blame, Jack. I can tell you really loved her.'

'Maybe.'

'What about your parents?'

Jack shakes his head. 'Foster care.'

'So, where have you been living?'

'I've been in and out of placements for years now. A few wards, like this. But it's my first time here.'

'What are they like? The placements?'

'Some are all right. Others are not. I get moved around all the time. But I'll be eighteen soon and I'll get my own place

if...' He pauses. '*If I show I'm not hurting myself. That's what Dr Dexter said.*' He looks at me hopefully.

'*You're not to blame, Jack.*'

He nods. '*Yeah.*' Then he holds up the rose. '*I love this.*'

'*Good,*' I say.

His fingers brush against mine. '*Thanks, Eli.*'

I link my fingers into his, just for a moment. '*You're welcome.*'

'*And not just for this.*' He bows his head so his hair falls over his face. '*I dunno. Just being with you. Around you. It feels good. I feel... I dunno. Like I'm in the real world.*'

He is looking at the rose, turning it in his hand.

Suddenly, the door slams open. Jack shoves it quickly into his pocket as Jane appears.

'*What are you two doing?*' she says. She looks mad.

'*Playing cards.*'

'*I've been watching you from up there.*' She points to the camera. '*What are you concealing, Jack?*'

His face crumples in panic. '*Nothing. It's not like that—*'

'*Show me your hands,*' she says.

'*Wait,*' I say. '*He wasn't—*'

'*Keep your mouth shut, Elias,*' she barks.

Jack looks terrified. '*I swear. I wasn't—*'

'*I've seen you two.*' Jane steps towards us. '*Getting closer. It's not good. We need to assert boundaries here. We don't want you influencing each other.*' She holds out her hand to Jack. '*Give it to me.*'

'*N-no,*' he stammers. '*I don't have anything.*'

'*Tell me what it is.*' She waits. '*Is it a blade?*'

'*No,*' he repeats.

She shakes her head. 'We're going to need to search you, Jack. You know your safety plan.'

'No,' he says.

'Turn out your pockets.'

'I-I...' he stammers.

Jane sighs. 'Then I'll have to call the team.' She pulls the alarm on her belt. Alarms blare, smashing into my skull.

'No!' Jack cries, scrabbling to his feet and backing into the corner.

People begin to pile into the room. Two, three, four of them.

I try to move, to stand next to him, but feel hands grabbing at my arms.

'Jack!' I yell.

I can see them piling on top of him, pushing him to the ground. One of the men puts his knee in Jack's back. He screams.

'Leave him alone!'

'Get into your room, Elias. This instant.'

'What are you doing to him?'

'He needs help.'

'How is this helping him?'

'It's none of your business, Elias. Now leave.'

'This is a joke!' I shout. 'You're hurting him.'

I feel hands on my arms.

I try to get to him – to help him – and throw a punch. It lands right in the person's face. Shit.

Suddenly I'm being pulled backwards along the corridor, in a blur of shouts and limbs. Pulled in the direction of the room I know I do not want to go into.

'No, please. I'm sorry – please. I didn't mean to – please, not in there! I just wanted to know he's OK.'

– CUT REMAINDER OF SCENE FOR USE AT TRAUMALAND –

DATE: MARCH 1ST
TIME: 14:03
LOCATION: BRIGHTON BEACH

'This is a good spot,' Cameron says, stopping in front of us. He places the box down next to him so it crunches in the pebbles. 'You ready?'

I nod. 'Yep.'

Jack stands still next to me, staring out towards the water. The sun dances across its surface as a gentle breeze moves across the beach.

'Come on, give me a hand.'

I help Cameron unpack the canvases and paints. Jack stays where he is, arms wrapped around him, eyes closed. He doesn't look sad. More, peaceful.

'Here, take these.' Cameron hands me two paintbrushes.

I catch sight of the healthcare assistant sent to watch us standing about ten metres away, texting on her phone.

'Here, Jack.' I hold out a brush.

Jack blinks his eyes open, a little startled, then takes it. 'Cheers.'

'Are you OK?'

'Yeah... I've just ... never loved the sea.'

'Why?'

'I dunno. It's kind of ... deceptive. And unreliable.' He looks at it for a moment, frowning, then turns to me and smiles. 'Ignore me.'

Cameron hands us each a blank canvas. 'Right, sit. Both of you. Face the sea.'

We do. Cross-legged on the pebbles, looking out across the water.

'Welcome to landscape drawing. Since you're the only patients who signed up to it, I thought we could come down to the beach, get some fresh air. All I want you to do is to paint what you see. Whatever it is, the point is to feel something as you do it. Anything. Anger. Happiness. Just focus on that one feeling and try and put it into the picture.'

I look left along the shore and see the long platform held up above the water, the white arcade with a sloped glass roof on top. I turn right. There's a second pier, further down, but this one is different. It's just a shell. A ruin. It looks like it's been burned down and is now just an empty metal structure, speckled with algae and worn away by the waves. It's held up by a precarious criss-cross of rusted rungs, jutting out into the water. The whole thing looks like it might suddenly collapse.

'Do we just ... paint?' I say.

'Yep.' Cameron opens up a purple packet of NHS raisin biscuits. 'Just paint.'

I watch as Jack begins to dip his brush into the paint, moving it across the canvas in long blue streaks.

I look out to the old pier, take the black paint and start to etch its outline. It looks ... nothing like the pier.

'What emotion are you feeling, Eli?' Cameron peers over my shoulder.

'Currently? Embarrassment,' I say.

He laughs. 'It looks like a spider. Now get angry with it. Anger is good.'

Anger is good. 'OK.'

I pick up the pallet, put dark blue, light blue, black – as many different colours as I can – on each finger and start smearing it across the canvas, pushing the paint to the edges, frantically filling the space. As I do, I feel a bubbling of something, maybe anger, maybe frustration, but definitely a release. I lose myself in it, until finally I stop and sit back.

It looks angry. It does. But also a bit … shit.

'Cool,' Jack says. 'Is that a bird?' He points to the m-shape that I appear to have drawn in the sky.

'Um… Yes.'

'It looks, kind of, I dunno…'

'Basic?'

He laughs. 'I didn't mean—'

'Like a child did it?'

'Ha! No. I like its simplicity.'

'Oh, God.'

He laughs again. 'Would make a nice little tattoo.'

'It would,' I say. 'Good shout. I've always wanted to try stick and poke.'

'No bloody stick and poke, please,' Cameron says from behind us.

I wink at Jack.

Then I see his canvas. It is … beautiful. The sky, the water, the reflection of the pale sun.

'Oh,' I say. 'You're really good.'

'What are you feeling, Jack?' Cameron says.

'Um… I dunno,' Jack mumbles. 'It's hard to describe. Something like nostalgia. Or longing. But I dunno if that's an emotion.'

Longing.

'Yeah, I'm sure it is. Why not,' Cameron says. 'That works, but your picture feels hopeful too.' It does. 'Good job.'

Cameron turns away from us, munching on his biscuit. When he's out of earshot, an urge comes over me. 'Jack can I ask you a question?'

He turns to me. 'Sure.'

'What happened to Rose?'

He doesn't answer. Just keeps looking out at the sea.

'Sorry, I shouldn't have—'

'That's OK,' he says. 'I just…' He stops.

Fuck. Change direction. Now.

'I'm going to go in,' I say.

He turns to me. 'What?'

'The sea.'

'Now?'

'Yeah. Screw it.'

'Eli,' Cameron says. 'Careful, please.'

But I'm already pulling off my shoes, my T-shirt. Then I'm running down the pebbles, wincing as they dig into the soles of my feet.

'What are you doing?' Jack shouts.

'Come on!'

'No way!'

I'm at the water now. My feet enter and I dive forwards. I hit the surface with a crash.

When I go under, a surge of ecstasy enters my body. I stay

submerged for as long as I can, feeling the prickling in my skin like needles. My brain opens – the water, the cold, the adrenaline wiping it of every thought, until I'm blank. Until I feel free.

When I come up, I see Jack standing at the shoreline.

'Come on!' I yell. 'It feels amazing!'

I watch him run his hand through his hair, contemplating.

The healthcare assistant tries to take his arm. 'Jack, don't—'

But he begins to pull off his shoes. I see Cameron behind them, smiling.

'Don't think about it – just do it,' I yell.

Jack nods. And then he's running towards me. When his feet meet the water, he yelps, hopping through the waves until he's knee-deep. He plunges forwards.

When he surfaces, he gasps, a huge intake of breath. 'Jesus Christ!' He starts coughing, spluttering, rubbing the water from his eyes. He trips and submerges again.

I grab his arm and pull him up. He starts to laugh.

I can hear the healthcare assistant yelling at us to come out, but I don't care.

'Wasn't so bad, was it?' I say.

'Fucking freezing!' he gasps, his eyes alight with adrenaline. Euphoria.

'Again?' I say.

He nods. 'Again!'

'Three… Two… One…'

We inhale deeply and together we go under.

DATE: MARCH 2ND
TIME: 03:00
LOCATION: SYCAMORE WARD

'Quickly,' he says, opening the door to his bedroom.

I check behind the nurses' station behind me. Most of the lights are off inside. There's just the low glare of computer screens behind the blinds, mingled with the faint fog from their vapes. They think we don't see.

We see everything.

It's been quiet tonight so they've kept themselves away from the patients. I heard the front-door buzzer go off about half an hour ago as their takeaway was delivered.

'Come on, Eli,' he says, and I can see that he's smiling. I slide into his room through the gap and step towards the little desk in the corner. He has a small lamp on, covered in a piece of material that Cameron gave him, so the whole room is doused in a dark green. There are pictures stuck up on the walls – pictures he's drawn, some I've drawn and given to him. There's even one that Fola made for him that says:

FOR HE NEVER GAVE UP, HE KEPT GOING, THE SCARS OF HIS PAST A REMINDER OF HOW STRONG HE IS AND WAS, AND ALWAYS WILL BE.

He pulls the door shut, then closes the slats in its square window.
'You've made it nice in here,' I say.
He shrugs. 'I guess that's a compliment for this place.'
I stand by the wall, suddenly self-conscious. I hold my hands together in front of me.

'What are you doing? You look terrified,' he says.

I am. In a good way. An amazing way. 'Just ... don't want to get caught. They'll go apeshit if they find us in here together.'

'Don't worry,' he says. *'They're too busy eating their KFC. I'm on general observation now and I've just been checked, so we've got an hour.'*

He sits cross-legged on top of his bed. I join him, facing him.

'How's it feeling?' he says after a moment, pointing to my wrist.

I pull up my sleeve to reveal the stick and poke tattoo I did last night after the beach, using a biro and a safety pin. An m-shaped bird. It looks a bit red at the edges. 'A little sore. How's yours?'

He pulls back his own sleeve to reveal the one he did. 'Yeah. Same.'

'Cameron will kill us.'

We hold our wrists out in front of us, so they're next to each other. 'Almost exactly the same.'

I look up at him. And then, for some reason, I put my hand on his. He doesn't flinch.

'Is that OK?' I mumble.

'More than OK,' he says.

I feel his other hand on my knee. There's something about the sensation that leaves more of an impression on me than the safety pin through my flesh. It does something to my insides, marks them with a heat, a pressure, that feels so big, so important, that I don't want it to end.

And I think, I'll never forget this. I'll never forget this moment. Or at the beach yesterday.

The bird on our wrists will always remind me. Always.

'Thanks,' I whisper. 'For being here.'

He smiles. 'What do you mean?'

'Well, I'm just glad... I'm just glad you're here. I mean... I don't mean I'm glad you're here here, in this hospital – because of what happened and everything. I don't want you to be here because of all that. I want you to be out there. Oh, fuck's sake. You know what I mea—'

And then he's kissing me. He's kissing me in the bedroom of a psychiatric ward between hourly checks, and although I should feel like this is incredibly wrong and bad, I don't. Because nothing about it feels wrong.

'Thanks,' I then say.

'You're welcome.'

And we laugh.

'Shh,' he hisses, looking back at the door. But we don't stop. We stuff our sleeves into our mouths, stifling the noise.

We kiss again and laugh again.

'I really like you,' I say.

'I really like you too, Elias Gordon Pew.'

I always thought when people said they had butterflies in their stomach it was a crass, hyperbolic myth. I prefer moths. Now I feel like there are about three hundred moths in my chest. 'Well, that's good.'

'Yeah,' he says. 'Everything is good.'

'Um... I spoke to my parents today on the phone. Told them a bit about you.'

He raises his eyebrows. 'Oh yeah?'

'Do you want to meet them?' I say. 'They're thrilled that I've met someone nice. They said it about twenty times.

And now that I'm a bit more settled or whatever, and we both have to leave, they thought maybe they could pick us up and you could come over for lunch or something.'

I suddenly feel very silly. Very formal.

'Yeah,' he says. 'I'd love that. They sound great.'

'Yeah, they are,' I say. 'They thought maybe tomorrow. What do you think?'

He shrugs, but I can see he's a little nervous. 'Yeah – if that's allowed.'

'I think the nurses should be cool with it, if my parents are there.'

Jack shuffles so he's leaning back with his back pressed against the wall. 'It's pretty nuts that your dad is Gordon Pew. I'm going to meet a politician. Jesus.'

'He's pretty normal when you get to know him.'

Jack nods. 'I'll have to be on my best behaviour.'

'He's going to really like you.'

'I hope so.'

He pulls his knees up to his chest, crossing his arms over them. 'What's your mum like? And your brother?'

'They're great. They've put up with a lot from me.'

He smiles. 'Obviously, I know who your dad is, but I'm interested to see what the rest of the Pews look like.'

I suddenly remember. 'I have a picture.'

'You do?'

'Yeah, they left it for me when I was admitted.'

I reach into my pocket, take the folded photograph, now battered and creased, and hand it to him.

When he unfolds it, I see him smile. 'Ah, you all look just like each other.'

'You think?'

'Yeah. Wow.' He shakes his head. 'I can't wait to meet them.'

'It should be nice.'

He sits, staring at the photo, then I see him frown.

'Jack? Are you OK?' I ask. But he doesn't respond. He just keeps staring at it. 'Jack? What is it?'

– CUT REMAINDER OF SCENE FOR USE
AT TRAUMALAND –

26

TURNING TIDES

The tube smells like sick mixed with deodorant. And weed.

The man opposite me reeks of it, and I'm so tired I could almost vomit myself. I pull my hood over my head, clutching my bag on my lap, making myself as small as I can. I close my eyes and replay the memory montage over and over in my brain, running my finger over the inside of my wrist, tracing the m-shaped line of the bird tattoo.

I didn't know. I didn't know it was there, underneath, hiding, all along.

Kindness. Gentleness. Perhaps, love.

Maybe a version of it. A version in its early stages, excitable and free, ready to grow into something brighter. Fiercer.

'*The next station is Brixton.*'

But as the tube pulls to a stop, I think *that's not true*. I did know. Because that longing, it never left. It was all for him.

It was so good. The way I felt was *so good*. And they tried to cut it all out of me. Of both of us.

I make my way out of the tube, and up the escalator. As I step out of the station, pulling my bag on to my back, I feel dizzy. I'm now running entirely off two Red Bulls, a packet of Quavers and pure adrenaline. I catch a glimpse of myself in the reflection of a bus window as it drives past. I look absolutely trashed. Like I've been punched in each eye and my skin is melting.

It's late afternoon now, the sun low in the sky. I fell asleep while rewatching the montage and woke much later than I'd planned. And then I had things to do (I'll get to that).

My family were already out. They think I'm at work.

I check my phone. No messages. I'll hear from my parents if they're worried. I always do.

I open Google Maps and type in the postcode from the website. Seven minutes' walk. I quickly message Nisha.

> I found where he is
> Turning Tides Supported Living
> Brixton

I see the dots appear as she replies.

> Be safe. If he's dangerous, call me.
> See you at 10 out the back.
> If you come in through the front
> they might recognise you
> Remember to dress up

I pause, wondering if I should tell her what I watched on the headset. I decide against it.

> 10 it is.
> Stay safe too.

I get up Maps again and begin to follow the blue line towards Brockwell Park. The air is ice-cold and bitter, but the sky is bright. It's one of those rare January days where the sun is out, but the frost still clings to the shadows. I pull my hoodie around me as I weave through the shoppers. Just before the park my phone tells me to take a left.

What did Jack notice in the photograph? Who did he recognise?

The smell of petrol fumes and noise of car horns disintegrate around me as my thoughts begin to race. There's no way they did this to protect me from him. He wasn't bad – he was the opposite… The voice on my phone suddenly chimes.

'*You have reached your destination.*'

I look up to see I'm on a quiet residential street, directly outside a large house. It's more rundown than the ones surrounding it. The window frames peeling and rotting, the metal handrail next to the steps leading up to the porch rusted.

A pang of nervous heat radiates inside me. It's the house from the picture on the website, the broken sign hanging above the door.

Beneath it, a girl is standing on the top step of the porch, hood up, with an open packet of tobacco and a Rizla in her hands. Our eyes meet.

She can't be any older than fourteen. 'Are you just gonna stand there and stare or what?' she barks.

I jump. 'Um, no…' I say. Quick. Try to be normal. 'Sorry, I was looking at the sign. I didn't mean to stare.'

She keeps rolling her cigarette. 'What do you want, then?'

she says. Then under her breath, but loud enough so I can still hear, 'Posh twat.'

Nice.

'Um...' I try to sound a little less posh twat. 'I was wondering if you could help me.'

She pulls a face, amused. 'Nah, mate, sorry. I don't have any more cigs.'

'No... It's not that.'

She pulls another face. This one says *right, and?*

'I'm actually looking for someone.'

She licks the edge of the Rizla, then expertly rolls the tobacco into a perfect cylinder. 'Oh, yeah? Who?'

'Um... His name is Jack. Jack Quinn.' She looks up at me. 'Do you know him? Is he here?'

The girl puts the cigarette to her lips and takes a lighter from her pocket. As she clicks it and moves the flame towards it, she inhales deeply. 'There's no one called Jack in here.'

I suddenly realise I hadn't thought of this as an outcome. I had not considered this would happen, because... Because I don't have another plan. There are no other options.

'OK. Sorry to bother you. Thanks. Cheers.'

I look down at my phone. Think, Eli. *Think*.

'Well, not right now, anyway,' she says. 'He just left.'

I look up. 'Left? What do you mean?'

She points down the road, towards the park. 'He's in there.'

'In there?'

'Yeah. He's swimming.'

'Swimming?'

'At the outdoor pool. The lido thing, or whatever you posh people call it.'

I feel the sting of the cold against my cheeks. It's freezing. 'He's swimming in this?'

'Yeah, he does it every day.' *Every day?* The skin on the back of my neck prickles. 'Something about the water making him feel stuff, feel alive or some shit.' She shrugs. 'It's all bullshit really. He's just tapped in the head.' Oh my God. Does he remember? *The beach? The water?* 'Anything else? Or can you please fuck off now?'

'No, that's it.' I'm about to turn, when – 'Wait. Actually, yes. There is. What's he like?'

She scowls. 'Like I just said, he's messed in the head. Do you not listen or something? He's weird. Like you.' Weird. Like me. 'But he's not posh like you.' Right. 'So, you might have the wrong person.'

He's swimming. *To feel alive.* 'I'm pretty sure it's the right one. Thanks so much. That's great. You're great. Thank you.'

She seems to have lost interest and is now typing furiously into her phone.

I turn to face the park. He's there. *Jack's there.*

A buzzing erupts inside me – a mix of fuzzy sleeplessness and anticipation propelling me down the street until I see the trees lining the edge of the park, a low mist still clinging to the bottom of them. I stand on the pavement, catching my breath. Directly opposite me is a red-brick building, unremarkable, easy to miss. A sign reads: *Brockwell Lido.*

A pang of giddiness takes hold of me.

I'm smiling. *Smiling.*

Excitement. *This is excitement.*

I can feel the good ones too.

I laugh.

I make my way up a set of steps and into the entrance so quickly that I nearly walk right past the man in reception.

'Sorry,' I say. 'Are you open?'

'Only for the brave,' he says. 'It's bloody freezing in there today.'

'How much is it?'

'Eight quid.'

I tap Dad's card to pay then walk past the changing rooms and out into the open courtyard where I'm met by a huge expanse of sky, hanging above a grey frame of concrete around a rectangle of striking blue.

I scan my eyes across the surface of the water, pushing my shaking hands into my pockets. A few people are doing lengths, some in wetsuits, others braving the cold in just their swimming costumes. I pace along the side of the pool, darting my eyes between the bobbing heads. Suddenly I stop. In front of me, on the concrete, is more colour – vibrant against the grey. A pile of clothes. A red jumper, a pair of blue jeans, some knackered trainers, a yellow beanie and a tatty green towel, all neatly folded. On top of the pile, right in the centre, is a small wooden pendant.

A rose.

I look up just as his head emerges from the blue, right in front of me. He gasps for air, dispersing the mist that hangs above the water's surface, and wipes the hair out of his face. He then pulls himself up on to the edge of the pool.

It's strange, seeing him.

His face, his hair. Skin bristling in the breeze.

I see the m-shaped bird tattoo, right there on the inside of his wrist. And the scars. White lines across his arms.

He glances up. His eyes meet mine. Soft.

My body shudders like it's being shaken awake. I feel a sudden burning sensation in my chest, making my eyes tingle.

Ping.

My phone. I look down at the screen.

Oh, God. *Oh, God, no.*

Dad:
Why are you at Brockwell Lido with my bank card, Eli?

No, no, no, no. Eli, you idiot.
Ping.

Dad:
I know you've been in the attic. I know what you've seen.
Do not speak to him.
You will be in serious danger.

27

DECEPTIVE AND UNRELIABLE

'You all right, mate?'

I look up from my phone to see Jack standing shivering in front of me, water dripping from his hair and swim shorts, making a pool at his feet.

I don't know how to start. Where to start. But first we need to get out of here.

'Jack,' I say. My voice is shaking. 'Jack Quinn?'

He raises his eyebrows slightly. 'Yeah?' he says. 'Can I help you?'

He doesn't recognise me. Not at all.

'My name's Elias. Elias Pew.' He frowns, confused. 'Well, Eli.'

I thought he might have some faint memory, but there's nothing.

'OK,' he says. 'Do you mind?' He motions to my feet.

'Huh?'

'My stuff.'

'Oh, sorry.' I step sideways as he reaches down to pick up his towel. When he straightens back up, drying his hair, then his torso, I realise how different he looks to the Jack in the memory montage. The Jack I knew. He's a shadow of that person – gaunter in his face, his chest – but what's most noticeable is that there's no light. No light in his eyes. They are black.

He's a shell. Numb. Blank.

Ping.

Shit.

Dad:
Stay exactly where you are.

I nearly drop the phone. I'm trembling. My whole body is—

'Mate, is everything all right?' I glance up to see Jack pulling down his T-shirt, the rose pendant now hanging round his neck. 'You seem a bit—'

'I need to talk to you. It's really important.'

'Right…' he says.

As he starts to pull his hoodie over his head, an urgency propels me. 'Something happened. Something happened to both of us and we need to get out of here. We need to talk…' I can't keep the panic out of my voice. I sound crazy.

Danger? Did Jack do something? Or is this another one of Dad's lies?

'Eli, did you say?' He's looking at me, arm mid-sleeve.

I nod.

He smiles politely. 'Yeah. I'm not sure you've got the right person, Eli.'

'I do. You have to listen to me. Look, can we just find somewhere quiet, private?'

He frowns like I'm some random nutcase, but I don't know how else to…

'Wait…' He narrows his eyes like he's taking me in properly for the first time. 'Have we met?'

'Yes, we have.' I glance over my shoulder at the entrance. 'We know each other. Well, we *knew* each other.'

'What do you mean, *knew* each other?'

Ping.

Oh, God. It's Mum this time.

Eli, stay where you are.
You're in danger. Don't worry.
Be with you soon.

'Hold on,' Jack says. 'You're that guy from the online support group.'

'That's right,' I say. Yes. Yes, that's right.

His body relaxes a fraction. 'Oh, so *that's* how we know each other.'

'Yes. Well, no. We knew each other before.'

'Huh? *Before?*'

Ping. 'Yes.' *Ping.* 'I just need a minute to explain—'

Ping. Ping.

Fuck's sake.

I look down.

Lucas.

Lucas…

Eli

I quickly type a reply:

Lucas – what happened?
What have they done?

It's so messed up.
I'm so sorry little bro.

Lucas – please tell me.

I wait for the text to send. Come on, come on…
A notification pops up, next to a red exclamation mark.

! MESSAGE NOT DELIVERED

I check my signal. Full bars. I text again.

Lucas – answer me

The same notification pops up.

! MESSAGE NOT DELIVERED

Damn it. I shove my phone in my pocket.
Ignore it. Ignore them. They're lying.
I can't stop shaking.

'You seem a little stressed, mate,' Jack says. He forces a smile, less polite this time. 'I'm gonna leave you to it.' He starts to pick up his trousers, socks and shoes.

'Wait. Jack—'

'I've got to get going.'

'No. *You can't.*' My voice trembles. 'Listen, there are things I know. Things about you that even *you* don't know.'

He stops. Tilts his head. 'Excuse me?'

I don't want to do this here, but I'm running out of time.

'When you did your share in the support group – all that longing, that blankness you were talking about, there's a reason for it. There's a reason you're not feeling anything, Jack. There's a reason you're not scared of water any more. That you're here, trying to feel alive again.'

His face scrunches up. 'Sorry, what did you just say?'

Keep going. 'I know that since last year, you've become numb. I know that nothing you're being told makes sense to you. That you're questioning everything that's happened. Because it was the same for me.'

He stares at me. He understands. *He does.*

A ringtone chimes through the air. It takes me a moment to realise it's coming from the jeans he's holding in his hands. He reaches into the pocket and takes out his phone.

Panic sears into my blood. I can taste it. Toxic.

'Who is it?' I say. 'Who's calling you?'

'Huh?'

'*Who is it?*'

'Hold on.'

Before I can stop myself, I reach out and try to snatch the phone from his hand.

'Whoa!' He dodges me. 'Mate, seriously.' He looks at me like I'm completely deranged.

I see the name flashing on the screen.

Melinda

'Don't answer that!' I cry. '*Please, Jack* – don't answer. Let me explain first.' I try to grab for the phone again.

'Jesus!' he says, gripping it tight. 'What are you doing?' He begins to walk away, hovering his finger over the screen, about to answer.

'*Don't!*' I shout, so loudly that he stops dead. I see people glaring at us, but I don't care. We need to get out of here.

Jack turns to face me. 'Leave me alone—'

'There was no bridge, Jack. There was no amnesia. You weren't found on a riverbank. That's why you have absolutely no recollection of it – because it didn't happen. They're lying to you. Last year you had your memories removed and it was arranged by my parents. I know how crazy this sounds, but it's true. They used a company who use a new experimental treatment which is designed to remove people's trauma, but that's not why they did it to us. Something happened – something bad – and you're involved. I think my parents are trying to silence you – us – by having us removed from each other's minds. Melinda is part of it too. They're trying to keep us apart.'

His eyes stay fixed on me. His mouth hangs open.

In the silence that follows, I see a man approaching us along the side of the pool.

'You need a hand, mate?' he says to Jack. 'Is this guy bothering you?'

'We're fine,' I say.

'I'm not talking to you,' the man persists, stopping right next to us.

Jack doesn't take his eyes off me.

'Please,' I whisper to him. 'Just give me another minute.

Trust me. Please. You know something isn't right. You know you've been lied to.'

Jack falters. I can see him computing what I have said, trying to process it. Then he turns to the man. 'We're fine,' he says. 'Don't worry, we know each other. Thanks.'

Thank God.

The man nods. 'Right, well try and keep it down. People are here to enjoy themselves.' He moves off, shaking his head.

Jack stares at me. Doubt. I see doubt.

There's no time for that. *Keep going.*

'Where did you get that?' I point to the pendant round his neck.

'What?'

'The rose.'

He lifts his hand, clutching it between his fingers. 'I made it.'

'Did Melinda tell you that, or do you remember making it?'

He stalls, thinking. 'She told me.' I can hear uncertainty now.

Good. *Good.*

'Do you believe her?'

'I…'

'You didn't make it, Jack. I did. I know things about you because we were once very close. We spent a lot of time together. I know that you were in foster care. I know you were there with your sister, in Brighton. I know that she died. I'm so sorry, Jack. I know you couldn't deal with the guilt of what happened to her – that you blamed yourself somehow. That you used to take her to the beach, to get away from your foster parents. I know smaller details, things that not many people would know. Like that you like crisp and banana sandwiches. And you prefer to use Doritos for the crunch.'

His eyes flicker like he's waking up. Yes. That's it. 'Jack, look.' I turn my head and point behind my ear. 'You did this. That's your handwriting, right? We wanted to remember each other.' My voice breaks. 'I just need a bit more of your time to show you something. And if you don't believe me after you see it, I'll never bother you again.'

I see something emerge beneath the black of his eyes. A glimmer of warmth.

'I did that to you?' he says quietly.

I nod. 'Yeah. Have you looked behind yours?'

'Behind my ear?'

'Yes.'

'No, why would I...' He lifts his hand up, moving his hair, brushing his fingers against the exact spot on the protruding bone where my own tattoo is. And as he does—

Yes. *I knew it.*

REMEMBER ELI

In my own handwriting.

'What is it?' he says, registering my expression.

'You want me to show you?'

He blinks, then nods.

I lift up my phone, zoom in on where his fingers are holding the hair back and take a picture.

'Look.'

When I show him my screen, he goes completely still. He stares at it, his eyes filling with terror. Then he looks up at me. That's the boy I remember from the memory montage. Scared, but strong. 'What the fuck?'

'I know.'

'This is... What the hell is this?'

'Just give me a chance to explain.'

He runs his fingertip over the tattoo like he's trying to read it with them. 'Was that your parents texting you?'

'Yes, they're coming... We need to leave.'

He flashes his eyes around the pool and for a moment I think he's going to turn and run.

He then inhales sharply. 'There's a bench where I sometimes sit,' he says. 'It's secluded. I'll show you.' He's shaking too now.

'Thank you. Thank you, Jack.'

'This is so messed up.'

'I know.'

We stare at each other for a moment and I feel ... relief. *Relief.*

He holds up his jeans. 'I need to...'

'Right, yeah. Of course.'

As he wraps the towel around his waist and begins changing out of his wet shorts, I turn my back to him, focusing on the blue of the water. *Deceptive and unreliable.* That's what Jack said about the sea. As people kick past me, doing lengths, I make a decision.

I will not be deceptive or unreliable. My stomach clenches. For the first time since last year, I've not been so certain of anything.

I hate my parents for what they did. I hate them so much. How could they do this to him? To us?

Someone shouts. 'Eli?'

I look up. Oh no. *No.* Dad stands on the other side of the pool.

I freeze as our eyes lock. My body won't move. I see Mum appear next to him.

'Jack...' I breathe.

I feel Jack's hand grab my arm. '*This way.*'

He pulls me along the concrete, away from Mum and Dad. People are staring at Dad as he strides towards us. Do they recognise him? Or is it because he's pointing at me? Everything blurs, panic robbing me of my clarity. Through the haze, I see Jack grab a plastic chair and push it up against the back wall.

'Eli!' he shouts. 'Come on!'

He clambers on to it and hoists himself up on to the top of the wall.

I can hear Dad yelling behind me. 'Don't go with him! He's incredibly dangerous!'

Jack holds out his hand. 'Eli – *quick.*'

I take it and he pulls me up. I follow him over the edge, landing in the mud on the other side.

'This way!' He takes my hand and pulls me with him.

We dart through the park, past tennis courts, through a little walled garden, winding our way into a thicket of trees, my legs burning, the cold air cutting into my skin. Finally we stop in front of a bench. It's tucked away in a mass of bushes, overlooking a small grassy area covered in rusty cans and bottle tops, empty vapes and exploded lighters.

My body is alight. I can feel my heart drumming in my wrists, my neck. As I glance around me, listening, I can hear him panting next to me.

'I think we're OK,' Jack says. 'For now.'

This is it. I swing my bag off my back and pull out the headset.

'What the hell is that?'

'I'll show you. Sit down.'

He does, his eyes remaining on the headset. 'That thing looks insane.'

'Yeah. Well, it gets more insane. This whole thing gets very, very insane.' I hand it to him and he turns it over in his hands.

'This looks like something a kid made.'

'I promise you, it's not.' I hear something. The snap of a twig.

We spin our heads round, towards the noise. Holding our breaths. We wait a few minutes. Nothing. Is it nothing?

I look at Jack. 'Are you ready?'

He doesn't look ready. Not at all. But he nods.

I attach the pads to their correct places. 'What the hell is this? Where did you find it?' he mutters, but I'm too busy making sure they're secure to answer. Just before I pull the goggles down over his eyes, he looks at me and I see it. Fear. Just a flash.

That's good. Isn't it? That he can feel fear?

He places his hand on top of my arm and as he grips it tight I feel a rush. In a fleeting moment I experience something so insanely warm and nostalgic, exciting and thrilling that I nearly gasp.

I've felt this before. And it is *wonderful*.

And then he's gone. Into his own past. *Our* past.

In the glow from my phone, I watch him watching the memory montage. He leans against the back of the bench, still gripping my wrist with one hand. The other grips the wooden armrest so tight that his knuckles are white. At some points he makes strained noises. Gurgling. Gasping. Laughing. At others he is completely silent.

When it is done – when he takes the goggles off – his eyes are red.

I think he's going to yell at me. To call me a psychopath.

But he doesn't.

He looks at me gently, *kindly*. His tone is soft as he says, 'Hi, Eli.'

'Hi, Jack.'

'Well … it's nice to meet you again.'

28

HELL

We sit listening to the wind, rustling the discarded wrappers at our feet and the constant pinging of my phone. Message after message from Dad, Mum and Melinda. No Lucas, though.

> We're in the park
>
> Where are you? Did you leave?
>
> Get away from him, Eli. He's dangerous

I turn off the torch and put the phone on to airplane mode. The sky is greyish blue now, still lit by the city glare. When the buzzing stops, we embrace the silence.

'Why have your parents done this?' Jack says after a while.
'I don't know.'
'Did I...' His voice breaks. As he turns to me, I can just make out his eyes glistening. 'Did I do something to you?'
'I don't think so.' I want to hug him, but it feels like I can't. Even though I know we have before.

He shakes his head. 'So, how do we find out what happened?'

I pause. 'There's a place I need to tell you about.'

'There's more?' he says.

I look at the clock on my phone. 18:30. Just a few hours till it opens.

I take a deep breath and begin with the hell rabbit.

~

Jack pulls his jumper around himself to stop himself shivering. 'I feel like I'm dreaming.' He turns to me. '*Nisha?* Christ, I haven't heard from her in years.'

'She remembers you.'

'She was older when she came to the placement. I think seventeen? She didn't speak much. We got told something awful had happened to her. She always kept herself to herself.' He shakes his head slowly. 'This is mad.'

'I know.'

'So, that's just a coincidence? That she works there?'

There are no coincidences. 'Yes, I think it actually might be.'

I want to rest my head on his shoulder to be closer to him. But that would be weird. Would it?

Yes. No. Yes.

My brain.

'So, we need to go to TraumaLand tonight? To watch the end of the story?'

I clear my throat. 'Yeah. Nisha's going to help us get in.'

'Right.' As he exhales slowly, I see the plume of his breath twisting out in front of us. 'When do we go?'

'Soon.'

'Soon. OK.' He looks exhausted. His eyes wide, like he's just returned from another planet. I think of the alien spray-painted on the back door of TraumaLand.

The truth is out there.

'But before we go, I want to try something,' I say.

He turns to me. 'Please don't give me another one of those head contraption things.'

For some reason, this makes me smile. Not his fear, more that he's here. With me.

He raises his eyebrows. 'What?'

'Nothing. Don't worry.'

'A bit too late for that, Eli.'

I take out my phone and pull up the screenshot of the webpage I found earlier this afternoon before I got on the tube. He looks at it over my shoulder. As he does, the faint smell of – well, *him* – moves over me. For a split second, I can actually see us at the beach together in my mind.

Is the memory mine? Is it in there somewhere, locked away?

Or am I remembering the memory I watched?

Christ, *my head*.

'Is that Cameron?' he says, pointing at a photograph of a man.

The heading says:

CAMERON TURNER
PRIVATE ART THERAPIST

'Yeah,' I say.

Jack squints at it. 'He's working privately?' He scans his eyes over the text beneath his headshot. 'He's in Wales now?'

'Looks like it.' I flick to the next photo – a screengrab of the CONTACT tab of Cameron's website.

'It's a mobile number,' Jack says.

'He might know more.' I shrug. 'He might be able to help.'

Jack nods. 'Worth a shot.'

I turn my phone off airplane mode, ignoring the barrage of messages. I then highlight the number from the screengrab and press *call*. I click the phone on to loudspeaker.

It rings. Once. Twice. Three times.

The phone clicks.

'*Hello, Cameron Turner.*'

His voice sounds far away, a bit muffled. I look at Jack. *It's him*. 'Hi, Cameron,' I say. 'It's um… My name is Elias Pew.'

A pause. '*Sorry, what did you say your name was?*'

'Elias Pew. Do you remember me?'

An even longer pause this time. Then, '*Sorry I don't. How can I help you?*'

Jack narrows his eyes.

'I was a patient on the ward you worked on last year,' I say. 'Sycamore Ward in Brighton?'

There's shuffling down the receiver. '*I don't work on that ward any more.*'

'No, I know. But you were there when I was a patient.'

'*There were lots of patients. And you shouldn't really be contacting me if you were.*'

He sounds different. Harder. Angrier. Less … kind.

Jack nudges me.

'I was there with a patient called Jack Quinn?' Silence. 'We were both discharged into private healthcare on the same day in March. You took us to the beach a few days before it happened. I painted the pier.'

The pause that follows is so long I wonder if he has gone. But then, '*No. Sorry.*'

I look at Jack. *He doesn't remember us?*

Jack takes the phone out of my hand, and holds it up to his mouth. 'Cameron?'

'*Is that Jack?*'

'Yes.'

'*You're together?*' He suddenly sounds different. I hear more muffling like he's moving quickly. A door slams.

'Yeah, it's Jack. Listen, something happened to us and we need to know what. We were on the ward together and then Eli's parents—' I nudge him. *Maybe don't tell him?* But he lifts his shoulders, *why not?* 'Eli's parents had a procedure performed on us both that wiped our memories.'

I can hear Cameron breathing. '*Boys, you need to…*' He stops. '*I can't speak with you. You don't understand…*'

'What don't we understand?' I say, leaning towards the phone.

'*Eli, your parents are… I can't…*' He stops again. '*Fuck. Listen, just – get away, both of you. Run. Hide. If you've found each other, they will do anything they can to stop you finding out the truth.*'

'What is the truth, Cameron?' My voice is louder now, echoing through the clearing.

'*Please… Don't ever call me again. They can't know we've been in touch. I can't be involved. I made a promise.*

I have a family…' His voice shudders. *'I can't put them in danger.'*

The phone clicks. The sound of the disconnect tone.

'Jesus,' Jack whispers as I hang up. 'He was terrified.'

'Of my parents.'

'Do you think they paid him off?' Jack says. 'Bought his silence?'

'I don't…' I hardly know them any more. 'Maybe.'

Jack shakes his head. 'What the hell did we do?'

I don't know. I don't.

I see the time on my phone screen.

19:42

'We need to go,' I say. I quickly message Nisha.

Nisha – we are on our way.
I have Jack.
Will be out back at 10.

I wait for it to send. Come on…

! MESSAGE NOT DELIVERED

Oh, Christ.

'What?' says Jack.

'Just… The message won't send.' Like Lucas. 'There probably isn't any signal down in the vault. I guess she'll be there now. She said to meet her out the back.'

Jack starts to stand. 'Wait,' I say. I lean down and unzip my bag, pulling out its contents. 'We need to put these on.' I hold up our costumes.

'What the hell? What *is* this place you're taking me to?'
You just said it.
Hell. I'm taking you to hell.

29

FIND YOURSELF

We are escapees from a psychiatric ward.

I thought Batman and Robin might've been fun – at least, the fucked-up version of them. But then I realised there were homoerotic undertones that could've been a bit, well, *awkward* and possibly a bit close to the bone. So, instead I found some bed sheets at home, which I tore up into gowns. I then scrawled PSYCHIATRIC INPATIENT all over them with my marker pen.

When we got into Central London we tried to find something to eat, but I didn't want to use Dad's card. Jack only had three pounds on him so we split a KitKat and a Lucozade. We sat on another bench – this time by the river – then put on our costumes.

We laughed as we pulled them on over our clothes. Hearing Jack's laugh did something to me that I can't fully explain. It wasn't some big swell of emotion, of joy or excitement, but a small echo, deeply rooted, of something I don't experience very often, if at all. Peace. In that moment, I realised that so much of me has been trying to fix the way I feel outside of myself. To get other things, other people, to change the way I feel. It's why I move so fast. My brain.

But the peace was in there all along – I felt it from inside me.

It was strange. But also, pretty huge.

I didn't tell him, though.

I used my face-paint set to give us bruised faces and bloody gashes on our cheeks and foreheads. People gave us funny looks, but it didn't seem to matter.

Nothing really seemed to matter.

We sat mostly in silence. But it wasn't really silent. The air between us seemed very full. Full of something that we shared without words. A history.

'Eli,' Jack says as we watch the lights of the buildings ripple over the water. 'It's so weird, all this.'

I stare back at him. 'Yeah.'

'I mean...' He trails off. 'Maybe we could just stay here?'

I like that idea. I do.

'But we need to know,' I say.

He nods. 'We do.' He exhales, looking down at himself. 'We look insane.'

'We do.'

And off we go.

~

The street at the back of TraumaLand is hard to find. Last night when I was there I wasn't exactly in my right mind. Then I hear the noise of retching.

Jack is taller than I am. Slightly. Being near him calms me.

I actually feel less terrified with him here. Why did Dad say he was dangerous?

He's lying. He has to be.

As we make our way down the alley, the thump of the trance music grows louder. Up ahead I can see a group of people dressed in a plethora of bloody and battered outfits.

'Are they being *sick*?' Jack whispers.

'Yeah,' I say. 'Some of it's...' I remember Amy. Her leg. Bella, finding her little brother in the bath. 'Some of the stories are pretty awful.'

'And all these lot think the people in them are actors?'

'Yeah...'

'Can't we just ... tell them?'

'I think Casimir might not like that.' I remember what Nisha said about him. *Particular*. The word feels oddly threatening tonight.

I see a row of bins. 'Here,' I say. 'We need to stash our stuff. If Casimir finds the headset on us...' I don't finish the sentence, but I know he understands.

'Eli...' he says cautiously. 'I'm...'

I turn to him. 'Scared?'

'Yeah.' And he looks it. Behind the face paint, I can see fear. Fear of what we have done. Or what has been done to us.

'Me too.' But we need to know.

I open the lid of the nearest bin and throw my bag into it. 'OK,' I say, looking at the people huddling by the back door. 'Nisha should be coming out any time now.' I step towards it. 'Just act like you've—'

'What? Seen something traumatic?'

'Yeah. Exactly.'

I scan my eyes over the crowd as we approach. Sweeny Todd, Count Dracula and Pearl, all vomiting into buckets. Freddie Krueger sitting on the pavement, wiping the sweat from his forehead, crying.

'This is nuts,' Jack says under his breath.

I see one of the bouncers from the other night standing by the door. The words on the back of it. The alien. But no Nisha.

'Let's wait here for a second...'

Come on, come on.

The door swings open and my heart jumps. A crowd of people file out, some laughing, some deathly white. I catch snippets of their conversation – *oh my God, that was sick, this place is insane.*

I suddenly panic. If we use Dad's bank card, he'll know where we are.

I turn to Jack. 'You don't have a bank card, do you?'

He shakes his head. 'There's nothing on it.'

Shit. We don't have any other choice. We'll have to get in, watch it, then run.

Like Cameron said. *Run. Hide.*

A hit of fear explodes in my stomach.

'You sure Nisha's coming?' Jack whispers.

'I...' No. No, I'm not. Why did my last message not go through to her? What if she's not here? What if she's been lying? What if she's told Casimir we're coming?

Come on, Eli. This isn't the time. Plan. I need a plan...

I see the bouncer – the one who was flirting with Zombie Mary Poppins last night (God, was it only *last night*?) – start chatting to Poison Ivy. His back is turned to the partly opened door.

An opportunity. Fuck it. I grab Jack's hand and pull him towards it.

'Eli…'

As the bouncer laughs at something Poison Ivy says, we slip through the gap. The door swings shut after us and the noise of it slamming echoes around the stairwell.

We're in.

Easy. *Too easy*. Where is she?

'Is everything OK?' Jack says. 'With Nisha?"

'Yeah,' I say as my eyes adjust to the darkness. 'I'm sure she's just caught up at the bar…' I turn to him. He looks terrified. A terrified psychiatric patient. 'You ready?'

'I dunno…' He squints at me through the half-light. 'You look completely mental.'

'So do you.'

I begin to descend the stairs.

'Eli…' he says, his voice quiet. Unsure.

I turn back. 'Yeah?'

A look of uncertainty flashes in his eyes. 'I'm sorry.'

'*What?*' Please don't leave. Not now. We're so close—

'Whatever the end of the story – I'm sorry if I caused this.'

Oh, God. This is awful. This is truly awful.

I step towards him and place my hand on his arm. 'No way,' I say. 'No one caused this but my parents.'

'But what if—'

'Listen, Jack. I could tell from the montage that you're an amazing person.' He drops his eyes. 'You're not capable of anything awful. You just aren't. This is all them. I know it is.'

'I hope you're right,' he says.

Side by side, we descend the steps towards the door to TraumaLand.

As I push it open, I notice the words on the back, marked in spray paint.

Find yourself
Or be lost forever

30

PRAYING TO THE STARS

The strobes blare. The music thrums.

I see the repeating doors in the wall surrounding us. The luminous words on the ceiling. The mass of bodies moving in time to the sound of the vault's beating heart. The neon rabbit everywhere.

The rabbit, the rabbit, the rabbit.

'Whoa,' says Jack. 'This is…' He trails off, his eyes fixing on to the clock.

02:32… 02:31… 02:30…

He points. 'What's that?'

I lean towards him. 'When the timer stops,' I shout over the music, 'we all pick a door. A story. The one I saw you in is called BUCKET.' He nods, his eyes scanning the words above each vault. 'Inside is a headset like the one you used earlier. We have to pay for time, so I'll make sure you have the maximum.' He turns to me, eyes wide. 'Unless you want me to watch it?'

'No,' he says. 'I want to.'

I look at the bar in the middle of the throng of people. Ajax is there. But no Nisha.

'Come on,' I say.

Together we move along the edge of the wall – past GRAVEYARD, BOAT, CHAINSAW, PARACHUTE, ELEVATOR – until we're standing in front of BUCKET.

'This is your story,' I yell.

Jack nods, watching the crowd jumping in a chaotic pulse – *dum, dum, dum, dum*. He looks disoriented. Like he might be sick.

Suddenly, the lights and music stop. The bodies stop jumping.

The warped voice echoes through the room.

I watch Jack's face as he listens, taking in each word. Blank. Like I was.

'*And so, welcome to TraumaLand,*' the voice finishes. '*It is now time for you to choose your story.*'

The crowd begins to move. People push past each other to reach their chosen door.

I feel Jack's hand on my arm. 'I don't know about this, Eli…' he says. He turns to me, his eyes searing. 'Can you watch it first?'

Oh shit. 'Yeah, yeah, course I can.'

I turn to the keypad on the wall. I push the up button to the max amount. Then I hold Dad's card over the card reader – *here goes*.

I tap it. £50.

Will it work? Maybe Dad's blocked it—

Card accepted.

The door swings open. 'My dad will know where we are. We can figure out what to do next once we—'

'Once we know what happened,' Jack whispers and I nod. 'Jesus Christ.'

Part of me doesn't want to leave him out here on his own. 'If you feel panicked or scared maybe go back up and get some fresh air. Or if you see Nisha, you can speak to her.'

'I'll be fine,' he says. 'I'll be here. I'm not going anywhere.'

'OK,' I say.

I turn away from him and step inside the vault.

It's the same as before. Empty room. Brick walls, concrete floor. A headset right in the middle.

I know what fear is now and I'm terrified. Completely terrified.

I exhale and pull on the headset.

> YOU HAVE CHOSEN BUCKET.
> YOU ARE NOW JACK.
> HELLO, JACK.
> YOUR STORY WILL START IN
> 3... 2... 1...

I leave the vault and drown myself in Jack's memory, which is familiar and horrifying all at once, until I reach the end of our story.

༺༻

– JACK –

'Eli?' I nudge his side with my arm. 'Eli?'

I put my ear next to his mouth. He's breathing, but there's so much blood, still pooling out of the gash on his head. The man with the bald head shoves me aside and places his hand over the wound to stop it bleeding, but the blood keeps coming.

I need to get Eli out of here. Now.

I look up at the man in the balaclava. 'Help him. Help your son!'

But he turns to the bald man, Karl. 'Go and get the car ready. They're waiting for us at the clinic.'

Karl steps outside.

I hear a scraping noise and watch Eli's dad as he picks up one of the wooden chairs, turns it over and places it in front of the door, trapping us in.

He looks down at his son and there's a flash of concern.

He turns his eyes to me. 'He needs help,' *he says calmly.*

'Yes, I know!'

'Then you must listen to me,' *he says.* 'That's the only way to save him. Or something is going to happen to you both that none of us want.'

'You're seriously messed up...' *I turn to Eli.* 'Eli, I'm here...'

I start pulling at my wrists, biting back a scream as the skin scrapes on the rope, until one hand slips out.

'Jack...' *Eli's father says as I scramble across the rug to Eli, my hands now free.* 'Jack, you need to listen. There's no point.'

I put my hands on Eli's face, shaking it gently. 'Come on, Eli. We're going to get out of here.'

'That's not going to happen, Jack, until you comply.'

When I turn back, I see Eli's dad is holding something in one hand – a ring binder.

'He's your son!' *I shout, my hands wet with Eli's blood.* 'Don't you care?'

'More than you would know.'

'Please… Just let us go.'

'I have something to offer you.'

'I don't want to hear it.'

'Well, I'm afraid you're going to have to. I hope you can see that you've put me in a very difficult position.' He tucks the ring binder under his arm, takes out a cigarette and lights it. 'If I let you go, you'll tell people what happened. And you must understand that if people find out, my life, my family's life, Elias's life –' he points a steady hand at Eli – 'will be completely destroyed.'

'That's the price you pay,' I say and his eyes darken. 'Eli needs a hospital – look at him.'

He stands, walks over to me and stops, looking down. 'It's a problematic coincidence that you've appeared in my life after so long, Jack.'

'I don't agree. There are no coincidences. You were meant to be found.'

'You need to realise no matter what happens here –' he holds my gaze – 'you will never tell anyone what happened.'

'The police have been looking for you for years.' He takes a drag of his cigarette. 'Please – let us go.'

Eli groans next to me as his dad takes the file from under his arm.

'What is that?' I say, keeping my hand on Eli. His breathing is shallow.

'I have a proposition for you. I want to offer you a kinder option than the only other way to keep you silent.'

'A kinder option than what? What's the clinic?'

'You can make all of this go away.'

'I don't—'

'Stop,' he says, holding up his hand. 'Yes, you do. We both want Elias to live, so I suggest you keep your mouth shut. I'm offering to pay you money – a lot of money – to leave right now and never mention a thing. You can have whatever you want. Your own flat, university, travel the world – things someone in your position could only wish for. I know how hard it's been for you. I know that you've had nothing. I can change that for you. There are conditions, but all I need is your name.' He holds out the file. 'Sign this and it's all yours.'

'So you can go on telling people how to live their lives? Those people deserve to know the truth.'

'We make the truth,' he says. 'If you're powerful enough, the truth can be whatever you want it to be. So, how does twenty thousand pounds sound?'

I shake my head. 'After what you did?'

'Thirty.'

'No way.'

He sighs, impatient now. 'All right, Jack – let's make this easy.' He leans forwards. 'I will give you fifty thousand pounds if you step out of this hut right now and never think of my family again.'

'No.'

'Jack...'

I clamber to my feet. He keeps his eyes on me, but he doesn't move. 'Do you really expect me to do that? Because of what you did, I will think about you and your family every day for the rest of my life, whether you like it or not.' I pause. 'Nothing will change that.'

'You're wrong there,' he says under his breath.

'What?'

'You don't know what I'm capable of.'

'Actually, I do. And I'm not leaving without Eli.'

'And if you leave here, what do you think you and Elias will do? Run off into the sunset together?' He laughs, shaking his head. 'You don't know him, Jack. You and Eli are incredibly different. He gets bored very easily. His mind needs stimulation and I'm afraid that someone like you just won't be able to give him that.'

'Fuck you,' I say.

He shrugs. 'I'm warning you. You should stay away from him. He's not been well and when it gets bad, he can be incredibly difficult.'

'I don't need you to tell me who he is.'

'You think you know my son better than me?' He takes a final drag of his cigarette and flicks it into the corner. 'I'll give you one more opportunity.' He steps towards me. 'Take the deal.'

I feel my blood pumping in my temple. 'No. Fucking. Way,' I say. 'I will never stop telling people what you are.' I move so my face is in his. 'Because you are a hypocrite and a mur—'

Suddenly his fist flies into my face.

The ringing in my ears is deafening. I'm laid on my back, staring at the solar system painted on the ceiling above. But then, in a flash, it's gone and his hands are around my throat.

'I told you,' he spits as he squeezes his fingers around my windpipe. 'I told you this wouldn't end well.'

I try to grab his fingers, but he digs them in harder, crushing my throat.

I try to shout, to scream, but I can't. The edges of my vision begin to darken.

I kick my feet, trying to lift my knees to knock him off me, but I'm too weak. His face is scrunched with the effort as he digs harder, teeth bared.

Then I smell burning. Something is burning. Behind him, light flickers.

I see the outline of a boy. He's standing. And there are flames behind him.

The curtains where the cigarette landed – they're on fire.

My vision swims. Everything is about to go black, when I hear shouts. Muffled thuds.

I realise the hands are no longer around my throat. I gasp for air, looking up.

Eli and his dad are tumbling on the floor together. I see their silhouettes, framed by the flames, as Eli reaches for the pole. His dad jumps for him, but Eli turns and plunges it into his stomach.

His dad drops to his knees.

Eli stumbles backwards and falls on to the rug. The rug that is now alight.

'Eli!' *I shout. I pull myself up and crawl towards him.* 'Eli!'

His jumper is on fire. He's screaming. Thrashing around. Trying to put out the flames as they spread across his chest.

Somehow, the bucket is in my hand. I throw the water at him, but as the flames die I can see the fabric is melted into his skin. I pull him off the rug as his cries pierce the air. The smoke is thick, clouding my vision. I drag his body, hauling him towards the door, the flames now climbing up the wooden walls.

'Help!' *I scream, but the smoke clogs my throat.* 'Someone help us!'

I feel a rush of air as the door swings open.

Gulping in the air from outside, I drag Eli up, sling his arm over my shoulder and haul him out on to the muddy ground.

I need to move – deeper into the woods. I blink the tears out of my eyes.

'Stop!' someone shouts and I lift my head.

It's a woman. A woman with a blonde ponytail, standing with Karl.

'Oh my God…' she screams. Her hand goes to her mouth. 'Eli!'

I try to drag him towards her, but I can't. I trip, landing in the dirt next to him. He writhes in agony, his cries cutting through the cold air.

Blood and burnt flesh. All I can smell is blood and burnt flesh.

The woman grabs my arm. Eli's mother. 'No one will know about this,' she says. 'Do you hear me?'

She looks at her son, her eyes filling with tears. 'Help is coming, Eli. It's coming—' Then she turns to Karl. 'Get Gordon, now.' She looks panicked. Terrified. 'They can help us at the clinic.'

And then she runs. Back to the house, leaving her son.

I turn to him. 'I'm here,' I say. 'I'm here.' I reach out my hand and gently touch his arm.

'Jack…' he whispers. 'Jack, I'm scared.'

'Me too. Me too.'

And I lie with him, on my back, praying to the stars.

31

OK. OK. OK.

I step out of the vault, my legs collapsing underneath me.

'What happened?' Jack grabs me, holding me up as I nearly topple to the floor.

The strobe lighting blurs my vision. The music shatters into my skull.

How is it true?

'It was...' But the words don't come out. 'Jack,' is all I can say. 'Jack, thank you.'

'What for?' he says, eyes wide. I lean my back against the wall, steadying myself. 'Eli, what happened?'

'My dad... My dad did this. All of this,' I mumble, but it hurts to speak.

I put my back to the wall and slide down it until my legs are splayed in front of me. I lean my head forwards between them.

We need to leave. Run. Hide.

I feel his hand on my back. 'Eli, what did he do?'

I stay still, regulating my breath. When I look up, I see the clock on the wall.

00:21... 00:20... 00:19...

'I'm so sorry, Jack.'

'Why? What happened Eli?'

The automated voice booms through the air. '*It is time to choose your stories.*'

Jack helps me stand and I turn to the keypad, my fingers trembling so much I can't press the buttons.

'Here,' he says, putting his hand on top of mine, steadying it.

Gentle. He's so gentle. How could my dad do that to him?

The keypad beeps. I tap the bank card.

I feel Jack's hand on my shoulder. 'Listen,' he says. 'It's not your fault.'

I can't look at him.

My family. My family are evil.

What did my dad do to cause all this?

Jack called him a hypocrite. And something else. He was going to call him something else.

'I'll see you in five minutes,' Jack says. He opens the door, then turns back to me. 'You'll be here, right?'

'Of course,' I say.

And then he steps into the vault.

As the door slams shut, I scan the room for Nisha. She's not at the bar. Where is she? I'm about to sink back down against the wall when I see something. A word above a door.

HOSPITAL

That's me. That's my story.

A deep, guttural, intense heat fuels me. I begin to walk

towards it, passing the remaining stragglers choosing their vaults.

'*Hey!*' I shout. Someone – a woman – is entering my story. *My vault.* To watch me, *me* getting held down and injected in that fucking seclusion room. 'You can't watch that!' I scream. I'm running now. I can't stop myself. 'It's mine! *It's my story!*'

When I reach her, she turns to me and laughs. 'Whoa, calm down. Wait your turn.'

'No,' I say, placing my hand on the door to keep it shut. 'You don't understand. *I'm in it – this is mine.*'

'This is all of ours, baby.' She smiles and winks. 'I've heard it's a great one.'

Then she yanks the handle, steps through the gap and slams the door in my face.

I begin to bang it, thumping my hand into the wood. 'Get out!' I scream. 'Get out. *It's not yours!*'

But then I stop as I see the word above the door next to mine. My fist remains suspended mid-air. A single word makes my body go still.

ROSE

Oh my God.

The receipt from the box in the attic. My parents paid for Jack to have an extra day removed. *One historical episode.*

I throw myself at the keypad, scrambling with the buttons, moving the up arrow to the highest it will go.

'*The stories will now begin.*'

I dig my hand into my pocket for the bank card.

Come on.

I tap it.

Come on, come on.

Payment approved.

It clicks open. I step into the vault, beneath the bulb, and take the headset as the door slams shut behind me. I pull it over my head.

But I know. I know before I see the words *you are now Jack* that it's his.

~

'What do you think?' I say to her, crouching behind the bush in front of the gravel driveway.

She turns her head, peering through the branches to the house, then looks back at me, eyes filled with awe. 'It's huge!'

'It's like a medieval manor.'

'Who do you think lives here?'

'I dunno. Maybe like a lord and lady.'

'Or the queen,' she says.

I laugh.

'Hey! Look at that!' She points longingly to a yellow bike leaning up against the wall by the porch.

'I have an idea,' I say. 'You want to go for a ride on it?'

She wrinkles her nose. 'But I can't ride.'

'I can. We could do a backie.'

Her eyes glint. 'But ... what if we get caught?'

'We won't. They probably won't even know it's gone.'

'Maybe.' She suddenly looks nervous. 'Is it fun?'

'Riding a bike?' I lean towards her. 'The most fun.'

She looks up at the sky. It's going to be dark soon. 'Don't we need to get the train?'

I shrug. 'Just five minutes.'

'OK.'

I take her hand and peer round the bush, checking each window of the house. It's quiet. 'Ready?'

She squeezes my hand tight as we walk quickly up the drive, the gravel crunching under our feet.

'Shh,' she whispers, but I can hear the excitement in her voice.

We tiptoe past the garage. As we get to the porch I can see four pairs of wellies lined up outside it. Even the wellies look rich.

'OK,' I whisper, letting go of her hand to take the handles of the bike. I turn it and begin to push it down the driveway, checking the house over my shoulder as I go.

I can hear her giggling. 'Quickly!' she says.

When we reach the end, I stop and sling my leg over it.

'Hop on the seat,' I say. 'Then hold on to my shoulders.'

I grip the bike as she pulls herself up on to it. I look down the road – a country lane lined with bushes and shrubbery.

'Jack, look.' I turn back to see a woman in the front window – blonde ponytail, white blouse – staring out of the shutters directly at us.

My eyes meet hers. 'Oh, shit.'

'Go!' Rose yells. 'Go, go, go!'

I kick the pedal and take a left out of the driveway. I feel Rose's fingers dig into my shoulders as she lets out a scream, piercing through the air, riddled with the shock of moving and the thrill of being caught.

I push with my feet as hard as I can, gaining my balance. It's been a while since I've ridden a bike. I find my rhythm and begin speeding up, twisting along the road, bushes and trees flying past on either side. The force of the air takes my breath away.

'You OK?' I shout over my shoulder.

'Yahoo!' she replies.

I push on round corners, along straight stretches, over dips, swerving potholes, which makes Rose shriek with delight. Up a hill, sweating now – the bike feels heavy. When we get to the top, I let my feet off the pedals and we start to career down the other side.

'Slow down, Jack!' Rose screams.

But everything feels so free. The air smells cleaner out here somehow.

Then I hear something. The rev of an engine.

I turn to see a car speeding down the road behind us. The handlebars wobble as I look round. Shit.

'Jack!' Rose cries. She's scared.

'It's OK!'

I keep moving, allowing the bike to race onwards, using the gradient of the hill to speed up. I glance round for somewhere to pull in, but the hedgerow is too dense.

The engine is louder now, so loud that I can't hear Rose screaming any more.

'Slow down!' I yell at the car.

But it doesn't. Its bonnet is now in my peripheral vision. Its horn blares.

Rose's fingers dig so deeply into my shoulders that I—

A sickening crunch. And then I'm in mid-air. Hurtling through it.

I hit the tarmac with a crack. My body bounces and I roll, twice, three times. I stop, just as I hear the screech of breaks.

I can't feel anything.

I hear ringing. A constant, high-pitched ringing in my ears.

I open my eyes. There's blood on the tarmac in front of me. And then I see the car, further down the road.

An old car. Green. A yellow stripe down its bonnet.

The door opens and a man steps out. Everything is blurry. I can't see his face.

Who are you? *I try to say.* What are you doing? *But no sound comes out.*

I watch him step forwards, towards the crumpled bike. Beside it is a bundle of clothes.

That's strange. I don't remember seeing clothes on the road.

The man leans down over it. He says something. 'Oh, God. Oh my God...'

Oh no. Oh no...

Rose, *I try to yell.* Rose! *But again, there's no sound.*

The man starts to pace back and forth. He takes out his phone and dials. He starts saying things I can't compute – it sounds all muffled – but I can make out someone on the other end. A female voice. Screaming.

'I didn't mean to!' he's saying. 'I'm not drunk – I only had a couple. The bike... You told me to get the bike back! What do I do?'

He listens for a moment. Then he hangs up and dials again.

'Karl...' I hear him say. Then muffled, quiet into the receiver. Pacing back and forth. Saying, 'OK. OK. OK.' Again and again and again.

When he puts the phone down this time, he picks up the bike.

I hazily watch him moving it into the back of his car, then getting into the front seat. It's like I'm underwater, the slam of the door sounding distant and muted. The engine starts again and the car begins to reverse, turning away from us. And then he's gone.

Rose. Rose…

I can't move my body.

I lie, staring at her, for what feels like a lifetime. She is still. Completely still.

I go in and out of faded darkness. The sky is almost black now. It's cold. Very cold.

I see the flash of headlights. I hear tyres stopping somewhere behind me. The slam of car doors. I flinch.

Voices.

Someone on the telephone. 'We need help out here. We're not far from Lewes…'

Someone leans over me. 'Are you OK? Can you hear me?'

'My sister,' I manage. 'Please help her…'

'Who did this?'

'I don't know… He came out of nowhere.'

'What did he look like?'

'I don't know…'

Then people are crowding round her. Round Rose.

Someone is pushing down into her chest – again and again. And then the sound of sirens.

TIME ENDED

32

PSYCHO

My dad's old Cadillac.

My dad's. My dad. That's why—

That's why he did all this.

Because when Jack saw the photo that day after the beach, it was the car he recognised. And he knew. He knew exactly who my dad was.

Murderer. Jack was going to call my dad a murderer. Jack must have confronted him when they met. And then my dad silenced him. Both of us.

The gaps in my brain keep filling like someone is pouring hot tar into them, sealing them together.

The night it happened – all those years ago – it was when Dad got in drunk. I heard him and Mum fighting in the kitchen, talking all night, Lucas joining them. Crying. *In the morning they looked grey.* They were making a plan. A plan to cover for Dad. The Cadillac was in the garage from then on. They got rid of my bike.

They were all in on it. They knew. Mum and Lucas too. They protected each other. To save Dad.

The whole time, I was upstairs, painting. While Jack and

Rose were lying in the road. And she was dying.

If you're powerful enough, the truth can be whatever you want it to be. We make the truth.

And he's coming. Soon.

He'll be tracking the transactions and he'll know exactly where to find us.

~

I push through the crowds of people emerging from the vaults. '*Jack!*'

I trip and stumble into someone. 'Watch it!'

Move, *move*. 'Jack!'

I see him through the flashing lights, sitting on the floor outside BUCKET, his head in his hands.

He looks up at me. Hurt. Terrified. Angry.

Everything, all at once.

'What did he do?' he says. '*What did your dad do?*' But I can tell from his voice, filled with trepidation and a weary unease, that he knows. I crouch in front of him and put my hand on his arm as people swarm around us. His eyes are red. I see panic. Raw panic. And hatred. 'Eli?'

'He…' I can't say it. 'Did Melinda tell you how your sister died?'

'Why, Eli?'

'Just… Please.'

'She told me Rose drowned in the sea.' They're all sick – completely sick. 'She said I blocked it out because of how painful it was…'

'She's lying, Jack,' I say. I feel ill. But he needs to know. 'There was an extra day my parents had removed from your memory. It was the day Rose died.' He stares at me in disbelief. 'And now it's here.' I point to the door across the room. The single word, 'Rose'. *Oh, God.*

I recount what I saw as clearly as I can.

When I finish, he wipes his nose on the back of his hand, his make-up smearing over it. He then looks up at me, eyes blazing. 'I need to see for myself,' he says.

'No, Jack. That's not a good idea—'

'*It's mine, Eli!*' he suddenly shouts. 'They fucking stole it from me! And now it's here for everyone else to see – everyone else to watch and *enjoy*. It's *my* memory. It's my pain – not theirs!'

As I watch him sob, I know.

This is so fucked. This is so, so fucked up. This place. It needs to stop.

I turn my head back to the crowd. And then I see her. Nisha. Serving drinks at the bar.

'Wait here,' I say to Jack. 'Just … give me a minute. OK?'

He doesn't answer. Just sits, huddled against the wall, clutching the pendant round his neck.

I stand and stride into the crowd, through the dancing bodies, giddy with adrenaline, until I'm at the bar. I push myself up to the counter right in front of her.

'Oi, queue-jumper!' Someone grabs my arm, but I tug it out of their grip.

She's writing something on a receipt. 'Violet!' I shout over the beat. '*Violet!*'

She looks up. 'Hi, what can I get for you?'

I lean towards her. 'We've seen it, Nisha! We saw what happened.'

She pulls back, pen in hand, frowning. 'Sorry. What did you say?'

'It was my dad. My dad killed Jack's sister. I need your help. They'll be coming any minute now.'

She stares at me. Blank. Completely blank. 'Wait...' she says. 'How do you know my name?'

'Nisha, it's *me*!' It must be the outfit. 'It's Eli!'

She tilts her head. 'Eli?'

'It's me, Nisha!'

I pull my sleeve back, revealing the bird tattoo.

She looks at it, confused. 'Sorry... Do I know you?'

Oh my God. *Oh my God*. No.

'Nisha, what did they do—'

Suddenly, I hear shouting behind me. I turn to see two bouncers pushing their way through the crowd, pointing at me. 'Hey, you!'

Nisha looks on blankly as I'm dragged away from her. 'What have you done to her!' I scream at the bouncers on either side of me, but they keep pulling me backwards.

The surprised faces of onlookers flash by as I'm pulled through the crowd – *he's gone wonky, fucking mad-head*. I try to squirm free, but I can't.

'No! Don't take me outside! Someone stop them! It's a lie—'

Then the recorded voice speaks again – *welcome to your worst nightmare* – and I'm hauled towards one of the vaults.

Above it the word:

PSYCHO

They swing open the door and throw me inside.

I hit the concrete floor, hard. When I look up, I see there are no goggles. No headset.

Just two chairs, facing each other.

In one of them is Jack. His hands tied behind his back, legs bound at the ankle.

'Hello,' a voice says. 'Please take a seat, Elias. I think you have something that belongs to me.'

Casimir steps out of the shadows and in his hand he's holding a knife.

33

THE GREATER GOOD

'What have you done to Nisha?'

Casimir doesn't answer.

The bouncers grab my arms, lift me from the floor and thrust me down into the seat opposite Jack. He's weeping, tears pouring down his face. They've wiped the make-up off with a rag that now serves as a gag. He stares at me, eyes wide, petrified. He strains against the ropes.

I'm so sorry. This is all my fault. Yesterday he didn't even know who I was. It should've stayed that way.

My arms are yanked behind me, around the back of the chair. I feel my wrists being tied together, my ankles. A damp rag is pushed roughly over my face, oily against my skin. The smell of the rag makes me gag. Sharp. Chemical. Fingers force my mouth open and stuff it inside.

It tastes bitter like turps, like it's been used to clean something. I try to force it out with my tongue, but it's tied too tight. My eyes begin to stream. The smell – the taste of the rag – making my vision blur.

The bouncers leave the vault, slamming the door shut behind them.

Casimir steps forwards so he's between us, stopping directly beneath the light bulb. He turns the knife round in his hands, touching the edge of the blade with his fingertips.

'Just the three of us,' he then says quietly. 'Now, this is how it's going to work. I'm going to talk and you're both going to listen.' His voice is calm, steady, but when he turns to me, his eyes shine a terrifying opaque black. 'It seems you've made a few mistakes. I'm able to forgive – *mostly* – but not everything.'

He points the knife straight at me. 'You.' The tip is a few inches from my chest. 'You made a promise. You signed something that I take very seriously. And because of what you've done, it leads me to believe that you do not take it very seriously. Is that true? You can nod your head,' he says softly, in a way that makes my skin prickle. 'That will suffice.'

When I don't, he steps towards me. '*Nod. Your. Head*,' he says. He then takes hold of my face with his hands so the handle of the knife is pressed into my cheek. He begins to lift my head up and down. 'That's it,' he says. 'That's it.'

He starts to laugh, the sound bouncing off the walls. I try to twist my neck, but he grips my head tighter, moving it up and down up like I'm his toy.

'Very good, Elias.' He stops, but keeps my face cupped in his hands. 'You *can* be obedient. However, you have got yourselves into a little spot of bother, haven't you?' He smiles, showing his teeth and I suddenly think of the Joker. 'And now you're in trouble,' he whispers. 'Oopsie.'

I try to lurch the chair forwards, but it's too heavy.

He tuts, wagging his finger. 'No, no, no, Elias.' He taps it on my nose. 'That won't help you. The only thing that will help you now is doing exactly what I say.'

He lets go of my face, steps back and holds his hands out to his sides like he's making a peace offering. He turns to Jack, then back to me, rotating between the two of us. He's casual, relaxed, in a way that feels unnerving. Unpredictable.

'So, here's the thing. This is my club and I like it. Lots of people like it. More than that, lots of people want it. *Need* it. We offer a service at TraumaLand that is increasingly necessary. We live in a world of addicts. So many of us desperately seek to fill a void. Drugs and alcohol, gambling, these things only work for so long. Take the edge off. But they don't quench the thirst. Because what people are missing is connection. Real connection. And with real connection comes emotion.' He pauses, looking me dead in the eye. 'We all want to feel. It's why we're here, isn't it? What is the point of any of this, if we don't feel alive?'

His eyes are manic. His hands play with the knife, turning it, moving it through the air.

He continues, enjoying his own words, the sound of his own voice. 'I assume you know from your little trip to my cleaner's office – and the headset and chip that you stole from me – that TEAR Solutions are performing what many might deem morally bankrupt healthcare.' He shakes his head. 'It's awful that it's gone this far. But parents are desperate. They want a quick fix. Neither of you had a choice in the matter. And I'd like you to know that's something I do not agree with. Some patients do get to choose, most in fact – but you two did not. However bankrupt that is, it is the future. And we must accept it.'

He stops in front of Jack and leans down towards him. He then places the tip of the knife softly on his arm and begins to run it over his skin. His scars. 'You'd been in so much pain,' Casimir murmurs. 'The agony you were in is written all over you.'

Jack lurches his body, trying to move away from him. But the knots are too tight.

'*Get off him,*' I try to scream. But the rag mutes it so it's just a pathetic, muffled yelp.

Casimir turns back to me. 'Did you have something to add?'

I try again. 'Leave him the fuck alone.'

It only makes Casimir laugh. That horrible laugh, reverberating around the vault.

'I recognise pain, Elias. It's my job to do so. I deal in pain.' His expression changes, his face weighed down by some unknowable force. He has experienced pain himself. 'And I am very good at my job.' He steps away from Jack, lowering the knife. 'Things are shifting. Changing. The world is starting to see different forces taking charge, forces that will soon be outside of human control. Technology is growing and we are hooked. It has its claws in us. It is both a blessing and a curse. It helps us, teaches us, even cures us. But there is so much darkness in it. It numbs us. Desensitises us. And then it starts to make us wonder if we are really here at all.'

He closes his eyes and inhales slowly. When he opens them again, he nods, resolute. 'I think it is only correct to balance the scales. I see it as my duty. I want to give back to people, give back what has been taken from them. But with this duty comes responsibility. It is vital for me to keep everybody safe in here. And that includes the people in the stories. Discretion is key.'

He turns to me. 'When you first came to TraumaLand and signed your name as Lucas, our colleague at the door upstairs assumed it was fine to allow you in. I have no stories of anyone called Lucas. And so, you slipped through the net.' He glances down at his knife in his hands. 'Don't worry, I've dealt with her for what she did.' He shakes his head remorsefully. But he's performing. I know it myself, all too well.

'You must understand that in order to keep this place going I need it to remain secret from those inside the stories. It's all for the greater good. For the people who come here to find their cure. That is why I do it. I do it for them.'

And for the money.

Casimir steps round to the back of Jack's chair and places his hands on to his shoulders. Jack flinches, his cries muffled by the rag. 'I know. I hear you, Jack. What about those people who have lost their trauma? It seems unfair, doesn't it? I know the procedure can leave you feeling a little numb yourself. I've seen the case studies.' Fuck off. Fuck. Off. 'TEAR Solutions will soon be a multimillion-pound, profit-making machine, endorsed by our government. So, if you think what I'm doing is wrong, you must see the bigger picture. I'm taking from the rich and giving to the poor. Like the…' He stops, smiling to himself. 'Like the Robin Hood of emotional balance.' He taps Jack on the shoulder pityingly. Performatively. 'But sadly there has to be some collateral.'

Casimir looks up. 'Elias, I know you doubt that a cleaner could ever do such a thing as this and yet here we are.' He winks. 'Privilege only gets you so far, my friend. Your lovely house.' You maniac. 'Those rhododendron bushes. That attic room. Those storage boxes.'

I squirm in my chair.

'What was that?' He puts his hand to his ear. 'How do I know these things?' He smiles. 'Well, your friend Nisha had something to do with it.' He crouches in front of me so our faces are level. 'I've learned a lot, watching, hiding in the shadows. Thankfully the memory-removal procedure is very quick and quite simple. Taking two days from someone's mind is not as difficult as it might sound. The technology is really quite clever.'

Of course, he watched it. A chill runs through me as I realise he knows everything.

I squirm in my seat, desperate to break free. 'You bastard.'

He frowns, feigning concern. 'I can see that this startles you, Elias. Don't worry, she's used to it. Nisha has had a long and troubled history. In return for taking the trauma of her past – which she asked me to remove – she works for me. It's win-win for both of us.' He leans right into my face again. 'She was in an incredible amount of pain, like Jack was,' he whispers. 'I removed so much trauma – files and files of it. It was so…' He falters and I see his eyes glisten. 'She deserved so much better. Life has been so cruel to her. She was incredibly grateful to me.'

He turns to Jack again and takes the back of his chair. He drags it so it screeches on the concrete until Jack is no longer visible outside the pool of light. He then heads to the door and knocks on it three times.

It opens and one of the bodyguards steps in. Followed by someone else.

'Hello, Violet,' Casimir says as Nisha emerges in the doorway.

'Hi, Casimir.'

'I won't take much of your time. I just need your help for a moment. Could you look at that gentleman over there.' He points at me and Nisha blinks. 'Do you know him?'

She squints. 'Yeah, I saw him at the bar about ten minutes ago. He was acting crazy, about to wonk.'

Casimir nods. 'Never seen him before that?'

She shrugs. 'Nope.'

'Thank you, Nisha. Sorry, *Violet*.'

'Don't worry,' Nisha says. 'Can I help you with anything else?'

She sounds so different. So compliant.

'Yes.' Casimir turns to me and smiles. 'Could you just explain to him about your name?'

Her name?

'Yeah, of course.' Nisha looks me dead in the eye. 'I go by different names. Always have. I used to do it a lot as a kid, made me feel safe. Still do it. I go by Violet at work. Nisha is the one I use outside of work, with people I don't know. Or for my phone, in case it's stolen, so no one can know my business.'

Oh, shit.

'Because there are some pretty evil people out there, aren't there?' Casimir says.

She nods, her face blank. 'I like being as anonymous as I can.'

Casimir shrugs. 'Makes sense to me. Thanks, Violet.' She turns to leave. 'Oh, wait. Just one more thing. Could you tell him your real name?'

'Sure. My real name is Amy.'

'Thank you. That's all, Amy.'

Oh my God.

Amy.

HAMMER.

In that shed? With that awful man? *That was her?*

She nods. 'Thanks, Cas.'

She then opens the door and disappears back out into the strobes.

As it shuts behind her, Casimir turns to me. 'So, Elias. I think you've already seen some of Amy's story. In fact, I think it was the first story you experienced at TraumaLand.'

'I...'

How? I never saw her face. Her voice was distorted.

When did that happen to her?

I feel sick. I think I'm going to be—

'Now tell me,' Casimir says. 'Do you really think she should have those memories back? She seems happy enough without them. And she consented. Now her memories are used to help bring other people back to life.'

You're evil, I try to scream.

I try to look at Jack but can only hear him groaning in the shadows.

Casimir steps towards me. 'I want my headset back, Elias. And my chip that's inside it. Sadly, those memories no longer belong to you. I'm going to remove the gag from your mouth and you're going to tell me where it is. If you so much as say another word, I will cut you.' He turns the blade, hovering it over my arm. 'Do you understand? Nod. Your. Head.'

I don't.

The blade slices into my skin. I scream into the rag.

He draws the knife down and I feel the blood trickling along my arm. My legs tremble with the pain. He waits until I've stopped screaming, then unties the rag and lowers it. I gasp, taking in mouthfuls of clean air.

'So, Elias,' he says. 'Where is it? I know you're fond of words. Just tell me and this will all go away.'

'You need to be stopped—'

He slices the knife. Deeper this time.

I scream as the pain radiates through me. 'What did I tell you about using other words?'

'Fuck off.'

'I see. Well, perhaps this will help.' He turns towards the darkness, knife in hand, to where Jack is. He leans towards him. I hear Jack whimper.

'Stop! You maniac!' Jesus Christ. 'I'll tell you! Just leave him alone—'

Casimir laughs. When he emerges back into the glow of the bulb, he's holding the rose pendant in his hand. 'This is your favourite thing, isn't it, Jack? Shame.'

Jack tries to scream, but Casimir ignores him, turning to me. 'Go on,' he says. 'Where is it?'

'It's in the bin.'

His face morphs into an expression of fury. 'What did you say?'

'I said it's in the bin.' He stares at me with his black eyes. 'It's gone. So, your new little project won't have us in it. Those memories will never be seen by anyone else, no matter how much you convince yourself you're doing the world a favour. No matter how much you *charge* for them. They're not yours. They're ours and we need them. We need them back. Just like we need the ones in here back.'

'You want them *back*?'

'Yeah,' I say. 'We do. All of them.'

My arm doesn't hurt any more. I'm numb. Completely numb.

He steps towards me, knife outstretched. 'You will tell me where those memories are right—'

Suddenly the vault door smashes open. It happens in a flash. A blur.

Someone is on top of him and the room fills with people – two, three, four of them – all wearing black, shouting.

'*Put the knife down. On the floor, now!*'

They pin him to the ground. As they pull his arms behind his back, he drops the pendant and his knife.

A woman appears behind me and begins cutting the ropes from my wrists. She then helps me up, letting me lean on her. I look over at Jack to see he's free now too, a tall man with a beard helping him up.

'You're safe,' the woman is saying. 'But you need to come with us. Now.' She is wearing a hooded coat, cargo trousers and boots, her short dark hair scraped back. 'This way, Mr Pew. Mr Quinn. Come with us, please.'

Then we're being led out of the vault. Back through the strobes and music and bodies.

I try to pull away from her, but she's holding too tight.

'We're here to help you, Elias,' she says as we step through the iron door and out into the holding area.

'Do you work for my father?' I say. 'Tell me!'

'Quiet,' she replies. 'Not here.'

We head up the twisting stairs, walking in single file – the woman at the front with me, the bearded man behind with Jack – up to the reception room at the top. Then we're out of TraumaLand.

Parked on the street in front of us, there is a van. A silver van with no windows in the back.

'Who are you?' I scream.

My brain – my brain is moving too quickly.

'In there,' the bearded man says, opening up the back doors. He takes out a mobile phone and begins to dial.

I hesitate, looking at Jack.

'Are you the police?' he says, his voice trembling.

'You don't have to worry,' the woman replies, putting her hand on my arm. I flinch. 'Jesus,' she says, looking down at the cuts.

And then she has something in her hand. A first-aid kit. She opens it and lifts out a handful of gauze.

'I just want to clean you up a little before we go,' the woman says, tearing open a small square packet with her teeth. 'This might sting a little.' She takes out a wipe and runs it down my arm. I can smell the ethanol, but I feel nothing, my body still numb. 'Nearly there,' she says, unfurling a bandage and wrapping it. 'OK, all done, sweetheart.'

Sweetheart.

'But...'

We can't trust them. We can't trust anyone.

'Now in the van,' she says.

'Tell me who you are!' I yell. My brain is moving so fast it feels like a forest fire spreading.

'Trust us, Elias. We know what your father has done, and we want to help you. You're safe now.' She smiles kindly. 'You have helped us more than you could know.'

I look at Jack.

He doesn't move. Eyes wide, body trembling.

'He's in shock,' the woman says. She steps towards Jack and places her hand on his shoulder. 'Hi, Jack. We are here to protect you, OK? Everything will be fine now. I promise.'

As we're led to the back of the van, I see the front door of TraumaLand, half open.

The rabbit gazes back at me. Its dark eyes staring, headphones lodged over its ears.

34

THE OMEN

It's pitch-black.

Everything is dark. Outside my head. Inside my head. Everything.

I can feel Jack huddled next to me on the floor of the van, trembling. He bumps into my side as we move, turning round corners, stopping sharply at lights.

'Who are these people?' He sounds completely drained. Empty, apart from the pain.

'I don't know.' I try to make my voice sound strong. Assured. For him. 'If they rescued us from Casimir, then they're going to help us.'

'How did they find us?'

'Dad's bank card.' My head feels like it's been put through a blender. My mouth is burning. My arm stings from the cuts. I try to block out thoughts of my family, focusing on the vibrations of the road beneath me. But they scurry like cockroaches through the folds in my cerebral cortex.

It was my bike.

My family.

My family of liars.

Murderers.

I'm a part of that.

Revulsion surges inside of me, making my stomach contract.

'Listen, Jack…' I move my hand across the floor until it finds the side of his. 'I'm so sorry. For all of this. I'm going to help you. We can go to the police, tell them everything. I never want to see my family again. I promise you – people will find out what they did.' I hear my words and they sound so stupid. So pathetic. Because no words are enough. They never will be. My family has put him through so much. Taken everything from him. I feel embarrassed. Ashamed.

Shame.

I forgot how terrible, how awful it is. A dark and twisted cloud, moving through me, suffocating me from the inside out. But I hold on to it. I allow it to consume me, to punish me.

I can hear his breath, shuddering next to me. He keeps his hand where it is, right next to mine. I then feel his fingers move. He places them on top of my hand, linking our fingers together, and softly squeezes. It does something to the cloud that has filled me. Pierces it with a momentary beam of light.

'It's OK,' he says. I can just make him out over the whir of the engine. 'I'm glad that you found me, Eli. I'm glad that I know. When I was watching that stuff on the headset, all that stuff in Sycamore Ward, you were really kind to me. You didn't judge me. Didn't ask about my scars. You really wanted me to get better. You talked a lot… But I can tell that I liked it. I liked being around you. It was so strange, watching it, experiencing feelings I never knew I'd felt.'

'Yeah, I know what you mean.'

As our bodies rock with the motion of the van, I feel him shift his weight, bringing his legs up closer to his chest. 'I think there was something about the way you were that made me feel a bit off-kilter. A bit on edge.'

'Oh...'

'No, in a good way. In a way that gave me something to be excited about. Your energy reminded me what life can be like. It was exciting. It was definitely ... fast. But free.' He pauses. 'I could tell that I wanted to get better that time. Ever since Rose died, I'd blamed myself. I couldn't deal with it. For years I was in and out of those places. But that time it looked like I did want to get out, make something of myself and move on. And having you there just seemed to... I don't know... Brighten things. It took me out of my head, which I'd been so stuck in. And then your parents removed it all.'

We make the truth.

'I'm so sorry about your sister,' I say quietly.

'Am I to blame?' He clears his throat, fighting the emotion welling inside it. 'I took her there. I stole the bike.'

I see him on the road, trying to say her name. 'No,' I say. 'It was them. It was all them.'

He exhales shakily. 'Good. That's good to know.' I tighten my fingers around his. 'I want to see it. I want it back,' he says. 'I was doing some crazy shit to try and feel again, you know? I was swimming when I thought she'd drowned. I was trying to feel something. Pain. Anything.'

'Wait – me too.' I pause. 'You haven't been watching *The Exorcist* on repeat, have you?'

I sense him turn to me. Is he smiling? '*The Omen.*'

No way.

The van suddenly lurches. We've stopped.

I sit upright and Jack's hand tenses in mine as we hear the thud of doors opening. The van shifts slightly, tilting as the man and woman step out.

They seemed kind. They did. But is that enough?

There's a clonk as the handle turns in the back door and it swings open, revealing the man and the woman in their hooded coats. The others must have stayed with Casimir. What did they do with him?

'Where are we?' Jack croaks, blinking into the light of a street lamp.

'A place of safety,' the man with the beard says.

The dark-haired woman nods. 'This is the best place for you to be. I promise.'

'Who are you?' I say.

The man holds out his hand to us. 'We're friends. Now, please, be quick. We don't have much time.'

I look at Jack. He's shivering. Do we have any choice?

We begin to stand.

'That's it,' the man says. 'Good job.'

The first thing I see are the McDonald's wrappers and Starbucks cups littering the ground. I then see a small door, a broken camera above it. A metal panel, and intercom buzzers numbered one to six.

The woman presses the one next to Floor 2.

'Wait,' I say.

'There's someone inside who wants to talk to you, Eli,' she says. 'Give them a chance to explain.'

'What is this place?' Jack whispers.

I glance back at the man with the beard as he slams the van door shut. Then I hear a voice answer the intercom. A woman's voice. One I know well.

'*Hello?*'

'They're safe,' the dark-haired woman replies.

'*Bring them up. We're waiting.*'

35

CLINIC ROOM 2

We stop halfway down the carpeted hallway, outside one of the many doors. I look up at the gold plaque.

Clinic Room 2

'This is where I leave you,' the dark-haired woman says. 'I'm sorry for what has happened to you both. I wish you all the best. And well done for finding each other again.'

She turns, heading back down the corridor into the darkness. I hear the door to the stairwell slam shut and we stand in silence together, the low hum of the generator pulsing from somewhere inside the walls. The smell of washed linen and fresh paint hangs in the air.

I watch Jack, taking it in, his face a mess of smeared fake blood and bruises. 'We can leave,' I say. 'We can just—'

Before I can finish, the door to Clinic Room 2 opens and a figure emerges.

Lucas. He stands in the doorway, wearing a fleece over his Cambridge hoodie. 'Thank God. *I'm so glad you're safe.*'

As he goes to hug me, I step back, fighting the urge to throw my fist at him.

'What are you doing, Lucas?' I say. 'Who were those people?'

He puts his hand out in front of him, trying to calm me. His eyes are red and puffy. 'Listen... I know what you both must think, but I need you to give me a chance to explain.' He looks at me. 'Please, bro.' Then at Jack. 'Please, Jack. I'm on your side. We're going to help you. But we need to be quick. People are looking for you.'

'*We* need to help you?' Jack repeats. 'What do you mean *we*?'

'Who's looking for us?' I say.

'Mum and Dad.' I hear the unease in his voice. 'And Dad's work.'

Dad's work? 'The government?'

He nods and however much I feel I don't know this person standing in front of me any more, I can see how serious he is. His fear is unmistakable. Lucas pushes the door open further and behind him I glimpse a large, dark room. 'Just come inside where it's safe.'

My brain reels. Why is he here? 'Have you always known about this place, Lucas?' My voice strains with the ache of his betrayal. 'Don't lie... Don't.'

His face fills with what I can only interpret as shame. Guilt. 'I've known about it since your memories were removed, yes.'

I feel my fist clench, but before I can do anything, someone steps out of the darkness behind him. Melinda.

My fucking therapist. Messy hair tied up like she hasn't slept, a large jumper on, eyes alert. Focused.

'*You*,' Jack yells, pointing his finger at her. 'You lied. You lied to me!'

She half whispers her words, but they are direct, strong. 'Calm down, Jack. Please—'

'You lied about my sister – about all of it. How could you? How could you make me think she *drowned*?'

'Please, Jack.' Melinda has the same look as my brother. One I've never seen on her face before. Shame. Guilt. 'I had to,' she says gravely. 'I had no choice. I'm so sorry.'

Jack shakes his head, unable to find the words. I can see his anger brimming over, about to spill out. But then his eyes flash down the corridor. He pushes past me, heading in the direction of the stairwell.

'*Jack*,' Melinda calls after him. 'You must understand that you have no choice now. If you step outside this building you will be in serious danger. As Lucas said, there are incredibly powerful people trying to find you at this very moment. This is where you need to be.'

He stops. Turns back, his eyes burning. 'You've taken everything from me,' he says quietly.

'I know, Jack,' Melinda says, keeping her eyes on him. 'Come inside and we can make it right.'

Lucas catches my eye. He nods. Reassuring. Strong. Is he lying?

'There's nowhere else to go, bro.'

I look back at Jack. Shit.

'Jack, please,' I say because Lucas is right. There's nowhere else to go.

He bows his head, despondent. Then he begins to walk back towards us.

'Good. That's good, Jack,' Melinda says. She glances at Lucas, and I see a look of relief pass between them.

Lucas puts his hand on my arm and guides me through the door, behind Jack and Melinda, into Clinic Room 2. The door shuts behind us.

It takes me a moment to adjust. Because it is not what I expected.

Four armchairs face each other on top of a rug in the centre of the room. The walls are lined by bookshelves crammed with books, some with broken and battered spines, some new and unopened. Golden bookends – heads of stags – hold them together, while other rows are broken up by expensive-looking ornaments. Vases, bowls and bronze busts. As I step further into the room, I can see trophies on shelves and framed certificates hanging on the walls – *Winner of the Progressive Healthcare Awards: British Psychiatry Institute, Advancement in Mental Health Medal Nominee: General Medical Council, Recognition of Innovation: World Health Organization.*

A low screen hangs on one of the walls displaying an image of a fireplace. It flickers gently, spilling out a warm, orange light. It looks cosy. Inviting.

'Please, take a seat.' Melinda lowers herself into one of the armchairs as Lucas takes the one next to her. Neither Jack nor I move. Next to each of the chairs is a small, circular table with a bottle of water labelled *TEAR Solutions*.

Lucas smiles. 'Come on,' he says. 'Just try and relax now.'

'Relax?' Jack repeats, glaring at my brother.

'Sorry,' Lucas says, and he sounds it. 'I just… We want you to feel safe.'

Safe. They keep saying it. *Safe.*

Melinda tucks her hair behind her ear and I realise she's nervous. Or embarrassed. The professional boundary that has separated us every time we've met before is no longer there.

On the table next to her chair, I see two small boxes, each the size of a jewellery box. Embossed on the top of each one, in a swirling font, are letters:

E.P.
J.Q .

'Why are we here?' Jack asks.

'We will explain,' Melinda says. 'Please make yourself comfortable.'

Jack and I exchange a glance. What else can we do?

'Bro,' Lucas says. 'You have to trust me.'

I look at him. He's smiling. Genuinely. Lovingly.

I step into the circle and take one of the chairs, perching on the edge of it. Jack hesitates, then takes the last empty one. We sit in silence for a moment, staring at each other. I'm so thirsty, my mouth still burning from the chemicals on the rag. I reach for the water, but Jack shoots me a warning look.

'It's sealed,' Melinda says. 'It's safe.'

Lucas nods at me. *It's safe.*

I unscrew the top and drink the whole thing in one go. A semblance of clarity returns to my brain. Jack does the same, guzzling the water until it's gone.

'Good,' Melinda says. 'OK.' She exhales slowly, her face flickering in the orange light of the screen. 'So—'

'What happened back in TraumaLand?' Jack cuts her off.

Melinda leans back, crossing one leg over the other. 'We were stopping them, Jack,' she says. 'We *have* stopped them. Thanks to you, we managed to locate the club. And we discovered that man – Casimir – was stealing the memories without our knowledge. He has been dealt with. TraumaLand is no more.'

'Just a sec.' I slide my phone out of my pocket and quickly google TraumaLand. I click on the link – it says webpage expired. No black page. No white text. No bunny.

'You've helped us hugely,' Melinda continues as I put my phone away. 'And now we're going to help you. It was very important to us that we got you out of there safely. Tamara and James run our security team. They brought you here.'

'How did you know we were there?' I say.

Melinda looks at Lucas. He shifts forwards and puts his elbows on his knees, clasping his hands together. 'This morning when we spoke in the corridor, bro, and I saw your tattoo and that you'd taken Dad's bank card – I knew. I knew you'd found him. And because of that, I knew what Mum and Dad would do to you both. I couldn't carry on lying any more. I contacted Melinda. I said we had to keep you safe. Melinda has always questioned what Mum and Dad have been doing. Despite the pressure they've put on her, I knew she'd want to help. And she did.'

'After Lucas came to me,' Melinda continues, 'he found your dad's passwords. We were able to intercept the bank card transactions and saw the ones you'd made at Feral Street.'

'It was after Dad followed you to the lido,' Lucas puts in. 'I'm sorry I had to turn my phone off. It was so they wouldn't see I'd been in contact with Melinda.'

'That doesn't make sense,' Jack says. 'It said the messages didn't deliver. They would still deliver even if it was turned off...'

'Dad must have disconnected my number,' Lucas says.

'To stop any contact.' Melinda nods. 'I tried to call you, Jack, but I can appreciate why you didn't answer.'

Jack sits completely still, staring into the distance.

'Why have you gone along with this for so long?' I say. 'Both of you?'

'This is bigger than us,' Melinda says. 'Bigger than any of us could have imagined.'

'You're working with my dad,' I say. 'He's *paying you—*'

She holds her hand up, stopping me. 'Elias, please trust me. Your dad is an incredibly powerful man.'

'Where is he?'

'He's at your home. He doesn't know we're talking. Neither does your mum. And they will not. I promise you.'

'But why...' I have so many questions. So many. 'Why were you working with them? Helping them to do this? Cover all this up? *He killed a girl.*'

I hear the starkness of my words. Lucas shifts in his seat. Jack drops his head.

Melinda glances at Jack, but he doesn't look up. 'I want you to know that I very much believe in our work here. When used correctly, this treatment could save the future of a crumbling system. Trauma relief is vitally important in a world that continues to harm our youngsters in unspeakable ways. That trauma manifests and grows into dangerous afflictions and is part of the reason we're losing so many. TEAR Solutions was founded to stop it at the source. Cut out the trauma and give people their lives back. This is not as new as you might think. Smaller trials have been going on for years and we've garnered incredibly positive results—'

'But that doesn't explain why you're helping a criminal,' Jack says quietly. 'A very powerful criminal. And it wasn't *trauma* you removed. It was an entire relationship—'

'Yes, Jack. You're right. We've removed many relationships in their entirety before, but I agree this was very different. This relationship was not traumatic and the removal of it was to help a member of the government escape having his reputation shattered.'

She looks down at her hands and begins to fiddle with her rings. I suddenly realise she's married. She has a whole other life out there. A family. 'I'm not proud of this,' she says slowly. 'But many of our investors have strong links to your father's political party, Elias. Advance Britain is spearheading the use of technology in the progression of society and TEAR Solutions offers them cost-effective options to bring people back from unhappiness. To get people back into work. This is what they want.

'They knew about us and that's why they suggested this option for you both last year. Financially we have our hands tied. They told us that if we refused to help your father they would shut us down with immediate effect. The government is powerful and we had to listen. We had no choice.'

'That's not true,' I say. 'There's always a choice.'

'Perhaps,' Melinda says. 'Perhaps that is what you think. We knew we could not let everything we've worked for come to an end. It was just not an option.'

'You should have.'

'Bro,' Lucas says. 'It's not that simple. Dad's party is investing so much into TEAR Solutions.'

Melinda nods. 'They're planning to roll it out to the public in the coming years – to change the entire mental healthcare system. If used correctly, we can help so many people – war veterans, abuse survivors—'

'But what if they don't use it correctly?' Jack says. 'They could do anything with it. It could get completely out of control.'

Melinda nods. 'Yes,' she says. 'You're right. And we have to hope that it remains regulated. But let me tell you something that may make you change your mind. I have a patient – her name is Bella.' Bella. The girl from the second story. FIRE. 'She has been through unspeakable things. Seen unspeakable things. The grief of losing her brother – of not being able to save him – was too much. When she came to us, she was desperate. On the verge of no longer wanting to be here. She was so damaged by her experience that she felt there was no option but to escape this life. But when we explained to her what we could do, she saw hope. We offered her *hope*. And now she is thriving. She's recently married and works as a florist. The trauma no longer haunts her every waking moment.'

I think of Nisha. Amy. Of what happened to her.

Jack shakes his head. 'But *we* had no *choice*. Our past was stolen. I would never have chosen that.'

'I know,' Melinda says. 'I know.' She pauses for a moment.

I suddenly realise something. 'If they never wanted us to find each other, why did they have you put us in the support group together?'

She tilts her head. 'It was a test, to see if it had worked. And it did. You'd never have known who the other was, if you hadn't made your way to TraumaLand and seen Jack's story, Elias. The government wanted proof that the procedure had worked. That meeting was set up to show them your dad was safe.'

Silence descends. I watch the shadows of the flames flickering over the rug.

'So, what now?' Jack eventually says. 'Do you expect me to go back to Brixton like none of this ever happened?'

'No,' Lucas says. 'You'd be in too much danger.' He looks at Melinda, who nods. 'We have a plan. We can run through the logistics later, but if we release the recording of Jack and Rose to the police, then Dad will be taken into custody.'

'Dad's party won't like that,' I say. 'They'll try and stop us.'

'By then it'll be too late,' Melinda says. 'We're already organising a safe house for you both where you can lay low for a while. Then we'll help you get your lives back on track. We will hold your dad to account, Elias – and ask the police for more regulation in the use of trauma removal. It will give the power back to us and hopefully help us to sever our ties with the government.'

I put my head in my hands. *A safe house?*

How has this happened? All of this?

'Eli?' Lucas says.

'Yeah.' I look up at him.

'This is our chance to get Dad for what he did.' He turns

to Jack, his voice catching with emotion. 'We can send him to prison, Jack. It's the right thing to do.'

I wait, watching him.

Jack nods. 'So, this safe house...' he says slowly. 'When do we go?'

'Tonight,' Lucas says.

'*Tonight?*'

'Until we release the video to the police, you're in danger of being stopped by Dad's party. We all are.' Lucas exhales shakily and I can see how much is at stake for him too. 'Tamara and James will take you. They're waiting outside.'

'But before you do,' Melinda says, 'I want to give you both a choice.' She picks up the two small boxes from the table next to her. When she unclips them, I see what at first glance looks like a set of hearing aids. 'You can have your memories back, if you want them. All of them. I've already downloaded the files that were removed from each of you. The procedure is painless.

'I'll place these on your ears and you'll feel sleepy. Over the course of a few hours, they will reactivate the dentate gyrus engram cells in your brain. In doing this, the memories will begin to come back to you. It may take a while, as we're still in the early days of perfecting the technology, but it works. They can be yours again, if you want them.'

I look at Jack. His eyes have lit up. 'You can have a moment alone together, if you'd like?'

'Yes, please,' Jack says.

Melinda rises from her armchair. 'I'll prepare the treatment, in case you decide to go ahead. We'll do all we can to keep you safe either way.'

'Thank you,' Jack says.

Lucas remains seated, looking at me. 'Do you want me to stay?'

'Um... No, it's OK. We won't be long.'

He smiles that same reassuring smile. 'OK, bro.' He stands and winks. 'I'll do anything I can to protect you.' He looks at Jack. 'And I'll do all I can to make up for being part of this, Jack. I really am sorry.'

'Thanks, Lucas,' Jack replies.

Lucas and Melinda leave together through another door – a smaller one in the wall opposite me.

For a moment we both stare into the flames on the screen. Then I turn to him. 'You want them back?'

Jack nods. 'I need them.' He sounds resolute. Completely certain.

'OK,' I say. 'OK.'

His eyes blaze red in the light. 'It might be difficult, but the way I've felt the past year – I didn't recognise myself. I had no idea who I was. I want it.'

I smile at him. 'So do I.'

'Your brother seems trustworthy,' he says. 'He seems like a really nice guy.'

'He is,' I say. 'He always has been. I'm glad his conscience won.'

Jack falls silent, thinking. 'Are you worried?' he says. 'About your parents finding us?'

'I mean, yeah,' I say. 'But my life is completely different to how it was a couple of days ago. And they deserve to pay for what they did.'

Jack shakes his head in disbelief. All of this is incredibly hard to believe.

'So,' I say. 'What about this safe house?'

'Yeah. What the hell will that be?'

'No idea. Maybe some little fishing hut by the sea.'

He smiles. 'That sounds nice.'

'Yeah. It does.'

'Well, whatever it is, we'll be there together. At least there's that.'

'Yeah,' I say. 'There's that.' I pause. 'Maybe there's a future where we can have all of the past and be OK.'

'I'd like that,' he says. 'I really would.'

Me too. That's what I want too.

A crack of light spills out of the wall as the door opens and Melinda and Lucas step out.

'Are we decided?' she says.

I nod. 'We are.'

'Would you like them back?'

'We would.'

She smiles. I see Lucas exhale, pleased. Excited for us.

'You're doing the right thing,' Melinda says as she goes to pick up the boxes. 'When you wake, you'll be somewhere safe.' She turns to me. 'Don't worry, Elias, you'll never see your parents again.'

Fuck. I'll never see my parents again.

I look at Lucas. *I got you, bro*, he mouths.

'You two have both taught me so much and I'm grateful,' Melinda says. 'I've been reminded that when it comes down to it, we only get one chance to be who we want and we mustn't let anything get in our way. Your bond is clearly very strong and I'm glad that it brought you back together. Now, if you would both lean back and close your eyes.'

As I sit back in the armchair, as Melinda puts the pieces into my ears and I hear a soft whirring begin, as my eyes begin to droop, I look over at Jack. At Lucas standing above me, his hand on my shoulder.

And then I realise something. Something that Melinda just said.

When it comes down to it, we only get one chance to be who we want and we mustn't let anything get in our way.

My dad said it. He said it to me at the foot of the stairs. Those exact words.

'Wait…' I begin to say, but the thought dissolves as sleep takes over.

36

FAITH IN GOODNESS

When *The Exorcist* was released, it made four hundred and forty-one *million* dollars in box office sales. And that was in 1973, so can you imagine what that would be today.

A lot of money.

I guess what that means is, trauma sells.

People want it. People will pay for it. They want to be terrified.

And I respect that, I do.

But I also wonder why. I mean, I know why *I've* wanted to be terrified, but not everyone has had their brain messed with to the point of numbness like me.

After some consideration, I've decided that ultimately it's about safety. I think that when we watch these films, these awful and scary films, we want to put ourselves into a position of such fear that when it ends, we suddenly feel safe again. We think *oh, thank fuck*. The real world is nothing like that. My life is nothing like that so I'm going to be just fine.

But *The Exorcist* leaves a lingering doubt, which I'm not sure people expected when they watched it. Because people do believe that evil forces exist. We put so much faith into goodness. Into those people that tell us they stand against what is bad and wrong, and can help us, like Father Karras does with Regan. But I think Father Karras started to get a bit allured by the darkness. To enjoy being around it. I think the power it held was seductive to him. The distinction between good and evil begins to blur, and for a moment you wonder if anyone is actually very good at all.

And to me, that is scary. Really scary.

I mean, I assume.

Anyway, that's all.

I'm in a bed. A bed I do not know.

In a small room. Just me.

And I'm wearing some kind of hospital gown. Interesting. It's kind of cute, though. I think I look good in hospital gowns.

It's very … *One Flew Over the Cuckoo's Nest*.

A sharp pain twinges in the back of my head. I lift my hand to touch it and see my arm is bandaged. The left one.

OK. Also interesting.

On the right arm there are stitches by the inside of my wrist like a chunk of flesh has been taken from it and sewn back together. How strange.

'Elias?'

I look up. A woman is standing at the door.

'Hi,' I say. It hurts to speak.

'I'm a nurse,' she says.

A nurse? Nurse Ratched? *That would be cool.*

'Oh, hi…'

She smiles kindly at me. Dark hair pulled back. Green eyes. She looks kind. 'Try not to talk too much, OK?'

'OK...'

'You're safe now. You have absolutely nothing to worry about. Do you remember what happened?'

'Yeah,' I say. 'Um... No, actually. Not really. Can you—'

'You fell off the roof of your house,' she says.

I *what*? 'Sorry, can you repeat that, please?'

'You fell.'

'Off the *roof*?'

'Yes. You're very lucky to be alive.'

What the hell? 'When?'

'Two days ago.'

'Two *days* ago?'

'Yes, on Friday morning. Your parents were out for a run. Your neighbours spotted you up there. You were appearing a little manic. It's OK, you're absolutely fine. You've been in the hospital recovering over the weekend.'

I feel the twinge in the back of my head again and touch it with my fingertips, pressing them into a long gash directly behind my left ear. I can feel stitches. Five, six, seven of them.

'Oh, don't touch that,' the nurse says. 'You were cut when you landed. We don't want it to get infected.'

Shit. 'And I survived?' I take in the look on her face that says *well, clearly*. 'Cool.'

'Listen, there's someone here to see you. But if you need anything, my name is Tamara and I'm here to help you.'

'Right. Tamara.' Tamara... A nice name. 'Thank you.' Tamara seems nice.

'Eli!' I look round.

Lucas. *Lucas.*

'Hi, Luc…'

He bounds over to me. 'I'd hug you, but you look a bit delicate, bro.' He has tears in his eyes. 'Jesus. I was so worried. I'm glad you're awake.' He puts his hand on mine. 'Mum and Dad have been worried sick. Just to warn you, there may be tears.'

'Tears?'

He raises his eyebrows. 'I know… They're really upset. Shocked. I'm sure you are too…'

I don't actually feel … anything.

And then I see them. Mum and Dad, making their way into the room, flowers in hand. Flowers.

'Oh my God, Eli…' Mum says, dashing towards me. She's wearing a white blouse, her hair up in a ponytail.

And yep. She's crying. She never cries.

'Hi, Mum,' I say as she leans down to kiss my cheek.

'Careful,' Lucas says.

'I know, I'm sorry,' she says. She touches the tip of her finger on to my nose. 'Oh, darling, we've been so worried about you.'

'I'm OK…' I say.

I think. I don't really know.

'Hi, son.' Dad is wearing his usual jumper-shirt combo that he thinks makes him look professional but relatable at the same time. 'Christ, son, you'll be the death of us.'

'Sorry, Dad.'

He takes my hand in his and squeezes it. 'Don't you worry. Everything is fine now.'

He's very wise, my dad.

'So many people want to see you,' Mum says. 'To know you're OK.'

That's odd. I don't know many people. 'Who?'

'Melinda, for one,' Mum says.

My therapist. We have a strange relationship. I like Melinda, always have. We understand one another. I hate her and she hates me, but we love each other really.

'Oh, right, yeah. I hit my head so she'll probably *love* this.'

They all laugh in unison. It's a bit strange but also kind of fun.

'Ingrid sends her love,' Lucas puts in. His girlfriend. I call her Intense Ingrid. Because she's really intense.

'And Peter,' Mum says. 'Of course.'

'Peter?' I repeat. 'Who the hell is Peter?'

'Um…' Lucas looks at me, a little concerned. 'Your boyfriend?' He turns to Mum and Dad. 'God, he must have hit it really hard.' He turns back to me. 'Listen, don't worry. Take it easy.'

Well, that's good. I have a boyfriend. How chic. 'Do you think he's into hospital attire?' I say.

'Eli!' Mum says, but I can see her smiling.

The door opens again. It's Melinda.

Oh. OK. So, we are doing this now? 'Hey, shrink.'

'How are you doing, Elias?' She has her hair pulled back all neat, like Mum's.

'I'm a little confused, I must admit.'

'Of course you are. You're very lucky.'

'Apparently so.'

'So, how are you feeling?'

Everyone is looking at me.

'I'm not.'

'You're not what?'

'Feeling.'

'Right. Well, it's probably something to do with hitting your head.'

'Can people be turned into psychopaths?'

'Sorry?'

'That would be kind of cool.'

'Elias,' Dad says and laughs gently. Or nervously. Both. But I'm serious. I see him glance at Mum, who smiles back at him. They're happy. Happy that I didn't die falling off the roof.

Dad places the flowers on the desk. 'For you.'

'Thanks, Dad.' I look at them all staring at me. 'Wow, there's lots of you. Big crowd.'

'Sorry, Eli,' Mum says. 'Let's give you some space. You need to rest.'

Melinda nods. 'I'll come back and talk to you once you've slept. How does that sound?'

'Yeah,' I say. 'Sounds great.'

Lucas looks like he might cry now.

Maybe I should try and do it myself. I can't remember the last time I cried. Everyone else seems to be doing it.

'Right!' Dad says. 'Sorry, Eli. I can't stay long. I need to get back to work. Busy, busy. You met Tamara?'

'The nice nurse?'

'Exactly. If you need anything, just tell her.'

'I will.'

'Any questions?'

'No. Actually, yes. Where am I?' They all laugh. They all laugh because they're relieved that I'm alive.

'You're in a private clinic.'

'Oh, right. Swanky.'

Dad winks. 'Don't mention it, son.'

'I never got this treatment when I broke my arm,' Lucas says. 'You're lucky.'

Everyone keeps saying that.

Mum kisses me on the cheek. 'We'll come back later. Don't worry about anything.' And then they all file out of the room.

I stare at the wall opposite where there's a picture of a field full of sunflowers. All I can hear is the ticking of a clock.

OK. So…

I fell off the roof?

I look down at the cut on my wrist. Feel the one behind my head.

Strange. I don't feel very bruised…

I look for my phone. I don't seem to have one. OK. Well, I kind of like that. I hate technology anyway.

'Hello?'

I look up.

There's someone in the doorway. Someone I've not met before.

'Hi,' I say.

'Can I come in?'

'Might as well, everyone else has.'

She steps towards me, letting the door slam shut behind her. She's staring at me.

Why is everyone staring at me today?

I like her hair. Kind of emo. Her purple nail varnish too. She looks like the kind of person I'd be friends with.

'Are you OK?' I say.

'Yeah,' she says slowly. Her eyes are a little … dead. It's freaking me out a bit. 'Is your name Elias?'

'Um… Yeah…' I say. 'Why?'

'I think…' She stops and looks back at the door, checking.

Then she turns back to me, pulls her sleeve up and shows me her arm. There's something written on it.

I feel a slight jolt inside me. A murmur of something. A flash of a memory, deep inside my brain. As I read the words, I feel a gap, a space, begin to open up inside it. For some reason, it makes me want to cry.

The truth is out there
And it's not what you think.
Signed,
Elias Pew
Property of TEAR Solutions, Floor 1, Harper House

It's in my own handwriting.

And there's a drawing of an m-shaped bird on the inside of her wrist, in the exact same place my scar is.

OK. Well, that's weird.

'Do you know someone called Jack?' she says.

I look up. Jack. *Jack.* Do I? 'I don't think…' But I stop as I see she's holding something in her hand.

Hanging from a chain is a wooden pendant. A rose. It looks a little odd, misshapen, perhaps home-made, but also kind of beautiful in a twisted way.

As I look closer, I see there's a name carved in it. Four little letters. And as I stare at them, I feel something, deep inside me.

Some sort of inexplicable *longing*.

'Wait…' I say. Wait.

Jack.

ACKNOWLEDGEMENTS

I have an incredible amount of gratitude for a number of people, without whom this book would not exist.

Firstly, my wonderful editor Katie Jennings. As always, your guidance, intuition and friendship are incredibly valued, and I love to keep learning with you. To Beth Marshall Brown, for your shrewd and current insights. Thank you for your editorial eye on this!

Becky Bagnell and Leah Middleton for your wisdom and steadiness throughout. I am very thankful.

To my agent Clare Wallace, for keeping me going with your excitement and enthusiasm.

My friend Leah Brotherhead. Having you read this as I wrote – and give the most incredible notes and thoughts – has been a joy. It's been a lot of fun. Liz Scott, always. Hayley for the amazing cover art. Everyone at OW and RTB, not least Mark, Lucy, Mati, Rowan, Paul and Laura. And Susila Baybars, our brilliant copyeditor.

To my friends and family, for your support.

To the 24-hour Tesco in Stretford that is not actually open twenty-four hours.

The Lake District, running and the sea.

All very helpful.

Thanks x

FRIENDS ...
WELCOME TO HAPPYHEAD

'One of the very best voices in YA right now.'
Benjamin Dean

'A truly thought-provoking thriller.'
Observer on *HappyHead*

'A rollercoaster of a read.'
Ravena Guron on *Dead Happy*

OUT NOW!